PRAISE FOR KR

"Another page turner! Kristy Cambr... ...s ...o ...
gripping tale of three uniquely troubled women from different centuries yet linked by secrets hidden behind the walls of an ancient English
castle. Enjoy the ride as Cambron uses her trademark skill peeling
away the mystery surrounding East Suffolk's Parham Hill Estate and
the answer to each woman's heart—one tantalizing layer at a time. *The
Painted Castle* is a story compelling, beautifully written, and sure to
thrill a broad range of historical fiction fans!"

—KATE BRESLIN, BESTSELLING AUTHOR OF *FAR SIDE OF THE SEA*

"Meticulously researched, intricately plotted, and elegantly written,
Kristy Cambron weaves a haunting yet heartwarming tale that spans
generations. With vivid descriptions and unforgettable characters,
Cambron draws her readers into a world full of secrets and romance.
Highly recommended!"

—SARAH E. LADD, BESTSELLING AUTHOR OF *THE GOVERNESS
OF PENWYTHE HALL*, FOR *THE PAINTED CASTLE*

"*The Painted Castle* is a richly layered narrative for readers of Pam
Jenoff, Rachel Hauck, and Sarah Sundin. Cambron's welcome knowledge of visual art as well as her penchant for marrying passion for
location with splendid descriptive construction create an ode to the
timeless quest for romance across the centuries. *The Painted Castle*
wields an artist's attention to detail, impeccable research, and sheer
soul that stir savvy readers to recognize they are being given the rare
opportunity to peer into an author's heart."

—RACHEL MCMILLAN, AUTHOR OF *MURDER IN THE
CITY OF LIBERTY*

"A brilliant ending to the Lost Castle series, *The Painted Castle* captivated me from start to finish. When woven together, each of the three
storylines created a beautiful tale of redemption, authenticity, and
courage. From the gorgeous setting to the sweet and gentle romances,
The Painted Castle is Kristy Cambron at her best."

—LINDSAY HARREL, AUTHOR OF *THE SECRETS OF PAPER AND INK*

"Enchanting and mesmerizing! *Castle on the Rise* enters an alluring land and time with a tale to be treasured. Ireland comes to life with as much vivid light as the characters of this dual-timeline tale of redemption and love. For those of us who love Ireland and its misty shores, its myths, and its mysteries, Kristy Cambron brings it all to life. More than once I wished to walk through the pages of *Castle on the Rise* and join Cambron's magnificent women on a quest for the truth, and for love."

—PATTI CALLAHAN, *NEW YORK TIMES* BESTSELLING
AUTHOR OF *BECOMING MRS. LEWIS*

"*Castle on the Rise* perfectly showcases rising star Kristy Cambron's amazing talent! Perfect pacing, lovely prose, and an intricate plot blend together in a delightful novel I couldn't put down. Highly recommended!"

—COLLEEN COBLE, *USA TODAY* BESTSELLING AUTHOR OF
SECRETS AT CEDAR CABIN AND THE ROCK HARBOR SERIES

"Cambron's latest is one of her best. Gripping and epic, this intricately woven tale of three generations seeking truth and justice will stay with you long after the last page."

—RACHEL HAUCK, *NEW YORK TIMES* BESTSELLING
AUTHOR, FOR *CASTLE ON THE RISE*

"Vivid visual descriptions will make readers want to linger in the character and time period of each chapter, but they will become quickly immersed soon after starting the next. Romance fans will appreciate how Cambron builds multiple love stories within this richly historical, faith-based tale."

—*BOOKLIST* FOR *THE LOST CASTLE*

"Cambron once again makes smart use of multiple eras in her latest time-jumping romance. Cambron spins tales of resiliency, compassion, and courage."

—*PUBLISHERS WEEKLY* FOR *THE LOST CASTLE*

"As intricate as a French tapestry, as lush as the Loire Valley, and as rich as heroine Ellie's favorite pain au chocolat, *The Lost Castle* satisfies on every level. Kristy Cambron's writing evokes each era in loving detail, and the romances are touching and poignant. *C'est bon!*"

—Sarah Sundin, award-winning author of *The Sea Before Us* and the Waves of Freedom series

"It's been a long time since I've been so thoroughly engrossed in a novel. Kristy Cambron grabs you from the start and weaves a fabulously intricate and intoxicating tale of love and loss. Her settings are breathtaking, her historical detail impeccable, and her characters now dear friends. *The Lost Castle* kept me spellbound!"

—Tamera Alexander, *USA TODAY* bestselling author of *With This Pledge*

"An absolutely lovely read! Cambron weaves an enchanting story of love, loss, war, and hope in *The Lost Castle*. Spanning the French Revolution, World War II, and today, she masterfully carries us into each period with all the romance and danger of the best fairy tale."

—Katherine Reay, award-winning author of *The Austen Escape*

"Readers will be caught up in themes of family, loyalty, and courage—as well as a mystery and even a bit of a fairy-tale romance—in Kristy Cambron's *The Lost Castle*. Cambron weaves together the lives of three very different women with vivid emotion against the lush backdrop of France."

—Beth K. Vogt, Christy Award–winning author

"Cambron's lithe prose pulls together past and present, and her attention to historical detail grounds the narrative to the last breathtaking moments."

—*Publishers Weekly*, starred review, for *The Illusionist's Apprentice*

"Prepare to be amazed by *The Illusionist's Apprentice*. This novel will have your pulse pounding and your mind racing to keep up with reversals, betrayals, and surprises from the first page to the last. Like her characters, Cambron works magic so compelling and persuasive, she deserves a standing ovation."

—GREER MACALLISTER, BESTSELLING AUTHOR OF
  THE MAGICIAN'S LIE AND *GIRL IN DISGUISE*

"With rich descriptions, attention to detail, mesmerizing characters, and an understated current of faith, this work evokes writers such as Kim Vogel Sawyer, Francine Rivers, and Sara Gruen."

—*LIBRARY JOURNAL*, STARRED REVIEW,
  FOR *THE RINGMASTER'S WIFE*

"Historical fiction lovers will adore this novel! *The Ringmaster's Wife* features two rich love stories and a glimpse into our nation's live entertainment history. Highly recommended!"

—*USA TODAY*, *HAPPY EVER AFTER*

"A soaring love story! Vibrant with the glamour and awe that flourished under the Big Top in the 1920s, *The Ringmaster's Wife* invites the reader to meet the very people whose unique lives brought the Greatest Show on Earth down those rattling tracks."

—JOANNE BISCHOF, AWARD-WINNING AUTHOR
  OF *DAUGHTERS OF NORTHERN SHORES*

"Cambron expertly weaves together multiple plotlines, time lines, and perspectives to produce a poignant tale of the power of love and faith in difficult circumstances. Those interested in stories of survival and the Holocaust, such as Elie Wiesel's 'Night,' will want to read."

—*LIBRARY JOURNAL* FOR *THE BUTTERFLY AND THE VIOLIN*

The
PAINTED
CASTLE

BOOKS BY KRISTY CAMBRON

THE LOST CASTLE NOVELS

The Lost Castle

Castle on the Rise

STAND-ALONE NOVELS

The Ringmaster's Wife

The Illusionist's Apprentice

THE HIDDEN MASTERPIECE NOVELS

The Butterfly and the Violin

A Sparrow in Terezin

The
PAINTED
CASTLE

A
LOST CASTLE
NOVEL

KRISTY CAMBRON

THOMAS NELSON
Since 1798

The Painted Castle

© 2019 Kristy Cambron

Published in Nashville, Tennessee, by Thomas Nelson. Thomas Nelson is a registered trademark of HarperCollins Christian Publishing, Inc.

Published in association with Books & Such Literary Management, 52 Mission Circle, Suite 122, PMB 170, Santa Rosa, California 95409–5370, www.booksandsuch.com.

Interior design by Mallory Collins

Thomas Nelson titles may be purchased in bulk for educational, business, fund-raising, or sales promotional use. For information, please email SpecialMarkets@ThomasNelson.com.

Scripture quotations are taken from the New King James Version˚. © 1982 by Thomas Nelson. Used by permission. All rights reserved.

ISBN 978-0-7180-9553-6 (e-book)
ISBN 978-0-7180-9554-3 (audio download)

Library of Congress Cataloging-in-Publication Data
Names: Cambron, Kristy, author.
Title: The painted castle : a Lost Castle novel / Kristy Cambron.
Description: Nashville, Tennessee : Thomas Nelson, [2019]
Identifiers: LCCN 2019018157 | ISBN 9780718095529 (softcover)
Subjects: | GSAFD: Christian fiction.
Classification: LCC PS3603.A4468 P35 2019 | DDC 813/.6--dc23 LC record available at https://lccn.loc.gov/2019018157

Printed in the United States of America

19 20 21 22 23 LSC 5 4 3 2 1

For Big Ed and all the heroes of the 390th—
You braved the skies.
We thank you.

After the day is gone we shall go out, breathe deeply, and look up—and there the stars will be, unchanged, unchangeable.

—H. A. REY, *THE STARS*

PROLOGUE

For the gifts and the calling of God are irrevocable.
—ROMANS 11:29

DECEMBER 3, 1833
216 STRAND
LONDON, ENGLAND

Thieves did not stop for a spot of tea—as a rule, they robbed and ran.

This one bucked convention though, as he lingered outside the tea shop door at Jacksons of Piccadilly as if he hadn't anyplace else to be just then.

Eleven-year-old Elizabeth Meade watched as snow drifted around the curious figure, dotting his shoulders. The flickering glow of gaslight cast shadows upon his face as he gazed up the cobblestone street. With one hand he tapped a walking stick in a cadence against the side of his boot, counting time to a private melody. The other hand he'd buried deep in his coat pocket.

Carrying himself with importance, as her ma-ma would say—a gentleman bestowed upon with high birth and noble rank—he owned a flawless posture that could have had him standing by a drawing room hearth entertaining guests instead of lingering on a street corner in a steady bout of snow. He'd tucked his face under an exquisitely tailored beaver-skin top hat pulled low over his brow, yet his patched and threadbare coat, the waistcoat noticeably devoid of a button down the front, and a candy-striped ascot that danced on a bitter-cold wind proved the oddest of contradictions.

He was common enough that passersby were content to see to their own affairs and ignore an aristocratic street urchin in their midst. But Elizabeth found him so clever a character that she'd reached for her case of drawing pencils on the coach seat—scolding herself that she'd not sharpened them beforehand—and opened her sketchbook the instant her pa-pa had stepped from their carriage.

The portrait would be a welcome addition to Elizabeth's sketchbook consisting mainly of flora and fauna from her family's Yorkshire estate. She'd drawn fox, the occasional deer, sheep that grazed on the hills, and the landscape outside their manor windows. And though her mother cautioned her against encroaching upon the winged army that buzzed around the estate, Elizabeth had done many an intimate study—and paid for it with wicked stings—to capture images of honeybees among rows of apple blossoms in orchards on their land. With the exception of the nuisance of a rogue bee sting here or there, it was by all accounts . . . *safe*.

Quite in secret, Elizabeth craved the opposite.

It was earnestness that proved capable of satisfying the ache deep in her core. If she'd been born a boy, perhaps Elizabeth would have run off to join the Royal Navy and sketch the great vastness of the open sea, in a cadence of waves that railed and toiled against the horizon . . . Or grown to be a gentleman of industry, like her father, and have the ability to go wherever she pleased, exploring England's secrets—the palaces and workhouses both—all tangled together in a web of sooty streets.

Elizabeth fantasized about near anything that would free her from the confines of a ladies' tea parlor. A second best to her imaginings was to accompany Pa-pa to his textile mill in Manchester City. "Mightn't it help for an heiress to have a rudimentary knowledge of the trade her husband would receive from her in marriage?" she'd asked. It seemed if she spoke of matrimony one day in the future it was enough for Ma-ma to acquiesce and allow her visits to the mill.

Relishing the opportunity, Elizabeth would slip away from Pa-pa's office as soon as they passed through the carriage-clogged streets along the Ashton Canal. While he oversaw operations, she could move about as a ghost in the mill's hidden corners and shadowed halls, sketching what she wished. There she'd fill endless pages with a fervor. Images of workers, their faces soot smudged, weary, and lined. The contrast of carding machines, clawing back and forth like cast-iron beasts, and cotton fluffs that danced about in the air like snow. Packhorses trudged through the cobblestone courtyard pulling shabby carts. Workmen muscled wares onto them, and all the women seemed to cough as they hurried by, their faces gaunt and clothing hanging off their thin frames until they looked like specters drifting on a breeze.

Once Elizabeth had hidden behind a stack of crates to sketch one of the scavengers—a small boy employed to clean out the machinery—and after, she questioned her pa-pa as to why children her age were set upon to work at all. When did they receive schooling? And whilst the machines were running they continued working . . . Was that not dangerous?

"Do not worry over such trifles," he'd said. "It is beneath your station." Elizabeth was clever, with a keen eye and a sharp pencil—he'd admit that. "But shouldn't you focus on pleasant things? England's rich landscape and our life in it. Why fret over the wretched plight of the worker?"

If that was pleasant, Elizabeth didn't want it.

She wanted real.

There was a world of it now to be found in just a few London blocks. Their carriage sat in the midst of it, she waiting while Pa-pa went about business, blissfully sketching what could be a true member of the grit and grime in London's underbelly.

Elizabeth pressed pencil to page, flitting her glance up and down, outlining the street urchin's strong jaw and broad shoulders upon a lithe frame, and shading the fall of shadows around him. She waited for the rare tip of the man's hat that might move the light just so, allowing her to capture the combination of street smarts and brash in his face, all the while he kept the walking stick *tap, tap, tapping* against his boot.

As if reading her thoughts, the figure stilled the cane, the army of snowflakes the lone movement around his silhouette. He seemed to have discerned a gaze rested upon him, as without warning he shifted his attention up to the carriage . . .

To her.

Their gazes locked for the briefest of moments, enough that Elizabeth held back a gasp. He was young—no more than twenty—and owned a pair of eyes in a rare and piercing stone gray, the left iris nearly halved by a jagged vertical line of bright golden brown that cut from top to bottom.

He seemed to understand their color was a rarity, so he broke away and tucked again under the top-hat brim. Elizabeth turned back to the page, wishing she'd brought her colored pencils to capture the intensity in his eyes, but continued sketching his face without them. She could add the contrast of hues later.

A ferocious *crack* awakened her from the spark of inspiration. She jolted upright, snapping her gaze to the street.

The top-hat urchin had vanished.

He was replaced by shrieking ladies and passersby who recoiled in the gaslight's glow. The horses lurched, jostling the carriage as Elizabeth tried to discern what the commotion was. She gripped a gloved hand to the window frame, fingertips battling to steady her.

And then there was a man . . . *falling*.

A cloaked figure absorbed what was assuredly a second gunshot fired from the alley shadows, then staggered back to hit the pavement in a dead flop. With the man's riding boots having fallen limp in the center of the pavement, crowds tripped to get out of the way.

And she watched in horror as her pa-pa lay motionless on the ground.

No!

Elizabeth flung the coach door open, uncaring if it caused the horses to bolt. She jumped down and ran, nearly turning her ankle on cobblestones as she pushed her way through the crowd.

"*Lady Elizabeth!*" Kinsley, their coachman, bellowed to her from behind. She glanced back, seconds only, to see he worked to calm the fright out of the beasts in harnesses.

Run.

It was the only charge within her.

"*Pa-pa!*" Elizabeth slammed her knees to the grimy slush when she reached her pa-pa. She parted his cloak, pressing her robin's-egg gloves to his waistcoat, finding a wound in his middle. Her palms darkened to crimson without effort.

"Pa-pa—what's happened?" she cried.

Elizabeth raised shaking hands to his wool cloak and gripped the lapels as if it would stop the flow of crimson darkening the stones beneath them. He searched the sky, with snowflakes catching on his eyelashes and drifting to rest in the amber bed of his beard.

"It's Elizabeth . . . ," she whispered, her breath freezing into a fog over him. "I am here, Pa-pa."

Cathedral bells rang across the distance, the few blocks between St. Paul's and them. Their chimes cut the ink sky with their ghostly song as snow fell and her pa-pa bled on the ground. Hamilton Meade, the Fourth Earl of Davies, looked through Elizabeth with a glassy stare as she held his hand. Watching. Numb. Lost.

He released a grappling, ragged breath and then . . . *nothing*. Just chimes and snow and strangers, and an eerie stillness that settled over the sidewalk like a dark fog.

Kinsley appeared then and fell to his knees in the gutter, leaning over Pa-pa to press an ear to his chest. He listened intently, but Elizabeth knew the effort was wasted. Pa-pa lay cold in death as an icy wind swooped around them. It toyed with the spilt tin of her mother's favored bergamot tea and rustled a bag of peppermint sticks that had fanned out on the sidewalk past his outstretched fingertips.

Elizabeth rocked on her heels. She gazed back to the carriage, its shadow a backdrop behind the cadence of thick, drifting snow and gathering crowds. Her sketchbook was still upon the coach seat, and she knew what was inside it.

The drawing depicted no clever character now—the rogue in the top hat and candy-striped ascot was more than that. Even in youth, she could discern who was an enemy. In that instant the man became the shadow Elizabeth vowed to chase until they knew who had done the bloodthirsty deed. There would be no escaping it, for the best clue was seared to memory: the devil's likeness in cool stone and a jagged line of gold.

Elizabeth Meade had just sketched her father's murderer . . . and those eyes would haunt her as long as she lived.

ONE

PRESENT DAY
10/11 O'CONNELL STREET LOWER
DUBLIN, IRELAND

"Who is that, an' why does he keep comin' in here night after night, ooglin' ye from across our pub?"

Irked shouldn't have described Keira Foley's older brother at the moment—not after Cormac and his wife just had a new baby girl and with their older daughter, Cassie, he now had a family camped out on cloud nine. He grumbled from their perch behind the vintage wood-topped bar.

Keira peered across the main dining room with nonchalance—past low-hanging lamps and tables packed with tourists enjoying a pint and a gab—as if the tourist Cormac spoke of was nothing more than a nick on the two-hundred-year-old wall paneling. The man had tucked into the far corner by the men's snug, opposite an ancient hearth with a steady orange glow, and had casually leaned his chair back against the wall of wood and frosted glass.

Act uninterested.

She shrugged. "Him? I don't know that he's ooglin' anything."

"He's a tourist. An' a Yank."

"Maybe." Keira swept a towel over the bar top—already clean

7

and bone dry, it didn't need it. "Why does that matter? We have tourists in here all day long. They keep the lights on for us."

"That one keeps comin' back, an' he keeps watchin' ye."

She looked back at Cormac, seeing the Foley green eyes she and her two brothers had inherited from their father—the owner and namesake of Jack Foley's Irish House. Like Cormac, her father was a mite enthusiastic about preserving the tradition of the famous O'Connell Street pub and had disappeared into the depths of the kitchen to inspect the delivery of potatoes they'd just received.

Thank goodness she didn't have to manage them both.

Where Keira was blonde and her brothers dark haired and the Dubliner's brogue she'd had as a child all but faded to a hint of a London accent now, that's where the differences ended. The Foleys were a bunch of Irish hotheads—stubborn and passionate in their own ways. It seemed Cormac had picked up on defending his little sister's honor that night and was running full steam ahead with the classic definition of a Foley's response.

Keira tossed the tea towel against the pub logo on his shirt. He caught it in a palm against his chest.

"I really don't know what you're getting after, Cormac. It's not a crime to frequent a pub for a pint, you know—especially for a tourist."

"But wit' a glass full an' starin' over here like the bar's on fire?"

"I hate to bring up the obvious, but I'm twenty-six years old. Even if that chap was ooglin' as you say, it really wouldn't be any of your affair. Unless you wish me to spend the rest of my life alone, you'll have to permit a bloke to glance at me once in a while."

Cormac groaned and leaned over the bar like he'd just ingested a side of bad beef. He gave her a standard paternal look, for he had ten years on her and, in many ways, had helped raise her since their mum died so many years before. Problem was, his heart was gold and she knew it. It's why the protective vibe never worked with her.

Almost never.

"When ye talk like that I'm reminded that I'm yer brother. *Older* brother. Who owns a nice pair of fists I wouldn' mind showin' off to any sod who steps out o' line."

She poked him in the shoulder. "Don't act meaner than you are or I'll tell Laine on you."

If anyone could soften Cormac's bristle and brash in two shakes, it was his wife. She was American. Unfailingly kind. And . . . she had Cormac's number.

"I'll show you some grace at the moment because I know Juliette has been keeping her dear ma and da from enjoying a full night's sleep."

Cormac looked up, half smiled.

Good. Mentioning your girls always softens you, dear brother.

"An' her older sister, don' forget. Cassie is just as enamored—an' sleep deprived—as we are. The cottage gets smaller an' smaller when Juliette cries middle o' the night."

"And that's exactly why I tried to convince you to live in that grand manor house at the Ashford Estate instead of building a cottage on the grounds."

"We wanted somethin' smaller. An' real. Maybe a little privacy— there an' *here.*"

"Which is why I can keep my smile and pardon you for being miffed. Look, I've watched over myself for quite long enough. There are dodgy patrons in New York and London pubs same as in Dublin. You can't think I haven't had to deter a few eager gents without you looming large in the background."

Cormac groaned again, as if the imaginings of his little sister's love life sent a fresh wave of nausea to cut him through his middle. "There are a thousand pubs in this fair country," he muttered and turned to stoop behind the bar—back to stacking glasses. "Why don' ye be tellin' him to go find one before I lose what's left o' my good humor?"

Keira bit her lip over a laugh. "Brilliant. I'll tell him."

In truth, Keira had noticed the man. Every six-foot-plus inch of him, with his perfectly pomaded ebony crown and coy half smile, the instant he and his button-down oxford and leather jacket waltzed in the pub at closing one night.

He was a tourist. That was clear the second he ordered "a pint of Guinness" without the knowledge that asking for a pint in any Dublin pub implied you wanted Guinness, full stop.

Tourists were respected for the American dollars they brought to the local economy, but it was a horse of a different color to be accepted into the closed world of a pub that had been an O'Connell Street staple for more than two hundred years.

This guy hadn't the first clue how to blend in. What's more, he looked like he couldn't care less, sporting a black leather jacket with racing stripes down the sleeves. But then . . . maybe that was exactly what he wanted. To stand out in a room of strangers so she couldn't pretend to ignore him, yet hold on to his air of mystery at the same time.

Keira crossed the wood-paneled front dining room, checking on tables of pubgoers as she went, meeting his glances every now and then. They both knew she'd eventually end up at his back corner table.

"Something wrong with your pint there, cowboy?"

"Ah. You're pretending not to know me because of your brother? I assume that's the famous Cormac Foley over there behind the bar." He tossed his glance over to Cormac, daring to smile at the fact her brother was simmering like a pot set to boil. "He looks irritated. Slow night?"

"Don't you think it's about time you went on your way, Mr. Scott? You obviously don't like our Guinness."

"I said you can call me Emory."

"And I said I'm not going to call you anything, except a Yank who should think about enjoying his pint . . . and then get on with all possible speed."

He set the full pint glass to the side, the thin foam layer on top long ago fizzled out. "I never touch the stuff."

"That doesn't explain why you've ordered it every night this week."

"Have I? Funny. I hadn't noticed." He smiled. Smooth, and a little too chill. Like he was playing a game she didn't know the rules to and fully expected to win because of it.

Keira peeked over her shoulder to find Cormac busy tending bar, but she knew better. He was watching them. What was more, they now had an audience. Locals who owned the precious real estate of ancient nail-head stools lining the bar front sat as a row of curious sweater vests and elbow-patch fisherman's jackets, now drinking in their cozy corner scene like an audience for opening night at the theater.

She pressed a palm to the tabletop and leaned in, dropping her voice. "Listen—the press has descended upon this place since word leaked about the 1916 Rising photos that were found at Cormac's Ashford Manor estate last year. And my brother is too private for his own good, so if he thinks for one second you're in that lot, he'll escort you right out the front door and send you packing with the number to his publicist. So what should I tell him is the reason you're still haunting our dining room? Because we both know it's not for the pints."

Emory shrugged and clipped two chair legs back to the hard-wood, the threat hollow enough to tempt him with little but to keep the game going. "I'm a paying customer. But to be honest, I'm debating whether to leave a scathing review online. Americans should be wary when they come in here, how tourists are treated and such."

Patience tested, Keira stared him down. "I told you on the first night, Mr. Scott, and that's flat. My answer is *no*. I'm not accepting employment offers just now."

"I'm not the type to give up easily."

"Neither am I. So hadn't you better find another prospective employee who won't toss your card in the rubbish bin?"

Emory slid a business card across the table with an index finger, like it had been itching to jump out of his hand. "Lucky I had a few extra printed, just in case."

The sleek blue-gray and black embossed card reflected a rectangle of polish to contrast the rustic wood table, but Keira made no move to reach for it.

"Look, I'm not trying to bother you, Miss Foley. But considering your job ended in New York and you've found yourself back under the thumb—forgive me, but an overbearing lot—of egocentric male family members, I would think you may be open to employment offers. At least one with better working conditions."

Caution warned Keira to retreat a step.

This Scott Enterprises chap knew more than could be attained through a simple social media search. No one outside of her family knew she'd just come home after things fell apart in New York, and few in Dublin knew the family history well enough to inquire about why she'd returned home to Ireland after a years-long hiatus from the family's cozy Irish holidays. If he was wise to all that, then he'd done some digging. And just how deep did the shovel descend?

No more games.

"You have about five seconds left before my brother endeavors to escort you out the front door by the seat of your trousers, Mr. Scott. Cormac's a steady chap, but even he has his limits, and you're testing them."

Emory tapped an index finger to the reclaimed-wood tabletop, calculating something. "Fine. Answer me this and I'll go—are you the same Keira Foley, doctoral candidate writing a dissertation on the link between painter Franz Xaver Winterhalter and a supposed lost portrait of Queen Victoria?"

Keira's throat tightened. That was one chapter she'd hoped was buried for good. Whatever this Mr. Scott was aiming for, she didn't like that it involved unearthing things she'd have preferred remained underground. "Your point?"

"I'm in the art business." He paused and tilted his head to the side. "So was it you?"

"It got me fired. But yeah. That was me."

His brow twitched. "How could a dissertation get you fired?"

Keira buttoned her lip. Not going there. That story was a closed book on a high shelf, and she wasn't pulling it down for the likes of him.

"Okay, don't answer that. But did you really believe there's a paint-ing out there—a sister to the infamous 1843 portrait Winterhalter painted of the queen, shall we say, in a more relaxed pose than was acceptable at the time?"

"A portrait of a woman with hair unbound, showing off a little shoulder action—meant as a private gift for her husband, mind you—isn't the least bit scandalous."

"It is if you're a queen."

Keira rolled her eyes. "For heaven's sake. You make it sound dirty. There are any number of paintings you might mention to accomplish that without tarnishing Queen Victoria's legacy."

"Legacy, is it?" He sat back in his chair, the wood creaking as he pressed his shoulders in a casual lean against the wall. "And what, Miss Foley, do you know of legacy?"

"I don't have time for this."

"Come now. You're a researcher. I'm sure the temptation of a name on a business card would be too much to ignore—especially for you. Tell me what you know."

"You flatter yourself."

"And yet you know you want to . . . Go ahead." He folded his arms across his chest with a smile. "Zing me back."

She took a deep breath.

Zing away.

"Fine. You were the curator at the Farbton in Vienna when a Klimt went missing four years ago—an irreplaceable portrait dubbed *Empress.* Investigators suspected the theft was an inside job but didn't have enough evidence to prosecute any gallery staff for the crime. So *Empress* vanished into thin air, the file remains open, and your name is tainted in the art world as a result. You have no home. A family who's all but disowned you. You're not received in any art circles in Vienna, Paris, London, or New York. And it seems the only establishment in the world that would put up with your cheek is a Dublin pub where your exploits at thievery are presently unknown—save for the barmaid who isn't the least bit impressed with a winning smile."

Keira eyed him, watching for a flinch of the brow that never happened. She crossed her arms over her chest to mirror his posture and lifted her chin. *Well? Good as you gave, Mr. Scott. Better, actually.*

"A winning smile? Is that your opinion or the internet's?"

"That's all you took from that speech?"

He leaned forward, elbows on the table. "Why? What do you want me to take from it?"

"I'd suggest you find another girl to listen to your fairy tales, Mr. Scott. I'm afraid I'm completely booked at the moment."

Emory nodded. And grinned. Enough that she could almost feel Cormac's frown intensify from across the room.

"That's why it has to be you."

"Why what has to be me?"

He pulled an envelope from his inside jacket pocket and slid it across the table next to the business card.

"Framlingham, England. Next Saturday. Five thousand euros just for showing at this address. Another five after the work is done. You decide not to take the job and we part ways then and there—no questions asked. But I can promise you, this is one fairy tale you won't want to miss."

Emory stood, straightening his height against her lack of it. He took a sip of the deep amber liquid, grimaced, and set the pint glass back on the table. "That stuff is terrible, by the way."

"You're asking for a clip on the jaw if you say that in here. Or anywhere in Dublin, mind."

He nodded, accepting her quip without an ounce of wounded pride. He took a handful of euros from his jeans pocket and tossed the pile of paper leaves on the table. "Tell your brother he can keep the change for the trouble," he whispered, then stared down at her in the firelight. "And I expect, Miss Foley, a fight will find me no matter what I do."

TWO

September 23, 1944
Parham Hill Estate
Framlingham, England

"Milady?" Darly tapped Amelia Woods's elbow, attempting to draw her attention from the hive she was inspecting.

"I thought I requested you please stop calling me milady? It's ridiculous." Amelia spotted the queen bee, keeping an eye trained on the activity of workers marching over the frame. They bustled around, tiny legs and wings glistening in the rays of early morning sun.

"Ridiculous or not, they're here." The old beekeeper tipped his chin in the direction of military-green trucks dusting up the road. He slipped a mahogany pipe between his teeth and turned his wrist over, inspecting the face of his watch. "And just shy of eight o'clock it is."

Amelia nodded. If trucks were headed for the front gate, then they must hurry.

No time for this now.

She placed the wedge top bar frame back in its pine box home. Pulling the veil over her head, Amelia drew in a deep breath of the

16

crisp air—so different from the coal-dusted air of London—loving how the bliss of it lingered in a mist over East Suffolk a bit longer in the mornings at that time of year.

"Well, I'd say we'll have our autumn blossom honey by week's end. But we'll have to harvest the propolis first—think it's ready?"

Darly inspected the uniformity of caps on the frame and nodded. "I'll tell the children to be ready for harvesting maybe by tomorrow or Monday next. As soon as you've settled the new arrivals in the manor, I'd wager Liesel will wish to begin lining up our honey crocks in the kitchen. But tell them we'll have honey cakes by then, and you'll have every child ready to harvest before sunup."

"Honey cakes? You talk as though it's still 1938. Honestly." Amelia picked up their tools, wiping off the brush and capping knife on her coveralls. "I can't make much out of what we are allowed, let alone cakes that won't last the week. Why, I'm surprised you can still smoke a pipe these days. You seem to live in a dream world that isn't rationed at all."

"Smoke keeps them bees calm."

"Henry Darlington—the pipe is more about keeping *you* calm and you know it. But I still haven't a clue where you manage to find an endless supply of tobacco after more than four years of war. If rationing rules are that easy to skirt past, I'd much prefer the children to be able to see some benefit from it. Extra flour. Butter. Heavens, even bacon rashers more than a pound if we're dreaming. Anything you can procure to put a little weight on Luca."

Luca. Among the littlest of the children. The one wounded inside with memories he might never forget . . . If only a good meal could fix all things.

Darly seemed to read her thoughts and smiled. "I shall do me best then."

Amelia eyed him in return, speculation winning. "If that's

confirmation of some sort of East Suffolk black market . . . then I don't want to know a thing about it."

"Squire Darly at your service. Always at your service, your ladyship."

The old gent bowed to her. And used the title Amelia had so often asked him to forgo. It was silly to be putting on airs of grandeur when she hadn't worn a title more than a blink. But he presented it as if he were a duke in the king's throne room instead of standing in a pasture in the frayed, moss-green elbow-patch sweater he always wore and Wellingtons liberally caked with field mud.

"One day, Uncle, I shall convince you to wear a veil and protect that priceless hide of yours. And perhaps a sweater that doesn't give such a convincing impression of a moldy swiss? If you have ration coupons left, why don't you use them to purchase one of those lovely tweed jackets you're always going on about?" She pushed back a smile.

It was a tease, of course. Darly's endearing combination of selflessness and eccentricity was unmatched, and the ratty scrap of a sweater he wore as they inspected the hives each morning only made him a rarer character.

And she adored him for it.

"Tweed will have its day again soon. Just wait. And wearing a veil would only toss a wrench in cogs that already turn in quite splendid fashion, *milady*. I propose we go on as we ought."

Amelia laughed and turned back to the manor. "Come along then, *Your Grace*," she said with notable cheek. "Let us see to our new arrivals."

Rays of light scarcely had time to climb behind the willows, but when they did and the sun was high over the pastures at midday, their Parham Hill landscape would come alive. The earthy smell of alfalfa . . . the perfume of sweet astilbe and English violets and white hawthorn hidden in the hedgerow along the tree line . . . the spicy backdrop of autumn clove. The sun would burn off the thick morning mist while the bees took over the orchards, searching for the ripe sweetness of apples that had tumbled from the trees and lay in latent piles on the ground.

And maybe another autumn in wartime wouldn't seem so grim because of it.

East Suffolk whispered of old English romance.

Amelia had been smacked with it the first time she stepped from her husband's auto to the front gate of his family estate. And how a humble coal miner's daughter and bookshop clerk living in London found herself a viscountess and mistress of a grand estate? She could scarcely understand that step up herself.

The land stretched out as far as the eye could see, yawning with rock walls and waves of green pastures spanning the landscape. Thatched-roof cottages dotted the hills. Arthur said the expansive manor house had seen better days, of course, when the windows gleamed and the gardens were tended with expert care. But at the time, there had been whispers. Too many of them, that war was coming soon . . . Who thought to repair a manor house in need when the world threatened to fall apart? They'd had each other, and that's what mattered.

Now an Allied air base was a stone's throw over the rise. Amelia could almost imagine it wasn't there at all. She chose to remember the seasons would change in Framlingham as they always had, but she'd pretend there was no war in the middle of it. No rows of bullet-riddled B-17s. No monstrous sounds penetrating the sky at night. No reason for rationing or blackout fabric pulled tight over bedchamber windows. Just the buzz of bees and crisp morning walks through the pasture, accompanied by an old uncle-in-law who'd become a dear friend.

Amelia had to sigh. Arthur's prediction had finally come true;

his estate had grown on her—and blossomed in her heart. After all they'd been through in a war that was wearing everyone thin, Amelia found in the midst of it roots had grown in a place that once had felt so far above her, and now it was just home.

Pity the understanding of it came years too late.

The first waves of Yanks changed everything when they arrived in January 1942.

Their "flying fortresses" invaded the skies like great winged beasts, and Amelia had to remind herself that it was but a good thing to look up and see them flying in formation over the estate. With the planes the flyboys brought decks of playing cards, pinup photos, stomachs that hadn't seen hunger like the average Englishman had for nigh onto three years, and enough bravado to think they could triumph over Hitler just by staring him down flat.

They brought all that and . . . *noise.*

Amelia rounded the hill with Darly but quickly lost him to his arthritic knees as she sped up, after having spotted a remarkable scene unfolding at the front gate.

Truck engines had been cut flat, but that did nothing to detract from the riotous hooting and hollering of their occupants. A steady stream of GIs hopped down from open truck beds, unloading military-issue bags and bedrolls like they were moving in . . . to *her* home.

"Pardon me?" Amelia approached the first in the line of trucks, waving her arms to gain someone's attention. "What are these trucks about? And all these men?"

A driver spotted her, winked, and went about looking over a few sheets of paper on a clipboard in his lap, as if she were no more than a passing wind.

"You there—" She countered with hands on her hips and bounced up on tiptoe to look into the driver's side window. "What is all this?"

The redheaded driver opened the door and swung his legs over as he leaned out. He was a young chap, freckle-nosed and wide-eyed, and couldn't have been much more than twenty. He took an unconcerned drag from the hand-rolled cig hanging off his lower lip like an old pro. "Orders, ma'am."

Amelia bristled inside. He couldn't be but a few years younger than she but was treating her as if she were an old country madam who couldn't possibly understand or even question an operation unfolding on her land, even if it was handed down by the United States military.

Such nonchalance about her home. Her life. *And what remains of Arthur's world.*

"Orders? What orders?"

"The 390th has an overflow," he said, his southern drawl a shade more pronounced, and tugged one of the papers from the clipboard to offer it to her.

Amelia scanned the typeset words.

Indeed, the telegram's explanation appeared final:

```
The United States Army has an overflow at the
Framlingham Castle base . . .
     Sending officers from the 570th and 571st
squadrons of the 390th Bombardment Group to
board at the Parham Hill Estate through the
winter campaigns. List follows . . .
     Rations will be increased to account for
the demand . . .
```

She shook her head. This wouldn't do. They were packed to the gills as it was. How were they going to accommodate—she looked up, tried to count a tangle of fatigues unloading crates from trucks and muscling supplies to her front door—some two dozen flyboys? Where was she to procure rooms, beds, and provisions on top of the scrimp-and-save lifestyle they employed to care for the children during wartime?

"I'm expecting children to arrive from the Brockhurst Academy in Lakenheath any day now, and we're struggling to accommodate even six more mouths to feed. No one said anything to me about the United States Army requesting to bunk squadrons of grown men at a country school."

"I don't think Uncle Sam makes requests, ma'am. We go where he tells us, whether it's to a schoolhouse or not. Though I had hoped we'd see a little more by way of jollies on the base, instead of being confined to a hedgerow with nothin' to do in the off hours."

He tipped his hat back off his brow, looking full face into the rising sun reflected by the manor house windows. "You got a jukebox?"

"*No*, we do not have a jukebox." Amelia stared at him, at the audacity of masculine exuberance. "This is *my home*. I am a private citizen, and I do not recall giving anyone—let alone the United States government—permission to unload an army on my front lawn. Kindly pack up your wares and travel on to the airfields. They're just over the rise, down the lane."

"Have to talk to the cap about that." He hooked a thumb, pointing to the line of truck beds stretching out behind them. "Back there."

"The captain, you say?"

He nodded. "Captain Stevens. He'll know what's what about it."

Darly caught up to Amelia by then, anchoring his walking stick into the mud and dew-soaked leaves. He paused, breathing as one too winded for his own good, and watched the spreading sea of green fatigues. The usual mellow demeanor he carried faded as he glanced back to her, replaced by a curiosity that set wrinkles across his brow.

"These children are . . ." He pointed. Counting? Good luck. She couldn't manage it either. "A mite more . . . mature . . . than I'd envisioned."

One soldier swatted at a bee buzzing around his face, then received another's toss of packed duffel as soon as he turned around and went careening into the rock wall like he'd just taken an over-size sack of flour in the gut. The soldiers' laughter that followed confirmed her judgment of the situation.

"Mature? They're swatting at my bees." She thrust the tele-gram into Darly's hand. "And if that's mature, I'm having tea at Buckingham Palace."

Captain Stevens it is, then . . .

Amelia marched through the mud lining the road, asking after their captain. The men mostly ignored her, except to say, "Back there," and "Keep goin'," or to give a whistle or two under their breath because a female was whisking by.

She filtered through fatigues until she thought the convoy might have no end, then stopped in the underbrush along the old stone fence, watching as they continued unloading stacks of wares on the front steps.

Fearing the noise was too great, Amelia looked up to the manor.

Her heart sank; the children were awake.

Their noses were pressed against the leaded glass on the upper floor as they watched in wonder at the invasion of servicemen at their front door. And after they'd had such a rough night with so little sleep. Further, if the men did not quiet down, they'd quickly have the bees in every hive swarming to a tizzy so they couldn't harvest on time—and her remaining measure of civility would be gone.

Her patience was bleeding down to the quick.

No . . . Please, not now.

Not when we've tried so hard to make this work.

Amelia crooked her pinkies between her teeth and let out a shrill whistle, just like her papa had taught her to do when she was five years old.

The bustle froze.

The men noticed her, alright. Every one of them that time. With eyes staring, brows lifted, and several astonished glances following the sound of the whistle that could wake the dead, all the way down to the petite Englishwoman who'd issued it.

A powder-blue, Peter Pan–collared shirt under weathered denim coveralls, with ash-blonde locks victory-rolled and tied by a rust paisley kerchief, probably wasn't the finery they'd been told to expect from the Englishwomen of London. But they were not in London. They'd invaded the East Suffolk countryside, where those who lived and labored did so on a real working farm.

She ignored their glances—or tried to anyway, shoving away the possibility of their judgments—and cleared her throat. "Excuse me, gentlemen . . ."

Gumption, Amelia. Show it now or you're dead in the water.

Amelia lifted her chin a shade and crossed her arms over her chest. "I'm searching for Captain Stevens."

One chap with a comical gleam in his eyes gave a quick point and a half-muffled snicker to a man standing next to him at the top of the truck bed. That man watched her, too, from a frame half a head taller than the rest. His tousled brown hair just tipped over his brow. He was clean shaven, like they all were, but judging by laugh lines peeking out from the corners of his eyes, he was older than the lot by a good five years at least.

"Right here," he said, restacking a crate he'd muscled in his arms so he could raise a hand in confirmation. He glanced up to the man at his shoulder before he swung down to the ground. "Lieutenant Barton—take over. And attempt to wipe that smile from your face, if you please."

The younger lieutenant with ebony hair and unusually jovial eyes gave a salute and a considerably wider grin. "You got it, Cap."

Tall but unassuming, the captain walked toward Amelia, dusting his hands on his uniform trousers as he went. He gave one of those smiles—the kind that wasn't humorous at all, just a press of the lips to show respect—and stopped before her. Dog tags dangled over the front of his army-issue tee, catching a glint of morning sun. The lightness of his hazel eyes focused down upon her.

"Hello, miss. I'm Captain Stevens, United States Army. Can I be of help?"

"It's *Mrs. Woods*, Captain, and yes, I believe you can. I'd like to know what you think you're doing, unloading on my front stoop."

He gave a tick of the brow—a little tell that he'd noticed the emphasis on the *Mrs.*

"Lieutenant Hale is in the front truck, Mrs. Woods. He should've given you the—"

"Orders? Yes. He did. But a telegram from the United States Army does little to explain what you're doing here when there is a base and airfield just over there." She pointed out where the road gave way to a rise, lined in rock-wall fencing all the way to where castle spires touched the clouds. "I'm sorry to be the bearer of ill news, but you've stopped about half a kilometer before your destination. Framlingham Castle and your airfield are just over the hill."

He tossed a glance to the castle spires rising against the horizon but didn't move. "Yes, I'm aware of that. I've been stationed at the base for some time."

"Oh, that's jolly good news. Then you should know your way

there by now. Please do tell your men to keep the noise down as they pack up—we have children who haven't had more than an hour's worth of sleep, and sixty beehives on the other side of this wall. Neither will take kindly to further disturbance."

"My apologies for the noise. The men are a little . . . loose today."

"To be quite honest, very loose. And if I see one more of them swat at my bees, I'm afraid I shall have to start swinging a broom at their heads to get my point across. The bees will not harm anyone unless provoked, but I'm afraid I will."

The captain nodded in appreciation of the lighthearted cheek she issued, though a somber bent still managed to overtake his features.

"And I am sorry for that. I'll tell them to be aware of the bees. But what I meant was we lost a few yesterday. Two fortresses down. Ranks slimmed a bit. And, well, swatting at bees and not standing at attention kind of helps to . . . keep up with it all."

"Oh," she whispered, raising her palm to cover her mouth. The men indeed went about their tasks with an affable air, as if they hadn't just had the finality of death claim fighting men in their ranks the day before.

He raised a hand, as if to soften the edges of his unintended chastening. "No, it's alright."

"I apologize. We didn't know. Well, we knew *something* had occurred because of the air-raid sirens in the last two days, just not that it was downed planes exactly. But it's why we lost sleep ourselves." She turned to the manor, looking at the shadows of the children lingering in the upper-floor window seats, as if they'd help her find the right words.

"Some Jerries managed to sneak in past the control tower. The RAF looked out for us last night though—gave chase back off the water."

Thoughts of spending the previous night crammed in the bomb bunkers rushed back to her mind. They were all in this together. Whether they spent the midnight hours in the belly of a B-17 or huddled in an Anderson shelter in the gardens, she couldn't chastise anyone for finding a way to pass muster through the worst of a Luftwaffe raid.

"I should have approached this better—forgive me, please." Amelia braced a hand at her temple. "We're still a bit frayed at the moment."

He nodded, as if he understood. "And I assure you, we didn't mean to add to that. It's the RAF boys who fly at night. That leaves daytime duties for the US Army. A round-the-clock operation it seems."

"Yes, the telegram gave a one-line explanation of your operations. But I'm afraid I don't understand what's happening here, except that it appears you gentlemen think you're moving in."

"We are."

"But that's quite impossible. I have a half dozen children boarding here aged four to fourteen years. From London. Norwich. Suffolk. And two children who have been with us since the summer of 1938. We've done everything we can to ensure the war stays over that rise—at your airfield and past the sea—but not here at Parham Hill. And while we're expecting a half dozen more to arrive from a school that was bombed last week in Lakenheath, we absolutely cannot accommodate officers from two squadrons in the midst of all of this. I'm terribly sorry. I wish I had anything else to offer but that you put up tents in the meadow."

"I understand that, and we'd be grateful for it. But . . ." He rubbed a palm to the back of his neck. Even winced a shade, like her argument was valid but only to the point he still had to defy it. "I'm sorry, Mrs. Woods. I wish I had something else to offer *you*. The RAF has sent orders down, and in joint partnership with Lieutenant Colonel Robert McHenry of the United States Army 571st Division, we're assigned here. For the next six months at least. Maybe longer."

"All of you."

"That's right."

She glanced at the swarm of fatigues moving about behind them. "Here."

The captain nodded. Firmly, though as one still sorry about it. "Yes."

"And do you have a superior officer with whom I might speak?"

"Not one who'd dare countermand a lieutenant colonel's orders. Though you're welcome to try. I can put you in contact with his office stateside."

Amelia exhaled, her breath hazing to a fog in the last of dawn's chill.

The arguments she'd brought were crumbling in her mind one by one. There didn't seem to be anything left to convince the captain against making Parham Hill their new servicemen's resort. And when he put it like that, how could their little farm fight the grandiose militaries of two Allied nations?

She'd lost.

The captain seemed to pick up on the caving of Amelia's resolve and took a half step forward. He smoothed his voice to a softer tone. "We won't be in the way. It'll just be sleeping, curfewed hours, morning and noon meals—the US Army will supply the rations. Even tables and chairs to set up in the great hall."

"Tables and chairs in the great hall . . ."

Crikey.

Arthur's mother would have had ten fits were she not in London. Having children boarders deposited on the front steps of the family manor was one thing. It was the duty of all British citizens to do their part for king and country. But Yanks hooting and hollering and buttering biscuits with their morning coffee instead of sipping Earl Grey in the family's ancestral hall? Amelia would have a heap of explaining to do in her next letter to the Dowager Countess of Davies.

The captain paused. "Don't these big castles have a great hall or some servants' wing off the kitchen somewhere?"

"The only servants we have here are ourselves, Captain. But yes. We have a great hall. And in light of all this, I suppose you're quite welcome to it."

"We'll clean up after ourselves. No mess. No misuse. The men will leisure in USO activities at the base or in town. And it'll be missions by day, sleep by night. I promise, you won't even know we're here. These men are officers, and that means they have the utmost integrity. If the United States Army trusts them to lead other men in formation cruising at thirty thousand feet, then you can trust they'll do the same with boots planted on the ground."

"That junior driver at the front of your convoy is an officer?"

"Ah." The captain smiled, tiny laugh lines sneaking out from the corners of his eyes. "That'd be Lieutenant Cebert Byron Hale—C. B. for short. Arkansas boy. He's young but capable. He may be outranked in age and experience by most everyone on these trucks, but I'd say he can hold his own with the radios. He's the last man I'd worry about—including me."

Amelia felt the hint of a blush warming her cheeks at his self-deprecating defense of young Hale. She didn't know why—and certainly didn't want to form a sense of familiarity with any of the men by exchanging backstories. But as their worlds would merge for the next several months, they'd have to coexist. Through bombing raids at night and the harvesting of honey by day.

It would be another adjustment they'd just have to get used to until the war was over—if it would ever end—and life could get back to normal. Not in every way, but at least enough to help them keep going.

Amelia pulled Arthur's cable cardigan tighter around her middle, the dark-ink weave swallowing her petite frame. "Well, I'd best go tell the children what to expect." She tipped her head in a slight nod and stepped off past him toward the bustle of fatigues growing on the front steps. "And I'll just ready the great hall so you can move in."

"Mrs. Woods?"

Amelia turned. His hazels were there, holding fast, looking back on her with an unexpected kindness.

"Yes, Captain?"

"It's Wyatt. And I promise—you won't know we're here." He gave her a polite nod and tipped an imaginary hat on his head. "Good day, ma'am." He faded back toward the ranks.

Won't know they're here indeed.

If the roar of Flying Fortresses overhead and the crash of bombs echoing through the pastures were any indication, Amelia had a feeling everyone would have a wicked-fast adjustment period— including the bees.

THREE

APRIL 20, 1843
PARHAM HILL ESTATE
EAST SUFFOLK COUNTY, ENGLAND

Deception played an elegant game.

To Elizabeth's mother, Eleanor Meade, the Dowager Countess of Davies, the matrimonial pieces were artfully placed so no one should learn the extent of depravity to which she and her only daughter had fallen. But to Elizabeth, a life reduced to scraping in society's shadows was less severe a reality than her mother's view of it.

In truth, she was not sorry to put distance between them and their crumbling estate.

An invitation to a spring ball in Mayfair would have been a tricky venture to navigate—even for an earl's daughter of good standing. But to attend such a one at the reclusive Parham Hill Estate nestled in the Framlingham countryside provided better odds that no one from Yorkshire—or London society, for that matter—would travel so far. That, her mother hoped, would preserve their ruse.

For Elizabeth, it might offer a chance to finally exhale.

Rail lines were springing up in the English countryside like ivy ornamenting a garden, yet the price of two train tickets to Cambridge might as well have been to the moon for what they could manage. They'd boarded a mail coach under cover of night, the deep lingering of shadows ensuring they'd not be recognized on their way down the north road. They'd spent the next several days and nearly every quid they possessed traveling to their destination. Another day of wheels cutting through mud, frequent stops for water though a spring rain was driving it down upon them in sheets, and three changes of horses had drawn out the last leg of the journey, now east, to an exhaustive degree.

The cramped quarters of the mail coach had been exchanged for a roomier coach that afternoon, and though her taffeta ballgown was starched and stiff, and made her feel every bump in the road, Elizabeth preferred it to sitting in a soiled traveling frock as she had for three dreary days in succession.

Outside the coach window, the final landscape beckoned with orchards primed for a fresh planting season. Rolling hills buffered the horizon in a vibrant Kelly green. Rock-wall fences cut geometric shapes of the landscape in a severe gray. And a long willow-lined road stretched a lazy welcome, transfixing Elizabeth with the unexpected peace of such a view.

It felt like home—almost.

Yorkshire was more than ten years behind them now—her childhood estate in its prime barely a blot on her memory. If Elizabeth could only take out a brush and capture the faint lines and play of light that now cut golden patches through budded limbs . . . Or the diamond flutter of ripples across the surface of the lake they'd passed by . . . Even the melodic *clip-clop* of the horses' hooves proved a diversion, helping Elizabeth escape the mire of her thoughts— enough that she wished the moment could last forever.

"We've arrived," Ma-ma announced, as though the looming manor of Parham Hill hadn't enough of a punctuation on its own.

Ma-ma patted the coif at her nape, making tidy what had once been rich chocolate brown now tinged with gray. She leaned forward, ignoring the ornate stories of beveled stone and leaded glass in favor of tugging Elizabeth's skirt into submission. She pressed a palm against a crease, smoothing the length of her gown.

"Do sit up, Elizabeth. You cause more wrinkles than the bench seat ever could. I cannot hope to save you from them all." Ma-ma spotted the inevitable sight of a leather-bound sketchbook in Elizabeth's gloved hand and grimaced. "What is that?"

Elizabeth slipped it out of view against the coach seat, used to the long-standing practice of defending an old friend from insult. "Nothing to fret over."

"Fret indeed. Do away with it or we shall feed it to the fire. I indulge your fancies with sketching because it is a proper pastime of gentle ladies, but not a substitute for necessity. Marriage is a tricky business, both to acquire and then to manage. You'd best remember your duties."

"I remember," Elizabeth whispered.

And she did, because she was allowed to forget nothing.

It was another ball.

Another gentleman of eligible age and situation.

Another glimmer of hope that had morphed into a dramatic scene played over and over: she must secure a match, and fast.

Her mother reminded her in regular fashion that she'd been blessed with fair gifts of honey hair and porcelain skin with only a few freckles to mar the bridge of a pert nose—which they could hide with the right maquillage. And she still possessed the glow of youth beset by rose cheeks and a radiant smile. But they would not last. With no dowry, no title, and one Yorkshire estate that had secretly fallen into utter disrepair, Elizabeth hadn't much by which to rescue them.

Save for one ballgown.

It was a muted cranberry from two seasons prior that was still presentable, but not bold enough to be labeled as showy. Even though that's what it was. All it was, really—a bit of show enabling her to play a part, weave a masterful deceit, and ensnare her a husband.

Time had wings and they knew it full well.

"Now, Elizabeth. The estate owner is a Viscount Huxley—one of the Suffolk Jameses. I believe he is the great-nephew of your late pa-pa's distant cousin."

"Has he any family?"

"Both parents dead. No siblings, so he'll inherit everything. The viscount is still young. Unmarried, but he'll have to acquiesce to that soon if he wishes to produce an heir—which he must. The invitation declares this ball is a birthday celebration in honor of his lordship's friend. The man is said to be an old bachelor himself. Whispers say he is a struggling portrait maker the viscount seems to have taken into his acquaintance. No doubt he is a disreputable man with a lot that cannot be redeemed even by such a grand occasion."

Even if it were true, something fluttered in Elizabeth's midsection.

A portrait maker?

Trying not to give note that her interest was piqued by the mention of an artist in residence instead of by the most eligible ball giver himself, Elizabeth cleared her throat, adding a layer of singsong to her voice. "To be a portrait maker, would this man not have some provision to be commissioned by clients who must be in a position to pay for his services?"

"Oh, they have their wretched ways. Painters . . . vagrants." Ma-ma wrinkled her elegant nose and Elizabeth could have laughed aloud. Her mother did believe such wild tales of those who did not fit her mold of polite society and its upper crust.

"Have you the artist's name?"

Ma-ma waved her off with the flick of her wrist, instead giving ardent attention to the ruffle encircling Elizabeth's hem.

"What are they all named? Sir something or another. Lord this, His Honorable that. An artist of no consequence, I'd wager, if he attends a ball this far into the wilds of the East Suffolk countryside."

"Does that reflect poorly then on those in attendance?"

"Certainly not for us. Though it is said the artist is quite eccentric, he and Viscount Huxley are close in acquaintance—to the tune of the artist offering counsel on matters of both a business and even a personal nature. And to date, the viscount has selected no bride. That cannot be coincidence. So this penniless artist could prove a profitable confrère in the end, if we draw him out early."

"Perhaps the artist's affinity for portraiture would give us something by which to converse. I've never met a real artist—not one who makes a living by the brush at least."

"Penniless is not a living."

Elizabeth exhaled, frustration battling to escape her and finding only a pent-up breath by which to do it. "Ma-ma, do you really intend to force me into this? Might we consider the fact that Viscount Huxley has no desire to wed?"

"Your father had no desire to wed when we were united either."

"What in heaven's name does that mean?"

"Not a thing, save that you ought to heed my warnings to mind your duty, and mind it well."

"What is duty, when I, too, have heard rumors that the viscount is most austere in the company of eligible ladies? I heard tell of Lady Michaels's daughters who were so ill received not two seasons back, they escaped the estate before dawn to avoid the unpleasantry of engaging him in the same breakfast room the following day. I suspect the viscount needs no acquaintance to speak for him if houseguests choose to flee his estate of their own volition, and in the dead of night no less. It appears his manners are able to accomplish that all on his own."

"Then it is you who will prove those rumors false by dutifully changing his mind." Ma-ma offered a polished smile, as if her efforts in encouragement were best served in their last moments before they stepped into the throngs of the big show.

When Elizabeth did not reciprocate, Ma-ma forfeited pleasantries in favor of a grim countenance. "Elizabeth . . . you know our circumstances full well."

"I do."

"And you face destitution because of them." She paused, as if to let the cold reality sink in to Elizabeth's innermost being—as if the loss of her father before her eyes had not done that on its own. "*We* face it."

"I know that. But I am not unhappy. At least, not due to our circumstances." Elizabeth turned her gaze down through the remark, hoping the true nature of her interest would be kept well hidden.

"Have you a wish to become a country schoolmarm?"

"The thought had crossed my mind . . ."

"You—the daughter of an earl—would presume to begin boarding round at the mercies of a county's charity or to submit to the cruel insecurities of poverty's whims? That is tantamount to ruin."

"What a relief," Elizabeth allowed, finding her mother's brand of destitution a far more intriguing prospect than she'd clearly intended. "I believed marriage to be my only option. Please excuse me while I search my reticule for a ruler and chalk."

"Do not attempt to be clever. That is not the life your father wished for you."

"And yet this is what it is. Pa-pa is gone. I have no title, no prospects, and an estate in ruin all because I had the great misfortune of being born female."

"*Hush*, Elizabeth," Ma-ma shushed, looking out the window as if the entire countryside were listening in on their plight.

"But, Ma-ma, if we could only go back and open an inquiry into Pa-pa's death . . . I believe there is more to what happened than a robbery. I told you, there was a man. I saw him standing by, waiting for Pa-pa to emerge from the tea shop, and if we just—"

"Stop this at once!" Ma-ma balled a fist in her lap as her voice caught on the ragged edge of emotion.

The coach jostled over a rut in the road, punctuating the silence her mother's outburst had cut between them.

Elizabeth had never told her mother about the street urchin's eyes. She'd never told anyone, in fact. A child wasn't thought to have any information of grand importance, and though he was an earl, her father's death was dealt with swiftly and in quite a forgettable manner. The authorities hadn't any inclination to investigate a man standing on a street corner. A vagrant had been charged. Justice was done, what little there was for them in it.

"We cannot go back, Elizabeth, even should we wish to. We must move forward."

"But inheritance is of public record. Anyone making a basic inquiry might learn of our present circumstances. We cannot hide the fact that we live in a grand hovel. An estate house with nothing left in it but empty rooms and a skeleton staff."

"Who would inquire? Your father's name still holds merit with these people, even ten years after his death. That name garnered an invitation to this ball, and the few we've received this season. But even that good fortune cannot sustain us forever. We must move quickly if we are to secure your future."

"And if I wish to be more than my father's name?"

"To be that name is the only hope we possess."

Reading the pain in her mother's look, Elizabeth tucked the

sketchbook in her reticule and pressed her fingers to her mother's gloved hand. Straightening her spine, she allowed her face to become a mask of serenity and her posture ready to submit to duty's demands.

"Forgive me, Ma-ma—it has been a tiring journey. I meant no ill reply. The sketches are away. See? And old ghosts buried. I shall be at my best."

Sated, Ma-ma squeezed Elizabeth's hand in return and then released it, hope back in her smile. She watched out the coach window as the horses slowed and they stopped at a grand portico. "I have a feeling this is the night we've been waiting for, Elizabeth."

"I pray you are right."

Elizabeth brushed her gloved hand over her reticule, feeling the sketchbook that held the old drawing she'd pasted in the back cover, right next to the solid metal of the tiny revolver she'd hidden inside.

Perhaps this *was* the night she'd been waiting for.

One day Elizabeth would find him.

She'd look into the eyes of a murderer, and though she hadn't a clue whether she was brave enough, bold enough, or made wretched enough to do so, she'd deal a blow of justice that was long overdue to the man who had ruined their lives. Until then, Elizabeth would hold fast, readying her resolve in subservience to her mother's game, as long as the invitations came in and her best gown stayed in fashion.

The façade would not crack until it was time. But when it was, Elizabeth would find a way to avenge Pa-pa's death if it was the last thing she did.

FOUR

PRESENT DAY
FRAMLINGHAM
EAST SUFFOLK COUNTY, ENGLAND

Where Dublin had been home, with its iconic blend of Old World tradition and modern sensibilities, the thriving metropolis seemed a world away from the quaint pastoral hamlet that was Framlingham, England.

Bridge Street curved in a long, lazy row past shop fronts of brick and vibrant façades of mint, sapphire, and buttercup yellow. Union Jacks hung from row houses with brightly hued doors, with dog walkers strolling by. Cardinal-red telephone boxes sprouted up every few corners. Tourists nosed about the pubs and a tea shop and dress shop, which seemed as original to the storied old town as anything could be.

The faint hum of chimes sounded in the distance, their melody spreading charm at just after nine o'clock in the morning. Keira looked left and right out the car windows—only shops, sidewalks, October's colors painted on the trees, and humble row houses greeted them. "Are those church bells?"

"'Tis services at the Church of St. Michael, miss," said Mr. Farley, a driver of perhaps fifty with peppered hair, a swift nose for side-street navigation, and a decidedly lead foot for the entire journey since he'd picked her up at the airport. She'd emailed Mr. Scott when she arrived, and Mr. Farley showed up right after.

He angled the sleek silver Mercedes around a curve and through tightly packed rows of shops, parked cars, and a brick-walled garden, until the lane suddenly blossomed and the buildings stretched wide again, giving them space to breathe.

Keira checked the map on her phone, pinpointing their location. *Brilliant.* They were just down the street from where she needed to be.

"It's just there." He pointed out the left corner of the windshield as he slowed the car by a clearing of autumn-tipped trees.

A cemetery of ancient limestone grave markers, all white and mossy and tarnished with age, bordered the immense structure of a cathedral looming behind the scene.

"It's beautiful." Keira glanced at it. Quickly. So wishing she could linger over it but knowing they must be close, and she'd have to give attention or miss their stop. "If you'll just pull up on the right. I'm booked in a flat on the second floor of a shop, just before the Theatre Antiques Centre. There's a red front door and—" Keira noted, even as the driver picked up speed again and the cherry-red portal she suspected was hers whizzed by the open window.

They breezed past the back side of the cemetery, with more of its collection of weathered and weary gravestones, and a bower of trees that gave way to a fork in the road.

"Excuse me, sir. But that was my flat." She glanced at the map on her phone and hooked her thumb toward the back window. "We passed it."

"We're going on to Parham Hill, miss."

"Parham Hill? Where is that?"

"'Tis not a *where* but a *what*—Parham Hill Estate is just down the road a few kilometers from Framlingham Castle. I've been instructed to take ye there."

"And who gave you this instruction? Was it Mr. Scott?"

The man shook his head, as if the name were as foreign as the idea that she'd stay in the flat she'd booked on her own instead of some estate grounds she'd never heard the first thing about.

"Afraid I do not know a Mr. Scott, miss. I've been employed by a Mr. Carter Wilmont, says the reservation. Don't know more than that. All I can say is I'm on the payroll with instructions to retrieve a Miss Foley from the airport and ferry her to the manor house straightaway."

"There's a manor?"

He chuckled. Seemed everyone thereabouts must have known of it by his reaction. "Aye. Parham Hill has a manor. And a church, a village, their share of cottage gardens, and a grand estate at that. The manor 'tis rumored to be one of the largest privately owned houses in all of England. And I'm told to deposit you on its front steps or I don't receive payment. And, miss, I've kids in the highbrow school their mother demands, with a sticker shock to match. So I'll be taking you on as the instructions bid. If that's not to trouble you, of course."

"No. That'll be fine." Keira backed down with a smile, meeting his hopeful glance in the rearview mirror.

Children in prep school uniforms and knee socks with bright futures at stake melted something inside, forcing Keira to exhale over a prickle of irritation that she was, in effect, being professionally kidnapped at Mr. Wilmont's request. But it wouldn't hurt, she supposed, to go on to an estate she was there to survey, have the driver receive his due, and at least find out what she had been enticed to cross the Irish Sea for.

She sat back, watching as they drew up on a little pub on the left. The Castle House.

It had charm with wide, street-facing windows bordered in country-blue paint and a memorable view of green hills and ancient castle spires just a stone's throw away. She hoped along with the view they had a warm fire, a thick stew, and a stout cider. If the estate was a dilapidated hovel buried in the East Suffolk countryside, then the Castle House just might have another patron by night's end.

If this was a sham, Keira was boarding a plane bound for Dublin that night—right after she gave Mr. Scott the what-for he'd deserve.

Between the hollows and hedgerow and an open gate of weathered wood tangled over by ropes of ivy, a hidden road sprang up so fast, she'd have missed it had she not been looking out the window. Instead of venturing on to Framlingham Castle—which loomed large and majestic on the horizon—the driver veered off onto this secluded road, through a heavy gate of stone and scrolled iron, into what Keira presumed were the estate grounds of Parham Hill.

Golden willows waving in the breeze stretched out on either side of the drive. Rock walls bordered the road, their dappled faces fading into a one-lane cobblestone bridge that spanned a rolling brook. She leaned forward, spotting the thatch roof of a humble cottage just peeking out beyond the hedgerow, its moss-green door dirtied to a patina sheen and covered in overgrowth that masked it behind bramble and bush.

And then, as if she could have prevented her breath from being stolen away, the trees leaned back, the grounds expanded in a lazy stretch of green tipped in harvest orange, and the road widened . . .

A construct of beveled stone, leaded glass, and towering stories became the showstopper one might imagine of an old English manor.

Sharp corners cut rows of windows—too many to count at first glance—along the ground floor. Three stories soared high with

Corinthian columns bracing the façade. Stairs flanked a grand stone canopy that arched over a cracked and cobbled drive. Gardens hemmed in both sides of the manor in the only weary and overgrown bit of the property she could notice straightaway.

Save for the arrival of carriages and ladies in empire-waist dresses, it was as if Pemberley had fizzled from the pages of *Pride and Prejudice* and managed to sneak, unannounced, into the realm of real life. But instead of a brooding Mr. Darcy character haunting the manor's landing, the faded-tee-and-jeans-clad figure of Emory Scott emerged from the front doors, tossing a casual open-hand wave and a smile from the top step.

"So this is it—Parham Hill," Keira whispered on an exhale.

The driver stopped under the canopy just as the clouds gave way to a soft, misty rain.

She peered up through the fogged backseat window, shoving back Cormac's reminders to *"be on yer guard with the Yank"* and *"Are ye sure ye want to be doin' this?"* as he'd driven her to the airport. And just as her brother had done when she'd been stubborn and rash and packed up her world to move to New York on a whim, he gave a quick hug and a kiss to her temple, whispering, *"Remember, ye always have a home in Dublin,"* as his last good-bye.

The longing pricked her heart. Having home fires burning somewhere was a luxury not everyone could afford to cast off. Even if hers might be a flat above a Dublin pub with family dynamics that had tripped them all up for years.

Home is still home.

How could a lavish manor tucked away in the countryside dare attempt to compare with the familiar comfort of that?

Knowing Emory watched from his perch, Keira crafted a veneer she hoped would read as professional, relaxed, and completely detached from anything but speeding this business along. The driver opened her door and she stepped out, riding boots to the stone ground. She flipped the hood of her yellow rain jacket over her head, protecting her neck from the chill of the mist.

"You're late," Emory called out with a hand cupped around his mouth, then checked his watch. "It's Sunday."

"Is it?" Keira rolled her shoulders in a shrug as she pulled the strap of her leather messenger bag up from the backseat. "You told me to email when I arrived at the airport, so I did."

"I thought we agreed on Saturday."

"*You* said Saturday. I didn't say anything except that you might wish to find a seat in another pub."

Emory trotted down the stairs with rain dotting the shoulders of his heather-blue ringer tee. He could have been coming down a flight in his own home for how natural the greeting was, like they weren't virtual strangers but old friends.

Once under the canopy, he slipped a tip into the driver's hand, then reached for the suitcase the man set out on the cobblestones. "Well, you're here now. Dublin's loss is our gain, right?"

"There's no need—" Keira reached out politely, but enough that her hand caught near his on the handle at the same time.

"I don't mind."

"But I'm not staying."

Emory flashed a look that read every bit of *Then why the suitcase?*, his hand still gripping leather in a brush against hers. He released it without a breath and stepped back with hands that drifted into his jeans pockets, then tipped his head toward the looming structure behind them. "I think you'll find we have an extra room, or fifty, at our disposal."

"It's not that. It's just, I'm already booked at a flat in town."

What Keira wanted to say, but didn't, was that there was no way she was going into that maze of Pemberley-esque rooms alone with him. If he was able to read her at all, he could have guessed why: she didn't trust him.

And she wouldn't be fooled by a packaged smile again.

Keira flitted her glance up to the immaculate spread of stone and glass, trying her best to show only marginal interest. But the sky had settled into the familiar English temperament of gray and blue layers of clouds that hung low and a steady rain that made the senses come alive. The rich aromas of earth and autumn were loosed by it, and the glow inside manor windows bespoke a welcome so inviting, Keira was fast becoming overpowered by the invitation to explore its world—despite the presence of a rain-soaked Mr. Scott in its midst.

"And yet . . . you still want to stay on." Emory smiled, a curious tip at the corners of his mouth that said he'd read the silence accurately. She'd been taken in. Either by the majesty of the manor itself or the lure of what could be inside it, he had her number.

"It's your choice, Miss Foley. In town or here. If you really want to go back, it's not too far a walk from the village up to the manor. We'll pay the driver and cover your expenses for the flat. But just so you know, the rest of the team is already here. You won't have to entertain anyone on your own." He paused, she was certain for effect. "If, in fact, that's what's worrying you."

"I'm not worried." Keira ignored the cleverness that was too easy for him. "What team? You didn't say anything about that in Dublin."

He tipped his brow in challenge. "Come in and find out."

Instead of the sound of their shoes hitting the black-and-white marble floor in a vast empty space, the faint melody of "As Time Goes By"

floated through the foyer as Emory led Keira out of the weather. She pulled off the hood of her rain jacket, listening as water drops trickled down to the floor.

"Do I hear music?"

Emory shook his head once he'd closed the outer door and fiddled with a security system on the wall. She peeked down the hall.

They have a security system but empty rooms?

Baritone notes careened off high-coffered ceilings to the checked marble floor, like the rich tones had every bit of business to invade the interior with their velvet rendition of *Casablanca*'s famous song.

"Not again . . ."

"The music's a problem?" Keira couldn't see it as that, not when the notes were inclined to drift so effortlessly.

"Not the music; it's Ben. You can't tell him anything. He's our historical adviser and is vintage to a fault. It's charming to start—and he says not a bad in with the ladies—but if I have to hear 'Here's looking at you, kid' once more, it'll be too soon for a lifetime. At least we make a game of hiding his fedora, and then he agrees to buy dinner because he refuses to go out unless he looks like Sinatra's twin."

Keira extended the handle of her suitcase and set it to roll as he started through the entry hall.

"You said Ben is your historical adviser?"

"He is."

"Of what? And why the attempt at making this place a second Fort Knox?"

Keira's heart skipped over her question as the music swelled, and they passed through to an empty hall lined with burgundy-and-gold damask wallpaper, gleaming hardwood, floor-to-ceiling windows with whitewashed shutters opened to the rainy landscape . . . The glow of crystal chandeliers stretched out before them, and an oversize marble fireplace stood smack-dab in the center of it all, with gold and orange flames dancing.

She paused, feet frozen in place.

Emory slowed beside her, looking down the same hallowed view as she—sconces aglow and view stretching for what seemed like acres in front of them.

"I know. Feels like you're lost in a scene from *The Shining*, right?"

"Something like that. Only more royal and slightly less terrifying."

"We should hope." Emory began rolling her suitcase before she could this time and tipped his head down the hall, leading again so she'd follow. "This way."

They walked, the sound of big band music growing.

Emory led them past the sparking fireplace along a span of windows dotted with rain. "So, the security around art—you must be used to that. I've been told you were part of a field team that handled the restoration of salons at Versailles. Is that true?"

"I'd say more of a glorified assistant who made the café and crepe runs. But yes, security is a necessary evil, isn't it?"

"You used the contacts from that job to secure a position on a team that restored paintings at Wentworth Woodhouse in South Yorkshire. You worked in curatorial at Buckingham Palace for a summer stint. Should I add 'master of persuasion' to your list of skills?"

"Maybe I didn't have to persuade anyone. Maybe my education speaks for itself."

He shook his head. "Right. Sorry. I tripped into that one. But what I was trying to say is you don't have the royal connections by family, but you've been on the inside of some of the art world's crown jewels. I'd still like to know whether it's true or just internet rumor that you once attended a royal ball at Chatsworth House. All that, and yet you've never been here?"

"It's not as glamorous as all that. In truth, a friend and I talked our way in a back entrance at Chatsworth and were very nearly thrown in the Tower of London as a result. And I wasn't even aware *here* existed. If this is a private family estate, it's been hidden well from the outside world."

"Forgotten more like, until the owner decided to air out some rooms and found a heck of a wrench had been tossed in one of them."

"Well, my last job was curatorial in a Manhattan gallery and you plucked me out of a Dublin pub, so it's safe to say I'm not here to put on airs about my résumé at present." Keira slid a sideways glance at him. "You may have named a few things I'd have to put on it if I wanted to update it. But my father and brothers didn't feel the need to check my experience when they decided I could fill a pint glass and ring up a sale."

"Big of you to say so." He nodded and led her to the end of the hall. "Here we are."

Tarps were spread where dust and buckets and piles of brick lay bare the entrance to a room, its polished wood doorway cracked with age. Emory held out his arm, inviting her to step through in front of him.

"What's all this?" Keira edged around the brick, careful that her boots wouldn't brush against the mounds of work in progress as she went inside.

"Ground zero for the restoration efforts."

The room lay long and shadowed, with corners enveloped in musty books and rows of wood shelves, and an iron ladder system that stood dusted over like flour had been tossed in the air. The ceilings were high—so lofty she felt they'd stepped under the vaults of a grand cathedral—with a painted surface that hinted at glorious hues they might uncover with a good restoration. And affixed to the wall at the far end of the room stood something obscured by brick . . . A wall of weathered wood? Standing on scaffolding, a young man in worn flannel and black-rimmed glasses removed its brick shield at a snail's pace, so close his nose almost touched the mortar.

A small crew bustled about beneath him, connecting wires to cameras and hanging lights in draped corners. Emory shouted out, gathering attention. Someone flipped the switch on a cell phone, deadening Ben's beloved big band tunes.

"Everyone—this is Keira Foley. She's joining up with us."

"Brilliant! Boss here said we should have been lookin' for ye yesterday." A young woman left a laptop on an antique sideboard and stepped forward, sprightly in size with chopped ebony hair, a deep lavender decorating the wavy tips, a bright smile, and an accent full of Irish moxie.

She stuck out a hand, which Keira accepted. "An' Emory wouldn' dare let on how worried he was when ye didn' show. Must have checked that expensive watch of his every few minutes for the last twenty-four hours. Way to keep him in suspense. Ye ought to try that tactic durin' contract negotiations."

Emory cleared his throat over the woman's blunt delivery. "Ah, so this is Maggie Jane Mitchell, our project manager on-site. Basically, she makes sure the world keeps turning while we're working."

"An' she's a wicked social media maven, don' be forgettin'."

"Right. She's recording restoration efforts. And we may tease her about being named after a famous American authoress, but M. J. suits her just fine. And being from Irish stock, she doesn't pull any punches, as you can tell—though she hasn't quite learned the art of English subtlety. But we're working on that."

"Ha. That from the loud subtleties of an American." M. J. gave him a mock squint as Emory moved out of earshot, over to another member of the crew who was inspecting the setup of monitors and cameras in the corner.

"Nice to have another gal in the mix to give these gents the what-for. If everythin' Boss here's told us about ye is true, 'tis an honor to work wit' ye."

An honor?

She cast her gaze over to Emory. What had he said about her? More than that—what did he know?

"Thanks . . ." Keira looked from their leader to the controlled chaos around them. Stacks of books. Library shelves with an iron ladder system. A skeleton crew of guys setting up filming equipment and untangling wires at their feet. "But what's this all about? He didn't set me up—just tossed some euros my way and told me where to show up."

M. J. smiled and leaned in on a whisper. "Not surprisin'. Ye'll learn that Boss Man o'er there keeps his cards close to the vest. *All* o' 'em."

"Keira? The rest of the crew's over here," Emory shouted and waved her over, then pointed out the guys with noses buried in technology, camera equipment, and to-go coffee cups. "This is Eli with the Red Sox cap—our videographer. And Ben is our historical archaeologist by the scaffolding—that's fancy talk for the guy who tries to dismantle a brick wall with a toothbrush without taking the entire house down with him."

"It's nice to meet everyone, but . . ." Keira paused after shaking the hands they'd stretched out in greeting, taking in the sight of production plans taking over the manor. "Am I here for some sort of art consult or a reality show?"

M. J. tossed a sideways glance over to Emory. "So ye didn' think to warn her?"

Emory shook his head and crossed his arms over his chest. "How could I? Would've ruined the surprise."

M. J. turned back to Keira. "Well, welcome aboard. Yer in for a treat. We'll flick on the lights an' roll film as soon as Carter pops in. Then ye'll see."

"See what?"

"What all this lot is for. Our guest of honor."

Keira didn't even have time to assess what they were looking at, let alone to know why a crew was mixing with the likes of Emory Scott. "Is Carter another member of the crew here?"

Emory shook his head. "Not likely. He thinks we art-lovers are all a little crazy. But Carter Wilmont—also teased as our Viscount Huxley—is the owner of the estate."

"An' yer best chap from prep school, don' be forgettin'."

"More partner in crime. He gives us free rein around here because we do all the work. So he indulges our whims to research musty old books and bricks, while he pops in every now and then to write checks and make sure we don't burn the place down." Emory shrugged. "Keeps us honest."

"Honest enough to tell me what's going on here, Mr. Scott?"

Emory glanced at M. J. and the crew, who'd heard her question and stood smiling with a shade of half knowing upon their faces.

"We need you to authenticate a painting. Simple as that. You tell us the who, what, and when behind it, then I can hand over the rest of your fee."

"Alright. You have my attention." Keira slipped the leather strap of her messenger bag over her head and set it on the floor at her feet. She looked around, finding only books, shelves, and shadows dominating the walls. "What painting?"

"Why wait? Carter's late and this isn't his show anyway. It's hers." Emory stepped over to connect an extension cord into a portable outlet. "Miss Foley . . . meet Victoria." He stooped to flip the switch, and the room exploded in light and color and spines lining book-shelves all the way back to the scaffolding. One last spotlight flicked on and then, under the glow of soft white light . . .

Queen Victoria.

The immaculate portrait of the queen had her royal shoulders bared, hair unbound in a rich brunette coil over her collarbone, and a subtle longing in the eyes that seemed to invite the room to delve into their cerulean depths. She hung surrounded by book spines and aged shelves, tucked in the corner so she was nearly hidden by the skeletal frame of an iron rolling ladder.

Keira abandoned her bags and stalked forward, aching to touch fingertips to canvas—though she never would do such a thing.

She stepped up until she was a breath away, inspecting the paint strokes. Barely visible but breathtaking at the same time. Hues had faded from years of existing unseen in the dark, with color clearly not what it once had been. But Victoria stared out, steady, with a presence so regal Keira's legs weakened because even a whisper that the portrait had once been in the presence of a queen was enough to warrant reverence.

"That is . . . Queen Victoria . . ." Keira breathed out on a ragged whisper before she could stop herself. Her skin prickled the length of her limbs as she collected her thoughts. "This isn't a Winterhalter, is it?"

"We don't know. That's why we need you." Emory had shoul-dered her leather satchel and rolled her travel suitcase along, then stopped it on the hardwood next to her boots. He stepped around the iron ladder into her line of sight and casually leaned an elbow against the metal tine as he looked at Victoria alongside her. "So it's back to town then?"

Keira shook her head, still transfixed by Victoria's regal domination of the immense room. "Not on your life. I'm not going anywhere until you tell me what in the world is going on."

A smile—free and knowing—covered Emory's profile as he, too, took in the image of the queen. "Like I said, Foley, welcome to the team."

FIVE

Men might say—even believe—they could go about unnoticed, but it was almost never true.

As the officers had moved into nearly every square inch of the manor's ground floor, the library at Parham Hill turned into Amelia's last remaining sanctuary. It had become an odd sort of companion out of volumes with cracked spines, pages yellowed with age, and faded rectangles on the wallpaper where her late husband's heirloom paintings had once hung.

Books were would-be fablers and old friends—the copy of *Peter Pan in Kensington Gardens* she'd pressed between her palms being one. The rust-red cover of the Arthur Rackham–illustrated version, with its gold-lettered title, showed wear, having become well loved and much faded since its 1906 printing.

"Mrs. Woods?"

Captain Stevens's voice stirred Amelia back to life, her hands jolting so she almost dropped the book. She swept her index finger against the row of her bottom lashes, tidying her face, then slid the book back in its glass case in the sideboard. She clicked the door closed.

"Yes, Captain." She turned, expecting him to engage her in conversation right away. Instead, he was enthralled. Speechless. Standing with hands pocketed in the center of the library, a veil of astonishment drawn over his features as he looked up to the ceiling.

It had to be the first time he'd seen it.

Amelia wished she, too, could walk into the Parham Hill library for the very first time all over again. With soaring timber-vault ceilings . . . Two-story, rounded-corner bookshelves in polished rosewood and an iron ladder system that spanned the length of the room . . . Crown molding outlined in gold that never seemed to fade . . . An oversize mantel and soaring brick fireplace . . . The Rococo scenes of English country life splashed in rich blues, golds, and greens across the ceiling . . .

The only glimpse of their current reality was the shattered glass of the grand Palladian window that had been boarded over from the inside after it had taken a hit from a rogue bombing early in the war. The room still held a secret beauty, even though it had been closed off from the rest of the manor. The heirloom paintings it had once housed had been crated up and stowed in the safety of an interior ground-floor storage room, and the furniture now was exposed after its ivory dust covers had been repurposed as clothing for the children.

"I didn't mean to disturb you, milady. But I was told I might find you in the library. I just didn't know it was like this."

Quite right. If she wasn't at work on the estate, she was at play with the memories of it.

Amelia loaded a stack of books in her arms and crossed the space to the opposite wall, her work boots clicking the hardwood. She climbed two steps on the rolling ladder and set the books eye-level on the shelf. "How may I help, Captain?"

When he didn't speak right away and awkwardness befell the room, Amelia turned to see if he was still there. His eyes weren't military then—all deference and leading drills. Questions hovered in their hazel depths, his obvious curiosity quite unexpected in the moment.

"Is something wrong?"

"No. It's just . . . It's true then? You're a viscountess?"

Darly. Amelia would have to kill him for perpetuating the lie that she was to be treated as royalty because of a silly title she'd obtained through marriage and only held for the year after. "Who said so?"

"The address for the rations was made out to a Viscountess Huxley. Is that you?" Wyatt tipped his brow, eyes teasing just a shade. "And you answered to *milady* without missing a beat."

Amelia felt a blush battle its way to the surface.

Perhaps she had.

"I'm afraid it's not as glamorous as all that. We just keep the 'milady' part quiet around here—especially when I'm mucking out barn stalls."

"But now you've opened your home to evacuated children, manage the estate grounds, harvest honey, and give the what-for to a bunch of bee-swatting GIs who stepped in to turn over your world. Quite the title earner if I ever heard of one."

"I believe titles are actually earned in one's actions *after* they're inherited, but that is not always the case in the real world, is it? And that's what we have here more than anything. Several of the children arrived years ago and haven't seen their parents at all in that time. We're lucky to have two teachers come in from the village school, or I don't know how we'd manage. The library got lost in the shuffle of honey harvesting and keeping things going, I'm afraid, and I'm backed up in my chores to get everything restacked. If that's not a triple dose of our real world, I don't know what is."

The captain turned a circle in the center of the ground-floor room, under a chandelier that twinkled from reams of morning sun. "A shame," he said, chin up, looking over the rich designs of gold coffer and baroque art spanning the ceiling vaults. "It should be used more. You could give tours, when this is all over of course."

When this is all over . . .

Tours of an English manor seemed a world away to think on, not when flyboys were sleeping on cots wall to wall in the drawing rooms, children from ramshackle lives in London were packed like sardines in the upper-floor chambers, and bombs fell from the sky like a stout English rain.

Amelia pushed the possibility of tomorrow from her mind.

"I'm just tidying up in here, Captain. So . . . is there something I might help you with?"

"Yes, actually. I'm looking for Mr. Woods—or should I address him as Viscount Huxley? I don't know how honorifics are handled here. I haven't yet had the chance to speak with him, and there's a list of essentials I need to discuss about the estate."

Amelia breathed in, her hand freezing to the first spine on the stack.

How long had it been since she'd heard her husband's name spoken by anyone other than the voice in her head or the longing in her heart?

Her mother-in-law mentioned "my son" in letters, but that was only in the occasional missive to check on the state of affairs at the manor. The children hadn't known Arthur well for how infrequently he was on leave those first few months of the war. Even Darly didn't say his name, and Arthur had been his great-nephew. It was as if the manor held its breath, keeping all from speaking of who and what they'd lost before they'd arrived.

Perhaps each expected their own world to start again after the pause of war, and the reasons why they were all tossed together in a makeshift family at a country estate would have been nothing but a terrible dream.

How she wished they could wake from it.

Captain Stevens cleared his throat. "Milady? Are you alright?"

"Yes, Captain. Do go on."

He held a scrap of paper in his hand, ticking things off aloud. "I need to see about bomb bunkers—are there any on the grounds? And there's a list of supplies coming in from the airfield we'll need to organize. Then there's security at the front gate and the men's schedules, how we can minimize any effect they might have on the children. And where do we park the jeeps we'll have to use to ferry men back and forth from the airfield? It's a growing list, I'm afraid."

Amelia stepped down the ladder, her denim coveralls brushing the iron rail and work boots touching back to polished hardwood with a *clip-clop*.

Very well. If he needed to speak with the trousers that ran the place, he would.

"That is a list with which I shall have to assist." Amelia faced him with an assuredness that surprised even her and took the list from his outstretched hand. "I'm afraid my husband died four years ago."

What former ease he'd shown faded from his face. He slid a hand into the pocket of his uniform trousers, his demeanor far less animated than before. "I'm so sorry . . . I didn't know."

"You couldn't have."

"I'm still sorry for your loss." He paused for a breath.

The scampering of shoes clipping the hardwood drew both their gazes to the doorway. A boy stood there, winded and smiling, his herringbone newsboy hat over a mop of burnished-brown hair that curled out from under the brim.

Luca's was that beautifully awkward, seven-going-on-eight-years-old toothy grin—messy and perfect they were at that age. These days it was one of the things she lived most to see. He graced them with it, taking off his hat to turn in his hands.

Amelia leaned against the bookshelves, waiting for him to ask this time.

When he opened his mouth to speak, she whispered, "In English, if you please."

He thought for a moment, fingertips running over the hat brim while his mouth moved, silently trying to place the words. "I am here for my book, milady," he announced, the shadow of a German edge to his accent.

She pulled the pocket watch from her coveralls pocket—noon.

"You are right on time. Barely." Amelia narrowed her eyes in play as she walked over to the sideboard and plucked a burgundy leather-bound journal from its top. "And do you see we have a guest?"

Luca looked to the captain, giving a polite nod as he accepted the journal from Amelia's outstretched hand. "You're an officer?" He glanced at the uniform, up and down the tall drink of water. "A flyer?"

"Try to be on a good day." Captain Stevens knelt, smiling on a playful whisper. "What are you reading?"

"I'm writing, sir."

Too many questions. Too much risk to have them form an acquaintance. "Uh, Luca . . . hadn't you better be off? Your sister will not take kindly to tardiness for your lessons. I'll see you back here after, and we'll see to your other studies. Yes?"

"And. . ." Luca shifted a side glance to the officer. He cupped a palm around his mouth, adding a secretive, "We'll check our painting after?"

"Of course we will. As usual. Now—shoo. Off you go."

Luca shifted his glance to the captain again, a mere second of notice. Was he deciding whether it was safe to leave milady with the stranger—maybe because of the uniform plus the smile? Then he fled back down the hall.

"He's a bright lad."

The former melancholy was swept away as a smile pricked Amelia's insides. "He is. Yes. And his sister will have his hide if he's late for lessons again. Already at seventeen Liesel's as strict as their mother is, apparently. As you can see, there's a manor of teachers and children, a pasture of bees, and now two squadrons of officers to tuck into the fold. I'd say we're about as full as can be expected, given the circumstances. So you'll have to bring your lists to me in future and we'll see what needs to be done with them."

"You add teaching Luca to your list of daily activities?"

"Well, that is our little secret, but I figured being an officer, we could trust you. He wants to learn to read in English, as his older sister prefers their native German. So I've agreed to help. We're tripping our way through together."

He nodded, accepting her answer without argument. And then his demeanor softened. He looked out one of the windows, to the green pastures stretching beyond the manor.

"I hate to bring it up, but for practicality's sake, how are you fixed at night?"

Amelia's attention snapped to him. "I'm sorry?"

"The raids." He pointed a fingertip up to the soaring ceiling. "You know, to see about the children?"

"Oh." She exhaled fast. "Yes, of course."

Air raids had occurred with such ferocity in places like London and Norwich, and though they'd had their share of close calls, the Luftwaffe wasn't frequent in threatening the country estates like they'd pounded the metropolitan areas. But being not far from the coast and with an airfield in such close proximity, they still needed to consider the reality that a German Dornier could slip through again . . .

She prayed—every day—it wouldn't.

"We get along."

"You have Morrisons in the manor? I didn't see any shelters outside, so I have to assume with so many children here, you have some indoors."

"Yes, we have Morrisons—they're packed away in the cellar, where we keep the bees in winter. And we do have Anderson shelters, but they're buried in the gardens and that's where they'll stay. Past the rock-wall fencing. We don't venture out there much, at least not unless it's absolutely necessary."

He looked out the windows again, as if he expected a formation of Luftwaffe fighters to loom large on the horizon. "But isn't that too far from the manor? If bombs fall, how do you get the children to safety in time?"

"We manage well enough, Captain." Amelia's heart closed up like a coastal town awaiting an impending gale.

The captain was nice enough, with kind eyes that looked but never lingered for too long, and the manners that came with integrity and maturity were easy to see over some of the other officers. That was a comfort. But in matters where he was attempting to tread—quite uninvited—Amelia wouldn't allow the liberty to dig any deeper than the surface of estate doings.

Parham Hill was their world, and she was willing to give her life to ensure the children remained wholly untouched by war in the midst of it.

"If you should provide me with a supply list, I'll see that Mrs. Jenkins is aware of the incoming rations. Preparing tea for a real army may come as something of a shock to our cook's sensibilities. I'd like to break the news as gently as I can, and a list that includes butter and sugar could be just the ticket to smooth things over."

If the captain noticed her deflection, he didn't comment or argue. Just nodded and handed the list over without another word.

He wasn't bullish, she'd give him that.

"I can have a cook sent over from the canteen."

"That won't be necessary, Captain. It's just a matter of getting organized." Amelia slipped the list in the front pocket of her coveralls and whisked past him toward the door, leaving the stacking of books—and private memories—behind for another day.

"Milady?"

Amelia turned, not wishing to appear rude but simply regretting she couldn't acknowledge a title she didn't deserve without an air of serviceable indifference. "Yes?"

"This may be a bit presumptuous, but . . . may I come back here?"

"To the library?"

He nodded. "If I promise not to disturb you and Luca, that is."

"Well, we're not often in here exactly."

"Oh. I see. Secret lessons require a secret space?"

The man—quiet in his responses, and with undetermined motives—wanted to come back to the library? *Arthur's* library . . . No one spent time in here but her. And Amelia's time was all packed up in the memory of yesteryears. Now this man wanted to share that? He couldn't have known what he was asking.

"You read, Captain? I mean, for pleasure."

"It's Wyatt. Please. And yes. I read."

"The kind of books one might find in a well-stocked English library?"

He leaned in, lowering his voice. "*Any* books. I try not to judge by the cover if I can."

"Alright." She paused, her feet almost tripping her back a step to put distance between them. The removal of stones from the walls around her heart was a painfully slow process—as was any new development that meant the world was moving on without Arthur. "As long as we can agree you will not call me 'milady'—that title belongs to my mother-in-law, and she's quite content to keep it to herself. 'Mrs. Woods' will do me fine."

"I believe I can remember that."

"Grand. Then there are the likes of Joyce, Keats, and Shelley, if you prefer, on the upper level. Plenty of Shakespeare. Dickens. The Brontës or Austen, if you really want to get the full English experience while you're here. Thoreau and Mark Twain—for the Americans in the room—are at the far end by the fireplace."

"Thanks. I'll take a look. Though, my apologies—I'm not what you would call a fan of Jane Austen."

"As an officer in the United States Army, I'm not sure I'd have expected you to be. But I'll leave the rest for you to discover on your own. You may borrow whatever you'd like and leave what you've read in a stack on the sideboard. Just please do not take any from the glass cabinet under the window."

He tipped an eyebrow.

Yes, you just saw me place a book back on its shelf, but please—don't ask me why.

"Secret stash?"

"No. Not secret. Just older." She smiled, brushing off anything close to an explanation. "They tell a good story, but it's one so fragile I'll not even take them out to relive it."

"To relive what?"

To relive time. Parham Hill's broken story. The library's legacy. Even Luca's very presence at the manor. Captain Stevens—*Wyatt*, as he seemed determined for her to call him—could have taken his pick. But the one story Amelia wouldn't relive was the yesterday when everything had changed.

When Arthur put his life on the line and lost it . . .

"It would do no good to relive a past that's best left on the shelf. If you'll excuse me then."

Amelia whispered a "Good day" and whisked out of the library, wishing the tiny decisions of yesterday weren't sometimes the very ones that could manage to change everything about the future in the blink of an eye.

SIX

APRIL 20, 1843
PARHAM HILL ESTATE
FRAMLINGHAM, ENGLAND

"You are lost, Fräulein?"

A man's thick German accent echoed against the high ceilings of the estate library.

Elizabeth jumped, then whirled around.

Impeccably dressed in an ice-gray coat with luxurious fox trim at the collar . . . Fair hair that mingled with gray at the temples, in his mustache, and in his tightly trimmed beard . . . Not unattractive, but a bit older than she'd anticipated. And severe.

"Lost?" Elizabeth wasn't lost. She was snooping in a private library, and they both knew it. "No, sir. I am not."

The gentleman had surveyed the crowd with mild interest from his perch by the ballroom's marble fireplace, almost since they'd arrived. Ladies had twittered past, fluttering fans and batting eyelashes under his deep-cognac glare. Yet he seemed to ignore the lot of them, as if the party both bored and irritated him in equal measure. He maintained a cool yet polished distance from the room.

Elizabeth had fallen into duty, dancing with several eligibles her mother had seen fit to introduce, until they could manage to draw an audience with the viscount himself. As usually occurred, the ballroom walls had begun to close in on her from all sides. The refuge of a quiet hallway beckoned and she'd stolen into its depths, the haven of an exquisite library the unexpected prize at the end. There she could finally exhale surrounded by books, dark-paneled walls, gilded chandeliers, and a fire that danced in the hearth, as if the room waited for a weary-hearted traveler like her to come hither.

And then . . . *the paintings.*

Canvases dominated walls between rows of spine-packed shelves, stretching toward the ceiling in gilt frames taller than a man. Portraits depicted generations of Huxley men with strong jaws and broad shoulders under various military regalia, and brushstrokes created the rich landscape of what she assumed was Parham Hill Estate behind. Yet, curious enough, not one lord was fair haired. Or decidedly severe, except for those in heroic, battle-ready posture. She'd looked over them all, her first habit to search their eyes, but found nothing save for oil on canvas and the dance of firelight against the hues.

At least until he'd found her.

"Whatever finds you in here?" He flitted his glance across the vast treasure trove of books around them. "The party is . . ." He pointed to a second set of doors at the far end of the library. The sounds of tinkling crystal, melodic reels, and general gaiety were muffled by the heavy oak, but alive in the background nonetheless.

"In the ballroom," she finished for him, her midsection generating a nervous tick under his scrutiny. "Yes, I know." She tucked her reticule at her side, out of sight, in the folds of her gown.

"Hadn't you better return to your line of dance partners? No doubt they are lost without the charms of your company." He stepped to a desk nearby and casually leaned against it.

"As we have not been introduced, sir, I will beg your pardon and take my leave back to the ball. I have yet to meet our host, and I should like to thank him for his generosity in arranging such an evening. I bid you good night then." Elizabeth bowed and, in a fluid motion, lifted her hem and quickened heeled slippers toward the door as if her feet had been put to a flame.

"Stay—" He rebounded like a shot, the desk creaking to signal he'd risen from it. *"Bitte."*

The protest arrested her. Elizabeth turned, found him standing with a hand out, half bowed and elegant, offering a leather wingback across from the fire.

"My apologies," he offered, keeping his post. "I welcome the diversion. We can be introduced and the doors will remain open, if that is at all concerning to you. But please do not leave me to the wolves out there. I fear I should not survive it."

Wolves?

Elizabeth suppressed an offbeat smile at the thought she and the stranger may have something in common. Marriage seekers in ballrooms could be wolves—including Elizabeth and her mother by very definition—but in the library, they both detested the packs with the same fervency.

Reading her smile as confirmation that his hook had worked to draw her back, the gentleman bowed. "Pardon, Fräulein. I am Franz."

Odd. One was never introduced with simply a Christian name and no title or surname to accompany it. No doubt they did things differently on the Continent.

She bowed in return, reluctance keeping her gaze upon him. "Elizabeth."

"Not *Lady* Elizabeth?"

This ball was a misstep. Another loss. Why not tell him the truth? They'd never meet again.

She walked to the fire and eased her gown down to the edge of the wingback's leather cushion, keeping her back poker straight. "In the ballroom, perhaps. My mother is the Dowager Countess of Davies, and she wishes me to remember that fact when I am amongst the peerage. But lost in a library such as this? No, sir. I assure you I am quite plain in comparison."

"Plain you are not," Franz scoffed, but nodded as if satisfied with her answer in some measure. He moved about the room, his tension appearing to ease as he took a decanter from behind the library's ornamental desk and held a crystal tumbler to the dance of firelight. "Would you care for one?"

She shook her head. "No, thank you."

"Then you won't mind if I indulge." Franz poured amber liquid into the tumbler and hesitated not at all before he partook of a deep drink. He eased into the wingback opposite her, his regal silver-fox coat melting against leather as he surveyed the room, a spell of orange cast by the firelight.

"And what is your reason for escaping the wolves, Lady Elizabeth?"

"I have no reason to be discontent—not in a ballroom such as the viscount owns here."

"That is not what I asked."

What purpose was behind the cat-and-mouse game he'd initiated? "You ask me to insult our host and fellow party guests by naming them ravenous beasts?"

"I suppose I did." He chuckled and offered an artful tip of the brow, signaling humor was easy for him. "But we should have nothing to fear in speaking openly. Not as we are both hiding."

"If you must know, I sought the artist. Then I saw paintings in here and wondered if he—"

"The artist? And who is he?"

"It is said there is a portrait maker in attendance tonight. I seek to inquire whether those rumors are true."

"Gossip? I would have guessed that above you, if you are not one of them." He twirled the liquid in his tumbler.

A thought sparked within her.

He was foreign. Direct in manner. Noticing of details others might overlook. And perhaps even playing the part in clothes borrowed from a wealthy viscount? It wouldn't have been completely unforeseen . . .

"You are not he . . . are you, sir?"

"What gave me away?" Franz gave off such an air of disinterest coupled with outright folly at the notion that the thought died almost as soon as Elizabeth had entertained it.

"Well, I fear I will remain disquieted until I learn the truth."

"The truth?"

"Yes. If he is, in fact, penniless."

"Penniless?" Franz let loose an easy laugh and stretched his legs, crossing one riding boot over the other at the ankle. "What manifold tales! Pray go on. What else has talk of the dance floor seen to produce but a sorry character as a penniless painter come to fritter away hours with England's noblest wolves?"

"You misunderstand. I seek only to learn if his plight is real, not to feed rumors of speculation."

"But what is your interest?" When she didn't answer, he continued, his voice a mocking whisper. "Perhaps . . . you are an artist?"

She tilted her head to the side, matching clever for clever. "Are not all accomplished ladies expected to be such?"

"*Ach*, I should be more direct with someone as witty as you. Perhaps matrimony is its own art form. Many a lady has mastered it and found herself far from penniless as a result. There is but a ballroom of eligible ladies beyond these library doors."

Elizabeth bristled at being smacked with truth. Even more at a stranger's boldness in judging her so completely. "That is quite a remark, sir."

"Forgive me. I am a foreigner. We know no better." He stopped, as if that explained all, and threw back a final gulp from his glass.

"I haven't a wish to marry into anything, sir—not a grand library or an estate."

Franz stood, as if he disbelieved her claim and had already lost interest because of it. "Revolutionary talk for a lady. And what makes you so much better than a ballroom of wolves? Hmm?"

"Better? I wouldn't think to—"

"Of course. We would never say such a thing." He abandoned the tumbler on the desk and turned back, amusement at play in his smile as he tapped his index finger to the side of his head. "But we might think it."

That's quite enough.

Her mother may have plucked and pulled her taffeta gowns and reared her for such a time as dancing the long hours through a gilded ballroom of gentlemen, but her pa-pa didn't raise a fool. Nor a milquetoast either.

Elizabeth stood, ready to quit the room and certainly to forget his abhorrent presence in it. "Pray forgive me, sir, for speaking with such sharp overtones. But I would not pledge to marry a man simply for what accompanies his name. I will be no pawn, not even if a gentleman possessed every painting in England. If you'll excuse me then. I find the air in here is a little *weak*."

Elizabeth bowed and quit the library in a singular breath, then whisked down the hall with the art of composure on her mind.

Brash and bombastic . . . How dare he! No one had ever spoken to her in such a manner of insult.

Not in any ballroom of polite society in London and Yorkshire combined. Perhaps East Suffolk was farther away from civilized society than she'd anticipated. But despite the biting rebuke, it steeled her resolve if anything could. Elizabeth was determined—now more than ever—that a contract of marriage would not be in her future. Not if she'd be forced into the tight little box of convention and expectation where the fairer sex was concerned.

Sketches and paintings may not purchase a future, but something would be salvaged of the circumstance fate had seen to level against mother and daughter. Whatever it was, it would be by her own hand.

The music continued, as did the jovial chatter of guests, an oblivious melody of high spirits greeting Elizabeth when she returned to the ballroom. She tipped her chin up, noble and serene as she could make it while weaving in between guests, though embarrassment coated her insides like wax. She'd been a fool, emboldened by the lump of a tiny pistol weighing down her reticule, and so prideful as to believe herself stronger and mightier than she truly was.

Had she no worth other than to seek revenge for something that could never be undone? Or in the same vein, could do nothing more with her mind, passions, or convictions than to adorn a gentleman's arm?

Both were prisons. And neither would set her free.

As the moments ticked by, Elizabeth sought her mother's form through the maze of gowns and dancing partners, flowing gauze and feathered coiffures, and the swirling of couples with whom she knew she'd never fit in. But soon, relief. Standing near the fireplace in quiet conversation with a gentleman of no particular notice stood Ma-ma.

Elizabeth could place nothing of the man beyond a tall frame, tailored white tie dress, and a crown of refined brunette hair that was somehow mussed as if the wind had toyed with it, even within the confines of an obstinately hot ballroom. She watched them, determined that once the gentleman had left, she would convince Ma-ma to make their excuses and part ways from East Suffolk for good. They could rest at an inn in the nearby market town of Framlingham, at least for the night, and then use the journey home to consider their next step.

Stringed instruments faded to a halt and couples slowed, leaving the center of the room a mismatch of dancers without partners. Elizabeth peered through the crowd, then in horror her heart sank as understanding set in.

The eccentric, loose-lipped foreigner from the library stepped into the ballroom and every head turned to gaze upon him. Ladies twittered with awestruck whispers and flopping fans. Gentlemen parted as he entered, their animated conversations giving way to bows and wistful smiles, so Franz might make his way unfettered through the crowd.

He glided through with an air of practiced elegance, smiling and boasting with playful eyes, but he wasted no time in stalking over to interject himself into the same cozy conversation Elizabeth so intently watched. He patted the taller gentleman on the arm in brotherly affection and bowed most elegantly to Elizabeth's mother.

Oh no . . .

Elizabeth tightened her grip on the reticule in her palm, feeling the cool metal of a gun barrel stinging through the satin of her gloves. While the gentleman spoke with Ma-ma, Franz talked and nodded in her direction as though they'd been in acquaintance for years instead of having just met. He paused, then leaned to whisper something against the other gentleman's ear.

The gentleman nodded—a quick flit of the chin at which Franz erupted in smiles—and patted his shoulder as a father might a proud young lad who'd just caught his first fox at hunt.

"Ladies and gentlemen! Good eve to you all." Franz clapped his hands to draw attention that had already been his. The echo of his shout seemed enough to tickle the teardrop crystals on the chandeliers, and even the service staff looked caught up in the man's felicitation.

"I, Franz Xaver Winterhalter, greet you—"

The blood drained from Elizabeth's head.

Franz Xaver Winterhalter . . .

Who wouldn't know the name of the most famous portrait maker for the crowned heads of Europe? It was he. Standing in that very room. And she'd just insulted the life out of him in his closest friend's library.

"It is my esteemed honor to attend your gathering this *Nacht*—a celebration I do not deserve but will no doubt indulge from the kindest of gentlemen on this the day of my birth. An artist's travels are never so enlightened as when he is in the company of dear acquaintances. So it is with even greater honor that I announce the Viscount Huxley—our very own Keaton James and our host this glorious eve—is to take a wife."

The ballroom erupted in a riot of gasps and clapping praise.

Elizabeth looked to Ma-ma, who was fairly in tears as the applause continued. She met Elizabeth's gaze across the ballroom, and as the throngs of guests celebrated, and more than one young lady wondered whether she was to be queen of such a grand estate as Parham Hill, Ma-ma nodded. Just once, with maternal pride glowing like fire in her cheeks.

Elizabeth knew exactly what it meant: their efforts had finally proved some worth.

The deal had been brokered, and Elizabeth had been sold.

Following the pronouncement of her name—Elizabeth Anne Margaret Meade, daughter to the Earl of Davies—she heard only a fog of voices. Her insides churned and roiled like she'd swallowed a caged beast battling for freedom.

This cannot be.

Not now . . . not ever.

The Viscount Huxley offered her mother his arm. Stringed instruments resumed their jolly melody, and the guests clapped around Elizabeth as he turned and then moved in her direction, presumably to claim her as his prize.

A man of seemingly careful manner and noble brow advanced toward her, yet nothing could untangle that moment. Eyes of the stormiest steel with a jagged line of gold bored into her soul with their decade-long familiarity, stealing the breath from her lungs. All Elizabeth could think was that her dear ma-ma had been proved right for the first time—it was the night they'd both waited for.

Mother and daughter had each found the man they hunted, never realizing he was one and the same, nor that the night would end with Elizabeth betrothed to her father's murderer.

SEVEN

What seemed only a few moments of time morphed into a long silence as Keira inspected the intricacies of Victoria's visage, absorbing the tiny strokes of light and dark, the blues and crimson and crisp white hues dulled by time to a creamy yellow.

Running her index finger along rosewood shelves, Keira walked the length of the room, cataloging titles in her mind. Then she peeked over Ben's shoulder, asking a few but not too many questions about a curious row of wood planks he was working to unearth from behind a patch in the brick wall. And in the midst of all the beauty and mystery of a forgotten library, as the rumbles of thunder outside had begun to drift away and the team had gone about their work, Keira had all but forgotten Emory was standing behind her.

She turned. Found he waited with a quiet presence, having faded into the background so Keira might have the freedom to gather what information she sought. He leaned against a doorjamb on the far wall, watching with one leg casually crossed over the other. "Have a question, or twenty?"

"You know I do."

Emory tipped his head to a tarp tacked up at his right, pulled it back like a curtain, and leaned in, gesturing for her to walk through. "Good. Let's get some air."

Feeling a bit like Alice stepping into the library's secret rabbit hole, Keira walked through and emerged from the cutout of plaster and wood into a gilded ballroom on the other side.

Coffered ceilings soared. Pristine robin's-egg walls gave the expansive room a regal but cool tone. And floor-to-ceiling windows let in natural light despite the gray veil of rainclouds outside. It was both vast and grand, but dispirited in a way without a host of settees or even a piano to keep it company.

Keira turned in a slow circle, boots clicking on the dull floor, imagining elaborate gatherings around the room's central fireplace and ballgowns that swirled as tuxedos led them in circles over the gleaming hardwood.

Had anyone a clue that such a treasure had been walled off right behind this one?

"And this is what's better known as the Regency Ballroom."

She had to hand it to Emory—he knew how to punctuate a moment.

A laugh slipped out of Keira's lips before she could stop it. "I wonder if you go through life pretending to be mysterious until the truth suits you, Mr. Scott. It's not usual to woo a prospect to a job while sharing almost no details of the work she'll be doing. You know you've hooked me with Victoria, even as you've told me nothing about her. What am I to make of that?"

"You can tell we're wooing you? That's good. I was worried we hadn't made that clear."

"You weren't worried." Keira sent him a squint-eyed glance that told him so, even if it was layered under lightness. "And you know you aren't being the least bit clear. Is it intentional?"

Emory stopped to look back at her. He waited before her like he was nothing if not entirely comfortable in his own skin. A quiet confidence defined him—so opposite from her that Keira felt it above all else in the room.

"Maybe. I'd like you to tell me what you see."

Victoria was a stunning hook to tempt Keira to stay on. But if she ventured too far into this thing with her answer, she could be in danger of reordering her life.

"Well, based on fade marks of the wallpaper in the library, several other paintings had hung in there with Victoria. That tells me light was allowed to flood in the length of the room for quite some time. For years maybe. But where are the windows? Or other paintings?"

"Windows—we're working on that. Paintings—a search is being conducted in the manor now. This place has quite an attic to sift through, if you can believe that. But if there's nothing to be found, it won't be for lack of trying."

"I can't understand why such a treasure was closed off from the rest of the world. The library alone is a masterpiece, even before considering the things it might have contained. At least the books are still there, though I'd have to see what condition they're in to say much more about how they fit in this puzzle."

"You authenticate books too?" He smiled, as if hoping to add to her role more responsibilities as the moments wore on.

"You don't want me to."

"Look, I'm sorry we don't have more answers. Not yet at least. Carter may not have found the library at all if he hadn't employed a clumsy contractor for renovations. He's been trying to decide what to do with this place—restore, sell off, or employ some combination of the two. When this all started, he just wanted to unload an old family manor he'd inherited. And if it wasn't for the crew knocking an errant hole in the wall, it might have happened that way. Then neither of us would be standing here now."

"Mr. Scott—"

"You can call me Emory, remember?"

"Right. Emory. I wonder if there's one thing at this manor you could show me—just one thing to make a lick of sense to an outsider. I'm intrigued by the library. And if she's real, Victoria could be like nothing I've ever seen." Keira swallowed hard, not wanting to reveal that this could be the thing she needed to get her career—her entire life—back on track. New York was a disaster. This didn't have to be if she treaded carefully. "What I don't understand is why you called me. Or how you even found me, for that matter. I'm on the fringes of the art world, so the fact that you dug up my name is astonishing."

He stood before her, arms crossed over his chest. "You want to see something real, huh?"

"Yeah. I would."

After a quick nod, he turned to the back of the ballroom. "Follow me."

Emory led them to the row of windows and opened a set of French doors in their center. They emerged onto a stone terrace where Keira could see rolling acreage behind the manor, dotted with rock walls and autumn rain that clung in mist over the fields. The willows held loosely to their leaves as wind and sky embraced its gray mood.

They walked down steps to a path shadowed by rock walls on both sides that stood at attention over Parham Hill like a great aged guardian of stone. Emory moved with purpose, that was true, but so did she. And Keira was far too direct for her own good—Cormac had told her a hundred times . . . She just couldn't let things go.

It was a fault, but she always wanted control.

Needed it, in fact.

"Why didn't you tell me about Victoria when we were in Dublin?"

"And you'd have come by Saturday if I had?"

Keira shot Emory a pointed look, though he kept face forward to the path ahead of them.

His profile was strong—he didn't seem one to flinch easily. But then, that would have been learned. She may have brushed elbows with art royalty in Paris, London, and New York, but Keira had done enough research to know he'd been born into it. Old money bred the same old connections. Being the son of a Wall Street tycoon meant Emory Scott was schooled in how to navigate under high scrutiny and when to jump through the gilded hoops of the art world.

By all accounts, he played the part well.

"You stated you're aware of my dissertation—how I don't know. But the queen wrote about the portrait she commissioned from Winterhalter in 1843, calling it in her journal 'the secret picture.' Even though several were made in miniature, there is a strong inference by some in the art world that the original portrait may have had a twin of equal size."

"But if it did, it was never found."

"And . . . this one looks remarkably similar to the only one history can authenticate, and that portrait now hangs in Kensington Palace. Knowing that, I don't care what it would have cost me. Had you said a word about it, I'd have been on the very next plane."

"Waiting was my call. I knew if I'd told you about her, you'd have jumped on a plane without blinking an eye. And I wanted you to join us not for her, but for you."

"Meaning?"

He shrugged, buried his hands in his jeans pockets as they walked through the misty rain. "Meaning, I know what it feels like to get socked in the gut and have to keep going."

Keira readjusted her gaze out in front of them, the horizon

proving safer than having a heart-to-heart with a stranger who owned a remarkable sense of the authentic about him. Better to shrug off the connection and act as if she hadn't a clue as to what he meant.

"Everyone gets socked in the gut sometimes. And everyone has to keep going. I'm not special about it."

"Maybe not, but when I took a hard look into who would be the best fit for this team, everything in me said you, Keira. You're not impressed with status or notoriety, yet you've got a résumé most in the art world could only dream of. You walked away from curatorial at the Met because you felt a stronger pull to the undiscovered talent you could see hanging in a Midtown gallery. And your own brother unearthed a major historical find at his Wicklow estate, yet you moved into a Dublin flat and were content to bus tables at a pub when you could have come in and told everyone at the National Trust where to go. That says you're in this field for the sheer love of it, and we need that on our team."

"I'm sorry to disappoint you, but I came for a paycheck."

Emory slowed his gait, halting in front of her like he disbelieved the comment as much as she did, even though she was the one who'd voiced it. "And now that you're here?"

"If you can answer me one thing, then I'll consider staying for that paycheck—and for Victoria."

The air had settled and a chill blew over the fields, but for some reason Emory didn't seem cold. He stood before her, waiting, relaxed in his jeans and worn tee like it was the height of a summer's day.

"Alright." He looked down on her, as if he'd been prepared for her to say something like that. "Shoot."

"Did you steal the Klimt? An irreplaceable 1908 golden goddess plucked from a wall in your gallery is something I find difficult to overlook."

Emory found his humor just then in a boyish smile that bled

down over his features. He appeared almost embarrassed about it. He tossed his gaze down at the ground before he kicked a stone on the path with the tip of his boot. "You already see yourself as Victoria's protector. That's good. She's lucky to have you on her side."

"I'd be any painting's protector. If you've asked me to come here to authenticate her, I need to know I won't be implicated in an art theft once I tell you what she is—or how much she's worth. I won't allow a repeat of Vienna on my watch." Keira stared back, meeting him eye to eye. "So, did you steal it?"

Emory studied her with a softness in his eyes that somehow whispered he'd answer her and that answer would be the truth.

"No."

"You were head of security."

"I was head of everything. But I didn't have anything to do with the theft."

She shifted her weight. "Then why . . . ?"

"You mean why was I shut out? Cut off from my family? And sequestered to an estate hidden in East Suffolk because the one person who won't abandon a shamed man is the best friend from his youth? I don't have all the answers, except that even those closest to us can become enemies when you tell a truth they don't like."

"What does that mean?"

The hint of a smile Emory always seemed to carry with him faded and something heavy replaced it. "It means enough time has passed that the truth doesn't matter now. Come on—it's just over the rise."

"How could truth not matter?" The concept was foreign to her. *Truth is everything.*

Had she wanted further explanation, Emory did not intend to give it. He led her across the brook, their boots hitting cobblestones on the bridge and continuing until the path faded to rain-soaked mud and the rock walls broke into a rusted iron gate drifting on an old hinge.

Keira looked up and saw it close up—the cottage she'd noticed hidden beyond the front gate.

A tiny path led to stone steps, a moss-green door covered over with a heavy layer of soil and grime, and window frames that had long since lost their panes of glass—only remnants of stained glass in faded evergreen and deep royal peeked out from the corners. It wasn't small by any stretch, but it was so heartbreakingly tired. The thatched roof had too many holes to count, with mossy tiles that had crashed down to the interior below. Raindrops collected and dripped in a soft cadence from the corners of the eaves, almost as if the cottage were crying over its own woeful state.

"What is this place?" she breathed out, enchantment reeling her in without fight.

Emory joined her at the gate. He pushed it with his palm, the iron hinge letting out a grating cry as though it hadn't been disturbed from its slumber for decades. At the sound a bird darted out the window and soared out over the meadow in a rustle of chirps and fluttering wings through rain. They watched it fly for a second or two, then turned back.

"Old beekeeper's cottage."

"There were bees on the estate?"

He nodded. "There are still. This is a working honey farm, though production has fallen to the owners of the Castle House pub down the road. It's not really much of a moneymaker now. More local lore than anything. Honey and beeswax candles feed the shops in town—for the castle tourists, what there are."

Keira ran her fingertips over the edge of the crumbling rock wall. Lovingly. As if she could relay with a touch that someone still cared about it. "What's happened here—other than the obvious?"

"The erosion of time. Best I could learn from the locals, some-one was killed inside when a Blitz bombing raid missed an Allied airfield and bombarded the tree line behind. It took out the entire side of the cottage with the damage you see there. And after that, it was never repaired. The owners just seemed to . . . let it go. It was abandoned by the end of the war."

Someone was killed . . .

The manor loomed over them like a great shadow, its grand walls and ballrooms and library seemingly untouched by time. All the while, a two-story beekeeper's cottage, its little arched windows with tiny shards of glass still poking from the corners and chimneys that looked like they'd once been harbingers of the warmth from inside, had withered with the ghost of it.

"Why has no one thought to restore it?"

"Seems like it's speaking to you the same way it did to me. But eccentric nobles do what they do, so that would be Carter's call. He has interest in many things, just not a burdensome estate in the East Suffolk countryside. He received the title and land upon his father's death, and being the son of an investment capitalist, his view of the estate is more in how to be rid of a burden at the most opportune price than to spend any real time unearthing its ancient history. But if you see some worth in restoring it, you might try to convince him. He's got a heck of a bankbook to work with. It's probably a lost cause, but you could still try."

"If that's true, then why did you want me to see it?"

"Because, Keira." Emory reached out and curled his palm around the top of the gate next to her, his fist clutching iron like he, too, was holding out hope for something. "This place has a story buried somewhere, and I think you can help dig it up."

"And why are you so interested in the story of an estate that isn't yours?"

The question died between them when a silver convertible tore up from Church Street.

The car kicked up sprays of mud and swirled fallen leaves from the lane that led from Framlingham. Its soft top was up—a sleek black on a silver bullet of a sports car that whizzed behind the rock wall, then revealed itself to be an Aston Martin when it emerged into the clear. It screeched to a stop under the stone canopy at the manor's front.

They watched half a pasture away as a man hopped out and tossed the keys in his hand before shoving them in the pocket of his navy sport blazer and trotting up the stairs.

"Carter?" she asked, though the answer was clear.

"Carter." Emory drew back, as if the magic cast by the cottage had fizzled by the mere reminder of the modern world. "That'd be our viscount. Posh, fast, and late as usual."

"Well, let's go meet him. I have more questions before I agree to anything."

"And he'll be glad to answer them for you. Though I have to admit he seemed a little too eager to have you come on board after he saw an actual photo of you. For the record, I find that highly unprofessional, even if it is warranted."

Thank goodness he'd started walking again or else Keira would have had to admit a tiny blush warmed her cheeks. She didn't know what that was. Maybe wounds left over from the last time easy compliments had been tossed her way? Whatever it was, it left alarm bells ringing in her head.

The contradiction of reluctant trust-fund kid, would-be art thief, and unexpected gentleman had her considering what kind of game Emory was playing. Or was it a game at all? Was the quiet team leader walking alongside her as innocent as he put on?

A Klimt was still missing. He'd given no explanation about that.

That left her on guard.

"A word of caution?" Emory whispered, looking over at her with a humored brow as they trekked back up the rain-sodden lane. "Don't fall in love with him."

"For a couple of school chaps, it sounds as though you two don't get on. And you insult me with comments like that, Mr. Scott. I'm a professional. You can't think that's the first Aston Martin I've ever seen in my line of work. I won't fall in love with anyone."

"You sure about that?"

She straightened her shoulders and tipped her chin up a notch. "Quite sure."

Keira fell in love with him.

Every inch of the six-foot-two, sandy-haired, Kensington-bred Carter Wilmont was as Emory had described. He was posh and perfect in manner, fast in wit, and fashionable at everything in between. And she fell in a New York minute.

By the time they breezed through the ballroom doors and back into the library, Carter's persona had managed to overtake the entire space without much effort at all. He'd caught up the crew in chatter by the scaffolding at the brick wall, the young viscount engaging in conversation with evident ease.

"Emory!" Carter approached them with a gleaming smile ready to greet his friend. He shook his hand, then turned to her. "And you must be Miss Foley?"

"Keira. Yes."

It was the oddest thing, but Keira wished she had a mirror just then. She hadn't thought to check if her hair was tidy when she and Emory had walked down a blustery autumn lane. And she hadn't thought about the literary tee, rain jacket, and jeans she'd worn that day until a viscount was suddenly standing in front of her with a tailored blazer, perfect smile, and outstretched hand angling in her direction.

"Emory said you grew up in London?" Carter asked, a sure grip taking over hers.

Whether by honed skill or providential talent, he had an uncanny ability to freeze out the rest of the world around them and slip into laser-focused conversation.

"Uh . . . yes. South London. Brixton."

He tipped his head toward M. J., who was working off to the side. "A friend of our Maggie Jane perhaps? Forgive me, but I thought I heard a bit of Ireland in you just now."

"We just met, so yes—fast friends. But I'm from Dublin, on my father's side. I've been living back there for the last six months or so."

"Mmm-hmm." Carter brought a palm up to his chin. "Well, Emory's recommendation is enough for me on a bad day, and meeting you makes this a good one. But I'm afraid I'm a bit on the skittish side. Past doings have made me a rather careful chap—for better or worse. So . . . you'll sign a contract for hire?"

"Of course."

"And a confidentiality agreement? As our art historian in residence, you'll agree to stay on at the manor while under contract, you won't leave Framlingham unless it's cleared with me, and you'll keep everything you see here in the strictest confidence. No contacts in the art world unless I'm told ahead of time, yes?"

Keira tossed a glance to Emory's place by the door. He didn't speak, but his eyes said, *I told you—eccentric.*

"I suppose I'll sign, if my professional word isn't enough."

"It's not that at all, Miss Foley. Everyone here has signed. It's just part of the hiring process. We have checks and balances in place on nearly everything these days. Pesky barristers and such, always try-ing to ensure the world is buttoned up to their complete satisfaction. The way they see it, wouldn't want a photo of our queen here popping up on social media before we can time our tips to the media just so, to find the right buyer at auction. That sort of thing. And all headaches avoided until we can plan a nice little unveiling at Sotheby's."

Keira drifted her gaze over to Victoria.

The queen hung there so regal in the glow of lamplight, her eyes gazing out at the span of room like Prince Albert stood behind them. Keira decided that signing a few papers meant little if she was given the freedom to dig into the story of the estate, starting with the masterpiece that hung before her, and maybe ending with the bee-keeper's cottage. By the looks of it, the cottage ached for someone to walk through its door again.

"If your world must be buttoned up as you say, then I'll agree. As long as I have free rein to research her the way I see fit."

"The rest of the crew is tasked with the structure of the manor, including the library, but you'll be in charge of authenticating what's in it, alongside Emory."

"Brilliant. I think we'll get on well enough. But I do have my own way of doing things. Hope that's not a problem for you, Viscount. When it comes to the art, I call the shots. *All* of them. And the deci-sions are mine until the contract says otherwise."

Carter nodded, just once, on an electric smile. "Done."

"And if I want to discuss further restoration of the estate—the outbuildings and such beyond the manor—what would you say to that?"

Keira glanced back to Emory, looking for support. But some-where in the last moments between Carter's requests and her survey of Victoria, he'd managed to slip away, like a specter gone to haunt another one of the hundred or so rooms at Parham Hill.

"Mr. Scott walked me around the grounds and . . . ," Keira began, searching the shadowed corners of the library, even though she had a suspicion she'd not find him among them.

Carter rolled his eyes heavenward. "Let me guess. The tour started and stopped at the cottage?"

"Mr. Scott feels it's important to the story of Parham Hill. And the history of the painting, though I can't see what connection there could possibly be."

"You and me both. Emory's been pushing me to restore that musty old shed from the moment he stepped onto the grounds, when it has no worth to us at all. Complete waste of time."

"He seems to think it's not."

"Well, that'd be our elusive Mr. Scott. He's a steady chap—the best, actually. Couldn't ask for a better friend. But when it comes down to it, once he gets something in his mind to grip, it's going to be a wicked-hard fight to get him to open his fist and let go. It was the same after that business in Vienna . . . I keep telling him the art world is fickle and he'd be much better served leaving the past in the past. But he's going to do what he wants. Living day-to-day and pressing in on the things he values is just his style."

"He doesn't strike me as someone overly concerned with style."

Carter looked up, surveying the high ceilings and painted scenes locked in by gilding at their edges. "Don't I know it. He's got a pair of faded trousers and an old tee for every occasion. Calls it some non-sense about living more simply. He won't listen, poor sod. Just jumps into the deep end with two feet wherever he goes. And here I've called him in to do the very thing he should steer away from—nosing about curating paintings for a world that trips him up at every turn."

"Well, feel free to bring me the contract and I'll sign. Mr. Scott can decide what to do with all this when he resurfaces. Until then, I'll keep a keen eye on Victoria."

Carter agreed with a "Welcome aboard" and an easy smile as he drifted off, charming his way out of the room. And it certainly seemed easy for him. But the friendship with Emory—trusting a rumored art thief with what could be a priceless find? That one would take longer to untangle.

Keira fell into historian mode. She found her tortoise-rim glasses in her carryall and slipped them over her nose, then pulled a protective glove over each palm. She plucked up vintage tools of the trade—a notepad and pen her preference for jotting notes instead of a smart device—and then went to work.

Though she had to set aside the unspoken tension between two men of completely opposite dispositions, in those moments, she saw only Victoria.

Even so, she expected the questions to keep up their assault—and it was her job to find the answers, wherever they might be.

EIGHT

The heirloom-silk gown teased the women in Framlingham from the window of Bertie's Buttons & Bows dress shop.

Amelia passed by each time she rode down Church Street on her old bicycle, creaking over every bump of uneven cobblestone, heading to Wickham Market for the weekly shop. The sight of it brought both bliss and anguish in equal measure, though she'd venture back by every Tuesday, riding the long way through town just to peek in the windows and see if it was still there.

And there it would hang.

The liquid-satin gown. Gleaming. And pin-tucked in all the right places, with gentle cinching at the waist and a wrap bodice that created a dangerously elegant V connecting up to structured shoulders. It swept to the floor like a bucket of cream had spilled over the inside of the window box ledge with a fishtail train gathered in a pool on the hardwood below.

The prime minister's government encouraged Englishwomen to "keep up standards"—solemn faces and scraggy buns tucked under prewar cloches would degrade morale, just as it was considered unfashionable to bop about in frivolous trappings. There was a delicate balance to strike, and so the high-priced beauty hung there day after day. Who could possibly surrender eighteen ration coupons for a length of satin a woman might be able to wear but once?

Practicality was the beast that ruled them all with a war on. Amelia spent her days in denim coveralls, a rotation of serviceable blouses, and the couple of herringbone skirts she mended to keep nice enough to wear in town.

Amelia rode by the shop toward Framlingham Castle, waving at sweet old Florence "Bertie" Bertram in the window, who was busily frilling her display of hats and sundries around her shop's token centerpiece. One last stop and Amelia could forget the gown for yet another week.

She pulled her bike up to the entrance of the Castle House, leaning it against the stucco wall of the public house before she stepped inside. The old brass bell above the door clanged its usual welcome.

The rich aroma of turtle soup awakened her senses—it was not her favorite, by any means, but if she was able to save a coupon or two for Darly's love of it, she did. She was greeted by the central bar of polished wood, humble tables with mismatched chairs, Tudor walls that stretched to low ceilings, and a playful fire sputtering in the hearth.

It was sunny but undoubtedly brisk that day, enough that Amelia was drawn in to stand by the warmth of it. Years of rations without replacing silk stockings meant her legs were bare and rightly covered with gooseflesh under the length of her midi skirt.

Thompson poked his head out from behind the bar. "Ho— milady!" The old man waved. "No rain today, eh?"

A blush warmed Amelia's cheeks.

Milady. Perhaps she was more used to it than she'd realized.

"Good afternoon, Thompson. No more rain, I'm delighted to report. I'm not certain I'd have fancied a ride through the backroads from the castle—all that mud left over from yesterday. I have but one good pair of buckle shoes left, and I'm afraid I'm rather protective of them."

"Ye'd be clever to mind yer step, milady. The cobbler's shop has a line down the sidewalk for those wantin' repairs. Best make it a wide berth when clouds start their gatherin'. But go on wit' ye then—warm yourself by the fire," said the fourth-generation innkeeper and cook, with a disposition as warm and wrinkled as the cheer in his face.

"Winds changing do make for good soup weather. And sitting by a fire." Amelia removed her dove-gray gloves, set down the old biscuit tin she used to transport his famous soup, then slid it across the bar top.

"The usual then?"

"Please. But with a spot of extra pumpernickel. There was a surplus at the butcher's and that put Mr. Clarke in a rather pleasant mood—enough that I was able to purchase rashers for the children and still keep one coupon back for Darly's favorite meal. He shall be delirious with this good fortune."

"It seems old Darly will be in for a treat tonight then—more than turtle and water stews in the back. We have potatoes! We received an extra crate in shipment, and rather than huntin' out what the mistake be about, they disappeared into the belly of our soup pot. Still had to use the armored heifer though. But bread we'll toss in at no extra charge as thanks for the autumn blossom honey ye sent over."

"Well, I don't think anyone is going to complain about canned milk to thicken a soup, especially when you have bread with honey to accompany it. Do you need more than two crocks? We have extra put by in the cellar."

"I'd take all if I had my mind." He smiled. "But no. Keep the extra sweetness for the children. They'll be wantin' somethin' special come the holidays."

Somehow the fire seemed more pleasant than usual. The dining room was calm as it awaited the flood of villagers who'd fill it come teatime. And on days like this, Thompson was eager to share news of what trickled in from locals. They hadn't a cinema in town, and since Thompson served as both postmaster and head of the Framlingham night watch, it was best to check in where stories arrived before the newspapers had set to print, and activities of the airfield were sure to be carried from house to house.

Thompson's sons were long grown and had missed the call of war, but that didn't mean the old innkeeper hadn't a keen heart for their village boys fighting it out overseas. Even the Yank flyboys had grown on him for how they frequented his dining establishment. It was in fact what Amelia bargained on in stopping by that afternoon. It had been nearly three days since Wyatt's crew had been seen after their last mission.

Three days . . . and no news.

"What news from the airfield today?" Amelia asked, hopeful as she eased into a wooden chair by the fire. She crossed her legs and unbuttoned her deep-merlot topper down the front. The fire sizzled its warmth like a blanket wrapped around her.

"A Combat Box of flyers went out in the wee hours. The watch counted them out from the roof of the butcher shop—a sturdy formation of twelve planes. Then we took turns standing out in the bitter cold and waited nigh until the afternoon hours for 'em to come back."

When his face grew serious, a breath locked in her lungs. She squeezed the gloves in her palms before she knew what she was doing. "And . . . they did?"

He nodded. "A mighty relief. Watched them come in not two hours ago. Counted the big birds one by one and didn' breathe until both squadrons come through, wit' Spitfires flying their escort. They all touched down at the airfield safe and sound."

Amelia let go of half the breath pent up inside along with her white-knuckled grip on the gloves in her hands—the Parham Hill officers were safe for now. That's what mattered. She just had to pray that when the post did come in, it didn't include any heartbreaking telegrams from the War Department.

"Well then, it's jolly good to have had such a large harvest this year. The wax will keep St. Michaels in supply so we can all light candles for the boys at the front. The children pray for them every night. They even remember our dear prime minister—Luca thinks him a rather formidable figure but prays our leader will see an end to this war so he might be reunited with his parents again."

"That young lad keeps his sister on her toes, eh?"

Amelia's heart squeezed. "Yes. And the rest of us too."

It wasn't likely the townsfolk would inquire about a little scamp bustling about their shops and pubs. The fact that Arthur and Amelia had secretly taken in a pair of German Jewish children as far back as Kindertransport in December '38 wasn't something she wished to explain to anyone outside of a trusted few. And the fact that she was hunting down the fate of Luca and Liesel's parents at the height of misinformation and roadblocks behind enemy lines . . . It was a monumental task that seemed to move at a snail's pace.

"I am quite certain God hears the prayers of those whose greatest wish is to be with someone they love, so He must hear ours—both for Luca's family to be reunited and for all the boys to come home safe."

The bell interrupted with a clear tone, ringing out as the front door opened.

Amelia looked up as the tall form of Captain Stevens breezed in and stole her thoughts away.

Several of the units had been on mission, Wyatt's among them.

The 390th was flying formation over enemy territory and Amelia knew little else, save that rumor had it Captain Stevens routinely volunteered for the more dangerous missions over the other officers. Yet he stood there in the flesh, clean cut and whole, clad in uniform trousers, button-down shirt, and flight jacket—even with the hint of a smile that said meeting her here was quite unexpected but not unnoticed.

"Captain. You're back."

"I am, milady. Just." Wyatt gazed upon her from across the dining room. He tipped his uniform hat with a thumb and index finger curled on the brim, then seemed to think better and took it off completely, turning it over in his hands. "And Wyatt will do me fine, ma'am."

"I suppose we did agree to that, didn't we?" she said on a light laugh that emerged without warning. "Though I'll remind you I'm not keen on the title 'milady.' A few gents get away with that around here, but they're too set in their ways to change now. We agreed to drop the formality since you're staying on at Parham Hill for the next months, did we not?"

"Of course—"

"Mrs. Woods." Then, on an ill-thought whim, she added, "Or Amelia is fine too."

Thompson intervened, breaking the cordiality between them with a jovial smile and a reach over the bar for a hearty handshake with Wyatt. And wasn't that always the way of it with pub owners and innkeepers? They seemed to understand the delicate art of what to say and how to say it, knowing when to keep mum about the particulars of others' business and when to balance it all with the simple act of extending a greeting.

"Captain! Welcome back. Sit down, sir." He waved a hand out across the empty dining room for Wyatt to join Amelia. "With milady over there. 'Tis not teatime yet but the pot's boiling. Ye get first of the special this eve."

Wyatt came over to Amelia's table and paused for a breath, in the kind of noble hesitation a gentleman exhibited when standing in the presence of a lady in the dining room. "May I?"

"Please."

He tossed a glance over his shoulder in the direction of Thompson's clanking and clattering in the kitchen, whispering low, "I'd hate to insult the man, but I've never actually prayed for my next meal of K-rations until I was served black pudding and haggis in this dining room. Please say I'll make it out of here alive, or I'm afraid I'll have to cut and run right now."

"I think you're safe this time," she whispered. "Turtle soup and bread."

Apprehension abated, Wyatt scooted up to the pub table, the chair creaking under his weight.

The fire popped in the hearth, toying with the silence of unfamiliarity between them. They'd passed in a great hall full of officers and smiled once or twice a day. They'd discussed matters of the estate as rations came in and orders carried men out on several occasions since the first morning they'd met in the library. But one on one, sitting and looking at each other across the space of a little table and barren dining room? That kind of conversation was new—and terribly stiff, as if the air itself were all thumbs.

"You've been to Parham Hill?"

He shook his head. "Not yet. Our crew just returned. Gave the men a pass so you might see a few trickle into town tonight."

A thought struck her. "Did you sleep?"

"I will. Later." Though he didn't have half-moons darkening

the skin under his eyes, the one-word answer made her guess his sleeping routine was more of catnapping spurts than actual rest.

"You can't say what it was that kept you away."

"No." He smiled. "But to be honest, you wouldn't want to know. We try not to think about what has to happen in the planes starting with the moment our boots touch back on solid ground through briefing for the next time we go up."

"Yes, of course. I'm sorry."

"I'd much rather hear about things here—the honey harvest, Darly's adventures in the fields, or Mrs. Jenkins shooing officers out of her kitchen with a swinging broom. Or what you're reading to Luca these days. How's the informal reading club going?"

"Slowly, but turns out it's enough to keep him distracted from the bombing raids at night. The journal he came to fetch in the library—it's his own making. A record of every air-raid siren and drill we've had. Seems he wants something to take home, a memory of sorts to show his mother how he and Liesel spent their time with us. And a makeshift reading club helps to pass the time between events."

"Do you take new members?"

She started, registering an unintentional pause. "I don't know . . . No one's asked yet."

"Maybe pose it to him then. See if he'll accept a third. What are you reading?"

"He wanted to read *Robinson Crusoe*, but I managed to convince him *Treasure Island* might be better suited to his age. I had to think his mother might appreciate that."

"Ah. *The Life and Strange Surprising Adventures of Robinson Crusoe of York.* Quite the literary work for a seven-year-old."

"It started with finding anything of interest to him—the sea proved to be it. Luca and Liesel had to leave their home. And family.

They traveled across the Channel before the war began, and it was the unknown of another shore that captivated him. It was meant to be a distraction at first—just reading aloud to get him simmered down at night so he could sleep. But now that he's got the bit between his teeth to learn, it's become our ritual to get through the days too."

Amelia shook her head, then turned her glance to the window. It was difficult to imagine a world thirty thousand feet up where sunshine and blue skies erupted with bomb blasts and planes busting to flaming bits among the clouds. How odd it was for her and the children to have some semblance of a normal life on the ground with all that turmoil exploding above their heads.

"I can see something is bothering you. Bombing raids? It would be alright if it was."

She turned back to him. "I wouldn't think to trouble you."

"By all means—trouble me. That look means something. Can I help?"

No matter how Amelia fought it, curiosity reigned. Arthur had been an RAF pilot. He talked about it once or twice, what it was like steering a metal beast to claw through the sky and losing the few school friends he'd enlisted with. But there hadn't been time enough to ask more before he'd been killed. And a host of unanswered questions plagued her.

If anyone would give her a straight answer, it might be the captain who seemed prepared, steady, and untouched by the brutal nature of it all.

"What is it like up there?"

Or to crash.

Or to watch planes fall out of the sky right in front of you . . .

If Wyatt wanted to explain what she guessed was fear-inducing about it, he didn't. Instead he wrinkled his brow as though thinking for a breath and decided on a quick answer that suited him. "It's very cold."

Deadly. Cruel. Terrifying. Unforgiving . . . Amelia imagined missions could be described as all of those things. But simply *cold*?

"Cold?"

"So cold the dash can freeze—and does, on occasion. Have to learn to fly without gauges in the event everything gets iced over. Men come back to the hospital with frostbite on a good day, lose fingers and toes on a bad one." He flitted a glance down to the gloves she was twisting in her palms. "We wear gloves too."

"Oh . . . these." Amelia loosened her nervous grip and untwined her fingertips in her lap. "Well, October fancies itself akin to January these days. I'm just cheered it's mild enough that the snow is holding off a bit longer. I imagine that's another obstacle to doing your job when the inside of a B-17 feels like a Frigidaire and the airfield is covered over with a sheet of ice."

"More than ice, I think the men battle waiting the most."

"Waiting?"

"Once you wave good-bye to England, it's about calming the nerves. Fumbling with the controls. Checking the oxygen umpteen times. Watching the sky until you finally see land again. And then the climax hits and the bomb bay doors open . . . but even then there's waiting. If not for all that and those pesky Jerries getting in the way, I'd say this job would be a walk in the park if you have patience to endure it."

Another lighthearted reply. It seemed if Wyatt possessed any manner of fear at all, he kept it buried beneath the surface.

Not like the other boys.

The younger officers joked and played cards and had pinups of their Betty Grables taped to the Regency Ballroom walls, but they walked around the manor with wide-eyed respect for how close death truly was—especially when chairs that had once been filled went empty at the breakfast tables. But Wyatt didn't. He seemed to stare fear down like an unflinching foe. He approached flying out on missions as if he were simply going off to an office job, not battling the clouds with Hitler's best flyers day in and day out.

It didn't fit.

"The children have become attached to the men already, though I've tried my best to keep them out of your hair. I hope they haven't added to any of the anxiety."

"Not at all," he countered easily, his voice a rough whisper. "But you're keeping them from getting to know officers first in order to shield them from loss after. That's probably best in the end."

Amelia shifted in her chair. "I didn't intend it like that."

"It's okay if you did. The RAF officers tell Yanks the truth when we arrive: you never make friends here because the moment you do, the next day they're gone."

Her heart sank.

Yes. They are gone.

"I wish it wasn't true, for everyone's sake." Her insides ached over it.

"The business of war doesn't mince truths though, does it? But we train hard, do our job well, and God willing, everyone comes home to tell the tales." Wyatt allowed a hint of softness to hold in his features. "And then one day you find you're sitting in a pub, talking books and bombs with a stranger by a fire, and for better or worse, you've set out and done exactly what those RAF officers said *not* to do."

He cleared his throat slightly, watching her kindly, since he'd just declared her a friend as the glow of firelight danced across his face. "If that bout of honesty means I'm disinvited to the book club, I understand."

She swallowed hard, tucking a lock of hair behind her ear. "Not disinvited, no."

"But not invited either? Maybe just as well. I'm afraid I may have inadvertently made an enemy out of your uncle and found myself banned from your library as a result."

"My uncle?" How could that be? Darly was the kindest, gentlest soul she knew.

"Afraid so. He ran me out of the library this week. Said a mindless barbarian had no business being anywhere near her ladyship's books." Wyatt leaned back with a cocky grin that made sure Amelia saw how he found humor in the interaction despite the fact that Darly had bristled quite badly. "I think he may have used a British expletive or two when he marched away, but I can't be sure. And do the British call everyone an 'overgrown Yankee scarecrow' in passing, or should I take that personally?"

Amelia did laugh then. And the smile bled down to her core.

Darly was only so frustrated by a few as to allow his propriety to slip. It seemed Wyatt Stevens had a unique way about him that clashed in so completely a manner that he'd shot to the top of the old man's list of vexations.

"It sounds as though we've had a simple misunderstanding. I'll just explain to him that you are free to borrow anything you'd like, and that should prevent any recurrence of the incident."

"Well, I was bred on an Iowa farm, so he's not that far off base. But what if I asked you to supply the books from now on?"

Silence washed over her, marking the seconds that ticked by on the clock between them. Darly was wrong; they weren't her books. They were her husband's beloved friends. And now if she agreed, she'd be placing them in another man's hands.

"You want my recommendations?"

He nodded. "If it's not too much trouble."

"Why, of course milady can recommend books!" Thompson interjected, appearing from the kitchen with a tray of steaming soup crocks in his hands. "She is our resident librarian, with her historic collection down at the manor."

Arthur's books.

The ones I love and am too afraid to share.

Amelia shot to her feet, cutting him off with a cheerful but hurried, "Oh, you do love a good gab, Thompson! But the time—I'm afraid I must be going. Mrs. Jenkins will be setting for tea, and she'll be in a state of panic should I not return to help."

Wyatt stood as she did, his manners more English by the minute. "But you haven't eaten yet."

"'Tis true! The captain's right. Ye can't leave before I give ye your basket, milady."

Thompson approached the table, a basket hooked in his elbow. He set the tray on the table, then the basket containing the biscuit tin of soup tied with twine but still releasing steam from the edges. Wax paper–wrapped mini loaves of bread sat on top. And a curious envelope balanced on top of that.

He smiled and crossed his arms over his chest in a happy "so there" stance.

"Thompson—you cannot mean . . . ?" Amelia clutched his shoulders and pressed a kiss to the old man's cheek before she could stop herself, delight gripping her hard and fast so she couldn't not respond in kind.

"Arrived today from Westminster."

"Truly!" Amelia swiped the envelope and read the address of the War Office, then hugged it to her chest. She could only pray it held the good news she'd been waiting on for weeks.

"Let me get this straight. You dole out kisses for . . . mail?" Wyatt's laugh wasn't masked. Not in the least. His hazel eyes twinkled as he looked down on her.

"For this kind—it appears I do."

Wyatt clasped his hands together. "An intelligent officer might make note to remember that."

Amelia tucked the envelope in the basket and gathered the wax paper parcels of bread safe around it.

"Tell your darling wife I'll return her basket tomorrow. If Darly's soup grows cold, he shall not forgive that folly easily." Amelia grabbed up the basket and bread and excused herself, buttoning the front of her topper in haste as she walked to the door.

"Amelia?" The way Wyatt said her name was too soft, too earnest to ignore.

She turned, nearly undone by the first time she'd heard it from him. "Yes?"

A pause. A look. And then, "I report again tomorrow."

"So soon? I thought you said you had leave."

"I'm subbing in with the RAF after one of their pilots fell out with a bout of pneumonia. Only enough time to sleep and eat before briefing, I'm afraid. And stop in here for a hot meal."

"Oh. I see . . ." Amelia paused, fingertips toying with the coat button at her waist.

She hated this.

Truly. Good men, brave men, flew out and sometimes didn't come back. It made minutes ticking by on the clock feel urgent when they shouldn't. And the few moments at a pub table mean more than they ought.

"You can't say when you'll return?"

He shook his head. "I'm sorry. But may I ask a favor while I'm gone?"

"Certainly." She hoped beyond hope he didn't ask for anything she couldn't give.

"I left a stack of books before your uncle, uh, escorted me out of the library. I've read them but didn't have time to browse for any others. Two or three should keep me busy for a short while."

"You're certain you trust me to select something you'd like?" She hesitated. "Books are a completely personal kind of journey. On the first page they ask us not only to be willing but to be moved, changed, persuaded, even made new by the time we reach the end. Everyone's walk through is different. It has to be. What if I choose the wrong sort of journey for you?"

"If that's how you really feel about books, I more than trust you—at least until my invitation to the book club arrives in the post. I have to find something to fill my time in between flights. And turning pages will keep my fingers warm to stave off the threat of frostbite."

"Alright then, Wyatt. When you return, your books will be waiting." Amelia nodded as she slipped the basket over her arm and hurried a good-bye, the bell clanging as she bustled out to her bicycle. She could wait no longer and tore into the envelope while standing with the wheels leaning against her skirt.

Blast.

Nothing but a bread crumb again.

Thompson's contact at the War Office had sounded promising this time.

They'd stumbled upon relocation lists—names of Berlin Jews who'd been transported to work camps early in the war. It had been a hope. But he reported only that there was no match with names for Luca and Liesel's parents. Looking for a German couple who'd vanished into the Berlin night in 1938 had once again thrown them back to square one.

Pedaling home, the threat of spray on her buckle shoes was all but forgotten as Amelia wove her way past Framlingham Castle and down the long lane to Parham Hill. She deposited the basket in the kitchen but hid the envelope in her pocket and slipped into the great hall, behind the few officers who were still on leave and children who'd joined them for dinner. She drifted along the back wall, then breezed down the hall to the library, finding how odd it was that officers, children, Darly, and an old English cook gave the remarkable impression of a makeshift family.

In the tucked-away treasure of Arthur's library, Amelia rushed to the small stack of books on the sideboard. A note had been left on the top, folded upon the front cover of *A Tale of Two Cities*.

She swiped it up and read the letters penned in sharp, regal strokes:

To the lady librarian of the house,

Dickens—not bad. A little dreary. What do you recommend next? Something with spirit. Please, if you have any pity . . . no Austen.

Back in a few days, ready to read.

—Wyatt

At least this letter had the promise of something good. Maybe one day she'd write one back. Or despite his protests, leave Wyatt a stack of Austen as a tease.

But not this day.

Amelia's heart was torn because she'd made a friend. And anybody in wartime would tell you that was a very dangerous thing to do—almost as dangerous as hoping for a letter from the War Office or longing after a liquid-satin gown in a town surrounded by roads of mud.

One never fell in love with something when it was far easier to pass by.

NINE

A revolver was not the usual utensil one brought to breakfast.

Not unless you were on the American frontier. But this was not a countryside of wide-open land and lawless men. They were in England. Queen Victoria's England. And there were rules.

A whim of brave insolence against a viscount seemed unlikely to end in Elizabeth's favor unless she could find just cause by which to accuse him of such a grievous crime. But it would take time to learn the game at play. The players. How in the world he'd elevated himself from street urchin to nobleman in a single decade. And especially the manor and the inner workings of Viscount Huxley's world. As his fiancée she may have liberties others would not to dig deeper into the mysteries of his private life. And though Elizabeth's insides recoiled each time she considered breathing air in the same room as he, she had but to remind herself she needn't go all the way to the altar.

Elizabeth could be clever and strong in the weeks the banns were read and put up a ruse of gentility if she needed to. All to the eventual end of the viscount's past crimes being brought to light and justice having its day.

The very existence of the revolver in her chamber, however, put all at risk. If it were discovered, her one ally could turn from a companion to a curse in the flap of a hummingbird's wings. That would not do.

Elizabeth tugged a salon chair over to the wardrobe in her primrose-papered chamber and climbed upon its cushion in stockinged feet. She stood against the beast of mirror and polished wood, inspecting the depths behind the scrolled façade with searching fingertips, and tucked her reticule behind it, into a dust-covered corner the maids' feather dusters had ignored for ages.

Satisfied it would keep for the moment, Elizabeth composed herself, slipping into satin shoes—one, two. Hands she smoothed against the braids that wound over her ears and tucked into an elegant coil at her nape. With a raised chin, steadying breath, and iron resolve, she ventured downstairs.

Butterflies winged a viscous dance through her insides as Elizabeth followed the sounds of idle chatter floating from the breakfast room. She forced the winged creatures to settle with each step down the open staircase, listening as the sounds of forks clinking against porcelain plates and teacups meeting their saucers grew more pronounced.

She paused in the shadow of the door, left ajar to the great hall. Elizabeth leaned closer to the edge of shadow until the Viscount Huxley came into view.

He presided over court at the end of the table, employing as normal a routine as reading a newspaper and drinking tea. Elizabeth was loath to admit the veneer of his profile was quite noble in the splash of morning sun, with brunette hair in a defiant tip over his brow, an iron jaw, and, she knew, remarkable eyes that so easily could have been beset with warmth and humor had he a character to match.

Ma-ma was close by his elbow, chirping on about something upon which he did not comment. She ran her index finger around the gold-embossed rim of a teacup before the rest of the house party guests, absently, as if the very fiber of her being could recognize what wares of luxury her daughter would now own.

The butler noticed Elizabeth's presence and hurried to announce her, and she was forced to pivot from engaging in a spy's deliberation in the doorway to floating into the room with all eyes upon her.

"Elizabeth! Do come in, dear," Ma-ma crooned, as if they needed an added layer of jam in order to keep the marriage arrangement in its locked position. "You are quite a dove this morning."

Gentlemen stood with sharp squeaks of chair legs against the hardwood. Viscount Huxley, too, stood—elegant in a riding coat of sleek royal blue, a crisp linen shirt that dared give no thought to a wrinkle, and a deep-crimson cravat tied perfectly round the neck. A gold watch chain winked in the sunlight, showing a glistening trail from waistcoat button to pocket. He watched. And waited. Those eyes revealing nothing as she breezed in, taking center stage in his world.

"Lady Elizabeth." Viscount Huxley gave an elegant but firm bow.

Elizabeth flitted her glance away as soon as she connected with the steel-gray and gold, fearing the memory of that night in Piccadilly would rise and spur her to confront him with the dull blade of a butter knife then and there, instead of how and when she chose.

"Good morning, Lord Huxley," she answered, proper and perfect, sweet and demure, but without an ounce of honest welcome.

Elizabeth moved to the sideboard. Took a porcelain plate of blue-and-white design, a rim of gold on it gleaming in the sunlight, and wispy willows dancing an ink-blue circle in the center. She filled it with anything that might prove edible: Fruit. Toast with butter and clotted cream. Rashers fried and crispy at the edges. She moved past the blood pudding and toms, yet with each set of sterling tongs she raised to plate, Elizabeth could feel the inspection grow upon the blush paisley shoulders of her morning dress.

Somehow she knew—his gaze followed her until she settled into a chair a moment later and spread an ivory napkin across her lap.

"Elizabeth, dear. Viscount Huxley was just engaging me in conversation about his immaculate gardens here at Parham Hill. They are quite extensive. Perhaps we should entertain a walk through them today. The air is quite clean and pleasant here in the country, is it not, Lord Huxley?"

"It is, Lady Davies. Though I regret I do not have time much to enjoy it, as affairs in London keep me occupied."

"London? Why, Elizabeth so enjoys the sights of the city! I daresay she will find it most enjoyable to accompany you on your future jaunts once you are wed." Ma-ma paused, as though calculating through the background noise of the less important party guests gathered around the table. "Have you a London home?"

"I do, Lady Davies."

"And where would that be?"

"St. James's, Westminster."

"Oh, how lovely," she cooed, turning to catch Elizabeth's eye. "We look forward to becoming acquainted with the rest of the estate grounds here, and in the London season, of course."

Elizabeth swallowed over the manufactured sweetness in her mother's voice. She sat straight, back a good ten inches from the chair back, and picked at her food like a dutiful little bird as she listened to her mother spreading syrup over the gentleman's mounting list of assets.

"You are most welcome to learn whatever you'd like, Lady Davies—you and Lady Elizabeth."

The viscount met Elizabeth's glance over the table in nothing more than a plain manner—not detached but still not connected. Yet knowing what she did, she wondered how a man could hide such evil intentions behind so elegant a veneer. Only in such stark eyes, she decided, and looked down at her plate instead of meeting his gaze a breath longer.

The door swung open then, flinging wide as Franz entered the breakfast room. He defused the momentary tension without care that the butler should announce him *before* he found his way into a room instead of *while*.

As was his folly, he'd dressed impeccably even for so early in the morning in a fur-lined morning jacket of red-and-gold damask and a cravat of shiny satin. He moved about with intention, curling his lip at the silver servers of cooked meats and rich sauces, choosing little for his plate—only the delicacy of fresh fruit and hot water with lemon that the butler seemed to know he must set in front of his chair.

"*Guten Morgen,*" Franz announced, then tossed a napkin on the table and sat—loudly, as if everyone should notice his entrance. He knew how to hold a room enthralled, carry the posture of a gentleman, and make polite conversation. Yet it was as if he entered every room and surveyed whether it was to his liking, and then would put his practiced manners into play only if and when he so chose.

"You are to be commended, Huxley," he continued with a preening smile. "A delightful evening has given way to a remarkable morning spread. As ever, you prove to be a most refined host."

It was a flagrant jest, given the meager sight of grapes rolling around on his plate. But Elizabeth was shocked to look up from it, just for a breath, and find what met her immediately after—*a smile*. Not from Franz, which would have been icing on the cake of his presence in any room . . . but upon the lips of the viscount himself.

A tiny flinch at the corners of Viscount Huxley's mouth revealed the battle to suppress an almost tooth-revealing grin.

His friend had entered the room and the gentleman must have found some solace in the presence of an ally, so much so that he dared become . . . real. And humored? Whatever the provocation, it lasted no more than a breath. So fast Elizabeth couldn't be certain it had happened at all, as she seemed the only soul in the room to have noticed his slip of character from austere to affable.

What to make of a man who held such a degenerate secret from his youth yet could smile so easily at the quip of a friend puzzled her to her core.

"Might we inquire, Mr. Winterhalter, as to the delights of break-fast tables at which you've dined before if the viscount's is so warm in comparison? They must hold remarkable tales," Elizabeth inter-jected, her mask of serenity firmly in place.

Toe to toe.

"My, Huxley, but you have won a prize. She is a clever Fräulein." Franz laughed and lounged with his back against the chair in a mild repose. "Please do indulge me with every detail of what I've missed with my fashionable lateness to this grand breakfast."

"We were just discussing the extensive gardens here at Parham Hill, Mr. Winterhalter." Ma-ma spoke up first. Of course. "Would you care to join us on a walk through them today? I should like to hear your view of how the color and light affect the blooms. I do find the artist's life to be such a fascinating adventure."

Elizabeth's insides churned. To accept anything of the viscount's world made her ill, especially given the ire that her mother had shown for artists just a day before.

"I wonder if Lady Elizabeth would prefer the library instead," the viscount challenged, his tone soft, perhaps even caged, but his words direct.

Elizabeth's attention snapped up and she stared back at him, his words stoking the need to challenge those eyes. "And why should I prefer the library, sir?"

"There is an abundance of sights that may hold interest for you. Art. Books. Stories. Haven't you such a library at your Yorkshire estate? It is said the late earl was quite the reader and that he valued knowledge like few men before him. Perhaps we should visit you, to inform the rest of us how a library ought to be properly cherished."

The countess dropped a fork to her plate. It clanged, and she of course made every delicate apology she could in the seconds after. A sea captain sitting opposite joined in, engaging her in conversation of the most animated inappropriateness, discussing the visceral trials of nervous complaints and dining while at sea. Her color turned as green as if she were on a ship deck herself.

"Could any estate in Yorkshire claim less, sir?" Elizabeth kept her voice low.

"I wasn't asking after any estate in Yorkshire. I was asking after yours."

Tick tock. He does shoot straight.

Perhaps she should too.

"And why should you care after ours?"

"I should take an interest in any venture of my betrothed's. Would not any estate you own fall to your husband's management once you are wed?"

"I assure you, sir, that any assets of mine would be managed quite well were there a marriage contract involved or not. But as this house party is coming to a close, would not our host choose to have his library back to the privacy of his own enjoyment?"

"How nonsensical would that be when the banns have not even been read yet? We've weeks yet to entertain the viscount's generosity as we plan the wedding," Ma-ma twittered, rejoining their conversation, her voice wavering though her smile remained steadfast. She turned to Elizabeth, her eyes chastening in narrowed slits. "Elizabeth, dear . . . Lord Huxley wishes to endear us to his estate, now that you are to be wed. Would you not wish to see the grounds of your future home?"

"Of course, we should be delighted to tour your gardens." Elizabeth nodded. "And any secret haunts you might wish to include us in."

"Lady Elizabeth is an artist, Huxley." Franz popped a grape into his mouth. "No doubt she would enjoy the view from your gardens. Give her something to paint, perhaps? So we might assess her skill."

The gaze of steel and jagged gold turned back, the viscount meeting her with piqued interest flickering in his eyes. "Is this true?"

Elizabeth shifted in her chair, under both the viscount's questioning gaze and her mother's harsh scrutiny, which was growing boundless as nervous seconds ticked by.

"All wellborn ladies are instructed in the art of drawing, among other studies."

"I would caution you. Mr. Winterhalter is quite the competitor. If he believes you are of the artistic bent, he will wish to engage you in a battle of wits *and* skill with a brush."

"Is that so?" Elizabeth flitted her gaze to Franz, issuing a direct challenge with the sweetest smile she possessed. "Then I would hope the gentleman arrives aptly armed with both."

Franz bellowed out a laugh and slapped a palm to the table, startling one of the ladies downwind so she yelped.

"You see? She attempted the same evasion with me in the library. I believe Lady Elizabeth is equipped to outmatch us all. And I suspect her interest in the brush is more than a passing affection. You must draw this out of her, Huxley, so we might know the truth. I desire a walk this morn, to shake off my inhibitions. *Gut*—we shall

all go," Franz added, a cool smile in place. "If you agree, of course, as our host."

The viscount looked across the table to her, though something hid away again, and his eyes forgot their openness. "I am Lady Elizabeth's humble servant. She has only but to wish something of me, and I will obey."

"Splendid! We walk. And, Travers—" Franz signaled the butler with a raised teacup and a wink. "You do prepare the perfect temperature of hot water this side of Buckingham Palace. You are to be commended, sir! When in this room, I'd have thought you only had ice water to work with."

If there was to be a row between the betrothed parties before they were a full twenty-four hours into an engagement, it appeared Franz wished to be front chair to witness the exchange. He goaded awkwardness like a zookeeper poking a caged lion with a stick. His smile said he read far more between the lines than what had been said. What was more, he seemed to revel in it.

Ma-ma twittered a squeaky laugh, finding the straightforwardness of their artist a tough pill to swallow. But Elizabeth, never. She conferred a soft smile on both men, revealing nothing save for the serenity of a dove who knew her place as a dutiful marriage match.

She sipped her tea, seemingly unaffected. But inside, a fire blazed.

One day Elizabeth would no longer be caged by the pain of her past or the rigid expectations of her future. One day she'd find a way to escape the gilded bars of both and then . . . she'd be free.

As Franz illuminated their party with talk of the throne rooms of Europe, Elizabeth spent the remainder of breakfast in the privacy of her own head. Which manor rooms kept the viscount's secrets well hidden, and just where might she uncover them?

Upon reaching her chamber to change for the afternoon, however, she found the reticule—and her revolver with it—was long gone, its place behind the top of the wardrobe bare, and the dusty corner void of any upper hand she'd hoped to gain.

Parham Hill indeed had its secrets . . . and unwittingly Elizabeth had added yet another to its ample number.

TEN

PRESENT DAY
PARHAM HILL ESTATE
FRAMLINGHAM, ENGLAND

Parham Hill must have a breakfast room, a dining hall, a kitchen—if it could boast any greatness at all, more than one of each. And with the American habit Keira had developed of caffeine first thing in the morning, she was up before dawn and on the hunt from the moment her feet hit the hardwood.

She slipped on boots over jeans and shrugged into an ivory tunic, and as it looked to take half the national debt just to heat the place, she wrapped a thick fisherman's-weave sweater around her shoulders. Entire wings of the manor might be without heat, and if she would be exploring them in the dark, it was best to dress for the occasion.

Keira poked her head into several rooms, finding the gem of a light switch on the wall in a few. Shutters were open in some areas, clamped tight in others. Curtains in evergreen and gold brocade hung with dust weighing the folds over some windows, while other panes were bare, with no obstruction preventing the viewer from looking out over the vast estate acreage. And most rooms, while immaculate in their Victorian styling, lacked warmth. Or evidence of once having had real people in them. Even less evidence of the modern world. Each room attempted a personality with papered walls, wainscoting, showcase hearths, and gilding but little else to show it had ever been part of a real home. Rogue pieces of furniture sat in random corners in a manner that conveyed no intention whatsoever.

The long hall she'd first stepped into appeared around a corner, and Keira knew where she was. It beckoned with sconces glowing through the arch from the marble entry hall, in a mix of light and shadow all the way down to the library door at the far end. It was where she turned and found Emory, sitting in one of the built-in window seats with his back up against the wall and legs stretched out, pecking away by the glow of a laptop screen.

"Morning, Foley," he said, thumbing through a book at his side and typing without glancing up. "You lost?"

"Oh—Emory, I'm sorry to have interrupted you."

"Not a bit. Just finishing up." He still thumbed through the book next to him. He paused, seemingly finding what he'd been searching for, and swiped a pen to scribble a note in the margin of the page. "I assume you're looking for the butler. We have staff here, but only to see to the housecleaning. If you want tea, you'll have to heat a kettle on your own."

"Coffee, actually."

"Really?"

"I'm afraid I might be an anorak about it now that I'm back in the UK, but I'm a typical coffee addict when in New York. Became more American than I expected, I suppose."

Emory pulled cordless earbuds out of his ears and tossed them in his backpack. "What hooked you?"

"A little shop on West 20th Street—Ivy Grove."

"Chelsea. Been to that part of the city a time or two myself."

"I'd stop in every morning on the way to the gallery. I befriended the owners and they'd save me a table tucked in a back corner by the window, where trees hid me from view of the sidewalk. I probably spent half my time in New York right there, watching the entire city walk by. And I still say that *no one* makes a better blonde Americano in all of Manhattan."

"Well, we don't have Americanos. What we do have is M. J.'s makeshift coffee bar setup in one of the drawing rooms. It's just a paint-peeled old door spread over a couple of sawhorses, but she said it would prevent the deaths of all men on the team were she to have a decent cup of coffee at sunup. And that's what we have until this place has a kitchen that's up and running."

"Seems like Carter knows how to get things done."

"Actually, he tasked his on-site assistant with it."

"Who's that?"

"Me." Emory tapped the laptop screen closed and set it and the book aside on the cushioned bench. He jumped to his feet. "Should I take that as a compliment? I'm not very sharp before I've had my caffeine."

"If you find coffee, then be my guest to receive it in any manner you choose." Keira peered back through the marble entry. Shadows lingered through the arched doorway, catching corners in a hazy blackness offset by the checked marble floor, but everything was still. Same down the other way at the far end by the library door. "Where is everyone?"

Emory grimaced, as if he were in pain on their behalf. "Carter stayed on. He and the crew, uh . . . they had a late night down at the pub. I tried to convince them otherwise, but I believe you English would call it something of a bender."

"Oh. Thick heads this morning. That explains the sleeping in."

She laughed under her breath. Bless them—they'd probably have a rough go of it when they did emerge from their chambers.

"They're young," he said, as if that explained all. "But then, so are you. And you didn't venture out."

"You forget—I was born on one side of a Dublin pub. That kind of thing doesn't interest me after years of living around the routine. Pubs are more gathering places than American bars anyway, and I'd rather go to eat a good meal. What about you?"

"I stayed back to clear debris from the entry to the library so we could move in more equipment today. And I actually enjoy waking up with the birds. You don't miss out on the sunrise that way."

"Sounds like you didn't get much sleep then either."

Emory ran his hand through his hair, mussing the ebony locks about his crown, and slid his palm down to his neck and squeezed. "Wish I had, to be honest. I don't sleep well in new places. Makes me want to fire up that espresso machine along with you if you don't mind."

Coffee with him was easier than without, especially since he knew where this elusive drawing room was. It wouldn't hurt to have one cup.

"Right then. Lead the way." Keira fell into step alongside him as he started down the hall.

"So, did you sign the contract?"

"Yeah. I did. So I'm bound to the estate and Framlingham for the next couple of weeks. With Carter's blessing I've already requested the borders for the original portrait—a friend still works in the archives at Kensington Palace and she owes me a favor, so she won't ask any questions as to why I'm looking into it. We'll start there."

"Will you have to go to London?"

"Maybe. Even if we can compare border images of the original portrait with Carter's, we'll have to send Victoria for a chemical analysis. After we have her x-rayed. It's a must if we want verifiable clues as to who painted her."

"Because . . . Winterhalter never sketched his canvases first."

"Right. He painted directly to canvas. Rather brilliant when you think of it. He was a camera before cameras had their time."

Emory stopped at a side hall that branched off the larger one, leading her to the end. He opened a door and flicked on a wall switch, and a trace amount of light shone from sconces on either side of an oversize fireplace. A gilded mirror hung over the mantel, catching the shimmer of light and their reflections in the room's warm glow.

Keira followed him into the drawing room of pinstripe wallpaper in rose gold. It was near empty like the other rooms she'd seen, save for a striped settee positioned opposite the fireplace, the makeshift coffee bar set against the side wall, and floor-to-ceiling windows that spanned the back.

"Welcome to the Rose Room, Miss Foley—Parham Hill's version of an old Suffolk coffee shop."

Through leaded glass, dawn was just breaking apart on the horizon. It cut the clouds like an explosion of fire, yellow and orange lacing through sweeps of a rare deep crimson. Hues spread like paint fanned from a brush and reached down to mingle with mist that still clung to the hills and hollows of the meadow.

Keira paused, breath arrested. "The Rose Room claims quite the view."

"What room doesn't in this place? And the crew never wakes for hours, so they miss this nearly every day."

"Ah . . . creatives. An unpredictable lot unless it involves early rising." Keira couldn't help but smile; she was one of them. Gladly.

Emory stepped over to the coffee bar and went to work in the little light they had. He knocked something over, and a bar spoon clanged to the floor. "Well, whatever that was, we'll find it later.

I'm still not turning on the overhead lights. For all its secrets and for lack of a table tucked in a corner, Parham Hill has one thing nowhere else in the world can boast."

"This view," Keira answered for him.

"Right. The view," Emory echoed.

Keira stood still as dawn continued its slow climb over the horizon, outlining the distant spires of Framlingham Castle against the clouds and layers of green hills that cut through the mist like ship sails through wind on an open sea.

"And seeing this, you sure a week or two is all you want to sign on for?"

She couldn't take her eyes off it. "It's all I promised Carter, even with the view. You?"

"However long it takes to finish the job." He paused the small talk, turning toward her. "Milk? Sugar?"

"Both. Medium." Keira looked from the view to the back of him as Emory worked, his shoulders squared to stainless steel, hands tamping grounds that would become espresso, and wondered at how swiftly he'd transitioned a nonchalant view of life to asking how she took her coffee. He continued working on their drinks, taking café mugs from a row of white lined up against the wall, and opened a mini fridge beneath it to retrieve some milk . . . without the least bit of play in him.

That showed he honestly meant what he'd said.

"Wait a minute—you're serious? But you must have signed a contract. Don't you have to return home at some point?"

"Framlingham is home at the moment."

"But where will you go when the job is over?"

He shrugged. Noblesse oblige. "I'm not worried about it."

Who was so cavalier with their livelihood? Keira wasn't one to stay planted in any one place for too long, so she understood the move-on mentality that came with wanderlust personalities like theirs. But didn't that roving spirit ever long to settle? Hers had. Even more when she'd come home with a broken heart and found two brothers married to the loves of their lives, and she still muddling through on her own. Dublin may have been a rebound home—and a temporary one at that—but at least she still had someplace that was dear enough for her to want to hang her hat on a familiar peg while she regrouped.

How could Emory toss that security about without a second thought?

"You're not at all worried about where you're to live?"

He steamed the milk like a pro, raising his voice over the loud whir of the frother. "Why? Should I be?"

"Most people are. It's a bit basic, isn't it? When I lost my lease in New York, I had to pack boxes and cross an ocean to move back in with my da. At twenty-six years old, mind. When I hadn't lived there since I was a girl in knee socks and a plaid jumper."

Emory stood in the growing cast of morning light, working but shifting his gaze up at her every so often. "That must have been hard."

"It was. It is."

"How so?"

She shrugged like it didn't matter, but of course it did. More than she'd dare tell him. Though it had taken years to come to grips with, Keira would give the abbreviated version.

No sob stories here.

"My parents divorced when I was young. Da chose looking after a ruddy old pub over his family. That's my view of it. He neglected his duty. He let us go, and then everything began unraveling in the aftermath. How do you backpedal from that? I had to come home now where I knew I could regroup from a few things— but we've never said a word about it. Da tends bar and we act like nothing happened all those years ago. He'd have the locals at the bar believing we're a right good Irish family, when all I want to do is tell him what I think of him."

"So you were just getting settled to deal with that, and I step in to lure you away with euros and paint. I hope you'll forgive me for the terrible timing."

"I might, if the coffee's any good." She took a drink—hot. Sweet and strong too, proving the perfect diversion.

"Well?" Emory waited.

"You're off the hook." She smiled. "Because so is this."

They stood by the windows. He was quiet as his smile faded and they sipped and watched the world wake, yawn, and come alive beyond the leaded glass.

"So what happened after you packed your boxes and braved the Atlantic?"

She smiled inside, warmed by more than coffee. "Cormac welcomed me back. He always does."

"Ah. Brothers can be good like that."

"My brothers can. I'm closer to Cormac—he's the oldest. But only because Quinn had a case of wanderlust and chose to indulge for several years. Before he married Ellie. I don't blame him completely; he's a different person now. And I was bit by the travel bug once upon a time. But Cormac was steady in a way few people in my life have been. I was still young and he gave up Trinity College to move to London with Mum and me, shortly after the divorce. She . . ."

Keira swallowed another deep drink of coffee, stalling.

It had been years since she'd talked of her mother with anyone other than Cormac. She'd not even been able to broach the subject with Alton—she should have, but her former fiancé didn't stick around long enough to find out what was ticking on the inside of her. And by the time she was ready to open up, he was gone.

"She what?" Emory spoke up, a little prompt drawing her back to the moment.

"Uh . . . Mum passed from cancer many years ago."

"I'm sorry."

Keira shrugged like it was nothing, even though deep down in the hidden-away recesses of her innermost, it was everything to her.

"It's alright. Like you said—just another sock in the gut, right?"

"I hope I don't sound that pessimistic. Life can sometimes be that, yes," he said, his voice softened to a whisper. "But it can have bring-you-to-your-knees beauty too. Grief isn't always a loss of any one person or thing. I think it's the loss of who we might have become had life not taken an unexpected turn. That needs some time to work out."

"You talk like you understand it."

"Maybe. But then I see a sunrise like this and I have to believe God's behind something so good. Why else would He paint the sky like that, knowing that no one else on earth would see it from this exact view but us two? There's intention in that."

Emory didn't elaborate, thank heaven.

Keira didn't know if she'd be able to talk about much more with him. It wasn't like her to open up, and certainly not to a stranger. They stood in silence for a while after that—who knew how long, save for the sun that made its debut in reams of harvest orange, gold, and white and after time had splintered the clouds with sharp rays that cut through the cloud of mist hovering over the meadows.

As the sun rose, Keira was struck with a realization.

"Emory, the sun streams in through these windows . . ."

"It does, yes."

"Across the entire back side of the manor?"

Emory stared at her, confusion showing in his glance. "Yeah. So?"

Keira set her mug on the windowsill and moved toward the French doors at the center. She wrapped her palms around the cold brass handles. "Can I go out here?"

He followed suit and set his mug next to hers. "Sure, it's not locked from the inside. But why?"

"Because I want to see the stone on the wall next to the Regency Ballroom. It should be down to the right, yes? Almost to the end."

"Yeah, it is." He followed her as she pushed the doors wide.

The crisp morning air filled her lungs as Keira swept out onto the terrace. She moved along the row of windows, counting rooms, finding the spot where he'd taken her down the stairs to the cottage the day before. She peered up when she reached a wall jutting out into the terrace, noticing its uneven stone soaring two stories in height above them and pitched sharp at the top.

It was the only span across the back of the manor that looked like it tried to fit but couldn't, not even with its dappled stone. A harsh wall faced the view of meadow and mist and castle spires that cut the sky—another clue that something didn't quite match up. Why in the world would a manor wall be built to cut off natural light and block out such a breathtaking view?

"Like the brick wall in the library . . . this doesn't belong either, does it?" Keira asked. Emory eased back at her side as together they stared up at the sweeping wall.

"It's not out of the ordinary for additions to have been added to manor houses like these, especially if they're owned for generations and the wealth grew at certain points among them."

"I know that. But this feels different somehow." She ran her fingertips over a line of the dappled stone. "You have the floor plans for the manor?"

"What there is of them, yes. There's the wood panel you saw. Ben's working to unearth what's behind it."

"When were the library shelves built?"

"1812? Somewhere around there. They're original to the manor."

She flitted her glance from windows to wall and back again. "And no shelving that was added later, hmm?"

"Not that we're aware of. The floor plans show a set of doors behind the brick wall that connected through to the ballroom. Pity the contractors had to be so negligent they punched a hole in the wall right next to them. But if they hadn't, would we even be here right now?"

"No. It's not the doors . . ." Keira stared, feeling something stir within her. She pointed to the junction of the high pitch. "I mean above them. What's up there in the floor plan?"

Emory stepped up alongside her and drifted his fingertips over the same corner she inspected, where stone met stone. He pointed out two lines to her, both marked by a stark variance in color, texture, and, evidently, age.

From afar, one might not have noticed—and they hadn't during their walk the day before. They'd known the library had been walled off from the inside, long after the manor had been built. But up close, it was clear: there was only one explanation for how the library had fade marks on the wallpaper if none of the shelving had been disturbed . . . "It used to have a window, didn't it?"

"Behind the wood paneling—it'd have to." Emory smiled wide, sunlight casting a glow on his face. "You know what this means, don't you, Foley?"

"We should be on the hunt for the other paintings that hung in the library. And we can't let Ben anywhere near that wall until we find out if there's glass behind it."

"Chances are he already knows. We just didn't think to ask where his nose is buried at the moment. But one thing's for certain—two weeks here won't be enough for either of us, no matter where we're going when it's over."

"Cormac's out just now, but why not try his cell phone?" Laine's sweet voice bounded through the phone.

Keira stood in her room—paced was more like it—around the simple but elegant furnishings. Under twelve-foot ceilings. From four-poster bed to marble mantel and fireplace, to the antique mirrored wardrobe and the salmon-colored salon chairs pushed up against the far wall. Step by step, heartbeat by heart swell. While she didn't have a clear understanding yet of what Carter Wilmont had in his possession, it was clear *something* was behind the library wall. Victoria's presence only added to the mystery of it all, and Keira couldn't possibly find out what it was if she bolted right at the beginning of this thing.

Calling home to give the news was all she could do.

"I tried his phone first. Got voice mail."

"Then he'll call you back, I'm sure." Laine paused. No doubt she was reading between the lines—her brother's wife was good at that. "As long as everything's okay."

"It is. It's just that this job may prove a bit more . . . involved than I thought."

"Oh? How involved?"

"Like a couple more weeks involved. I can't see any way around it."

Laine paused again, silence echoing over the phone. "What's he look like?"

"What?"

"You know—the guy. The one my husband pitched a fit over? I couldn't get a straight answer out of him. He just kept grunting disapproval so I read between the lines. So, what does he look like?"

"Laine, I'm stuck out at a manor in the East Suffolk countryside, in a town the size of our entire city block there in Dublin. I'm not thinking about men."

"If you're stuck out in the middle of nowhere, then I say all the more reason."

"I don't have time for that and wouldn't want to even if I did. Who'd have guessed an old manor could pose such a unique problem? No, not a problem. A brilliant opportunity. I have a chance to redeem myself from the fiasco in New York. If I can rewrite that chapter of my life, I just might find a career out of it. They have a painting here that needs authentication, and I need time to work out exactly what that means—with no distractions of the male type—so get that out of your clever little matchmaking mind right now."

"Well, that's fine with us, Keira. You're an adult. You don't need our permission to spend extra time with . . . the painting." Keira could almost hear Laine smile through the connection. "Or with whatever else might present itself as an opportunity."

Of course she didn't need their permission.

Keira knew that. She'd moved to New York for a high-profile internship only to find herself drawn to work at a Chelsea art gallery instead. It was only supposed to be three months. Then six. Then a year, and in the midst of it all, when the timing couldn't have been worse, she'd met Alton Montgomery . . . and the secure part of her world came crashing down.

Cormac had tried to warn her off an entanglement with the gallery owner's son, but Alton's easy compliments, ardent attention, and heart-stopping smile formed a toxic combination that spelled disaster in the end.

She didn't want a repeat, thank you very much.

"Look—just tell Cormac not to worry, yeah? I'm grateful for the support, but this could run into Christmas and I know I'd hoped to be home long before that."

"And Jack? What should we tell him?"

Keira chewed the edge of her thumbnail at the mention of her father. "I don't know. Maybe nothing. Da won't notice I'm gone. But I promised Cassie I wouldn't be gone for the holidays. If I let my niece down, she'll never let me hear the end of it."

"Well, that'd be part of her charm I think. But I'm biased as her mom. I'll just say you're wanted for Christmas, Keira, but Cormac wouldn't lay down any firm expectation on it. Even if we're planning on hosting this year. If Ellie and Quinn have a break in their renovation schedule on the Sleeping Beauty, they might come over from France. But you know there's always an extra room for you."

A thought hit, and Keira remembered she needed to ask. She'd only met her sister-in-law, who happened to be Laine's best friend, when Laine and Cormac were married the year before. It was then Ellie had been in the throes of a tough cancer battle.

Keira finally halted her back-and-forth, sitting on the edge of her bed. "How's Ellie?"

"She's much better. Has another doctor's appointment with her oncologist next week, so we should know more then. And in the meantime, she's apparently delighted to goad your dear brother with every zealous plan of restoring their fairy-tale castle to its former French glory. She wants to rush through and open to the public in the spring even if it's not picture-perfect ready yet, though Quinn's do-things-right attitude is feeling the tension of it. Apparently he thinks they can do much better if they wait and open with a bang in the busy tourist season in the fall. Ellie's just as determined it's got to be spring, so they're at an impasse.

"But Quinn's changed through it all, as you know. He'll tell you the globe-trotting side of him has finally died out. It seems the cancer battle did more than just affect Ellie, because she says now he grips tighter to the things he hadn't before. He's forged a closer relationship with the family and the land, putting down roots. He's overseeing everything alongside Ellie and even pledges to stay on and manage the vineyard with your grandfather, which is all new for him. So we'll have to see what they make of it."

"What is it with this family and castles?" Keira laughed low. "It seems everything we try has one hiding in the background somewhere. Seems we can't one of us say no to the stories in a pile of old stones."

"You're right." Laine paused as a baby cooed in the background.

It was beautiful to think of Cormac and Laine having a new daughter—Juliette—named for their mother. Keira listened as Laine soothed the child with honeyed words and soft, velvet tones.

"Sorry about that. Juliette's a little restless these days. But if you want me to, I'll tell Cormac you called. And if I can do anything to soften the news—which, by the way, you should only be excited about—you know I'll go to battle for you. Anytime, anyplace."

And she would. Keira had learned two things in the time she'd moved back home: Cormac had a wife who was absolutely perfect for him and who was beloved by everyone else too.

"Thanks, Laine. I'll keep that bit in my back pocket for a day when I need reminding."

"It would be wonderful to have the family all together for the holidays, but we understand if you can't. You have a job to do there. No matter how he might try to grumble about it, Cormac will understand that." Laine paused, and Keira could almost hear the warmth in her smile through the phone. "He's just gotten used to the idea of having his little sister home again and doesn't want to let go. That's all."

"And I'm not letting go of anything. I'm just . . . stepping away for a few more weeks. I promise I'll be home soon."

"And I'll tell him and Jack that our girl is coming home soon."

Seconds of silence ticked by against the connection. "Your dad misses you too, Keira . . ."

She swallowed hard against old wounds and broken dreams.

"I know he does."

"Well, as long as I said it. I'll just let you two come together on your own. So let's leave Christmas on the table, okay? You just do your best there, keep us updated, and we'll talk soon. Okay?"

They said their good-byes, and Keira sat on the bed, phone in hand, savoring the silence and the view out the windows.

The crew was bunking in the wing facing Parham Hill's border with Framlingham Castle, with a view of the rock wall–lined road that led to the village. But a bit of odd action snapped her attention from the landscape and drew her to the window.

And there, far off on the horizon, she saw a dark-headed figure—*Emory*.

Clad in his usual tee and jeans, his hair hanging in his eyes, he swung a scythe, cutting through bramble and the thick vines at the cottage gate.

Keira watched, peering around the side of the curtain at the furious clash of man and nature that erupted before her. Emory swung and struck at the thorns of time as if the overgrowth were his mortal enemy and he the lone protector of the cottage's fate. He was too far to judge by his face, but if she read the unmistakable layer of fury in his muscled swings, Keira saw the distinct shadow . . . of pain.

Parham Hill seemed to own the strange combination of both peace and pain. Beauty and bitterness. A lavishness surrounded by a coldness . . . They were strange bedfellows to find hidden in the shadow of Framlingham Castle and its quaint little country hamlet. It made little sense. And for how quickly Keira had stepped into the role of Victoria's protector, she was just as certain the old bee-keeper's cottage had a champion of its own.

ELEVEN

The sputter of a plane engine was the cry of Amelia's nightmares. It grew louder, screaming through the sky until she jolted awake.

An eerie stillness settled over the manor and she lay for several breaths after, just listening. Watching the ceiling from her bed. Willing the jarring noise to fade into the darkness and reveal itself to have been just another terrible dream.

Most nights Amelia slept in tiny spurts of time, drifting in and out, listening to the sky overhead while she tossed and turned, still clothed—just in case they should need to make a run for cover. Waiting up for several crews of the 390th to return that night, she'd stayed up after midnight. When they hadn't, she'd checked the library and found no stack of books waiting for her.

She'd poked her head into the doorway of the Regency Ballroom as a last resort to calm her nerves. Finding Wyatt's cot and several others still made, she said a prayer for their safety, left a key in the lock of the kitchen door, and lay down for another harrowing night.

As fire danced and crackled in the hearth in her chamber, Amelia listened.

The whistle ended with a resounding boom out in the fields. There was no mistaking it that time. Bombs were falling somewhere, and being so close to the airfield, the manor could be an inadvertent target.

Then the sirens began their wail.

Not again . . .

Amelia threw off her quilt and swung her trouser-clad legs down to the hardwood. The chamber door crashed open at the same time and she jumped, not remembering for a moment that the manor house was full of officers who would react to the sirens same as she.

"Oh—Wyatt," she breathed out, hand resting in a palm-slap against her middle. "It's you."

He stood in the darkness of the hall, also trouser-clad, unlaced boots open at the ankles and breathing as if fear had gripped him, too, for the seconds it took to run up the stairs to her door.

Praise be she was always prepared and so rightly dressed. He seemed to have picked up on the possibility that she hadn't been, having diverted his gaze the instant it landed on her through the moonlight.

"Alright in there?"

"I am, thank heaven." Amelia still fought to catch her breath as she tugged on the work boots she kept, unlaced and readied, at the foot of the bed.

"That one was close."

"Too close." Amelia pulled a mustard cardigan over her work shirt, the thick cable weave she'd left hanging over the metal rail of the footboard. "But then they always are. I apologize for being so blunt, but your blasted airfield keeps us on tenterhooks. I'm afraid it's not always easy to decipher bombs from plane engines, no matter how experienced we are with the burden of air-raid sirens." She swiped Arthur's pocket watch and tiny framed picture from the bedside table and tucked both in the front pocket of her work denim.

"It's not the airfield tonight. Time to go to the gardens."

"I think I knew that." She knew it was right, though reluctance plagued her heart. "Let's fetch the children. They know what to do. We've done this midnight march before."

Amelia slipped into the hall, ready to clear the chambers room by room just as they'd practiced in their drills. But what she didn't expect was to see blackout curtains drawn back at the end of the hall, spilling enough moonlight to illuminate open chamber doors all the way down the first-floor hall. Fully clothed officers bundled children in their arms and hurried the older ones down the grand staircase in orderly fashion.

"How did you . . . ?"

"We drew up a plan last week, remember? I gave it to you with the list of rations. We made it so we're ready to go before lights-out. It's more efficient to involve the officers so every man knows the room he's assigned and which Anderson is his to get the children to the garden. And if any man is out on mission, or if . . ." He hesitated for a split second over what she suspected was the wretched reality of when flyboys flew but didn't come back. "He knows which officer steps in and takes over in his stead. So the hall is clear on any night if need be."

"I'm afraid between the honey harvest, the baling, and everything for the children, I missed that completely. You'll have to forgive me."

"I'll be keen to forgive you, but at a far more opportune moment."

Wyatt had itchy feet. She could see it in the way he watched as the last officer carried a child down the stairs, then turned back to her as he edged tiny steps that way. He held a hand out to her, palm to ceiling. "Do you need anything else?"

Amelia looked back in her room. "No. I have everything, but—"

"Good. Let's go." Wyatt held his hand at the small of her back as he ushered her down the stairs in front of him.

Amelia tossed Wyatt a look that said had it been daylight, she'd have given him the what-for that he dared push in at all. The United States Army officers were guests and that was flat. But as they couldn't switch on a light without drawing the blackout fabric over the windows and given the pace he'd set to trek through the manor, she doubted Wyatt could have seen a displeased glare anyway.

As long as the children were safe, she could abide in the moment. In the morning . . . well, that was another matter entirely. Wyatt tried to lead them past the library, but she held him back and slipped inside the door. "Please—one moment."

Amelia ran to the sideboard and grabbed a book from the glass-walled cabinet, leaving its door open in the dark. She whispered a silent prayer for the library's safekeeping, then followed Wyatt through the adjoining ballroom full of officers' empty cots, their woolen blankets spilling onto the floor, and maneuvered down an aisle set between mess hall tables in the great hall. They fled to the farmhouse kitchen spanning the back of the manor, where she stopped them at the butcher's block before they made a run to the gardens.

Tears stung Amelia's eyes, drawing her back. "You're certain all the rooms are clear? We can't leave anyone behind. And Luca—he's terrified of the bombs. If he hears explosions . . ." Tears threatened to choke out her words. Amelia hesitated, finding them over the quell of emotion. "He'll be traumatized. They all will. We must check the ground-floor rooms to be certain no children are left."

"Luca's already gone to the gardens with C. B. I made certain I'm the last one out. Or, we are." Though his attention was focused on a distant point out the span of windows at the back of the kitchen, he paused for a split second, entreating her with, "Can you trust me?"

Amelia hadn't time to think. No time either to conjure an answer, not with sirens screaming like a banshee across the meadow. Another pulse cut the night, an explosion so loud she thought it could shred her soul from the inside out. A loud boom followed a half breath after, bringing such pressure and pain she thought her eardrums might burst.

The upper half of the kitchen's Dutch door squealed and clanged on its hinge with the explosion. Wyatt yanked Amelia through the door to the butler's pantry and shoved her under him as they tumbled to the floor. Walls shook as Amelia's face slammed into the stone floor, sending white-hot pain from her cheekbone up to her temple and ear.

Bucket and broom, stone and sprigs of drying herbs tied up by twine across the ceiling fell with them. Had any canned goods been left on the shelves or bottles of cleaning supplies tucked in high corners, they'd have come crashing down too. Thank goodness honey crocks were lined on shelves in the cellar, or it might have spelled disaster. As it was, there was little to contend with save for a jumbled mess of plaster dust and dried lavender, and baskets of onions and root vegetables that had been tossed down over their tangle of limbs.

The pungent sweetness of cordite hung on the air. Amelia could almost taste the lavender and feel the tinge of heat that blasted through the open door. But then everything screeched to an eerie . . . silence.

"Wait," Wyatt cautioned when Amelia tried to rise from under him.

They lay in the stillness, palms to the cold stone floor. Breathing together. Hearing nothing outside. No cries from the children or the popping of gas lines to signal that secondary fires had roared to life. Just the deafening silence and the thundering of her heart slamming in her chest as Wyatt kept his arms around her.

The blasts had been too close.

They'd only had one other venture so near the manor. It had scared them out of their wits one summer night and shaken their Anderson shelters like they were dice jostled in a cup until dawn. It had knocked out a side of the barn, but praise be, they'd lost only one cow and three hives in the blast.

No one had been hurt then.

Amelia clung to hope they'd come out unscathed this time too.

"Are you alright?" He released her, pulling his arms back from her shoulders.

"I believe so." Amelia sat up enough to cough through the dust but couldn't hope to stand, her balance lost by having her bell rung so soundly. She felt the floor moving, the room spinning, and brought her palm up to rest on her brow. "If I can just . . ."

"Don't move," he whispered through the dark, taking the hem of her sweater and raising it to her head.

"But the children. They'll be terribly afraid. I must go to them." Amelia stared through the door, dust clouding so she could scarcely see anything outside.

"Just hold on. I need to see to their mistress first." Wyatt examined the side of her head. He brushed her hair back against her shoulder, wiping dust away from her temple.

She leaned into his shoulder, head swimming, trying not to cough through the haze of plaster dust floating on the air. Though he tried to be gentle, the feel of cable weave pressing down on the tender skin of Amelia's temple caused her to clamp her eyes shut for a moment and wince on a deep breath.

Wyatt sparked a flame from a silver Dunhill and held it up to illuminate the side of her face. The golden glow splashed over his features, concern marking his brow as he studied her. He finally smiled a shade as he ran his index finger along her hairline, then leaned back, holding the light out between them. "It's not bad. Doesn't seem to need stitches."

"So it's to be one of those 'looks worse than it is' nuisances, yes? Grand. Though it certainly fights for attention with the sting, I have to say."

"We'll see to that. Keen to stand?"

Amelia nodded and sat up enough to right her feet under her. "I believe I can."

Wyatt held fast to her hand, palm sure but gentle as he raised them to standing together. He kept a grip on her, looking through the tiny light invading the darkness.

"You look fine—you're fine," he breathed out fast, his words spilling out in a nervous jumble like she'd never heard him suffer with before. "The bleeding's already slowing, but we'll take you to the base hospital to be sure. I'm sorry, but you'll need to give the sweater a good washing to get rid of the stains. But you're going to be fine."

Fine.

Three times in succession, mind—the captain sounded as rattled as she felt.

Amelia drew in a deep breath, steadying herself against him.

Truth be told, even in the flicker of a single flame that was nearly drowned out by the darkness, she could see the depth of concern in his eyes. Wyatt stared back, breaths no longer racking in and out of his chest. He was settling. The more he looked at her, his eyes drifting back up to the throbbing spot on her temple, he seemed to ease back into the assured officer she'd known from their first meeting.

"How did you know we were the last ones out?"

He found her book on the floor, went to it, and dusted the cover with his forearm. He held it out to her. "Told you—we made assignments. I'm always the last one out. And this time my assignment was you."

In the midst of catching her bearings in a disordered butler's pantry and trying to sort out what the flame revealed was at play on Wyatt's face, the flurry of what had just occurred came flooding back. Amelia took the book, hugged it over her chest, and gripped his elbow so she could borrow his strength and angle around the wares strewn about them.

She'd have made it out the door had Lieutenant Hale not darted inside.

"Cap? You in here?" C. B. shouted, then halted at seeing them emerge together in the flicker of Wyatt's lighter flame.

Lieutenant Barton trailed him, both filling the door frame.

"We're here." Wyatt braced Amelia at the elbow, helping her navigate overturned spindle chairs, shattered porcelain dinner plates littering the floor, and a large splinter of wood that had broken free from the back door. "What was it, Hale?"

"It's not the children?" Amelia begged before the lieutenant could even answer them.

"They're all fine, milady. Tucked in the Andersons with the men. They sent me back for you both, Cap. Hear tell the little ones wouldn't settle until they knew milady was accounted for. And the men were a mite concerned about you too, sir."

"We're quite fine, Lieutenant." Amelia looked past him to where night held fast, its darkness pervading the pastures.

The distance was outlined by a blazing orange glow in the center of the pasture. Wyatt must have seen it too, because he advanced to the empty window frames and surveyed the fiery scene before them. "What is it?"

"Pathfinder wreck, sir. Full bomb load. That was the first blast. Word from the airfield is it was chased in by a Ju 88 that got past the towers. Ended up in the far pasture."

"How many on board?"

C. B. looked sickened to say it, but he stood tall, added a sharp, "A full crew, sir."

Amelia shuddered again.

No doubt it was blood and bombs and twisted metal burning with charred wreckage in the back fields. Flames illuminated a span of rock wall that had been knocked out, and a giant willow afire with orange flames licking the starry sky.

Wyatt patted a hand to Amelia's cheek to draw her attention back.

It caused her to start and stare at him, not because of the warmth of his palm soothing her skin but because he'd never touched her before this night. Not for a handshake. Not in exchanging rations lists or even in passing a platter of food across the table in a packed dining hall.

He'd always kept his distance. But perhaps close calls had the power to change that.

"Go with Lieutenant Hale. He'll take you to your children, alright?"

"You're not coming?"

Wyatt shot his gaze to the window.

Time was precious, but lives were infinitely more dear. She had to understand if he felt that. But wasn't it wanton to run toward the flames without thinking it through, or at least seeking assistance from the airfield?

"Wyatt—a full load . . . If there's a wreck, that means bombs could explode at any second."

"If there's a crew down, then I can't stand by and watch them die. Just do as I ask, please. Go with Lieutenant Hale so I know you're out of harm's way. Watch over the children. I'll come back for you after, and we'll go to the hospital together. Get you checked out."

He brushed his hand over her cheek a last time, and with that, he left her standing in the estate kitchen, coughing from the dust and the surreal smell of burning metal and sweet lavender that invaded the air.

She watched Wyatt run toward the mass of flames.

Disappearing into the night was one thing; it was what flyboys did. They took orders and obeyed, taking up fortresses to defy the enemy. But to watch as Wyatt gave the orders to run toward incredible risk instead of shying away from it—that kind of courage upended any fortifications Amelia had built up around her heart.

She'd told herself Wyatt was just a nice officer.

A fellow reader who appreciated the merits of a fine English library.

But then why had she tucked his notes away in the Bible she kept in her bedside table? Why was it so easy to memorize the list of books he'd read? Why had she watched him run out over the fields, squinting through the darkness so she could follow his form until the very last second it finally disappeared into the night?

Amelia played it over in her mind as they neared the rounded, earth-covered roof of the Anderson and the metal doors that opened.

Inside, tiny eyes stared up at her with a mix of relief and terror.

She counted heads inside the shelter. Gripped little hands. Hugged shaking shoulders. Amelia called out names in the dark and confirmed that all were accounted for. And as yet another boom shook the ground beyond the manor, she took Luca in her lap and tried not to think of the danger beyond their garden blooms.

Something shifted in her pocket when he stirred, and only then did she remember the photo and watch she'd tucked there. Amelia removed the frame and ran her fingertips over the shattered front. The glass cracked in a streak across the smiling faces of a honeymooning couple who in the spring of 1938 had no idea how short their happiness would be.

She set it on a metal shelf on the inside wall and opened the precious copy of *Peter Pan* she'd snatched from the library.

As she read those precious "fly on wings, forever, in Never Never Land!" words aloud, she remembered the talk with Wyatt at the Castle House. The reality that death chose where and when to land upon the living without mercy forced her heart to whisper over and over, as bomb blasts shook the countryside . . .

Wyatt Stevens is not a friend.

But that, too, was a lie.

TWELVE

An odd thrashing drew Elizabeth's attention from sketching ropes of ivy, marigolds, and camellias that had entwined like a painter's palette along the water's edge.

Water tripped over the stones in the brook and birdsong sounded overhead as she paused, stilling the pencil tip to page. A breeze carried across the cobblestone bridge where she stood, tugging wisps of hair loose in a playful dance against her neck as she listened.

Light mornings like this one had provided an escape from the manor and her dear ma-ma's every whim to make Elizabeth's the most celebrated walk down an aisle since Queen Victoria but three years before. It was the blushing twenty-year-old bride who'd made ivory the fashion in such demand that Elizabeth's gown, too, must have lace trimmings of the Honiton variety and the fabric woven of the finest silk and satin from Spitalfields.

She'd have allowed, maybe even enjoyed, Ma-ma's marriage meddling under normal circumstances. But cares choked like thorns loosed in an untended garden. The revolver . . . a quite enigmatic groom . . . the slow, aching simmer of long-nursed pain and Elizabeth's pursuit of justice for her father made her chase the only solace she might find at Parham Hill—with a sketchbook and wide-open landscape to keep her occupied.

Vengeful shouts erupted from the trees, startling her to certainty this time.

The thrashing of leather upon flesh continued, so violent that Elizabeth dropped her pencil in the binding, certain the estate must be under some sort of attack.

A workman emerged from the tree line into the open meadow, his shirtsleeves rolled and vest flapping in the breeze as he muscled a series of whips to a stallion's hindquarters. Impulse forced Elizabeth to pull the blush skirt of her morning dress free from her ankles and burst out at full speed. Her slippers pounding over cobblestones, she took to the meadow, not stopping even as her hair loosed from the heavy coil at her nape.

"Stop this at once!" she cried, breaths racking in and out of her lungs as she became a shield between the poor creature and its attacker. Elizabeth pulled the reins free from the man's grip and flung her arm out—palm open in front of his face.

"Mind yerself, miss. This 'ere horse kicked a groom an' near put 'em to the grave. He's a beast, he is. An' mind he gets what he deserves. Won' be long before he takes a saddle, or a series of licks on the road back to the stables."

The horse bobbed its head in an angry spurt, eyes wild and defiant as it pulled the reins she'd fisted. Elizabeth re-coiled the leather around her palm, firming her grip. "Shh . . . shh . . ."

She turned back to the man. "This is the way you choose to break a horse—by beating it into submission? Is it not better to pursue gentling a horse's spirit instead of breaking it completely? Have you no mercy?"

"You are a sprite wit' mighty opinions. Out o' the way an' back to his lordship's parlor. Ye 'ave no business 'ere." He advanced a step on her and reached for the reins.

Oh no you don't . . .

She hid them behind her back. "You make it my business, sir."

"I warn ye not to interfere, *miss*." He eyed her, hand still clutching tight to his leather strap—which he raised a shade higher as a warning. "The groom kicked by this shod beast until the undertaker near be summoned is me brother. So I will do what I see fit so it doesn' happen again to no man."

"I'm terribly sorry for your brother, sir. But even an accident such as that does not warrant your actions. I cannot allow you to continue."

His scoff carried on the breeze. "Ye cannot allow?"

Elizabeth noted the viscount's crest branded in gold upon the bridle. She countered with a raised chin. Though the breeze blew strands of loose wisps across her neck and cheek, she issued a blazing stare that said he'd have to go through her if he wished to administer one more swing.

"Viscount Huxley would not allow his horses to be treated such. It is in your best interest to quit this estate, sir, before his lordship hears of this grievous offense upon his property." She paused, adding truthfully, "I do not know what he'll do to you when he learns of it."

The man flinched, his brow tightening as if the words were a jest. He was all bristle and brash against a defenseless horse. But to challenge the cool indifference of a real murderer . . . The man did not know what fate could await him. But she did. And if it were proven, she may well be saving his ungrateful hide from the temper of his master.

Ignorant to her deliberations, the man took a brazen step forward. "Just who do ye think ye are to speak to his lordship?"

"She is my wife," the viscount thundered from behind, his voice as raw and real as Elizabeth had ever heard it. She turned to see him emerge from the shadows of the tree line, where the road cut the willows in two. "And I would consider how much you value your life before you dare speak another word to her."

The viscount shed his coat and tossed it on the ground without care, giving a brisk roll to his shirtsleeves. Though his hands flirted with making fists at his sides, he stalked forward with eyes that raged a wicked warning.

He was not to be challenged.

Not by anyone.

Gray stone and gold pierced the man as though he were a foe on a battlefield, so deadly the groom might have mere seconds left in which to flee with his life. The viscount stopped when he was anchored at Elizabeth's side, his shoulder just teetering on the edge of brushing hers as he crossed his arms over his chest.

"You heard Lady Elizabeth. Go." The viscount flitted his glance to the road bordering the meadow where a coach had stopped and its door flung open. Franz lingered out front, leaning against it in the pomp of full traveling regalia in royal blue and satin top hat, but without the usual posh smile.

"But me brother!" The groom's cry was urgent. Insubordinate. And woefully lost.

"Your brother will retain his position, should he wish it. Once his injuries are sufficiently healed I will welcome him back as long as he can respect what is owned on this estate. But you, sir, are dismissed forthwith. I consider it forgiveness of a debt that you do not find yourself before the magistrate as it is."

"That creature is a beast. Mark my words—"

Elizabeth gasped as Lord Huxley lunged without warning, twisting the groom's arm behind him to tear the strap free.

"Beasts are made," he gritted out, edging fully in front of Elizabeth so she only saw around the haven of his shoulders. "By a temper that cannot be controlled and so it sickens everything around. That darkness has no place on this estate. Go before I forget that a lady is present and lose what civility I have left."

With little choice the groom huffed and stalked from the meadow. Franz tipped his hat in a jovial manner that said, *As you like, my good man!* as he reached the road.

"*Gut!* And quite a turn, Huxley," he called out. "Am I relieved this did not degrade into my aid being rendered in an uncomfortable exchange of fists. As it is your courage has saved the day. And I shall make myself useful and see that the uncultured *Schweine* is tossed from the front gates without delay." Franz tipped his hat to Elizabeth before strolling down the road behind the groom who was dusting his heels upon it.

The viscount couldn't temper a smile as the portrait maker disappeared, his top hat moving fast beyond the rock wall in his zeal to remove the offending party from the estate. Elizabeth could hold back neither and battled the relief with an unconscious smile of her own, almost forgetting in whose presence she remained.

She breathed deep, palmed the pleats of the morning dress across her middle, and banished the smile so he would not see it. "Franz would have fought a man. Was that a jest?"

Viscount Huxley shook his head. "It is a strange contradiction—a painter with an angry right hook. But don't let the peacock bit fool you. Franz can handle himself. He's as comfortable in a palace as he is in a roadside inn, though his sensibilities much prefer the luxuries of the former."

Before she had a chance to inquire about the circumstances in which either of them had been drawn into a bawdy brawl, they were alerted by the horse's whinny. The viscount's smile melted away, replaced by a serious furrow to his brow.

"You are not harmed?" he asked her, palm open, asking for the reins.

Elizabeth's heart drummed in her chest and her fingers ached from clenching so tight. She released them, placing the leather in his hand.

"No—I am well. Thank you." She looked to the bridge, remembrance making its presence known. "I heard the commotion and I fear your horse has been injured because of the man's actions. I'm afraid I didn't think better of getting involved. It just . . . happened. I saw it and had to react."

He nodded, eyebrows raised a shade. "Yes, it seems Cisco here has found himself a champion. I fear his affections may not lie with me after this." He raised his hands, ever careful, and approached the animal. "Aye, Cisco," he whispered under his breath. "Calm. Shh, shh . . ."

The animal stirred and bobbed about, stamping its hooves to the ground as the viscount whispered the words in a low cadence, over and over as he reached for the gold ring on the bridle. He grasped the reins that dangled in front of the stallion's shoulder, slow and steady, then knelt on the dew-laden earth, uncaring that his trousers would be soiled as he inspected Cisco's flank and leg to the hock.

He ran his palm over the horse's stifle. "He'll not suffer permanent damage. Not on the outside at least. But I don't know how we'll break him now. It will take quite a bit of work for him to learn to trust again." He stood, sighing as he patted the horse on the mane. "And we were nearly there."

"And your stable master? Should he not have been here?"

"He was otherwise engaged." The viscount turned his attention to the road, the coach abandoned along it. "I've business in London and Franz has a commission in Belgium. I sent a missive through your maid but received no reply. My apologies that we could not wait.

But we heard the commotion and then with you blazing across the field . . . it stirred worry."

"Oh. I see."

Nary a doubt entered Elizabeth's mind that it was the man before her and not the horse that might have been labeled a beast. Up to that very moment, she'd have believed it without question. But the contradictions in his character were mounting in swifter fashion than Elizabeth could see fair to work out. The eyes that once seemed so capable of depravity now looked on her with something akin to softness. A genuine, unbidden worry overpowered her defenses to see him as what she knew him to be.

Surely a man could not be so convincing in strength of character yet still possess a murderous intent at his core.

"You needn't be troubled, Lord Huxley. I shall be more careful in future."

"No—you misunderstand. I want to thank you for stepping in. Pray forgive me if I was shaken." He ran a hand through his hair, like he was thinking with his fingers. "But if anyone had harmed you, I would not have . . . And referring to you as my wife when we're not yet . . . I apologize. Unreservedly. This arrangement is new and I don't yet know how one responds in such matters."

Elizabeth stood under his gaze, unable to find a response to the tripping of his words. Until he stopped trying to find them. He allowed the slow fade of a smile upon his lips and a slight tip of the head in notice of something. "You have . . ."

"What?"

"There's something in your hair." He stepped forward as carefully as he'd done with Cisco moments before and raised careful fingertips to the loosed braid at her temple. He plucked a tiny breath of a white flower from it—the petals no bigger than a pin's top— and dropped it to float away on the breeze.

"Oh—I was in the gardens, and the wind . . ." She tried to smooth her mussed coif with a palm against the spot where he'd pulled the flower. "But I should go in. My mother will be anxious after me."

"You needn't feel you must be tracked here. I open every door to you. Give you every right of property to come and go as you wish. Though I might request in return that you inform me in advance before you throw yourself in front of any more horses. Just so Franz and I might be at the ready."

Humor? On top of everything else?

She stifled the tiniest twinge of familiarity that attempted to settle into her heart.

"I will be honest with you, about anything." Pausing as if he'd been ready to lead Cisco away but something drew him back, he took a step closer. "I wish these things, and yet . . . it is to no end."

"What is?"

"Attempting to pretend we do not know exactly who each other is," he whispered.

Her throat very nearly closed up. "I'm sorry?"

"We're strangers, are we not? I can see that pains you considerably. And our treatment can't have been welcoming. Franz is an acquaintance who even for his eccentricities and rather unpredictable tongue has become a trusted friend. I apologize if he caused you discomfort with his forthrightness in the library that first night. I'm afraid I haven't many intimates, and a friend's follies are not enough to excommunicate his arrogant hide from this house."

"I was not offended. I can see Mr. Winterhalter does not mean any real harm. Do you, Lord Huxley?"

"Do I mean you harm, Lady Elizabeth?" He tipped his brow, questioning, and shifted his weight sharply as if surprise ran the length of his limbs. Truly, he looked almost wounded by her question. How on earth could that be?

"No . . . I meant, do you not also see Mr. Winterhalter's nature is without harm?"

"His nature, perhaps. But an addiction to his art causes trouble at times. He has difficulty keeping acquaintance. As do I." He stopped, turned to her, this time the sun playing in shadows at their backs and the light fully shining upon his face so she could see every feature upon it. "Forgive me, Lady Elizabeth, but I am direct in nature. And I find in this circumstance, I must be such with you."

"Very well."

"I have been made privy to your circumstances." He hesitated. "All of them."

Elizabeth swallowed hard.

If the viscount knew of their circumstances, he'd believe her identity as a fortune hunter. A wily woman without character. That was enough to send both her and her mother from Parham Hill in the next coach and could preclude any future invitations in society—a circumstance Elizabeth wouldn't have shed a tear over, but one her mother surely would never recover from.

But if he referred to the other . . . to the death on a sidewalk in Piccadilly in which he'd played a part, Elizabeth was prepared to be as direct as he. "And those are?"

"My steward was able to confirm your father's title passed to the new earl some years ago—a cousin from Preston, Lancashire. He inherited all the land, the property, and capital, save for your manor in Yorkshire. But it has fallen onto . . . difficult times."

Why should I mince words?

"Ruin, my lord. It has fallen to utter ruin. I should bring nothing but a pile of rotting stones to a marriage."

"The manor's disrepair is indeed the report that has reached me."

Elizabeth nodded. "I wonder now why you ever agreed to a

marriage contract with me, had you suspected our aim in coming to Parham Hill was an advantageous match."

"Was that your aim particularly?"

"No. But like your artist friend, my ma-ma, too, means well, and her zeal to improve our future prospects is not enough for me to excommunicate her from my life. So if you'd prefer, we shall pack our trunks and quit this estate by teatime. There is no reason to further the discomfort of this association on either side."

"While I appreciate your candor, Lady Elizabeth, you misunderstand. I do not accuse you. I was attempting to share a confidence. It is in part because of your circumstances that I requested your hand."

A wave swept over her—the last thing Elizabeth expected was that the gentleman had not been tricked into a contract. Instead . . . he'd asked. "You requested?"

"I know you do not love me. And I do not ask for it. In fact, it is my requirement if I take a wife that she have no affection for me at all—even less for my estate or how many pounds I earn per year. When I learned of your aversion to any similar arrangement, I knew you would be such a match. So, yes, I did ask for your hand."

"I am of age."

"And may make your own decisions, yes. But you are also dutiful to your mother. I see that tension in you and it is commendable. So I should like to make you an offer. If you wish to leave I will arrange a carriage at once. But if you should require more time to consider the proposal, I offer that as well."

Everything in Elizabeth reviled at the thought of marriage to him.

It was what kept her pacing a hole in the hardwood of her chamber floor through the night, and why, if she could manage sleep, it was with a letter opener under her pillow. Had she the stomach to enact justice of her own volition? No, heaven help her. But perhaps she possessed enough gumption to find restitution in another way.

If he offered more time, perhaps that was exactly what she needed.

An entire manor of secrets loomed before her. If Elizabeth were to tread carefully, she might have every opportunity to find evidence that pointed to her father's murder. And if not that, then some other misdeed that might draw out his true character. A letter tucked away in a drawer, a conversation overheard among the staff—anything might prove fruitful. If she could just bide her time, then justice may yet be served.

With shades of indecision pushed aside for the prize she sought, Elizabeth nodded. "Very well. I will consider your proposal."

Something in him shifted, with softness at the corners of his eyes that said he'd placed an odd sort of hope in her answer. He looked over to the rock wall as a satin top hat was making its way back in their direction.

"May I assume we'll keep this arrangement between us?"

"You assume correctly, Viscount. I'd much prefer it, for everyone's sake."

He nodded and walked on to lead Cisco back to the road but turned back, his eyes searching hers. "And you might call me Keaton from now on. If it suits you. Good day, Lady Elizabeth."

The ghost of his touch lingered at Elizabeth's temple in maddening fashion as she hurried across the meadow, the great spires of the manor house looming large before her.

Nothing minimized the great loss she'd endured. And nothing he could do would ever make it right. But for the first time, she felt the anger and bitterness that had been companions the past ten years dare to consider a gentle thaw. The viscount had just given permission to do two very opposite things: to call him by name and, without his knowledge, to lay the path for his own downfall.

Time would tell which the better choice might be.

THIRTEEN

"Got your text, Dr. Foley. What's the verdict?"

Keira peeked over the tortoise rim of her glasses as Carter breezed into Parham Hill's Rose Room. She eased up from her stool in the space behind the easel and horde of standing lights she'd semicircled in a safe environment around Victoria.

"Viscount. Nice of you to remember we're here. And I told you when we met that I'd not completed my doctoral studies."

"Close enough. What do we have?"

After days of absence, no response to repeated texts or emails, and a relaxed saunter with a to-go cup of coffee in hand, Carter Wilmont gave a pretty accurate sense of the man Emory described as his friend by slipping back into their world without warning, first thing in the morning.

"I sent you messages with all that. Days ago."

"Right. My secretary said I should 'return the art doctor's calls already!' or she would promptly quit her post, which she's been threatening to do for the last five years." He leaned in, his cologne refusing to let her focus. "Until I send her a Burberry handbag as a

154

Christmas bonus and we start the cycle over again. This is a down month apparently."

Keira squashed a laugh by biting her bottom lip. "Beatrice? Yes. Lovely woman."

"You've spoken to her?"

"A few times. Trying to procure a response from her employer. While she thinks the world of you, she is a bit . . . miffed, shall we say, at what she claims is your classic lack of follow-through on any matter that concerns another human. I think those were her words."

"Blessed woman. She'd scold a tree trunk given the chance."

"And yet she invited me to spend my Christmas holidays with her family when employment with you does in fact fall through. What in the world should I make of that cautionary tale?"

"Whatever you'd like. Just don't tell me you've found out the painting's botched. This beauty's going to Sotheby's in the new year, and she needs to make waves when she does. That's why I'm counting on you. Emory said you moved into the pink room because of all the windows. So here I am. Give me the goods."

"The *pink* room?"

He gazed around in a slow survey, the corner of his mouth inching up in distaste before he took a sip from his cup. Keira could imagine that despite the stunning sunrise from the wall of windows and the glorious Victorian touches about the room, the space would no doubt be the very first Carter Wilmont would gut when he set out to remodel the manor for a more modern world.

"Pink—my word. Not his. Listen, I had to skive off before I stop in at the office today, so I'm not overly concerned with the color of an outdated room, or offending my darling old secretary. Emory says you're bound for London. I came to find out if that's true." Carter stopped beside her stool and leaned in, the crisp shirtsleeve of his shoulder nudging hers as he squinted at the painting. "So what am I looking at besides a dishy highness in old duds?"

"Well, for starters, this is not a Winterhalter."

"You're sure."

"As much as we can be. Yes."

"Classic. So that diminishes its value considerably." Carter backed up to expand his view, as if that eased the blow of bad news.

"I know this is a disappointment, but it may not be over."

"I believe I slept through art history class in prep school, so I haven't the first clue what that means." He flashed a heart-stopper of a grin. "Tell me you've got something else or I'll be forced to pay you for your charms alone."

"Well, this painting certainly has the hallmark of a Winterhalter—rich contrasts of light and shade, a royal setting and lavish textures—the gauze of Victoria's gown and the flower petals at her bodice show that, and here—" She pointed to the curve of Victoria's neck with her gloved pinky. "See this? Up to the chin? These lines are noticeably softened while the lines of her face, even in the same light, are quite sharp and deeply contrasted. It's like the artist wants us to look right at her, but while she's fully focused away on something—or someone—else. And given the fact that Winterhalter did paint an almost identical sitting with her hair unbound and the intense longing of her look 'off-camera,' it gives every indication this should be his work."

"But it's not."

"No—for a big reason. Winterhalter was known not to make preliminary sketches of his work, but this artist did. That's what puzzles me."

Carter straightened, the concern seemingly hitting him now. He crossed his arms over his chest and rested a pensive palm against his chin.

"Then the obvious questions are, whose is it, and what might it be worth?"

"I don't know. Not yet."

"Emory said something about Winterhalter having a studio of apprentices who worked under him, to mass-produce his paintings. Real twenty-first-century guy to have the foresight into a booming industry. Maybe this is one of those copies."

"Highly unlikely. He did that later in his career, as his work became more well known. And this portrait is intimate—a birthday gift the queen herself commissioned Winterhalter to paint for her husband. It's said Prince Albert was so moved and found it so private a gift that he closed it up in his personal office and wouldn't allow it to be viewed by others—even though it was his favorite portrait of her. Kind of sweet, actually. But he'd never have agreed for it to be mass-produced."

"So the people behind these paintings actually had a heart beating underneath all that taffeta?"

"You may be closer than you realize. If this work isn't his, then we need to know what's under the surface, so I had a portable X-ray machine brought in."

"You found something."

She nodded. "Yeah. We did. And it's big." Keira stood, peeling off her gloves as she went for her cell phone on the mantel. She flipped through her photos until she found it—the sketch image detail from the X-ray analysis—and held it out to him. "Here."

Carter held up the phone, then with doubt pinning his brows in toward the bridge of his nose looked back at her. "You're serious."

"Completely."

"This is what you're so excited about? A bee?"

"Not just a bee. A honeybee—the same variety as on this estate. And this one's remarkably detailed, like the artist was as interested in sketching it as the preliminary portrait itself. And look where it is—in the same spot over Victoria's right shoulder but buried under the paint as if it would never be seen. I have to wonder if you have any additional information about your family legacy at this estate, because I believe the artist had a connection here."

He shrugged, noncommittal about the estate's legacy. "I know enough to be dangerous in the right circles. There was a viscount in the late nineteenth century who thought it a clever idea to get the honey business started on the estate. They've had honey production ever since, though it's not thrived for years. Kind of a nuisance now, actually. I keep swatting at the mad things. Other than that, there's a story of an heir who was killed in one of the wars. I don't know much else."

"Is there a local historian? There must be some records of its history, being so close to Framlingham Castle."

"This place was always a thorn in the side of my father's family. An old summer estate I remember coming to as a boy, but with a hefty price tag to maintain. It didn't seem worth delving into its history if I was never going to inherit."

"But you did inherit."

"Seems I did, yeah. My father never did anything with it, and now I'm stuck with the grand headache of it all. I have to recoup something for the trouble."

Footsteps echoed in the hall, and Keira turned to find Emory in the doorway, two empty mugs in hand.

It had become their unspoken ritual of sorts, coffee in the Rose Room as the sun came up. But no clean mugs meant Emory had gone off to fetch them, and Carter had unknowingly broken into the solitude of their private world. He slowed at seeing the two of them, his smile fading back to professional courtesy in a blink.

"Found a couple." Emory gave a quick nod to his friend.

"Carter—welcome back. Didn't know you were joining us or I'd have brought another."

"I've my own, thanks." Carter held up his to-go cup.

"Ben will be glad you've resurfaced. The brick's come down fast, and he's got something to show off in the library—just a boarded-up wall, but he's hopeful about what may potentially be behind it. They're also doubling-down efforts on searching the attics for anything they might find to connect to the library."

"What could connect to the library up there? I'd wager it's only musty old trunks and broken-down furniture."

"Even so, he'd like to loop you in, that is, if Miss Foley is about finished here."

"Foley here's been telling me that our painting could be worthless because of some bee drawing underneath the paint."

"Worthless?" Emory set the mugs on the makeshift coffee counter and tidied up the bar with his back to them. "Is that so?"

"Not worthless. Not yet," Keira corrected, trying to infuse something positive back into the conversation. "Just different than we expected. There's a small sketch behind the portrait . . . just above the queen's right shoulder."

Emory stopped and turned, then smiled.

At *her*.

Yes, they knew the secret.

Carter picked up on the temperature change and fired back, "What?" ping-ponging his glance between them.

"What Miss Foley is trying to tell us is she believes it's the artist's signature."

"A bee is a signature."

Keira nodded. "In the original, Winterhalter's signature is just over the queen's shoulder. Whoever this artist is, they signed in the exact same spot—only they did it with a sketch." Her heart fluttered, and she grabbed up her phone again, then flipped through images to the photos of the original painting's borders.

"Here. After we compared the borders of this painting to the original, we found they're different, of course, but too similar to be discounted completely. But there are also too many inconsistencies in the overall composition to judge it as a replica—shading, paint strokes, even the variation in color. The paintings are close but intentionally altered so they can't be mistaken as by the same artist. So instead of a replication, it appears we may have something rarer."

A shiver ran through Keira, exhilaration at what could be in front of them. "I believe the portraits were likely painted by two different artists, but at the same time. If one sat in the presence of the queen, it's very likely they both did. Together."

"So what you're saying is, we should go to London."

"Um . . . the painting should go, yes." Keira cleared her throat, sweeping her unruly blonde waves behind her ear while she thought of how to pivot from the assumption that he'd go to London with her.

"You've made plans? What about your contract?"

"Not yet. But I can arrange for a chemical analysis the day after tomorrow. If everything goes as we hope, then we should know a lot more after that. But yes, someone should study the paintings together if possible, side by side."

The reasons why weren't clear even to her, but something inside prompted Keira to look at Emory. "What do you think?" She willed him to say something.

"Em? He won't set foot in London. Not for a million quid, eh?" Carter slapped Emory on the shoulder. "But we'll go. I've a company helicopter. Shouldn't take more than a few hours, and we could catch dinner and head over to Mayfair for a show after."

Alarm bells began ringing as Emory remained silent next to her. She wasn't disinterested in Carter—she had a pulse after all—but caution kept whispering inside in a "Watch it—you've been burned before, Keira" kind of way.

"I'm not certain I'd have time for all that, what with transporting Victoria safely and the tests we have to run. I'd have to stay with her the whole time."

"How long does it take to eat? Minutes."

"Well, I'll just see what M. J.'s up to then. Maybe she can go with us. An extra set of eyes to help out from a historical perspective?" Keira offered, turning back to the card table she was using to stack her things. She looked to Victoria, her only ally in the moment, and even her gaze was fixed on the other side of the room.

No help there.

"Whatever the doctor orders, right, Em?"

Keira turned back, ready to blast Carter with his own brand of cheek. Only he didn't seem to be talking to her. And he wasn't smiling. He stared at Emory, the tiniest flicker of challenge growing in his eyes.

"I'm the gaffer here so I don't mind making it a London party. We can stay at my flat a few days—the group of us. That is, if you decide Kensington isn't as dodgy as it used to be, Emory. Call Beatrice. You two know how to get this set up, I trust. Kensington W8 address. Good enough?"

The room could have lit like touch paper. Neither man moved. Nor spoke, but she wagered they might have rather talked it out with their fists in each other's faces. And Keira hadn't a clue as to why.

"Yes. Of course," she cut in. "I'll make a few calls today."

"Brilliant. I'll just drop in to hear Ben's tales from the library and then meet you back here tomorrow. We take our queen to the palace and celebrate our good fortune with a Sotheby's auction soon after."

Carter winked on a gentle turn that said he was cultured and practiced, and mostly innocent in what he was asking. But Keira was no fool. There was something not completely up front about him, and whatever it was couldn't be completely hidden by charm and a perfect smile.

He left just as quickly as he'd popped in, his footsteps echoing off the high ceiling of the Rose Room as he breezed out.

"He comes and goes with ease."

Emory nodded. "As he pleases, yes."

"So you wouldn't mind if I go to London?"

"Why would I? It's your job. He's paying you. He's paying us both, actually. We're at his beck and call."

"My job, maybe. But I get the sense that you have some apprehension about Carter and me working together on this. Is there something you're not telling me about the two of you? You're supposed to be friends, but if I gave looks like that to mine, I'd be shopping alone for the rest of my days."

"Nothing to worry about."

So there was something.

Why was it you could feel the elephant when it lumbered into a room, but no one wanted to comment when it stepped all over their toes?

In some odd way, Keira and Emory had found an unspoken rhythm in the days they'd worked together and had just fallen into it. Coffee together in the mornings. Discovery and work through the afternoons. Crew dinners at night and starting again the next day. They'd been elbow to elbow since she walked through the manor's front door. But every time Carter stepped in, he upended the balance.

Instead of elaborating, Emory pulled a folded sheet of paper out of his front jeans pocket. "So, I found what you asked for. Victoria penned a journal entry on 13 July 1843. It was one that was left out when Princess Beatrice sifted through the queen's journals after her death. Had to do some digging, but you were right. The queen mentions the portrait and how Winterhalter came to Buckingham Palace to paint it. To quote her, 'I find that I'm quite exhilarated to sit for the "secret picture" again tomorrow. Winterhalter has said he'll bring his little bee back for the occasion.' And in another journal entry from 2 January 1873, Victoria referred to it as 'my darling Albert's favorite picture, though I am gratified to have sent a copy home with her as the artist.'"

"So the 'little bee' is a woman? I must admit, I'm gratified too." Keira took the paper from him when he'd finished reading and scanned the words herself.

With this, they were one step closer. Whoever the artist was, and whatever her connection was to Victoria and the manor, and perhaps a pivotal place in history—they may have the opportunity to find all the answers.

Emory must have seen the excitement bubble to the surface, because when Keira looked up, she saw he'd been watching the emotions play out on her face all along.

"Emory, this is amazing. Truly. After all you've done, don't you . . . don't you want to go with us? To see what happens?"

He shook his head. His hands made their usual drift to his jeans pockets. "Victoria's got enough friends without me tagging along."

"You don't care for London?" She pulled at any straws that might reveal something about the rivalry dynamic between the two men.

"I don't care for a lot of places these days. Must be getting cantankerous in my old age," he said, his voice laden with something heavy, though a smile still made its way onto the fringes of the last word. "Well, I'll just see myself out."

Emory walked to the end of the coffee bar, where he'd laid his laptop and book on the windowsill. He picked them up and headed for the back doors.

Keira stepped forward before she could stop herself. "Wait—no coffee this morning?"

"Not today. I have a few things to do. But I'll see you when you get back. Alright? I'll learn what I can about the history of the estate, and we'll compare notes when you turn up again."

It was the oddest thing, to watch Emory step out the back doors of the manor to be swallowed up by the vast acreage and the autumn sun. Keira stood at the window, watching as he trotted down the terrace steps and out to the path toward the cottage.

Somehow she could feel sadness follow, though she hadn't a clue why.

For two men whose manners were so opposite and whose interactions were increasingly layered with ice, Carter Wilmont and Emory Scott didn't seem to be lifelong friends at all. If there was one thing she'd have paid money to know—almost more than who painted the masterpiece hidden in the manor walls—it was what other stories had been buried at Parham Hill.

A trip to London wasn't likely to untangle all that.

FOURTEEN

Amelia jumped at the strong-knuckled *rap-rap-rap* against the cottage's front door.

She checked her pocket watch—only half past ten.

Maybe Luca was so excited to move on to their next chapter that he'd managed to sneak away early that day. She crossed to the door and opened it, only to find it wasn't Luca who stood on the stoop under the canopy of golden willows.

"Wyatt . . . What a surprise."

Her jittery exhale was a certain telltale sign she hadn't expected him to find her at her cottage hideaway, and in such a state of disrepair as laboring over a pot of melted beeswax, making candles for their winter stores. She whisked her hair back at the temples, smoothing the locks behind her ears.

"Hello, Amelia. I'm sorry to disturb you."

Wyatt looked past her to the collection of beeswax candle jars drying on wooden racks above the worktable, then to the row of leaded-glass windows open along the back wall. If he trailed that glance all the way through the cottage, he'd see back to the private office, the rows of bookshelves, and the prized painting hanging on the wall with them.

Amelia slipped out to the stone front steps and pulled the brass knob closed with a *click* behind her, leaving the view behind. "You only disturbed my mad candle making, and I needed a break anyway."

"Is there anything you don't do on this estate, milady?"

"With an estate this size, who'd have time for leisure? Besides, if we don't keep St. Michaels in supply of beeswax, how would the townsfolk light candles for their boys who are off at war? It may be a small effort in comparison to the RAF or the US Army, but we still do what we can."

"You mean to say we're all fighting our own war."

"Something like that."

A smile, rather sheepish, softened his face in reply. "I actually wondered if Luca is about. I have a bribe of sorts, for consideration that I might join the book club."

"No. He's not. But I expect him anytime. He left his journal here again, and he always seems to find his way here when he can sneak away from the dreaded school lessons. So he should be about looking for it."

Wyatt held out a rust-red book. "We found a stack of children's books tucked in with the others shipped to the base from overseas. I set this one aside special."

The cover bore the title *Curious George* in black ink. A tiny monkey and a tall hat were illustrated on the front.

"*Curious George* . . . I've seen it. It's quite a popular book in America, yes?"

"It is. In fact, my nephews loved it."

It was the first time he'd mentioned anything of himself. Of home. And of what he'd left behind. Wyatt seemed to smile at a secret memory, and something flip-flopped in her midsection. Thinking of him reading a children's book to young nephews? Amelia cast the tenderness of the image aside, opting to keep the few feet of distance firmly in place between them.

"I'd like Luca to have it."

She accepted the book and turned it over in her hands. "It's very thoughtful, of course. He'll be delighted—even if it's not of the seafaring bent. But shouldn't you wait and give it to him yourself?"

"I wish I could . . ." He glanced over his shoulder to the jeep stopped by the road, as if a clock ticked through the time he had left. "But I brought it for another reason than the book club. You see, the author, Hans A. Rey—Reyersbach—and his wife, Margaret . . . they're German Jews."

The book seemed to pulse with electricity in Amelia's palms. "They are?"

"I've been thinking of the Pathfinder crash." He stopped for a breath as his gaze shifted to her temple. "You're well?"

"Quite. No damage. And what scar I might have is hidden by my hairline, so I get to keep my girlish looks despite the scratch the enemy tried to inflict upon me."

There may have been the ghost of a scar peeking out from her hairline, but the rest was a memory already. No stitches, no harm done. They'd all lived through it, and anytime you could say that after falling planes and a hail of bombs, you moved on with gusto and not a second thought about what might have been.

Wyatt cleared his throat, as if to shed his voice of its natural husky undertone. "You said something about Liesel and Luca having to leave their home and family to come across the Channel. Is that true?"

"They did, yes. In 1938."

"Do you know anything of their family?"

"Well, we're actually trying to find record of their parents, but we can't seem to find any sign of a Jürgen and Lea Schäfer—at least not that they're still in Berlin. It seems all the Jews have been moved out long ago. Thompson and Darly are both helping in the hunt, calling in favors from anyone we can. Contacting the Red Cross. But digging from a distance isn't the best approach, and we've had no luck so far."

"What brought the children here?"

"All I know is their father was a third-generation butcher and shopkeeper. They lived in a flat above their family's shop. Details are fading, but Liesel said soldiers arrived in trucks one night. The Germans shattered the shop windows and burned the building to the ground, with everything the family owned inside. Their father and mother were dragged into the street. Jürgen was beaten in front of his family by soldiers with clubs and taken away, so the kids thought they'd never see him again. And their mother . . . Soldiers inflicted horrific crimes against many of the women. I'll spare you what Liesel does remember of it all. It was Kristallnacht—'night of broken glass'—because so many Jewish businesses and homes and even lives were shattered. More than a hundred people were killed in a single night outside the windows where they should have been safe, and their innocence. That died too."

Wyatt shook his head and looked down at his boots, as if sickened. "There was coverage in the American newspapers—international reporters could still move around some before Hitler invaded Poland. But all that seems to have stopped, and what's happened to the Jews of Europe is just a trickle of reports over the wires. I remember reading about it when it happened. It didn't seem real. Still don't want to believe it is."

"Liesel said they were shortly reunited with their parents, but they set out for the coast soon after. They put their children on a boat and waved good-bye from the port as they sent them across the Channel. When the children landed in England, Liesel carried her younger brother as they boarded a train bound for London. They were taken into a home in the city where they knew no one, had no family but each other, and could barely speak the language.

"When word circulated that an invasion could be imminent, the Red Cross loaded thousands of children on trains. And one brought them here, with nothing but a paper tag on their coats that said *Framlingham* and a postcard to send word back home once they'd reached the safety of a country manor. Only I haven't an address by which to send it—just names: Jürgen and Lea Schäfer. So they stayed with Arthur and me . . . and now with just me. And until I can reach the parents of every single child in our charge, Parham Hill shall remain their home."

Wyatt nodded, understanding heavy in the purse of his lips. "Now I understand why I felt so strongly that Luca should have it."

"Why is that?"

"Because the authors have a similar story."

Amelia hugged the book—an unconscious reaction, or connection somehow, to the beloved family the children had been separated from for so long and with so many kilometers in between.

"Are they alive?"

"They are."

"What happened to them?"

"Hans and Margaret were a young married couple living in Paris before the Nazis marched in. They found two bicycles and in June of 1940 rode hard for the Spanish border—some four hundred miles with nothing but the clothes on their backs and a manuscript for a children's book in a wicker basket.

"They reached the United States after having been stopped along the way several times, and made it through by the skin of their teeth only because they could show drawings about a curious monkey and a man with a yellow hat—some kind of odd authority for their cross-country journey. But because of George, they made it through. And barely a year later arrived in New York, where they found a publisher. And here you are, holding the very book—proof that any story can have an ending worth risking everything we have, just to share it with someone else."

"They're safe in America now?"

"Yes. And grateful for it every day. The number of Jewish refugees the government is allowing in has been shaved down, so they're lucky to have made it at all. Fortunately, those Jews on US soil were given the assurance they can stay even if their visas expire. So now they live in New York, sharing stories with children who desperately need something to cling to in this broken world. They'd tell you that in many ways, *Curious George* saved their lives. And through their survival to share this book, they may have saved countless others too."

"How do you know all this? Was it in the American newspapers?"

"It may have been. But I know it because . . . I published them." Wyatt shifted his weight on the stone steps. "Wyatt Stevens. Associate Publisher, Houghton Mifflin, New York office, at your service."

"You never said, so I just assumed—"

He smiled—dashing, heart-stopping—humbling her with the seeming ability to read her thoughts that if he'd grown up on a farm, he must not have read a book in his life until he'd landed in an English library.

"Common misconception of Iowa farm-bred boys. But there's a great big world out there, and I once wanted more than anything just to see it. And here I end up standing on your doorstep, reunited with the story once again as we're fighting the same evil that allowed it to be shared with the world."

"So that's why . . . in the library? You wanted to read all the books."

"That's part of it. But I suppose in some offbeat manner, they're a comfort when I'm not in an iron fortress, dropping bombs on what could be my last day on earth. It's a sobering duty. But if I can walk into a library half a world away from home and still find a reminder that makes me feel *at* home, I can forget the rest for a little while."

"Whyever didn't you say something? You asked me to recommend books. What a fool you must think me to select them for a man who's publishing them."

"You could never be a fool. Not to me." Wyatt took a step forward, just shy of crossing the space between them.

Amelia drifted back until her shoulders grazed the cottage door.

"I haven't read all of them. How could any man, with the number of shelves in that library? It would take a lifetime to do it."

A lifetime . . .

Arthur should have had that.

A lifetime to read books and keep bees and harvest honey. To grow old with her and have a manor filled with the sound of children of their own. Those had been their simple dreams. But he was gone. And Wyatt stood before her—alive, breathing, looking back at her with such openness that she couldn't bear to break the connection of his eyes fixed upon hers. However well-intentioned that connection was, he wasn't guaranteed to walk away unscathed either.

"I pray, every day, that you and the rest of the men have a lifetime—and every ounce of joy in it that God allows when this is all over."

"I'm not asking God for a lifetime. I'm realistic about what I have right now. Here." Something so honest and raw weighed down his voice. "This moment to say it's not often you meet someone who has more than a passing fondness for the very same thing that impassions you. Please don't think I have anything but the utmost respect for you and your recommendations. I'll read whatever you give me. As long as I'm here, I'm *here*."

Amelia heard what he said—really tried to hear it. But flyers didn't have the choice to look beyond the now.

That wasn't the way war operated.

And it wasn't what life gave.

What they prayed for and sat around radios each night to hear spoken in Churchill's own voice was that the war was over . . . And blessed day when that did come, Wyatt would go home. The library had stories to keep him entertained, even comforted for a time in between missions, but that would eventually fade and the world could get back to marking a lifetime with joy and births instead of lamentations and death.

Amelia couldn't see any end save beyond it.

One day he'd go back to publishing books. The children would be reunited with their parents, one by one. And the manor would be passed on to the next owner—the heir she and Arthur should have seen birthed. It would be a cousin come back from war, maybe with a new bride like she, and Amelia would be pushed out to . . . She hadn't a clue.

They were both on borrowed time.

"Thank you, Wyatt. I'll ensure Luca receives the gift." She turned to go, one hand cradling the book to her chest, the other clamping down on the escape hatch of the brass doorknob.

"I didn't see blackout fabric over the windows," he said from behind.

"That's because there is none."

"They've run out of it in town?" Wyatt's tone was weighty. Careful and concerned.

She half turned, only able to give him a quarter profile, lest he see how hard it was to look away from him. "No. I never inquired because I refuse to hang it."

"But your government issued the directive that all windows must be covered so as not to arm the enemy with a target on English soil."

Darly had been insistent too, questioning why Amelia refused to add the veil of protection against the Luftwaffe's bomb-laden iron bellies. Though she tried, Amelia could hardly explain it to herself, save that something inside withered were she to have no memory of the world before war blew in and decimated the view from British windows.

Wyatt scanned the cottage's façade, inspecting the leaded-glass windows on either side of the arched front door, then looked at her again.

"Is that wise? Given we had a JU-88 sneak past an entire airfield and wreak havoc on the countryside? We can't account for your safety with the back of the cottage exposed. It could happen again. If it did, the Luftwaffe would have an easy target."

"And yet I was not the one to run toward plane wreckage filled with bombs." Amelia arched her brows, challenging him with the lightness of humor edging in between them.

"Amelia, I had to."

"I know you did. And I mean no disrespect of your courage. I wouldn't have asked you to be any less than you are by trying to convince you not to go. But in a similar way, I'm asking for your understanding that it's necessary I leave these windows undressed. I seldom work at night, so there's no real danger." A sudden smile curved the corners of her mouth. "I thank you, Wyatt, for thinking of Luca. Though, are you certain you wouldn't like to wait? I have to believe it more meaningful if the gift comes directly from you."

He looked pained, rubbing the heel of one palm on his other, like words ached to come forth, but whatever was on his mind he couldn't—or wouldn't—say. "Not this time. I'm afraid . . . I have to go."

Wyatt nodded. Once. Tipped his uniform hat and slowly walked away. But he hesitated on the path, stalling his footsteps at the gate. He curled his fingers around the top of the gate, squeezing hard to the scroll of rusted iron, then shoved it so the hinge cried out and it clanged against the wall of stone.

He turned back, no veil between them as he took wide steps back toward her. "Amelia?"

The hesitation required no explanation; it was the first time he'd ever said her name like that.

"I . . ." Wyatt dropped his hands into his uniform trouser pockets as he stood under the trees' mingle of light and shadow.

"You're going up again, aren't you?" she whispered.

"Yes."

Autumn had clung past its due to tired old limbs overhead but finally gave way, leaves dancing on a gentle breeze between them. And all Amelia could do was hug the book in her hands.

Perhaps she could protect it until Wyatt came back.

If she was pretending, an image of Wyatt sitting by the fire in a humble cottage, reading *Curious George* to Luca like he would have to his young nephews in the States, would become as normal and beautiful a scene as any a makeshift family might have had together. If Amelia and Luca could let him into their secret world of coping with war, and grief, and the potential for loss, she'd stand back and look on, beaming from behind a worktable. And in the soft glow of firelight she'd listen to that same husky voice telling stories of adventure and the bravery they all so desperately needed to believe was possible. And Wyatt would gaze at her across the cottage, their souls connecting in a single glance, and they'd be able to say everything in the silence that they couldn't seem to say in that moment on the path.

"When?" Amelia managed to utter, even the one word testing her will to speak it aloud.

"Briefing's tomorrow."

"And you'll return?"

"Can't say. I'll be training men at the airfield and might not be back for a couple of weeks. But . . . I wondered if you'd allow me to take some books."

Would he see if she dug her nails into her palms around the safety of the book she held in them? She hated war. Hated that she was beginning to care about one captain in particular.

"Of course. Take what you like."

Wyatt stared back at her, the wind toying with his brown hair similar to the way her emotions toyed with her insides, from the friction-build between them.

"We have books at the base, but . . . it's not the same as knowing they came from the library—or from you."

Amelia nodded, the air suddenly feeling warmer than it ought. "There's no restriction on whether you read from a cot in a ballroom or in a hangar at an airfield. The library doors are open to you and the books freely given as long as you're here."

He brightened, his countenance sending a twinge to her heart.

"I returned the last stack in our usual place. I'll come back by tonight to pick up the new ones before I go."

"They'll be waiting."

The wind kept up its dance, freeing a lock of blonde hair from its barrel roll to whisk about her cheek and fly across her nose. Amelia brushed it away, knowing it was decidedly inelegant but allowing a faint smile anyway, which he seemed to like.

"Good-bye, Amelia." He beamed a smile back—the first time

he'd been so open—and she reciprocated, without needing a clamor of words between them. "And thank you."

Wyatt walked away this time, his steps sure and shoulders high as he marched through the open gate. He jumped into his military-issue jeep and sailed off down the road, in the direction of the airfield.

It took everything in Amelia to walk the path instead of speeding at a full run through the meadow. *Stop. Think clearly.* The tension between them was imagined—only a reality because fighting men were, on the worst occasion, dying men, and they could ill afford to form an attachment. It couldn't be that her heart was awakening after the long sleep of four years.

Amelia hurried into the manor through the doors at the back of the Regency Ballroom and crossed to the library and the antique glass-doored sideboard where a stack of books waited only for her.

The aged volumes of Sherlock Holmes were there, just as she'd hoped, piled atop one another with spines worn to a lovely fade. A note sat on the stack, folded but coming unfurled upon the cover of *The Hound of the Baskervilles.* Though Amelia hadn't enough within her to face the reality that she'd come to long for his penned words, she took the paper in hand, unfolded it, and read quickly:

To the lady librarian of the house,

Sir Arthur Conan Doyle . . . bold. Intriguing. And every Sherlock Holmes story starts in a remarkably different way. More like Curious George than I expected. Luca may have to read one next so we can discuss it.

Still avoiding Austen, if you please.

Back by Christmas—I promise.

—Wyatt

A long pause followed, Amelia's heart beating in her throat, and then:

P. S. There's a USO dance at the base on Christmas Eve. Will I see you there?

Few things in Amelia's world terrified her more than the sputtering of a plane engine overhead or the whistle of bombs raining from the night sky.

Odd, but in her heart, attending a USO dance with Wyatt Stevens came dangerously close to both.

FIFTEEN

"Ah, Lady Elizabeth. Just the artist I was looking for." Franz bustled out of the Regency Ballroom, catching Elizabeth as she'd hoped to go unnoticed, and slipped from a drawing room door to the hall.

With his jacket discarded, silk waistcoat undone over a wrinkled linen shirt, and hair in a disarray of odd angles that stuck out about his crown, Franz presented quite disheveled. Not at all the picture he so routinely displayed.

"Mr. Winterhalter," Elizabeth said, swift to give a practiced curtsey. "Are you quite well, sir?"

"Well indeed." Franz gave a hurried bow, then looked behind her as if searching for a companion. "I've disturbed you in some endeavor?"

Thinking quickly, she held up two books she'd borrowed from the library. "No, sir. Not at all. I've been about the library. But it won't be long before luncheon is served, and my mother will wish me to be on time for it. She can be exacting about such matters of propriety, even if our host is away."

"But you are not presently engaged?"

"Not presently, no."

He nodded. *"Das ist gut."*

She needn't tell him the library was a ruse to afford her the opportunity to walk the long hall spanning the back of the manor, off which she'd step into rooms and search about quite without revealing her intentions. That was the plan, anyway. To find the viscount's private library and search it unobstructed—until Franz had found her there.

"Forgive me, sir. I thought the viscount stated you had a commission in Belgium. I did not expect you'd still be with us. We are delighted, of course, but have you and the viscount returned so quickly?"

"I regret that I was forced to postpone my trip. Something has come up here. But Huxley remains in London—business affairs hold him fast, I'm afraid."

London. And business affairs . . .

"Oh. I see. And does the viscount . . . frequent London?"

Franz didn't reply, instead just stood with hands pinned at his hips, surveying her face and morning dress. "You wear yellow often?"

"I suppose. On occasion." Elizabeth smiled. She couldn't help herself. My, but he was eccentric.

"I wonder if you would come in here. I have need of your assistance." He eased the books from her hand and extended his arm for her to join him in the Regency Ballroom. "If you please."

Elizabeth gazed past him into the depths of the room. The floor-to-ceiling windows had been laid open along the back, spanning the wall where white wainscoting met the rich robin's-egg wallpaper. She thought she remembered there had once been gold brocade curtains hung along them, but he'd had them taken down? Elizabeth didn't doubt Franz might have yanked them down himself, one by one, if it improved the light. He did appear to be working on something—an easel and canvas were set up in the center of the room with a beech pochade box standing beside it, the wood grain bespeckled with all manner of paint hues. A long brush was angled over the wooden top, its coarse bristles loaded with paint in a rich azure.

"I could come in for a moment, I suppose. But what is all this?" She followed him inside.

Franz moved about, lines furrowed across his brow and cognac eyes serious as his gaze penetrated the space between then. "This is the innate predicament when an image must come to life—it needs a spark for the fire to begin its slow burn. Paint alone cannot tell the story. It must first be born within the artist in order for him to put that life to canvas. And to be born there must be the spark."

Elizabeth nodded, though she wasn't entirely certain what he was referring to. "A spark, you say?"

"*Ja.*" He clapped his hands together. "A spark—exactly."

Fresh air enveloped Elizabeth when she crossed the dance floor to the easel, the open windows welcoming the cool spring breeze, and the melody of birdsong brought the outdoors inside. How did a celebrated portrait maker craft his masterpieces? Elation coursed through her as she turned behind the painting, imagining the richness of the forms taking shape from the artistry of Franz's brush.

Finding nothing but blank canvas, she turned back. "You have not begun?"

The rolled linen of his shirtsleeves appeared to be in his way, so Franz shoved them back off his wrists and crossed his arms over his chest. "*Nein.* I do not sketch first. The image—" A measure of agitation seemed to weigh his shoulders as he paced a few steps back and forth. He tapped two fingers to his temple. "It lives here until it is born. But it is being difficult."

"I see. And you need me to do what exactly?"

"Sketch for me."

A slow smile built within her—interest coupled with disbelief. "You wish me to sketch upon your canvas . . . ?"

Franz tipped his head toward the opposite side of the room. "Nein. On yours."

For the first time, Elizabeth saw a second setup nearly identical to the first. Franz moved to the fireplace and deposited her books upon the mantel as she approached behind.

Another easel and pochade box—this one appeared new—and a blank canvas waited opposite the fireplace. She walked over to it and ran her fingertips over metal tubes tucked in neat little rows— oil paints in fiery titian and deep crimson, an array of sea blues and the luxury of creamy neutrals. She tapped her fingertips against the pencils and brush heads sticking up from a wooden cup in the corner of the tray, smiling as the boar's hair tickled her skin, then ran her palm over an ivory canvas smock draped across its top.

It was a miraculous setup—an artist's dream. And this man was inviting her into it. "What is all this?"

"You prefer to sketch outside? It is not *en plein air* but close to it with the windows open. It will have to do, as I must remain indoors for this painting." Franz ignored her question as if his own thoughts raced about and he couldn't notice anything outside of his own head.

"What am I to do? Mr. Winterhalter, you're being quite mysterious, even for you."

It was then Elizabeth noticed the tea table next to the fireplace. Upon it, a black leather-bound sketchbook lay bare, open to the last quarter of its pages. She recognized the splay of images from Parham Hill: flower studies of marigolds, camellias, and tea roses. Horses and willows. Castle spires cutting lines against the clouds. And a few sketches she'd done from memories of home in Yorkshire . . .

She sucked in a desperate breath.

One of the most famous artists in the world had stepped into the privacy of her childish imaginings. With horror she slid her glance from him to the images, wishing she'd never sketched them. "Where did you find that?"

"Oh, this—*ja*." Franz moved to retrieve the sketchbook from the table. He thumbed through the pages like he was in a hurry about something. With a sudden slap of his palm to a page, he flipped the book around and presented it to her. "Here. I was quite taken with this one. You have used oil paints before?"

"I have."

"And can you duplicate this?" He pointed to a drawing Elizabeth had done days before, of a honeybee drinking nectar from an apple blossom branch.

Elizabeth reached for the book, begging to take it back. But he resisted, slipping it out of her reach.

"I don't know where you found this, sir, but I am not in the habit of sharing my work with anyone."

"The viscount fetched it from the bridge—before he left."

"Oh," she breathed out, half relieved to have found it but half terrified the sketch hidden in the back might have been discovered by prying eyes. "My drawings may be a trifle, but they are important to me. And private."

"A trifle? Is that what you think?" Franz shook his head, a coy smile upon his lips, and pressed an index finger to them as if to shush her out of such talk. "*Nein.* They are not."

"Forgive me, Mr. Winterhalter, but I do not believe the viscount would approve of this. If you please, I should like to have my book back and not speak of it again. And then I shall go. It is almost luncheon and I will be missed if I do not appear presently."

Franz returned the book, which she battled not to take with an intentional swipe from his hands. She curled her palm around the binding, intent upon fleeing, but he held her at bay with a booming laugh that echoed off the high ceilings.

"Approve? Who do you think requested that I work with you?"

The reality arrested her, and Elizabeth turned back.

He smiled wide. "Though I'd have twisted Huxley's arm on my own in seeing this. Yours is a rare talent, Fräulein. Has no one told you how gifted you are?"

Searching his face in earnest, Elizabeth waited for him to reveal the jest that never came. Though Franz's manners were flamboyant at best, there was one thing he did not appear to take lightly—*ever.*

That was his art.

The maturity with which he stood before her—open, serious, and without an ounce of arrogance—made the words ring as truth. Elizabeth had never considered herself any kind of talent, let alone a rare bird. Nor that the viscount would see it in her and request that Franz take her under some sort of wing because of it.

She shook her head. "I've never shown my drawings to anyone, save for my father many years ago. It is just a memory of home—the orchards and honeybees on our Yorkshire estate. Perhaps I remember the way things used to be."

"You have had no formal training?"

"None at all, sir. You cannot mean to judge me any kind of proficient because of a few simple drawings."

Franz paused, then crossed the dance floor with slow steps and eased the sketchbook from her hands.

The drawings were nothing particularly special, not compared to those of an accomplished artist of his stature. But he flipped through page after page, exclaiming over Elizabeth's use of light and shadow, the deep expression she was able to bring to inanimate objects, and the way her eye was able to extract exquisite beauty from even the most mundane of subjects.

"You are correct. I cannot assess the scale of your talent based on a mere book. I must see more in order to judge more."

Elizabeth gazed around through indecision, the sun catching in a cascade of light against the rows of colored tubes. She looked to the open windows, birdsong providing a backdrop of peace to the vast space in a cheerful melody that carried through the frames. The breeze moved about again, toying with the edge of the smock draped over the pochade box.

"Did you tear down the drapes in here?"

"Of course. An artist must remove whatever obstructs his view from seeing the world through the lens of light." He began to button his waistcoat, as if buttoned-up meant back to the business of masterful creation in his mind.

"The viscount really requested this of you?"

"Not the drapes, *nein*. But the rest—he did. In quite determined a manner, I might add, requesting I provide him with the list of items you'd need in order to begin."

Elizabeth's heart triggered in her chest. "Whyever would he do such a thing?"

Franz's demeanor shifted from serious back to humored, and he chuckled as if the answer should have been plainly known. "I suspect it is because our dear viscount is attempting to woo you, clever wolf that he is. Though he would never admit it, not even to himself. But that is no concern of ours at the moment. We have much work to do."

He smiled and reached for the smock, pulling it free from her pochade box. He held it out to her, bowing as he waited. "So what's it to be, Lady Elizabeth? Will you but help a struggling artist with his craft?"

"Struggling you are not, Mr. Winterhalter." She eyed the smock in front of him with conjecture. "I once thought you to be penniless. Much the fool me."

"Ach, but that is where you are wrong. Artists only starve if they do not feed the fire within them. Every master must begin somewhere on the road to greatness. May she be bold enough to step out in pursuit."

Elizabeth gauged his sincerity with a measured glance.

The temptation proved too wild to ignore, and she eased the smock from his outstretched hand, slipped it over her dress, and tied the canvas strips tight around her waist. She exhaled low, unbuttoned the festoon sleeves of her dress, and tucked satin pleats back off her wrists while she challenged him with a direct stare.

Franz stepped back to his own easel, paused to look over the top of empty canvas, and nodded to her from across the room. "*Gut*. Let us begin." He picked up his brush.

Ma-ma would come searching sooner or later, likely when Elizabeth did not appear in the dining hall within the hour. But she hadn't the ability to stop herself from drowning once in the perfect rhythm of creating light, color, and shadow on a blank canvas . . .

All the while she sketched, painted, and fell deeper into her first glorious taste of the artist's world, somehow the bitterness of her early memories diminished.

No more Piccadilly . . .

No more falling snow and broken dreams . . .

The memory of steel gray entered her mind, but this time she would not see the eyes as she once had. Instead they'd softened, and what had been jagged and sharp was now cut by a hopeful line of gold.

SIXTEEN

Present day
19 Pembroke Place
London W8, England

"He knows how to work a crowd like Houdini on a stage. I'll give him that," M. J. whispered at Keira's side as they stood on the fringes of the reception room in Carter's London flat.

Their host mingled about, weaving through the clusters of guests he seemed to have wrangled from all corners of London, sipping champagne with a practiced air and cutting a suave profile against the crème of British society. Every now and then he'd look up and scan the diamond tiaras across the space until he spotted the two Irish girls in a corner. And then he'd give a nod in their direction to show he hadn't forgotten them completely.

"See?" M. J. practically melted at the latest wink. "He's even workin' us."

"He's trying to." Keira watched M. J., who was fast falling under their dear viscount's spell. "There's a difference."

"Tryin' to? Would ye look around? I've never seen anythin' like this. Art historians are used to books an' musty old ledgers—but stately manors an' old money too. We assistants don' get out into the real world to see the likes o' this very often. I come from a tiny

flat in County Wicklow. How am I supposed to compare anythin'
like that to all this?"

"Oh, this isn't the real world. They think it is, but it's *their* world.
They only let us in so far. We might be invited to the party, but we're
still not one of the club. Not really."

M. J. glanced around, seeming to absorb the sights in the sparkling flat while she talked. "Well, call me a fish because whatever that
man is sellin', I'm in line to buy—hook, line, an' sinker."

Keira could see why. A gal would have to be dead and buried not
to have her heart stirred by the view around them. It looked like New
Year's Eve at Buckingham Palace there was so much glitz and glitter.

Carter's flat was a little lap of luxury tucked back in a court
off Kensington High Street, on the edge of Edwardes Square and
London's famed Holland Park—three stories of stately rooms with
a perfectly manicured garden terrace on each floor. All pristine
white wainscoting and herringbone hardwood, polished to an
impressive sheen, and lofty arched windows that beckoned guests
to pause and view stars twinkling in the London sky. It was gilded
chaos with tuxedos and trust funds floating around, and they'd
found themselves plopped down in the marvelous center of it all.

"Remember, M. J.—*work*. That's what we came to London to do.
Not to fall in love with Carter Wilmont and his . . ." Keira looked up
to the cathedral-height ceiling for the right words.

"Absolutely brilliant life?"

When she didn't agree, M. J. leaned in and shrugged her shoulder up against Keira's in a light bump. "Snap out o' it! Forget about
Victoria, will ye? Keira, she's tucked in tight at Kensington Palace.
An' here we are in designer duds at a party wit' actual royals. Between
this gown from Harrods an' your little gold number from that vintage shop in Notting Hill, I'd say we more than fit the part. Quite a
turnaround from a Dublin pub or a stodgy old manor in the Suffolk

countryside, yeah? We're more than within our bounds to enjoy the fruits o' Carter's generosity for one evenin' at least."

"Just one evening?" Keira whispered, wishing that was all it would amount to.

Carter had food catered last minute and a chef on loan from The Savoy. She didn't even know that was possible. A string quartet played in the space between the reception room and French doors open to the terrace. Crystal champagne flutes caught the light as guests moved about, their glasses reflecting like diamonds on parade. Harvest bouquets of black calla lilies, lavender, and soft mossy greenery covered fireplace mantels, and vanilla candles perfumed the air with sweetness. Every person here seemed to be wearing what would have amounted to Keira's yearly salary at Jack Foley's pub, and without batting an eyelash, they'd do it again tomorrow.

An absolutely brilliant life . . .

That's what it was all right. Until it wasn't.

Keira had been bit by it before—the intoxicating lure of the way the other half lived. And as M. J.'s eyes sparkled and she chatted on, giggling like a schoolgirl invited to dine with the queen, Keira's old wounds battled not to reopen.

How was it she'd tried to cut and run, hiding away in Dublin to lick her wounds after she'd been left in pieces, and all the while she'd been pulled through a door that would dare tempt her back? She'd have rather stayed on the straight and narrow than explore any further into this world.

M. J. looped her arm around Keira's elbow, sighing into her side. "Who is Carter Wilmont? Maybe he's 007 an' the tux is just a clever ruse to throw off all the hoity-toities. But how in the world is he still single? That's the real question."

Keira rolled her eyes, a smile taking over. "You really want to be a Bond girl?"

"'Course not. But maybe our other boss is the real mystery man to ye?" It was M. J.'s turn to wink. "Don't deny it. I've seen the way ye look at him."

"Emory?"

A knowing smile curved M. J.'s mouth. "Yeah. Emory. A real-life Simon Dermott if ever there was one."

"Maggie Jane . . . don't make something out of nothing. We're talking about your potential love life—not mine."

"Oh yeah? Well, in *How to Steal a Million* even Peter O'Toole didn't do cagey an' coy as well as our Mr. Scott does, unless I catch him starin' at ye."

"What in the world does that mean?"

"Nothin'—just that I'm allowed to notice a thing or two," she teased, eyes sparkling. "At least ye know where ye stand wit' Carter. Ye can' tell me yer not watchin' the same magic spell cover everyone around us that I am. Ye may be immune to the viscount, but I'd say the rest o' us are duly smitten."

"Watching, maybe. But participating? No. I'm no Audrey Hepburn. And if you remember the film correctly, she took out a pistol and shot the chap in the arm at their first meeting. Doesn't bode well for a lasting relationship."

"Don' say that too soon. Ye know how it worked out between them. An' Parham Hill does have a heap o' closets . . ."

"None of which I'm eager to step into with anyone, thank you very much. I'm here for the painting and the paycheck—in that order. But if you're inclined, I give you my blessing. My extreme caution where our viscount's charm is concerned, but I suppose a blessing nonetheless."

M. J. exhaled as Carter smiled at something, and Keira watched as another guest crossed paths with their charismatic employer.

A woman in her fifties approached in a gown of soft black gauze frosted over by a multistrand string of pearls at her nape, with a perfect chignon of chocolate peppered with gray. She greeted him with an elegant kiss on the cheek and a stalwart air. Truly, had they been dropped down into another era, Keira might have suspected Coco Chanel herself had arrived to mingle in Carter's world.

They talked for a few moments, the pair of them, until he whispered something, the woman's glance shot up, and they both stared over—at *them*. In a breath Coco's face changed from bearing a regal air to holding a suspicion that had no place in such affable surroundings. She nodded, pursing her poppy-red lips before Carter offered his arm. The woman accepted, hooking her elbow around his as he wove them through the crowd.

"For the love of all 'tis holy—look out." M. J. nudged Keira's side as she smoothed the wavy ebony hair at her nape with a quick flip of the palm. "He's comin' over."

On closer inspection, the woman was even more regal than she appeared across a crowded room.

Carter led the fashion icon to stop in front of them. "Ladies, I'd like to introduce you, if I may. This is Miss Maggie Jane Mitchell, our jack-of-all-trades at Parham Hill. She keeps us caffeinated, among other things like managing our world at the estate. And this is Keira Foley—our resident art historian."

"It is a pleasure to meet you both. Working at that old manor our Carter has finally inherited? He is being secretive though—will not share a bit about what you're doing as far out as East Suffolk. It does set one to wonder." She turned to Keira, those red lips curling in a soft smile, her eyes seeming familiar somehow, revealing shades of sympathy in their depths. "But I hadn't expected to meet you, Miss Foley, so this is a pleasure. I believe you may know my son—quite well, in fact."

"Do I?"

"Yes . . ." She pressed her lips into a deeply creased smile—as poised and polished as could be before laying down the hammer. "I am Marion Montgomery."

Keira glanced up at Carter, who stood by, a sudden statue in a pristine tuxedo. He didn't explain how he knew her former fiancé's mother. Didn't speak at all, in fact, just stood and waited with hands buried in the trouser pockets of his tailored suit.

Then the humor shot back to his lips, a grin light and feathery, and he turned to M. J. "Care for a turn about the room?"

Her eyes lit up like a firecracker, sparkling as she looked to Keira, then to the center of the crowded room. "But no one's dancin'."

Carter shrugged. "Never stopped me before. You know, I once danced down the Champs-Élysées in a snowfall, from the Arc de Triomphe all the way to the Grand Palais, without losing my footing once. I believe we can successfully cross the length of this room and give the rest of these guests something to gawk over. Want to give it a go?"

"Right." She handed him her champagne glass. "Lead the way."

He set hers alongside his, discarding them on the fireplace mantel. M. J. tossed Keira an elated look, just biting the edge of her bottom lip as Carter led her away.

"It's a pleasure. Are you sure?" Keira asked Marion when the couple was finally out of earshot, making sure she held back from pumping venom into her words. She wouldn't go back to past hurts, nor would she allow them to own her present.

"A manner of speaking, my dear."

"And no, we haven't met." Keira tried to read the woman. "There wasn't time, was there?"

"Of course there wasn't. You know men. Fickle and fast. Do you think we've ever met one of my son's girls?"

Keira swallowed the bitterness of a snap-back reply.

She'd unwittingly become one in a long line of impressionable gallery interns—young and stupid young ladies, the searching-for-something, easily-drawn-in kind—who thought themselves special in the eyes of the high-society prize that was Alton Montgomery.

"That's not the way he explained it when he was down on one knee."

"Alton's father and I would have stepped in while he was in New York had we known how far things had gone. But we were out of the country at the time. If we'd have known before our son made such a rash decision, it would have saved you a lot of hurt in the end."

"You mean had you known Alton proposed to me you'd have stopped a grown man from showing how shallow his character truly is? It was me or the money, and he chose what he loved more."

Marion sighed with an acquiescence that said she knew Keira had fallen for her son's promises. And what Keira had thought was something real and exciting and completely fairy tale–esque instead became the cautionary tale of her life.

"My dear, it never would have worked." She stared back, not with cold indifference exactly, but with what Keira could only read as something she ardently believed was true. Money was the way the world worked, and it blotted out human emotion every time. "You know as well as I that Alton's position carries . . . certain expectations when it comes to marriage."

"I thought love had some bearing on the conversation."

Marion bristled under a sleek smile, fingertipping her pearls. "If only that were true."

"Oh, I know what you mean. I'm a working-class girl from an O'Connell Street pub—not a pedigree that works in rooms like this, is it? But I was researching for my dissertation and it took me to an internship at a Manhattan gallery, where I met the boss's son. *Your* son. And after a whirlwind few months of five-star restaurants and

Broadway shows that ended with a Tiffany ring on a very important finger, I woke up one day to a pink slip and a fiancé who refused to answer my calls. No explanation—no job, no marriage, and certainly no love. Just ghosted out of a future with the man I thought actually cared for me.

"I had to meet his assistant in Central Park and hand over that little blue Tiffany's box because he couldn't muster the gumption to do it himself. So if you'll forgive me, I have no interest in raking it over. It's done and believe me, I'm better off."

The night was a bust. Keira turned to leave only to feel Marion's fingertips graze her elbow, a soft, pleading request to stay.

"Miss Foley, I had no intention of raking anything over. I am sorry, but now that we are both here, I must speak with you on another matter."

"What matter? There's nothing else to say."

"Oh, but there is. For Carter."

Keira glanced up, saw Carter keeping an eye on them as he twirled the impervious M. J. around in circles in his reception room. No help there. He was aptly employed, and apparently very happy to be occupied instead of enduring a well-meaning scolding from her former fiancé's mother.

"Look, Mrs. Montgomery. If you're implying that there's something between Carter and M. J., I don't see how that's any of your business. They're adults. While I will do everything I can to caution my friend from making the same mistake I did—"

"No. Carter's able to manage his own love life. I mean the Scott boy."

A wave of uncertainty washed over Keira.

Had she heard that right? How in the world could this be about Emory?

"Who—Emory Scott?"

"Carter says he's hired that young man to manage the restoration efforts at his estate. It seems the two of you have become . . . friends in recent weeks. Is this true?"

Friends?

It was difficult not to think of drinking coffee while watching the sun rise over Parham Hill's meadows and taking walks through the pasture to the beekeeper's cottage—of doing any work at all in the last weeks without Emory at her side. It was all innocent, at least in her mind. But something familiar had settled in, for those were things friends did. And the memory of the times she'd spent with him was something she'd carried all the way to London. Maybe hadn't realized it was still with her until that very moment.

"I suppose so," she whispered.

"Miss Foley, let me be frank. The Wilmonts and the Montgomerys have been close for many years. I consider it a duty to Carter's mother to check on her son anytime he is putting himself in a situation, let's say, that is less than acceptable. Since his father's sudden passing, Adelaide Wilmont has become more anxious about settling her son's future."

"Sudden?"

"A heart attack. Leading mergers and acquisitions one day, gone the next. And Carter has to pick up the pieces and run with all of it. An association with Emory Scott is not advisable if Carter is to take his father's place in their business affairs."

Marion ran manicured nails over the rim of her cocktail glass. She cleared her throat, whatever spell that held her all of a sudden broken.

"Mrs. Montgomery, I don't understand . . ."

"I would like you to convince Mr. Scott to leave the Wilmonts alone."

"You want me to convince Emory to walk away from Parham Hill?"

"Exactly. Carter won't listen—he's much more equipped in the charm department, bless him. But that boy is as hardheaded as his father was. I know you must be aware by now that this is a small world. The art. The parties. Look around this room and it's the same list of players whether it's London, Paris, or New York, just with a few new wives and a bit more Botox. But since the fallout of the theft at the Farbton and then the funeral . . . Emory has had little by way of explanation for his actions. It's as if the day his fiancée died, he did too. And no one has seen him since, until he reemerged at Parham Hill and begged Carter for a job. Rather suspect, don't you agree, for Carter to hire an art thief to manage an inheritance of potentially priceless fine art?"

The revelations felt like fire in Keira's veins.

A fiancée . . . and a funeral?

The room felt steaming hot all of a sudden, the garden terrace and its fresh air looking altogether too inviting a place for Keira to run. She breathed deep, shock traveling her limbs. The lines on Marion's face suddenly took on a starkness that didn't match the elegance of everything else about her persona.

"He didn't tell you then."

"No. He didn't. But then, we're not . . ." Keira paused, started again. "Emory doesn't talk about his personal life. He's only interested in business—which he's quite dedicated to, by the way. I've never seen anything in his character that warrants judgment like this."

"No? Wait." Marion's smile was easy, slithering through her elegant image. "Emory Scott has many secrets. I'd tread very carefully if I were you. Regardless, if as Carter says you and Mr. Scott have formed an attachment, I must ask if you'd agree to sway him from any further association with the Wilmonts."

The last thing Keira imagined when she'd carted Victoria off to London was that she'd spend an evening in the company of her former fiancé's mother. And instead of giving Marion Montgomery an earful about the vices of her despicable son, she felt a deep sorrow over Emory's loss that triggered something completely different than anger.

It gave the scything battle she'd witnessed at the steps of the beekeeper's cottage some measure of sense when it hadn't any before.

She needed to know why.

"What makes you believe I would step in at all? It's really none of my business. Give me one reason why I shouldn't walk out this door and leave you wondering what might have happened had your son not been such a coward and you stayed on my good side."

Marion's eyes twinkled in the flicker of candlelight, the slight glimmer of authenticity trying to sneak through her polished veneer. She lingered on the spread of The Savoy's best—caviar and buttered toast, strawberries and wheels of brie, scores of canapés and rows of crystal champagne flutes with pink sugared rims—all lined atop a long olive wood island in the kitchen.

"Would you care for something to eat, Miss Foley?"

The prospect of eating with this woman felt like it could have been a last meal with a boa constrictor. But Keira studied Marion Montgomery. What had she tucked up her Chanel sleeve? Alton was gone—that was over and done with. Keira would not revisit the last year in her heart. But to have the opportunity to dig deeper into what Emory wouldn't say . . . The woman was offering veiled information, but still something that intrigued her.

That Keira wouldn't walk away from.

"Dinner? Yeah, I think I would."

SEVENTEEN

DECEMBER 24, 1944
PARHAM HILL ESTATE
FRAMLINGHAM, ENGLAND

Amelia sat on the library's lone settee, staring through the glass door of the cabinet to the spine of the prized *Peter Pan of Kensington Garden* volume that had been a gift from Arthur their first Christmas together.

A fire danced in the hearth, radiating its golden glow into the vast room as rain clapped the roof in a steady downpour. She could hear it over the crackling and popping of fresh logs—a depressing drudge of water. It had the nerve to rain on Christmas Eve! Shaking the sides of the manor with wind and stinging ice pellets that would turn into knives against the windows. And where there jolly well should have been bright, fluffy snowflakes drifting about the sky, instead they had puddles of water, and mud, and a dour forecast to contend with on such a spirited day.

Had she been able to summon the nerve, Amelia might have imagined digging her best dress out of the back of the wardrobe—several years out of season. The soft merlot gabardine with golden shell buttons on the cuffs more than made up for its age. She would barrel-roll her hair, use the one prized tube of poppy-red lipstick she kept back for the most special of occasions, and slip on the last pair of stockings that might have existed in all of England, their silky smoothness a long-forgotten luxury against her skin.

For that, Amelia might have been brave enough to defy the weather with a joyous heart. But the sideboard was bare. Every morning she'd checked. No stack of books. No note. And no word meant . . . *no Wyatt.*

The tension between the past and her memories of Arthur—the pain of letting him go to a plane that was shot out of the sky—battled the something new that fluttered in her midsection whenever Wyatt walked into a room, or when she held a note of his penned words in her hand. It was why she so often found herself in her late husband's library these days. Reliving memories. Doubting her own ability to heal. And wondering whether fate sought to punish her with thoughts of a man who was just as courageous, just as kind and steadfast as her Arthur had been, but very different at the same time.

Thinking of the way Wyatt had dared to smile at Darly's up-turned nose over his lowborn status and of the way he had taken to supporting Luca's mischief around the manor, she feared Wyatt might have begun to awaken the heart she hadn't expected to share with anyone again. And there was an almost insurmountable risk associated with attending a USO dance in a dress with poppy lips and the one last luxury she had in silk stockings . . .

"'Tis Christmas. He'd want you to be happy, milady."

Darly's voice cut into Amelia's internal deliberation. He stood behind her, hovering in the doorway but with propriety too stiff to allow him the benefit of leaning against the jamb.

"And just how did you know I was thinking of Arthur?"

"Who said anything about Arthur?" he whispered.

She stood and walked his way. "Well, who else would we be talking about?"

The light of the hall cast a halo around him.

There was that same threadbare cardigan Darly always wore—she thought she spied a fresh hole pulling at the notched collar. His shoulders were a dampened evergreen, the sweater having absorbed the rain. His hair glistened wet in the light, gray-tipped ginger curling out from under the brim of his newsboy cap. The old tweed trousers he'd preferred for the last many years were not topped with a thick wool coat as they should have been.

He'd have been dubbed shabby in dress only because of rationing and a heart that was as selfless as any she'd known, who gave his coupons for the benefit of the children. But to her, he could have been a king for the presence he added to a room, waterlogged or not.

"Look at you, dear uncle! Whatever happened?"

"It seemed pleasant enough for a walk to town."

"You never! In this downpour?" She laughed, his stubborn eccentricity a tonic even on the heaviest-of-heart days. Only Darly would dare walk down the lane instead of taking a trap, trekking through stinging rain and ice as if he were above it all. "Come in and sit. You need a warm fire and dry clothes or you'll catch your death. And we certainly cannot have that."

He pulled a letter from his pocket. "I stopped in town to see about a few things. And brought the post along, milady."

Amelia took it in hand—why she thought it could be from Wyatt, she didn't know. But the looping script was not his. It was postmarked London, and the elegant address marked on the front could belong to only one person.

She ran her index finger under the envelope crease, took out the paper, and scanned the letter from Arthur's mother. "Nothing from Thompson today?"

Darly shook his head. "No, milady. I'm sorry. But will the dowager be gracing us with her presence this holiday?"

"It appears affairs in London keep my mother-in-law aptly occupied. She informs us in this letter that she is leading a corps of the women's Royal Voluntary Service in the city. Helping feed and care for those who have taken to sleeping in the underground. It's just as well, I suppose. She's needed where she is and would not care for the manner of disrepair in which we must survive at Parham Hill. The idea of children teeming about the drawing rooms and now servicemen playing ping-pong in her family's illustrious great hall . . . I'd much prefer the war to end and us to have the ability to patch up the manor before she sees it in its present state, lest she feel I've allowed Arthur's legacy to fall to ruin."

"Her protests over your marriage were unfounded, milady. And fell upon the deaf ears of my most intelligent nephew."

"Well, thank you for that. But it doesn't matter a scrap now."

"It matters still, just to know someone was on your side."

Amelia replaced the letter in its envelope and tucked it inside the pocket of her coveralls. "I'll answer her later, when I've time to pen a good, long letter. As it is, we have yet to bake honey cakes, hang socks along the mantels in the children's chambers, and light candles in the windows before darkness falls. Come now, Uncle. Why not warm yourself by the fire?"

"It's three o'clock." Darly broke into her attempts to evade, to divert, and to ignore the great elephant in the room.

"So it is. I'm afraid I lost track of the time. The library owns its own brand of magic, doesn't it? Come on then. Let's go see about you, stubborn old man." She hooked her elbow around his, pulling him toward the hall in a gentle tug.

He stood still in the doorway, cast by a subtler vulnerability than was usual for him. He patted her hand, released his elbow from her grasp, and took off his hat. He smoothed what hair remained atop his head and turned the cap about in his hands. "Not just yet, milady."

Darly was stalling. Why?

Panic stung her heart. Perhaps there was news in town? News of fortresses that had gone down in the poor weather? "What is it? What's happened?"

"I don't mean to worry you. All is well. And I don't mean to pry—it's not the way of a gentleman."

That wouldn't stop him. It hadn't before, in fact. "But . . ."

"But hadn't you begin readying for the dance?"

A wave of embarrassment washed over her.

How he'd known or assumed she would attend the USO dance—whether it was with Wyatt or on her own—it gave the implication that she was romantically inclined again.

She waved him off, relief popping out as a laugh. "A USO dance? In this weather . . . Are you mad? I'll be the only one there."

"Yes, milady. I speak of the dance. In this weather and on this special day. You ought to go."

"But I can't leave. Not now. I shouldn't even have lingered in here as long as I have. We've baking and decorating to do. And I'll be needing your help, sir. Shall we go?"

Amelia tried to mask the fact that she was terrified of something as trivial as a dance, putting on a brave face as she smiled and moved to walk by him. But Darly arrested her by producing a box he'd kept just out of sight in the hall—a large, pastel-pink rectangle with the name *Bertie's Buttons and Bows* splashed across the front, dotted with raindrops that hadn't yet dried after the return walk from town.

"You'll be needing this instead, Amelia."

She looked up at him, tears pricking her eyes with strong emotion. "What is that?"

The aged bachelor smiled with a fatherly warmth that shed all propriety but held fast to mercy and benevolence.

"It's your invitation to live again."

"To live . . . how?"

"Only you can answer that. Your grief speaks to how much you loved him—any fool can see that. But Arthur was a good man, and he would not want you to hide away in his library for the rest of your days." He replaced the cap on his crown and tipped his head in a bow. "I've put the cover on the tram. I'll hitch the horse and drive you over when you're ready." He left her then.

Just like that.

With shock prickling her senses, Amelia opened the box and couldn't breathe for a moment.

A liquid-silk gown lay inside careful folds of pastel paper, the ivory shining and more exquisite in person than she'd ever imagined it to be by simply looking into Bertie's shop window. She ran her fingertips over the familiar folds of the cinched bodice, the fishtail train, and the mother-of-pearl buttons that sat in a delicate row at the wrists of elegant sleeves.

A bill of sale signed by Florence Bertram herself indicated that all eighteen of the clothing ration coupons Amelia had thought went to keep their children warm, clothed, and in high spirits through the winter months had instead been put by and spent on a lavish Christmas gift . . . for *her*.

EIGHTEEN

MAY 16, 1843
PARHAM HILL ESTATE
FRAMLINGHAM, ENGLAND

When it came to uncovering murder, one could imagine herself doing just about anything to accomplish it. If Elizabeth had to tiptoe about the manor and peek into closed doors as a would-be sleuth, so be it.

Sunlight streamed through the windows of a room far down the main hall, light hitting against walls papered in masculine navy and grays. Judging by stacks of unopened correspondence in a tray upon the desk, it appeared to be a private office, and if the look of the articles inside gave any indication, it was one in frequent use.

She was arrested by the fact that she could not find a single shred of evidence that the viscount was any less than who he claimed, nor that the staff or Mr. Winterhalter had even a single harsh word to speak of him. By all accounts he was as upright a nobleman as any. And the memory of the moments that had passed between them in the meadow played over and over again in her mind.

This room of his personal things proved to have an entirely different feel—one of intimacy that all the other rooms she'd seen could not boast. If it was his private study, there may yet be something to provide answers.

She slipped in, clicking the door closed behind her.

Deep-cognac wingback chairs of leather anchored a fireplace. A globe sat upon a sideboard on the far wall, next to a potted plant and glass domes with smaller plants sunning under the window. Shelves boasted an abundance of books. Feathers . . . rocks . . . even a collection of dried honeycombs—all with no visible dust. Pressed leaves and butterflies hung in frames upon the wall. And where a portrait of some distant member of the Huxley line should have hung in prominence over the hearth instead hung a landscape in rich greens and grays—what looked to be the vast expanse of Parham Hill's rolling acreage.

Even so, was it Franz's work?

She leaned in, inspecting the paint strokes before remembering why she'd stepped into the office at all. Time was short and art couldn't be the lure that tripped up her endeavors.

Hurrying over to the desk and hesitating but a breath over his chair, Elizabeth began the hasty opening of drawers. She thumbed through a stack of letters from some names she did not recognize—a business associate by the name of Thomas Whittle and several from what appeared a closer relation by the name of Fenton, though all were dated from years ago. Nothing current. Still, for him to hold on to them for so long made Elizabeth think they could have some merit in the end. Other names she did recognize—including Franz—his looping script as fanciful as an itinerate portrait maker's could be—and another in fact signed by the prime minister, Sir Robert Peel, himself.

Heavens, he does have high friends.

Keaton had never mentioned an acquaintance with the prime minister before. Wouldn't a gentleman of station have boasted of such a thing? She made a point to commit as many names to memory before she searched through a stack of books and musty old ledgers lined up with bookends along the desktop. Anything in hopes she might find some secret connection to where his path had crossed her own so many years prior.

Where are you?

A low drawer revealed editions from the *Illustrated London News* newspaper from the year prior.

She sorted through them, finding the commonality of articles about thespian troupes, of all things. Most noted productions at the Adelphi Theatre near Piccadilly. Others at Covent Garden gave mention of a Miss Kelly's Theatre and Dramatic School that had been constructed in May 1840 . . . And several articles discussing "illegitimate drama"—those burlesque and melodrama shows that had become more frequent across London, with the crop of nonpatent theaters that were gaining popularity with the theater-going masses. And one article, strangely enough, placed one Keaton James—not listed as the Viscount Huxley—alongside a man named Thomas Whittle, the latter in a performance at the Theatre Royal, Drury Lane. Whatever the connection, it had to be from some point in his youth, before he inherited the title of viscount.

Whyever would he be interested in theater news?

Elizabeth sighed and dropped the newspapers back to the desk. Maybe Keaton fancied the diversion of entertainment that was the theater. Many gentlemen did. But newspapers . . . old letters . . . and not one personal effect of substance. So it was as nonsensical a find as any. If that was the extent of his secrets, she'd have to admit the search into the viscount's past was all but a lost cause. It was very likely she should have no recourse but to confront the man head-on and pray she'd have enough gumption to stand up to whatever outcome may result from it. Had she been able to find the revolver, Elizabeth was certain she may have enough of it left in order to see her through, no matter how fearful his rebuttals might become.

Heaven help her, Elizabeth wished Pa-pa were here.

He'd know what to do.

As it was, Elizabeth was alone. And she'd have to make the decisions she thought best—then live with the consequences.

"Pardon, milady. I did not know you wished to use this room."

Elizabeth whirled around to find one of the maids standing by an open door. She'd entered without warning, a slightly surprised bent to her doe eyes, her arms loaded down with a bucket and cleaning wares. She curtseyed with difficulty, trying not to drop the lot on the hardwood as she did.

"Oh, not at all." Elizabeth closed the drawer of newspapers in haste and turned back. "Nettie, yes?"

"Yes, milady. I've been sent in to open the room. His lordship has lately returned, and he wishes us to ready it for his use. But do you wish me to leave?"

"No. Of course not. I'll just move out of your way," she fluttered, moving past the viscount's desk to the door leading back out to the hall. "I have an engagement elsewhere."

"But if you please, milady?" Nettie added, calling her back.

"Yes?"

"I might ask that you join his lordship in the library at present."

"The library?"

Nettie bobbed her golden crown under her maid's cap. "Yes, milady. He's asking for you. Should we see you, we were to make the request right away."

He's asking for me?

"Thank you, Nettie. I shall join his lordship directly." Elizabeth stepped out into the hall, battling to calm her breathing on the walk from Keaton's private study down the long hall to the library.

It was not a brief jaunt by any account, but somehow she'd

traversed it almost as if she were running a marathon in crino-
lines. He'd invited her to be about the gardens and manor, even the
stables when it came down to it—wherever she wished to go. That
was acceptable in theory, but she doubted it an expectation that
his betrothed intended to nose through private affairs in his own
office.

To be unaccounted for in her betrothed's manor was not a good
showing at all, so she must hurry.

Elizabeth paused at the library doors at the far end of the hall.
She peeked through them, finding the viscount leaning with a hand
braced on the fireplace mantel, interestingly staring down at logs
in the hearth as if they danced with flames, when on this warm
spring day a fire had not been set upon them. His gaze watched the
memory of a fire that had gone cold.

"Viscount?"

"Keaton, please," he said on a bow when she stepped in. "You
needn't be formal with me. And not in here. The library is . . . well, it's
the least pretentious room in the manor for a number of reasons,
that is, despite the gold trim."

"Keaton." The familiarity still tripped off her tongue. "I was told
you wished to speak with me?"

"Yes, I do. Please. Come in."

Elizabeth scanned the room. No dowager countess. No portrait
maker in residence. And no service staff. It was quite unorthodox
for him to have reappeared so quickly, and then to request an audience with her when they'd not spoken since the day he'd found her
defending a horse in the meadow.

Being in the same room with him again was a fluster-inducing
occasion, especially given the fact she'd just been elbow-deep in his
private correspondence. He was the one to have secrets to admit to

her, that was true. But Elizabeth still felt a measure of guilt at being caught in his study, even though it was for a valiant cause.

Somehow she felt the twinge that he didn't deserve her mistrust, though that couldn't possibly be justified. She knew the truth.

"I understand while I've been in London you've—" He paused to sort through a stack of books on a sideboard under the window, and she held her breath. "Been taking lessons from Franz."

"Lessons. Yes, I have. For many days in succession now."

"And you enjoy this?"

"I do. I cannot account for it, but he seems to have the impression that I am an artist of some talent. I fear I'll let him down when he discovers how normal I am compared to his brilliance. But if you have any concern of my continuing . . . ," she said, uncertainty mounting in her middle.

"No—it's quite alright. I simply wished to relay that should you enjoy your tutorial and wish to continue it, Franz is inclined to do so. However, the lesson for this afternoon has been canceled. That's all."

"Oh. I see. Mr. Winterhalter is not ill, is he?"

"No. But in his own constitution, he may be soon. Our Franz is about readying his trunks—meaning, he is quite troubled by the state of his wardrobe at present. He set about to ensure the staff is educated on the merits of how to, as he put it, 'adequately starch a shirt and steam-iron cravats for a successful journey by coach.' Something to that effect."

And with that, he turned human again before her.

Keaton smiled, a calm, fluid, and very real action of the lips that showed he actually enjoyed teasing her, and perhaps being found in her company again. He stood, hands gathered behind his back, waiting for her to respond.

"Oh dear. That sounds . . . quite serious."

Keaton broke character, allowing the casual reaction of a laugh under his breath. "It is to him. He leaves the day after tomorrow, and I daresay he will find that wrinkles cannot be held at bay for that long. I fear for the safety of all involved in this venture."

"Is he off to Belgium then?"

"Yes, but on a diversion first. He's been called to London over the summer. Buckingham Palace, as a matter of fact, to take audience by the queen. I was sent back to relay the request and bring a missive outlining a new commission for him there. He is much sought after by Her Majesty and the prince consort."

It shouldn't have surprised her—Franz received commissions from royalty regularly. But still the news sent a little ripple of excitement to wave through her midsection.

Her Royal Highness. Queen Victoria. She'd summoned him just like that, and the request was so commonplace that he'd gone off to see about packing for the coach ride?

Elizabeth had to shake herself out of her stupor. "Of course he must go. I will keep up until he returns, that is, if he wishes to continue. He may return from the palace and find a distaste for the simple artistry of the countryside."

"I do not think Franz capable of engaging in your lessons if it were simply a passing breeze. I would be on your guard before he attempts to employ you as an apprentice in one of his studios." He tipped his head to the side, studying her more intently. "It seems as though Parham Hill may have competition for your affections. I'm aware that puts our impending marriage at a disadvantage."

Elizabeth felt her midsection wither—talk of affections was dangerous business.

"My affections?"

"Yes. Franz has asked if you might accompany him to the palace."

"Me?" Affections melted, and the shock of the unexpected settled in. "But why?"

"He believes you have a gift and wants you to have the opportunity to share it."

The air was sucked out of the room.

She swallowed hard, unsure of how to process what he'd just said.

Never had Elizabeth imagined meeting a gentleman who would offer space for a woman to decide her own fate in accepting or rejecting a proposal. But his offer now was fairly a unicorn—that she should not have to be forced into a ladies' drawing room at all but instead could step into an artist's studio if it was what impassioned her innermost.

There were few working females in the upper class of British society—even fewer artists in employ. It was nearly as scandalous as a lady singing opera or touring about as—*gasp!*—an actress. He would be prepared to support her in such an outlying venture as pursuing a profession, even as she was to step in and become mistress of all Parham Hill?

"You've time to think it over. Should you wish to go, Franz would accompany all of us to London and then make his departure to Belgium for his commission there. And after, he will return and take up his commission with the queen—with you as his apprentice. If it's what you want, of course."

The prolonged silence after Keaton gave the offer spoke volumes.

He stepped forward again, this time to stop in front of where her feet were iced to the floor. Steel gray and gold looked down on her in a show of tenderness Elizabeth had not thought possible before.

Not from him, ever.

"I apologize, sir. I'm not certain what I want. Not now."

"Yet I wonder whether I was wrong to have encouraged this."

"Why?"

"I may yet lose the opportunity to hear you give me your answer one day."

Keaton made no move to reach for her, but she imagined it. That a hand intended to grasp hers . . . Or that his eyes looked on her not with malice but with openness. That he was willing to consider affection. And heaven help her, Elizabeth wanted it. Some measure of closeness. A reckoning that said he wasn't the monster she'd once believed but a different man entirely.

The realization caused a sickness within and sent her flinching back before the ghostly fingertips of her imaginings could reach her.

Forgive me, she mouthed, and nearly tripped over her skirt in her haste to move back from him. An oddity, as he'd not even moved from his place.

"I'm sorry. I didn't mean to imply—"

Elizabeth balanced a hand on the sideboard, digging her fingernails into the wood so she could stand, this time the familiarity so different from when they'd met in the meadow. Confusion and guilt stripped her insides bare, emotion winning because it was clear there had been a shift in her affections. Above all things, this could not happen.

Not with him.

"Oh, my dear! I passed our Mr. Winterhalter on the way to oversee the laundry of all wretched things, and he has just shared the prodigious news!" Ma-ma hurried into the library, oblivious to anything in the room as she flitted about, taking up and patting Elizabeth's hands in elation. "Have you told her, Viscount?"

Keaton nodded, his composed veneer back in place. But he did continue watching Elizabeth as if she were a doll, porcelain and feeble, perhaps ready to break. "I have, Lady Davies."

"And is this not magic, Elizabeth? You are to go to Buckingham

Palace. To the palace to take audience with the queen herself! Ah, if your father were here." Ma-ma dabbed the corners of her eyes with a kerchief, puttering on about the bliss of an impending marriage and an audience with the queen too wonderful to absorb so close in succession. "He would be but proud, my darling. So, so proud. Almost as much as he would be on your wedding day, of course. And now the wedding must be in London. High summer. We will have much time to plan in the city. Oh, is it not a kindness that the viscount has given permission for you to do this?"

"I do not give Elizabeth permission, Lady Davies. She is free to make her own choices as long as she is here."

Keaton looked at her—a quick glance that said he meant it.

Every word.

"I'll just go see to our trunks." Elizabeth stumbled over the words as she stared across the space at Keaton, she knowing but he not having a clue as to what had passed between them. "There is much to be done before we leave. If you'll excuse me then."

Leave indeed.

Elizabeth excused herself on a weak bow and slipped from the library in a flurry, steeling every muscle in her body not to run all the way to the safety of her chamber.

One thing was certain—she would not waste another moment peeking through desk drawers like a shadow or haunting drawing rooms like a ghost. Keaton James knew as well as she what he'd done. And distraction couldn't change that.

He'd never fool her enough to make her truly care for him.

NINETEEN

Italian string lights threaded around the wooden rafters of the roof of the beekeeper's cottage, creating a bower against the twilight sky.

The golden yellow of the willows was losing its battle as November wore on, and a cold wind blew leaves to stir in a whirlwind against the garden gate. Keira pulled the collar of her canvas jacket tighter around her neck and grasped rusted iron in her palm, pushing until the hinge gave. Machinery buzzed loudly for long seconds—a power saw?—its cry reverberating across the meadow until it stopped again, and only the autumn wind remained.

The front door was cracked open so Keira climbed the steps and nudged it, rapping her knuckles against oak as she walked through.

There was no answer, save for another buzz of the saw.

A humble entry greeted her with weathered stairs that wound up tightly to a second floor. She passed under a rustic beam that hung low and stepped into an adjoining sitting room where a wood fire burned in a hearth against the wall. Instead of furniture the room boasted buckets and metal toolboxes, a pile of cast-off wood scraps collecting dust in a corner where the roof crumbled at the eaves, and a man bent over an old craftsman's table with his thermal shirtsleeves pushed up to the elbows. Sawdust collected on his arms as he measured a plank of wood for the next cut.

"So this is where you go to hide." She folded her arms across her chest in mock accusation.

Emory stood tall and faced her with a wary smile, like he'd been caught in some sort of crime. He pulled safety goggles back from his face. "Keira." He tossed the goggles on the table and wiped sawdust on his jeans. He walked toward her a few hesitant steps. "I, uh, didn't expect anyone out here."

"I followed the lights." She looked to the stringed magic above their heads. "What are you doing?"

"The crew's gone into town for dinner and Carter texted that he was staying on in London. Seemed like a good time to sneak in some work with everyone gone."

Keira walked in a few steps farther, unable to stand on the fringes of something so beautiful instead of being in the thick of it. She glanced up at the sinking sun through the open ceiling, the string lights growing bolder and brighter against the sky. "What is this room?"

"A parlor once upon a time. Or some sort of workshop in the latter years. There are paint droplets on the floor."

Keira nosed into a dark hall beyond the staircase, peering into the dark shadows. "And through here?"

"A small library at the end with rotting shelves. A converted kitchen, butler's pantry, and dining nook, though the ceiling has some serious water damage. I wouldn't hang out in there during an English spring, if you know what I mean. It'll have to be stripped down to the studs and rewalled. Then bedrooms and a bath on the upper floor. And a loft on the floor above that."

"Not bad," she whispered, wrapping her palm around one of the wooden spindles that led upstairs. "You know, I had the strangest bit of guilt at keeping Victoria away from here."

"You two have become good friends in all this, hmm?"

"I'm not sure why it seemed right to bring her back, but it did. I just can't shake the feeling that there's a story—something we're missing. We won't have the chemical analysis for a bit, but I'd say Victoria is very likely as old as we'd hoped. And that means we should be close to dating her. I haven't any firm ideas about an artist yet, but I'm hopeful."

"That's good. Then you're closer to finishing up your job and you'll get to go home. Maybe by Christmas? No doubt your brothers will be happy."

"And what about you for Christmas? No home to go to?"

He shrugged, hands drifting down to slip into his jeans pockets. "Maybe I imagined I'd stay here in some dream scenario—at least until Carter sells the estate."

"Does he know you're restoring the cottage?"

"He couldn't care less about this place. If anything, it'll improve something of the value in the end. That'll keep me safe for the moment." He stepped around a bucket, pulled a wooden stool from under the worktable, and patted its top in offering to her. "Here. Sit. Do you want some coffee?"

"You made coffee out here?"

"Hardly. Stretching extension cords for the lights and power tools is all I can manage across the meadow. But the thermos keeps the coffee hot most of the night. That way I can work through." He poured her a cup into the thermos cap, steam curling as Keira took it in hand.

"Thank you."

He sat on a stool opposite her and poured a mug of his own. "So what brings you out here, Keira?"

You. You bring me out here . . .

"Told you. I saw the lights and I was curious."

Emory tipped his brow, that little way of showing he didn't believe her one bit. "Has anyone ever told you you're a terrible liar? Something's on your mind. Go ahead. Spill."

It wasn't sunrise, but for the moment the ease of their coffee meetings battled for domination. Keira hated that the conversation was about to take a turn for the worse, especially when the cottage was so peaceful and the coffee hot, and a man she didn't want to hurt was waiting so patiently right in front of her.

"Okay . . ." Deep breath. *Go.* "You weren't even in Vienna the night *Empress* was stolen, but you seemed to take the fall for it. I wondered why."

Emory's face fell, the mood shifting from light to heavy in a blink. "Carter decided it was a good idea to drag you into this?"

"No. I met someone else in London who did . . . Marion Montgomery."

"Really." He laughed, though it was humorless—a rake that said he wasn't surprised and certainly wasn't upended by the mention of her name. "And how is it you're graced with knowing the great matriarch of the Montgomery clan?"

Keira paused, debating over how far to go . . . How much candor had their friendship earned her? And would she be sorry if she let him in?

"Because . . . I was jilted by her son and fired from the family gallery when I had the nerve to think I could marry above my station. You?"

Emory sighed, looking down as he swirled coffee in his mug. "So that's it. The spineless Alton Montgomery is the reason a dissertation got you fired? I should have known."

"In a manner of speaking. A dissertation took me to study in

New York where I met Alton. But it's more than that. Marion spent quite a bit of time trying to convince me to sway you out of your job here at Parham Hill. That'd be a polite way to put it."

"Or direct."

"Either way, why would she do that unless there's something you're not telling me?"

He set the mug down—hard, so coffee spilled over the lip and made a ring on the workbench wood. Then crossed his arms over his chest.

"And what did you say? I hope it ended with something close to 'he's tougher than he looks.'"

"Emory, when I read about what happened in Vienna, I just assumed your family had pushed you out because the painting went missing. To be honest, it made me angry that anyone would treat you that way. It made no sense then but even less now that it seems to be the other way around—you've walked out on them. At least according to Marion. And Carter confirmed the same when I asked him after. If you could spend Christmas with people who love you, why would you stay away? For years? Do you know what a gift it is to have family, when so few of us have that?"

He didn't argue. Didn't mention her mother's death or the uneven relationships she'd had with the men in her family for the last years. Keira was ready to defend those things with her life. Instead, he stared back into the depths of her eyes and whispered, "They want the *old* me. There's a difference."

"How?"

"Those people you met in London see who I was before, Keira. I don't even know that man anymore. I don't *want* to know him. Fast cars and faster women and swirls of paint hanging on museum walls . . . Nothing was sacred in that world. Not to me."

"Even you have to admit it's not a crime to have means."

"No. Wealth is not a crime. But it is a lure for some. Carter sticks around because he honestly believes one day I'll wake up from this bad dream and he'll get his friend back. But it's not that easy. Not anymore. And when I say you can't win with these people—you can't. Believe me, if I could get my hands on Alton Montgomery now, I'm afraid I wouldn't be the definition of posh these people seem to remember. I'd wring his neck and that would put a nice bow on the end of our association."

A tiny clench of Emory's jaw just showed in the firelight, and he looked down at the scarred wood of the worktable top. "Marion told you about Elise?"

Keira felt something twinge in her chest and she whispered, "Yes."

"And there you have it. That should tell you all you need to know about the character of the man before you."

"But it wasn't your fault." Keira stood on instinct, feet drawing her a step closer to his side. She set the thermos mug on the worktable and turned to him. "She died of cancer, Emory. How in the world could you have controlled that?"

He clamped his eyes shut for a split second and braced his arms on the table, head sagging. "Elise died, but it was my choice to leave her," Emory challenged her, his eyes pained. "I flew home to London as I pleased because I was too arrogant to think she could die without my being at her side. I honestly believed if I pretended it wouldn't happen, then it wouldn't. No matter what the doctors said. The great name of Scott was so built up in my mind that I couldn't see anything else. And Carter was there with her instead—my friend had to stay with my fiancée while she took her last breath. What does it matter that a painting was stolen from a museum when I'd lost all I had that mattered in the world?"

"I know you can't get that time back, but what good is it now to push away the people who are still here?"

"You don't know what you're talking about, Keira, only what you've been told. There's more to it than that."

"What more?"

"When a hundred-million-dollar painting vanishes into thin air and everyone walks out on you as you stand at a graveside, I'd say that's a pretty good indication of what your life is worth. Even my family didn't believe me. They pitied me but didn't believe a word I said."

"And now?"

"It doesn't matter if they believe me or not," he whispered, and he stared up at the lights. "Because I have right now. Right here. I told God I wouldn't hate Him for taking Elise and for everything else being stripped away, as long as He could still show me one good thing in every sunrise. And so help me I've looked. Every single day. That's why it doesn't matter what comes after this job, because my life is no longer my own. I'm four years sober and a lifetime away from the old Emory Scott. I won't go back to who I was. Not for all the money in the world."

A small measure of softness took over Emory's face and he stepped closer, slowly, with marked intention, until the tips of his boots could have brushed hers. Something in him spoke of understanding as he gazed down at her, that she couldn't blame him for wanting to cling to something that was solid in their crazy, mixed-up world.

It was the same thing Keira had clung to since New York—faith in what was good over what hurt like fire. The same thing she was holding so tight to now.

"What if I said I agree with you?"

"You want me to stay, Miss Foley?"

"Of course I want you to stay. I'm tougher than I look too. And I like to think a bit smarter." A smile found its way to her lips. Keira couldn't have held it back if she wanted to. "Isn't it obvious? She wants the painting, Emory."

"Marion? How did she find out about it?"

"Through Carter. Through his mother. It doesn't matter. You say you know these people? Well, I do too. And if Marion thinks we've found something, she doesn't want you anywhere near it. Not because you're a thief—because you're *good*. And you know this business like nobody else. So I told her the fact she wants you out says more than she realizes, and you ought to stay here and fight in Victoria's corner. Make all the Montgomerys out there eat their words when you clear your name."

Emory shifted his weight, like surprise had thrown him off balance. "You actually said that?"

"Yeah. And you should have seen her face when I told her I was coming back to fight with you." Keira tried to laugh it off, but he didn't join in.

Emory just stood there. Looking down on her as the wind kicked up, breezing through the holes in the roof and under the open eaves. He drifted a fingertip to catch the waves of hair that swept against her cheek, taking them dangerously close to something Keira promised herself she wouldn't allow to happen again.

The Scotts weren't that different from the Montgomerys— London or not, Victoria or not . . . her heart wasn't ready to get trampled in that world twice.

"I'll, uh . . ." She stumbled back on shaky steps, searching for a way to escape to the entry. "It's getting late, so I'd better go."

"Keira—wait." Emory followed, then stopped by the mantel, its wooden beam thick and well weathered. "You say you want to fight in Victoria's corner? Come here. I found something today and I couldn't wait to show it to you."

He ran his fingertip over a rounded embossing in the ivory

tile surrounding the hearth. She squeezed in beside him, a thrill of connection charging through her. Keira brushed her fingertips to the same place he had, the carving smooth beneath her skin, then trailed the line of carvings that repeated across the top. "It's a bee?"

He nodded. Smiled. Heart-stopping a bit in a way Carter or Alton never could have been because the emotion behind it was real. And unforced. He'd genuinely been waiting for her to come back just so he could share something with her.

"Your artist's signature is right here, next to the initials *A. W.* And you know where else I saw it? The tile around the library hearth where Victoria was found. It's the same design, Keira. There's something that links this old cottage with that bricked-off library."

"You believe a bee could mean something more than the fact this estate was in the honey business?"

"Why not? Since you admitted to Marion that you're invested, and if you don't mind a little rain coming through the roof, I'd say we work together to find out who A. W. is—on principle if nothing else."

"I've been thinking . . ."

"Just what have you been thinking, Keira?" He turned to her, too close. Inspected her face, too long. And had whispered with a blatant softness that nearly stole her ability to string two coherent thoughts together.

"We should search through the books."

Emory was cool enough to suppress the look he'd given her— that little tip of longing in his eyes retreated back behind his detached veneer. "The books?"

"Yes. It'll take time to go through the library, but maybe we start with the ones in the glass sideboard. In a library that's been hidden away and a manor emptied and forgotten, there's one constant— the books. They've been meticulously cared for. If they're the only things left alongside Victoria, there has to be a link that ties them together. And if we fancy ourselves clever researchers, we'll find it."

"*We'll* find it?"

The bower of lights proved entrancing. It was as if everything conspired to decide for Keira that she wasn't going anywhere. Maybe it was a lovely little cottage with a broken side and forgotten past, or the artist's signature embossed in tile, or the tiny flicker of a flame within her that said Emory Scott hadn't given up.

Not yet.

And neither would she.

Keira turned, found her coffee on the worktable, and dragged a bucket closer to the fire. Then she sat and sipped, waiting until he did the same. Emory picked up a bucket and sat too, stretched his legs out in the space between them, crossing one over the other.

"So—Carter and M. J., huh? That's a development."

"I don't know, but I think I saw that one coming a mile away." Keira couldn't help but laugh, warming her hands around her cup.

"Better watch out, Foley. You're sounding more like an American every day."

The sun drooped low on the horizon as they talked, until its rays were gone and only an ink sky and coffee by firelight remained. The trip to London wasn't all she'd expected—not for Victoria or for her. But answers would come later.

For the moment, sitting with the unguarded Emory Scott was enough.

TWENTY

Rain had long ago turned to pellets of ice that racked the freshly replaced kitchen windows like pebbles thrown against glass.

Amelia sat at the farmhouse table, stirring a spoon around the spray of tea roses lining her mother-in-law's Crown Staffordshire bone china. Perhaps she shouldn't have added honey to her Earl Grey when it could have been used for so many other things. Still, a tick past midnight on Christmas could afford her a little bit of sweetness, wherever she might find it.

A pounding thumped the kitchen door, nearly startling the life out of her.

Amelia jumped to her feet, snatching up the closest weapon she could—a scrolled jam spoon that hadn't seen jam in ages. She brandished the dulled blade in front of her and cracked the door open.

The shoulders of his flight jacket were covered in ice, his hair wet at the tips and face pink from the cold, but it was not an agent of the enemy or an apparition that had been sent to toy with frayed nerves.

Just Wyatt.

His breath flowed in and out on a heavy fog, like he'd landed a plane and sprinted all the way from the airfield.

"Wyatt!" Amelia dropped the spoon where it bounced from the wood countertop to clang on the stone floor, disappearing in the darkness.

"Did I miss it?" he breathed out, a hush falling over him as his breathing calmed.

"I didn't expect you tonight. Not now at least. But come in." She pulled him inside out of the cold. "I'm sorry. You've missed Christmas. I'm afraid the children have all gone to bed."

"No—a call should have come in from the base. There's an emergency situation at the airfield. I tried the front doors. No answer, so I came around to this side."

"What do you mean? We've had no call. Last I heard the telephone lines are down from when the ice storm came through."

Wyatt finally focused through the darkness, squinting in the moonlight.

It was then the arrow struck and he paused, surveying her head to toe with a sudden softness that had her look down, remembering.

Except for services at St. Michaels, he'd very likely never seen her in a dress. And certainly not one of liquid satin that swept down in a train, fanning out at the tips of golden-toed heels. Her hair she'd rolled in sumptuous waves and left down to flow over her shoulders. She'd even kept the diamond teardrops in her ears, maybe her subconscious stalling because she just hadn't wanted the night to end without him in it somehow.

Hanging a dress back in the closet and dropping earbobs back in the jewelry box would have done it.

"Oh. Yes—a dress." Amelia blushed, feeling her cheeks warm, and touched a palm to cover it.

"That's not just a dress. If I'm honest, I think that's every dress ever made."

"Darly seemed to think Christmas was the appropriate time for a gift worthy of dancing, frivolous as it is." Amelia played off the praise with a shrug of the shoulders and a slight roll of her eyes to the ceiling.

He started, a tiny flinch of the face indicating a track had just shifted in his mind. "You went to the USO dance?"

"Not a particularly clever move, especially given the cost of such a gown. I can't believe I went out in this weather. What was I thinking?"

Either the blush in her cheeks or the tiniest bit of waver in her voice caused it, but Wyatt stepped up to her. Fast. Saying nothing as he took off his hat. Just stopped, a breath away, looking down at her in the gown shimmering so innocently in the moonlight when it had started the whole moment.

"I would have come, if I could," he whispered, hazel eyes searching hers, ardent even through the shadows. "I would have done anything to have been there tonight."

A wall fell, and Amelia allowed her heart to receive the honesty of his words. "I know that. I know."

She shook her head, trying not to think of where he'd been, the devastation he'd seen, or why he'd been so very late.

She wiped her mind clean.

Forget everything but what it feels like to see him again.

"I didn't have a choice. I was sent straight from the airfield as soon as our wheels hit the ground. We have a problem."

"What is it?"

"Two hundred soldiers. Stranded—fortresses circling in air or landing God knows where because runways are iced up all the way down the coast. Framlingham is the last airfield able to take planes from the Channel, but the army doesn't have barracks enough for all the men who might need to come in."

"And they're asking us to take them here?"

He nodded. "We don't have space for a squadron at the base, let alone a fleet of hundreds. They've nowhere else to go. Nowhere else to land safely."

The chill from the windows ran over her, but Amelia defied it. "We may have to feed fireplaces with the last of the furniture, and it may be a feast of popcorn balls and cranberry strings from the Christmas tree, but the men won't go cold or hungry tonight. They are all dear to someone, and they need their own promises remembered tonight." She pressed a palm to the front of Wyatt's coat over a trail of water that had melted from his shoulder, then slid her hand down the front. "Go back. Tell them we'll open our doors."

Amelia worked in a dress that night for the first time in her life. As the clock ticked into morning and scores of airmen began to filter through the front gates of Parham Hill, Amelia unbuttoned pearl cuffs, rolled sleeves to her elbows, and covered satin with a plain canvas apron.

They lit candles in the entry as a flurry of RAF pilots and Yankee flyboys trudged up the path. They settled tired bodies in as many corners as a makeshift cot could fit in the elegant Rose Room, pushed beds closer to make space in the Regency Ballroom, and lined pallets along the balcony of Parham Hill's great ancestral hall.

Amelia opened the cabinets and handed out the best bone china to warm freezing hands. Steaming tea they poured into porcelain and all the extra honey for winter stores was brought up from the cellar. And with blackout curtains drawn tight, they lit Amelia's beeswax candles the length of the stairs up from the ground floor, in a flickering trail of circular magic that overtook three stories of the grand entry space.

Handing out a stack of woolen blankets as she looked up to brush a stubborn wave of hair back out of her eyes, Amelia just caught the sight of Luca, his mop of brown curls weaving through the crowd of displaced servicemen. He hugged a special book in his arms as he filtered through fatigues and officers and drifted over to stand at the captain's side.

Wyatt didn't need much to notice—he seemed aware of the boy's presence already and responded by placing a hand upon Luca's shoulder and keeping it there, much as a father would.

As if her previous imaginings of fireside readings in the cottage could possibly come true, Wyatt looked up. Amelia watched as he searched through the happy madness until he rested his gaze upon her and smiled.

"Silent Night" flowed from somewhere in the entry. With no big band or shiny instruments necessary, a clear, soft tone rose to the ceiling in a bittersweet combination of peace meeting war and banishing it from their world, if only for that one night. Voices floated up to the vault of their ceiling-sky in a soft chorus of hundreds, and to Amelia, it became the holiest night she'd ever known.

When silence had again befallen the halls and ballrooms, and the children ventured back to their beds in hopes a jolly elf would yet have time enough to fill their stockings, Amelia drifted into the sanctuary of library shelves and her beloved books. She found Wyatt kneeling before the hearth, adding logs on the fire—like he knew she'd eventually meet him there when all the work was done. Flames fanned wildly with each toss, licking at the kindling along the back of chimney bricks and sparking up to carry into the night sky.

At the sound of her heels clicking on the hardwood, he turned. She sighed, settling into the welcome corner of the open settee. "You know, I sat in this exact spot yesterday morning, wondering what would become of Christmas. And now look at us—a manor packed full with children tucked in their beds, half the country's servicemen sleeping on the stairs, and I served tea in a gown worth more than this manor. What a beautiful, topsy-turvy holiday."

"Seems you're the last one up again."

"You're awake too. I'm convinced by now that you never sleep, Captain. You just keep going, defending the world like a machine in the sky."

Smiling at what she thought was her lighthearted jest, Amelia slipped her feet out of the gold lattice heels and gave the shoes a playful toss on the floor, then tucked her legs up under her. What she did not expect was for weight to settle upon his shoulders on the hinges of her words and a somberness to drift down over his face.

It melted the ease within her.

"Amelia—if I hadn't come back late, you'd have still been there?"

"Well, I almost didn't show, if you must know the truth. I must have walked up and down the manor steps umpteen times in those horridly uncomfortable shoes. Maybe I feared this silly dress would have been ruined in the rain. And now look at it—splashed with tea and honey and I couldn't care less because I'm so happy."

Amelia tried to cap the admission with a noncommittal laugh but fought to calm the racing of her heart when he didn't buy it. Instead, Wyatt paused on what seemed a clear decision, then stood and walked over to join her.

He knelt before the settee—before *her*—his arm casually draped over the armrest so the warmth of his fingertips curled in a graze against hers, then took the liberty of staring directly into her eyes. "You really waited?"

How honest could she, should she, be? Amelia couldn't find the words. They choked out within her so she couldn't utter a reply.

"How long did I make you wait?" he whispered again.

She swallowed hard. "I stayed until the band packed up their instruments and the last light was turned out."

Wyatt shook his head, angry at a fate he couldn't have controlled. But it was sweet nonetheless. And telling, because he leaned in with apology in his voice that the weather dared alter best-laid plans. "Amelia . . . I'd have done anything to land on time."

"You don't have to apologize."

"No, I want you to understand. Framlingham was the last airfield open for miles, so it's by sheer luck we found a place to land at all, let alone to find an airfield that was already home. I need you to know it was a risk landing on ice and being late or running out of gas, crashing in a field somewhere, and risking being . . . well, really late."

"A better excuse for tardiness I don't think I've ever heard. You are forgiven, Captain."

"It's no excuse. But crash or not, it still would have been worth it. I promised a lady I'd come back by Christmas. And I always keep my promises."

"If that's true . . . then someone convinced me today that it's time."

"Time for what?" It was tender, the question and the way he allowed his fingertips to stroke her hand.

Amelia looked back at him, into the eyes she hadn't realized now had begun to feel so like home when they gazed upon her. "Not to waste a chance when it's been given."

Wyatt looked to the faint scar at her temple, like he'd done before, but this time he didn't hold back. He moved to edge back one of the barrel curls she'd styled so carefully at her vanity table earlier in the evening, and she allowed him to do it, his fingertips brushing her hair so it rested over the delicate rise of her shoulder.

"Did you dance? I mean, should I anticipate any mounting competition because of my lateness?"

She shook her head. "I might have—and mind, I had to turn away more than one eager Yank—but no. Just on the off chance my dance card was already full, I chose to keep my dancing shoes at the ready."

He dropped his hand but held his breath.

"Would you dance with me now?"

Amelia raised an eyebrow in play. "You forget, sir—the band has already gone."

"I didn't land that plane for music."

"I haven't any shoes." Amelia glanced at the rug and the golden heels glittering in the firelight. "See? I flung the sorry lot over there where they belong, never to be worn again in this lifetime—miserably uncomfortable things."

"Leave them." He rose, hand out, eyes serious as they waited for her to accept. "I'll hold you up."

Amelia almost couldn't breathe as a grandfather clock ticked time behind them. Wyatt waited, patiently standing with his hand out, where she could reject him if she wasn't ready.

Or brave enough.

"Dance with me?"

Amelia was barefoot and not at all polished after hours of work, but she couldn't care less that the gown would likely never be worn again after that night. All she wished was to lean into the crook of Wyatt's shoulder, breathing in his scent, absorbing the warmth through his shirt. They swayed by the melody of the fire. Ticking time with the clock. His thumb brushing her back every few steps in a gesture that felt so like home.

He didn't kiss her—maybe he knew she wasn't ready.

There was nothing to say of tomorrow or the next day, or of the missions that were sure to call him to the skies once more. No more promises were made—none that might be broken. And no more wounds unearthed from the past.

Even to heal, some secrets refused to yield.

TWENTY-ONE

MAY 24, 1843
ST. JAMES'S PARK
LONDON, ENGLAND

If Twining's Tea Shop still stood, its doors would face the street—and the nightmare of the sidewalk—at 216 Strand.

As the horses clip-clopped their coach along the Thames, Elizabeth pictured the layout of the streets and the shop mere blocks away.

Even a decade later, they were burned upon her memory.

The sidewalk with cobblestones was just as uneven, the shop windows just as fanciful as they were so many years before. She remembered the snow. The lamppost. Even the younger version of the stoic viscount who with Franz sat opposite her on the coach bench.

Keaton peered out the glass window at the Thames and then the mass of foliage as they rolled into St. James's Park, uttering not a word. Franz on the other hand commented on the fine array of carriages moving about in the park and on the ladies who were plucked and primped like peacocks left too long in the sun. My, but he was snobbish at times. And translucent. And for the life of

Elizabeth, oblivious to the tumult of thoughts running through the minds of the rest in the coach. Her ma-ma scheduling appointments and calculating pounds in her mind. Keaton drifting from staring out the window to glancing at her and back again, offering only the occasional reply out of propriety. And Elizabeth barreling down into a tunnel of confusion at it all.

"Do you not agree, Elizabeth?"

Always to be counted upon, her mother twittered in conversation, the question a nervous discourse that snapped Elizabeth back to attention.

"Forgive me, Ma-ma. I am afraid you find me lost in the delights of our surroundings just now," she whispered. "What was it you said?"

"Lady Davies was inquiring after the excellence of the view," Keaton said, his voice low and weighted but not unkind.

"The view?" Elizabeth nodded, a trifle lost under the weight of his look. "Yes, it is lovely. Is your home near here, Lord Huxley?"

"Not far," he offered. Slow. Cool. Matter-of-fact.

"It has been quite some time since we have passed these sights." Ma-ma reached over to pat Elizabeth's gloved hand even as she looked to the men. "How do you find London, Viscount? Oh, but then you have just returned, haven't you? It must be tiresome to you by now, traveling back and forth on the horrid road to East Suffolk. No doubt you shall wish to take up residence here when you and Elizabeth are wed. But we must find an objective point of view. Mr. Winterhalter—is London not a wonder of innovation and pleasure?"

"Pleasure? On the contrary, I have been here many times, Lady Davies. I find the streets of London bore me to tears. Inside the palace? That is the real wonder. The queen has nothing but the epitome of elegance to boast of. Crimson carpets. Gilding in the most exquisite designs. Buffets of sugared plums, tarts, Cornish hens—all of the delicacies of taste one could imagine. But outside?" He wrinkled his nose as he gazed at a carriage, a man in top hat and a lady cloaked in haughty puff-up as they passed by. "Reprehensible wolves. As you stated to me once, Lady Elizabeth . . . I believe the air is a little weak." He smiled, a faint shadow overtaking his lips. "Let us believe in the presence of Her Majesty there will be an abundance of elegance— all we will capture with a brush in the most animated fervor. *Ja?*"

Ma-ma cut in, her zeal an expected nuisance. "Quite right, sir! And then there are the parks. The opera. The theaters . . . every possible amusement and folly a guest could wish for, that is, if one had a single thought to leave the elegance of the palace. I wonder whether we should venture outside at all. My dear Elizabeth is not used to the harshness of city air."

"Ma-ma, I believe you forget I used to visit the mill with Pa-pa. Was not Manchester City as industrial, as forward-thinking, and as bustling as London? And I suffered no ill effects from the city then."

Keaton perked up, his attention drawn from the window like a shot. "You accompanied the earl to his mill?"

Elizabeth nodded, thinking of the puffs of cotton on the air. The workers. The horrid raking coughs that echoed through the mill floor. And the sight of children scuttling along the rows between chewing cast-iron machines. "I did on countless occasions. It was to learn of industry, but I'm afraid I learned more of the plight of the working class than I'd expected."

"Yes, of course. Elizabeth wished to learn of the industry she'd have brought to a marriage. A pity the mill closed down or you'd have had another venture to entertain, Viscount," Ma-ma purred. Approving, though she hadn't a clue as to the direction Elizabeth wished to take the conversation.

"And did you sketch at this mill, Lady Elizabeth?"

Leave it to the artist in the coach to keep his mind glued to a singular love.

"I did, Mr. Winterhalter. But industry is not the same as the artistry London boasts. Theaters, for example. There must be quite a society of theatrical establishments in London." Elizabeth looked to Keaton, noticing the tiny flinch in his jaw. "Do you enjoy the theater, Lord Huxley?"

"Not particularly."

Elizabeth tilted her head, questioning in body before her mind could stop her. Had she heard correctly? "Not at all? How so?"

"I haven't any great scheme to take in a show while we're here, unless of course you should wish it, Lady Elizabeth. And then I am but your servant in such matters. But as a pastime, no. I do not enjoy theater in the least."

"You never go?"

"No," he said, firm as the ground beneath the coach. "I have no desire to."

"That is truth. Huxley allows no distractions—at least before you became his betrothed, Lady Elizabeth. The theater is an idle curiosity in his mind compared to matters of substance. Why, he'd much prefer a dreary dining room of distinguished wolves with all their dreary conversation. He indulges an acquaintance with the prime minister himself, taking up matters of politics. And the common good. And the plight of the Englishman sentenced to a cruel fate in a poorhouse. Or a Manchester mill, perhaps? *Phish . . .* Not colorful talk at all."

The discourse on the theater and the seemingly harmless newspaper articles she'd found burning on her mind, Elizabeth looked down at her gown. The low-pointed waist and bell skirt were appropriate, and the deep-royal paisley was quite in fashion. It would be quite serviceable for greeting a queen. But a thought struck, and she seized the moment to ask, "Dear Ma-ma. Forgive my capricious-ness. I lost sight of your request when we left Parham Hill. I am a wicked daughter!"

"What's this? My request, dear?"

"Of course—that I visit the dressmaker to have a suitable gown made for the audience with Her Majesty. I fear you are but right. This old frock is quite unsuitable. I should hate to be a matter of disappointment to you."

"Oh dear! Why yes, of course. But you needn't put pain to it. We are in London—the city of most fashionable endeavors. It is not Paris, of course, but I believe we can solve this problem without the least disruption to your audience with Her Majesty. How delighted I am that you've changed your mind! And all this time I believed you to be indifferent on such matters."

Keaton glanced up, his brow tipped a hair. "As did I."

"Not at all, Lord Huxley. You've generously offered a dress allowance, which I rebuffed in error. I wonder if we mightn't ven-ture to one such shop or another—at least to inquire after whether there might be anything suitable to be fitted for. And if we haven't time to have one made, perhaps there will be something put by in one of the shops. I'm confident we can find something to make up for this oversight and bring your household honor when I do bow before the queen."

"It must be yellow." Franz smiled and winked with a wickedly delighted bent. "She is quite the flower in buttercup, Huxley."

Keaton ignored his friend and the ill-timed tease. "Of course, Lady Elizabeth. Once we reach my home and you've had time to rest, we may venture out at your leisure. The coach is at your disposal."

"Oh no, I would but sooner see us tossed in the Thames than to sully your time with the prime minister for the likes of ribbons and bows. How tiresome for you, Viscount. I assume you have an audience with the prime minister, on matters of Parliament perhaps?"

Elizabeth bristled a touch inside when Keaton reacted to the sugar she was coating onto her words, as if he knew better than to find it authentic. But for Ma-ma to acquiesce, she must play the part to the best of her ability and looked to be succeeding, as Ma-ma appeared utterly delighted in the turn of events.

"Perhaps, at some point."

"And there we are. Ma-ma and I will be quite content to see about procuring a suitable dress, without tarnishing one moment of your stay with such inconsequential matters as female frivolities. I shall enjoy the diversion immensely, and when we are summoned, we will arrive at the queen's dining table with every possible luxury in a dress that you can afford, sir."

Franz flipped the talk from the tiresome exchange to another sight out the window, drawing attention to a lady's fashionable hat as they rode by. He'd switched back to jovial conversation, noticing hue and shape, commenting on the way the light trickled through space between the trees to illuminate the artificial bird flapping fake wings on her crown.

Elizabeth might have thought nothing was amiss in those moments as the carriage pulled to a stop at the front stoop of a Georgian town-home in crisp, gleaming white. Windows boasting high arches looked down on the street. And ivy bedecked with glorious red and pink roses climbed up to dress the sky.

Alighting from the coach proved to be quite a production, with greetings from the butler and housekeeper and the curtseys of maids in a neat little line as Keaton presented his bride-to-be. But as he reached for her hand to help her from the carriage, something shifted. He'd removed his glove so his fingertips held hers and lingered a breath or two longer than necessary for her to find her footing on the sidewalk. And he kept his fingers on hers. Bold. Deliberate. As the service staff bustled around them, and as Ma-ma and Franz broke away to direct the activity in concern for their own trunks and the unfortunate outcome of wrinkling should any unnecessary jostling take place.

Keaton held fast, gray depths with a jagged line of gold searching her face, ignoring everything in that moment but *her*.

In a gaze far more open than she'd expected, he sought connection somehow, as if he was not afraid to hide his eyes from her this time. As if they both recalled the same London connection and that was why, all these years later, he wouldn't do her the disservice of trying to hide it now.

"Forgive me," Keaton whispered, as if holding her hand too long had been the trigger of an apology.

But she knew better. They both did. For in the depths of those eyes she'd hated for so long, she read the astonishing emotion of unmasked pain. And an apology for an offense she couldn't determine the root of.

Whatever the moment had been, it was whisked away on a blink. Keaton released her, breezed up the steps, and disappeared into the depths of his London world, leaving her shocked and breathless on a sidewalk for the second time in her life.

MAY 26, 1843
DRURY LANE
LONDON, ENGLAND

For days Elizabeth had been up to her eyebrows in satins of rich royal blue and cottons in bright primrose and chartreuse, in addition to the elegant simplicity of ivories in wool, linen, lace, and silk that felt like water to the touch—all of the fabrics in reams so that they might choose whatever tickled their fashion fancy most.

Ma-ma wasted no time in summoning the carriage the moment they'd settled in Keaton's townhome. Poor, wretched horses—they'd had a rest of only minutes before they were off to cart them away again, seeking out the most fashionable spots in the heart of Mayfair and Covent Garden and venturing to shop after shop for four days in succession.

Most recently they'd stopped at a two-story establishment the name of which she couldn't hope to remember, with high ceilings plastered over with gold rosettes in evenly placed domes, street-side windows that stretched two stories tall with displays of chapeaus in pinks and lavenders for spring, and an interior that looked as though it had spawned an army of children in brocade, crinoline, and lace on all surfaces.

Elizabeth submitted as best she could to being plucked and pulled, measured and fitted for an endless wardrobe of fashions fit for a queen, always smiling but watching for that slim moment of time in which she might slip away to the grand Theatre Royal they'd passed a block down on Drury Lane. Questions plagued her about the inconsistency in Keaton's character—particularly why he wasn't forthright about his connection to the theater.

A stack of crinoline skirts and gowns of all manner of pattern was fluffed on the counter at her side, creating a wave of perfume in the air when it was set down.

"Elizabeth, dear. Which one do you prefer? Or perhaps more than one . . . ?" Ma-ma's fingertips already trekked a journey through the pile like an expert tracker.

"I'd thought yellow, Ma-ma."

"Yellow? Indeed." She laughed, tossing whites and blush pinks and ivory tones about like blankets of snow. "Why not one of the new colors? Look at this sapphire!"

She held the striped blue up to Elizabeth's collarbone, then laid the fabric over her shoulder and nodded. "This is far more suited to your coloring. We'll take a dress length and a half, and then let's see what we'd have you do with it."

"I should think yellow, Ma-ma." Elizabeth swallowed hard, knowing she hadn't a true care for whatever hues they walked out with. "It is the viscount's preferred color."

Ma-ma froze, began a slow nod that built to an eager one, and turned to the shopkeeper. "My daughter is right, madame. The viscount does favor yellow. I've heard that in conversation. Pastel . . . Gold. Or buttercup, perhaps? Did not Mr. Winterhalter mention that when we were in the carriage?" She flitted behind the counter like she was the owner, then disappeared behind a curtained doorway, her voice trailing off into the depths of the modiste's world. "What do you have in a deep saffron satin for evening . . . ?"

Elizabeth tugged the striped sapphire from her shoulder and laid it over the counter, and as the other shopkeepers bustled to find hats in every shade of sunshine imaginable, she slipped through the front doors.

The street was alive with carriages and drivers and working lads bustling about in tweed suits and woolen caps. A repair crew labored about a hole in the street. Shoeshines worked on the sidewalks, polishing gentlemen's boots until they shone like mirrors. And little scamps wove in and out of the crowd, pickpocketing the wealthy perhaps and running off to enjoy their spoils on a different side of town. A nearby bookshop boasted posters on a brick wall—*Charles Dickens back in form!*—indicating that the famous author had lately returned from an American tour and was penning a ghost story of Christmas tradition that would be available closer to the season—*Post orders now!* It predicted a rousing success of the author's next penned work before a page of it had been printed.

Elizabeth hadn't any luck attempting entry by the front doors of the other theaters she'd stopped at, so she kept a keen eye on the side of the multistoried Georgian theater, watching what appeared to be a stage door on the corner of the bustling Catherine Street.

With a quick breath and a confident air that said, *Of course I belong in a theater. Whyever would I not?* Elizabeth eased through the door after a gentleman had stepped out.

A man in a red vest with gold pinstriping, with thinning salt-and-pepper hair and an impressively groomed mustache, bent over a wooden crate, then rose carefully, as though his back had a crook that had worsened with age and a lifetime of backstage theater work. He took a candle knife from his pocket, scraped the wax from an iron wall sconce, and replaced the melted candlestick with a fresh one.

"Excuse me, sir?"

"Oh, miss," he said, not with a curt tone but certainly one of surprise. He gazed beyond her, finding no one else in the shadows.

Yes, yes. I haven't a husband. Not a father or a lady-in-waiting either. It's just me, and I haven't time to dicker about it.

"Are you lost? The ladies' services are just down the hall—"

"No. Thank you. I'm looking for a . . ." She paused, memory tripping over which name to choose out of the ones she'd committed to memory in the viscount's study. "I'm looking for someone who may work here. A Thomas Whittle?"

The man was quite unaffected. "No, miss. Isn't a name known around here. Might I ask if you're lookin' after the owner?"

"The theater owner . . ." She raised her chin. Confident. Clear-headed. "Yes. Of course. I'm seeking the owner. His name? My apology—I've stopped in to inquire after a business matter, and I seem to have misplaced his name."

"It's Mr. Churchill, miss."

Elizabeth nodded, brightening with a smile that would encourage the tale to keep on its present course.

"Yes. Of course. Mr. Churchill. That's his name. I need to speak with Mr. Churchill, please. Is he here?"

"Oh, he's always here. Churchill doesn't go out much."

The man set the extra candlesticks and knife in the belly of the worn wooden box, wiped his palms against each other, and held an arm out for her to follow down a red-carpeted hall to an open area. The hall was a bit dark and grainy to look at, but it was better than standing in a back hall with no option but to be ushered back outside.

"This way, miss."

Backstage, sets and ropes and wooden backdrops were piled against a high brick wall. A workman bustled by, calling up to a man on scaffolding. He tossed a coil of rope to the floor and hurried on his way without noticing them. And then, breathless, Elizabeth stepped out onstage.

The man led her across what seemed like miles of polished wood flooring, with gaslights flickering on the side walls and an entire auditorium of plush seats and empty aisles—four stories of balcony space for London's greatest plays to debut before crowds of thousands.

"'Tis the first London theater with gaslighting innovation throughout the entire building—save for the actors' corridor, which we keep up wit', as it saves a pretty penny to light with candles. Quite an expense. But this view is worth it, no?"

"I believe it is, sir. Very worth it."

"Your husband has never brought you here then?"

He chuckled while he led her down the stairs to the center aisle, as if he had a secret delight in asking a question he must have known the answer to.

She straightened her spine. "No. Not yet. I haven't had the pleasure."

He laughed again, under his breath. "Perhaps you need to find a real husband first?"

Elizabeth walked along behind, holding her skirt a shade higher off the ankle, in case she had to make a run for it if her inquiry went poorly. Who knew where he was leading her? Being at the ready was wise. "I'm not certain that's any of your affair, sir."

"No. 'Tis not. But I assure you that none round here care to meddle too much in affairs that aren't our own. We theater crowd don't care much for backstory. It's what happens under the lights and on the stage that matters most. So if'n you see fit to nose about the back halls and tell a tale to gain audience with our Mr. Churchill . . . well then, I thought you might like the grand tour. You might be a storyteller yourself, eh?"

Heavens. What was she to say to that brash?

"Just through here, miss."

They came to a hall—the entry by the look of it, with the grand portico on Catherine Street shadowing the front through the windows. The central staircase was nearly as wide as the stage itself, with gold spindles and chandeliers dripping teardrops of crystal from lofty arched ceilings. The man brought her to an alcove tucked behind velvet curtains and a frosted glass door that read Churchill in stark block letters.

He tipped an imaginary hat and smiled under that trimmed mustache as he tapped the glass.

"Enter," came the bark from inside.

"I'll just be out front, miss, should you need an escort to see you safely back to the street."

Whatever the man had thought of her or the mystery of her obviously manufactured story, Elizabeth had somehow managed to win favor with him. She smiled and nodded, turning her hand to the brass knob.

She hung in the doorway, waiting to be acknowledged.

"What is it?"

Mr. Churchill was no stodgy old thespian, attracted to hard drink and harder living. It was what her mother had always said with a lip curled in disdain—it was proper to wear an appropriate gown and attend a show on occasion, but never, *ever* was one to associate with the likes of the theater crowd. It just wasn't done. They were the absolute degenerates of society's bottommost rung. But the picture Elizabeth had built in her mind was one of an underworld character with a toady smile, a smelly cigar, and perhaps the most uncultured of sensibilities.

Not so of the gentleman before her.

He was young—entirely too young to own a grand theater. He mightn't have had but ten years on her at the most. But he seemed at home in his hideaway.

A starched shirt, black satin tie, and double-breasted waistcoat of red to match the velvet in the entry hall pegged him as a gentleman of means. Honey-brown hair tipped over his forehead as if a touch of him liked the unruly side, and he looked down a pert nose, with eyes of what color she didn't know—just scribbling something with fountain pen to paper without care that a woman perched in his doorway.

Elizabeth cleared her throat and he looked up, a slight air of impatience sneaking out through a grimace. "Who are you?"

"I am—" Oh dear. She hadn't thought of that. Elizabeth couldn't give her real name. And couldn't very likely tie anything to the viscount.

The clock was ticking on her story.

Think, Elizabeth. Think.

". . . Mrs. Eleanor Davies."

He paused for a breath, then replaced his pen in the wooden holder on the desk with marked intention and stared back. "Mrs. Davies, is it? How may I help you?"

"I'm sorry to trouble you, sir. But I am in a hurry, so I'll get to the point. I'm looking for an employee of yours—or someone who may have been employed by this theater some years ago."

"The gentleman's name?"

"Thomas Whittle."

"Thomas Whittle, you say?" His eyes narrowed a cinch. He stood, taking his time about slipping shirtsleeves into his coat. "And why would you believe Thomas Whittle would be employed at this establishment?"

"I'm not certain he is. I'm seeking a gentleman who may have had a business association with someone close to my family, and all I know as of yet is a name and that he may have worked in London theater at one time." Elizabeth felt small under his scrutiny, clearly able to see his eyes in a cool blue staring straight through her. "It is a business matter of great importance."

The man adjusted his waistcoat and coat and smoothed wrinkles from his cuffs as he walked toward the door. "I have a Royal Patent on file, miss. Nothing illegal goes on in my theater."

"I'm not inquiring after your operations, sir."

"Aren't you? Now that Her Majesty has seen fit to culture the urban masses, I hold no argument with the smaller theaters that they, too, should try their hand at the stage. You may go back to your employer and report that Christopher Churchill will not be bullied. Not by anyone—especially with a manufactured name sent to stoke my temper."

"Which name?"

He started like she'd smacked him. As if she should know the name Thomas Whittle would have lit a fire within him and anger was a completely natural reaction.

"As if you don't know?" He smiled. Grinned with arrogance that he'd peeled back enough layers of her story and wasn't buying a fraction of it. "Eleanor Davies? Please do try to be more imaginative than that."

Eleanor Davies . . . That's what this was about?

How in the world would he have recognized a conjured form of her mother's name—Eleanor Meade, Dowager Countess of Davies, was somehow known to him?

"I'm sorry if I—"

"You are not sorry, miss. And I pity you your present task. Sent here to ferret out more information. Or more money, which you will not receive." He crossed his arms over his chest, confident. Irritated. With eyes that stared at her as though she were the scourge of London. "How much is she paying you to come here and dig into my business affairs?"

"You know someone by the name of Davies?"

He laughed—booming enough to shake the glass panes in one of the bookshelves against the wall.

Something in Elizabeth said to ask more. Find out what manner of fate brought her to a theater—of those she'd stopped by in the city already and hadn't the faintest luck—and all of a sudden she'd selected a name that generated some sort of vitriol in a complete stranger.

"I don't understand. Do you know the Countess of Davies?" When he didn't budge, Elizabeth felt something awaken, and she took a desperate step forward. "How do you know her?"

A miscalculation seemed to have caught him off guard, for something shifted in his face. A furrowed brow, a deep swallow, and a terse line forming at the jaw—they combined in a manner that left him almost crestfallen.

What had just happened to change the temperature of his persona from the edge of enraged to backtracking now in wide-eyed fear?

The sounds outside were amplified by the silence that had swept in and flooded the space between them. A breeze caught white gauze curtains, shifting them out like a specter had entered the room.

"You should go, miss." He flitted a glance to the busy street beyond the glass. "Surely you are expected by someone."

The incomparable flutter of boldness—the need for answers—rippled through her. "And do you know a Viscount Huxley, perhaps?"

He stood still, staring her down in her afternoon dress of blush satin as if weighing something in his mind. It was only a moment, but a long one. And after she'd braved mentioning the name of a onetime street urchin with rare eyes who'd grown up in ten years, followed the activities of London theater, and then professed an aversion to it at the same time . . .

It was a rare secret, of which they both seemed to know something.

Churchill stepped past her to the theater alcove, then shouted through the door to the gentleman who'd allowed her entry. "Dorchester?"

"Aye, sir!" the man shouted back from his post washing windows. He dropped his towel in a bucket at his feet and scrambled in their direction.

"Show this lady out. Now." He gave the command in control. "If you allow her entrance here again, it will cost your position. Do you understand?"

"Aye, sir. Of course."

"Good. Then we understand each other," Churchill said, then turned to her, the same cool veneer showing upon his face that said all he wanted was for her to be gone. "Go. And do not ever come back."

TWENTY-TWO

Keira breezed through the front door of the Castle House and fell into the scarred wood booth at their vintage pub table, in a complete but wonderful daze.

Emory didn't look up. He didn't need to. They'd fallen into a rhythm since London that said they were past the awkward first things—how to make small talk or what to say so you didn't sound like a dolt to the person across the table. Since they'd shared their messy backstories and were working side by side, there wasn't much by way of discomfort to worry over.

Emory took a hearty bite of a blueberry-lemon scone, then dropped it back to the porcelain while he chewed and began flipping through photos on his phone, comparing something to words on the page of a notebook he held.

Keira stared at him—a creature content in his element, too focused to notice she hadn't said a word since she'd rejoined him.

"Here. I ordered you a latte the way you take it." He slid a cup and saucer over in front of her, still without glancing up. "Like a hopelessly sugared-up New Yorker. Should have seen the glare the waitress gave me when I had to explain the details."

"I don't think I'll have any."

"No coffee? That's new. Turning back into an actual Brit by switching over to tea, are ya?"

Keira twisted her blonde waves into a loose knot at her nape and wrapped her fisherman's sweater around her middle. The fire crackled behind them. It was more than enough to keep her warm. But tugging at the cable weave was more of a distraction than any- thing. To absorb what she'd just heard on the phone, her hands needed to think too.

"I managed to sweet-talk the waitress into bringing the owner over while you were gone. May have promised to leave her an exor- bitant tip, but . . ." Emory turned his laptop at an angle so she could see it better. "It'd be worth it. The owner of this pub is something like an eighth-generation innkeeper and confirmed what I've been hoping to hear. Says his grandfather apparently knew the estate owners back in the late 1930s—a Viscount Huxley and his wife. Same title Carter now lays claim to. So the last couple who stayed on at the estate before it was boarded up— Hang on. I have their names . . . Here. An Arthur and Amelia Woods. And you're not going to believe what I found in the library this morning that ties it all together."

Emory finally connected his glance with hers, victory in his smile. But it faded fast behind the napkin he brushed over it. "What's wrong?"

"I just received a call I did not expect," Keira whispered. She bit her bottom lip with her front tooth, trying not to cry.

"What—about Victoria?" Emory asked, his attention so arrested that he froze with the scone in midair.

"No. Not that. This is personal, actually."

"Personal. Alright." Emory tossed the scone back to its plate, then pushed the laptop out of the way and folded his hands out in front of him. "Not bad news, I hope." He hesitated again, this time as if choosing his words very, very carefully. "From London . . . or New York?"

Thank heavens the call had nothing to do with Alton. Or his pearl-strung socialite mother. Or the fact that Keira hadn't listened to one word the woman pushed on her in London and, instead, stepped in league with the art world's enemy numero uno.

"No. This is good news. The best. My brother Quinn—you know, the one you haven't met?"

"I submit that I haven't actually met the other one. Not officially. Cormac just tried to stare me through the wall of your father's pub. But if that's being introduced to one of the Foley men, I guess, yeah. We've met."

Classic Cormac.

"He did do that, didn't he? Sorry." She squinted, the apology subtle but sheepish at the same time.

"I'm not convinced you really mean that. By your expression, I'd say you're remembering it much more fondly than I do. I still believe I had a bull's-eye on my back halfway down O'Connell Street after I left that place. But what's this good news? I could use some right now."

"Well, we've been waiting for this prognosis for a while and today we got it. Ellie, my sister-in-law, has been battling breast cancer for the last year, and they've just learned she's in remission. Cancer-free. Quinn said the oncologist told them she doesn't need any more treatments. He told her to go live her life." Keira tried hard not to cry in front of him. "'Go live your life.' How many people are aching to hear those words, and they did. They get to. I can't imagine what it must feel like to face something so precious as your future with your spouse being taken from you, and then it just comes rushing back . . . in a blink. And suddenly you have all your tomorrows again."

And then the connection hit her, and Keira thought of how he might construe it with his own loss of Elise. "I'm so sorry. I should have remembered how insensitive that would sound . . ."

"No, it's okay. I'm happy for them. Happy for you too."

"Quinn asked if I can be home by Christmas. The library and the painting have become more of a project than we initially thought, haven't they? I don't want to bail out on you before we have answers, but it feels like this is important to them and I need to honor that."

"We're working on it, aren't we? I think being home for Christmas is a definite possibility, if it's what you want."

"I can't believe I'm saying it, but I think yeah. It's time I go home to Ireland because I choose it—not because I have no place else to go. Ellie and Quinn live in France, but they've been in the States for treatment. So they're coming over to Dublin. With Da there, and now Laine and Cormac, they want to spend the holiday together as a family before they go home for good."

"For good?"

"Yeah. It's this mad thing. We Foleys seem to have an affection for castles the way you Scotts fancy . . . What is it you Scotts fancy?"

"I still maintain that my father was entirely disappointed that I didn't end up on Wall Street like him. He still can't stomach that his son took a liking to fine art instead of getting that old MBA from Harvard. He seemed to think chasing down paintings would ruin my future. He was right at least in some measure."

"I'm sorry."

He shrugged. "Don't be. I'm not. You know that. But tell me more. Tell me something good's come out of this and it'll make my entire day."

"It has. The good picks up where they left off. Ellie and Quinn were restoring a château at our grandfather's home in the Loire Valley. It's called 'The Sleeping Beauty' by locals—this forgotten little castle with a moat and a storybook forest around it. They got married on the grounds last winter. I couldn't make it over from the States, but Laine says it's really lovely there. There was an ancient chapel with stained glass windows and candlelight and snow falling all around—girlish fairy-tale stuff I won't dare bore you with. But they had to set aside the restoration when the shock of the cancer diagnosis happened. And now, well, they want to get back to living. I can't even believe they want to open the château up to the public in the spring. Imagine that. An old castle will breathe new life again. I really hope I get to see that one day."

Keira hadn't even realized how she was rambling, talking about fairy tales and snowy French castles, until she looked up and saw him watching her.

Emory's gaze had softened in the sunshine that streamed through the windows, studying her as the fire crackled behind them and the chatter of the dining room hummed like a forgotten drumbeat.

Remembering the coffee saved her.

Keira lifted the rim to her lips, the sugar and real cream he'd ordered in it exactly the way she preferred, and drank deep. How could she ignore the ease that came with understanding the quirks of someone else's presence, enough that he listened when you ran off with your words? And knew how you took your coffee? And ordered it without having to ask? And then sat quiet, content, and smiling in your presence—happy only because you were?

Was that what happy did—made you feel so light it bubbled over without warning? Too fast to stop it, Keira felt her cheeks warm.

"This news is one of those good things, isn't it?" He raised an eyebrow.

"Yeah. One of the good things you're always on the hunt for. This is my cottage, I suppose."

"Then today has been worth it. And tomorrow, we look again."

"What's next then? We're in a holding pattern until we find out more about Victoria. Until then, I'm at your disposal, Mr. Scott. What's this connection you found in the library this morning?"

"Okay. I said I talked to the owner here and he confirmed a few things I'd been tracking down. The initials A. W. from the tiles? Found out those are the initials of the former viscount who was killed in 1940, an Arthur J. Woods—RAF pilot downed in the war. I tried to match that up by searching through the books—a dead end there, but it wasn't a half-bad idea for another reason." Emory reached over to his backpack and grabbed a book from inside. "I sorted through the glass case this morning, did a quick catalog of what's there."

Keira stared back, tipped her head a shade. "Wait a minute. When? I got up when you usually do—sunrise. As usual."

"Told you—I don't sleep much in new places. Doesn't matter. The point is, the books are definitely vintage. Some first editions. Mostly classics. Dickens, Sir Arthur Conan Doyle, Austen . . . What you'd expect out of a proper English library. And one vintage children's book—*Curious George*. Nice choice. And then . . ." He split the journal, spread-eagled his palm over the binding to keep it flat, and slid it across the rustic grooves of the tabletop in front of her. "There was this."

The binding was a worn burgundy leather, the paper yellowed and still clinging to the musky-sweet smell of age. Letters were penciled in, some jumbled over the lines, their shape and size consistent with the penmanship of a young child. The historian in her wanted to smack her own hand away from touching it without gloves, but Keira suppressed the urge, somehow needing the touch of running her fingertips over the lines to connect with the past.

German.

It seemed to have no connection whatsoever—not to a cabinet of carefully preserved books by some of the most celebrated authors in history. A child's journal penned over with German and pages of practice in the English alphabet alongside? "This was in the glass cabinet in the library?"

"On the top shelf." He spun it back so he could flip through the pages, three-quarters of the way through to the end. "My *Deutsch* is a little rusty, but you can make out what it is here. Something about planes. And Framlingham Castle."

It was easier to sit beside him, or they'd be passing the journal back and forth all day. Keira slipped around to the space on his bench and leaned in, shoulder grazing his. "Why in the world would a child's German study notebook be kept in the cabinet?" she whispered, scanning the pages.

He started a bit, curiosity seeming to have captured him. "You read German too?"

"Add it to my résumé without sounding so surprised, would you?" she countered, running her fingertips over the lines on the page, reading as best as she could translate.

"I think I'll be surprised when I find something you actually don't know, Foley."

"Historical records aren't all in English. A girl has to have more than one trick up her sleeve if she's going to make it in this business. You know that."

"Okay, Professor. We both know I couldn't read it to save my life. So what does it say?"

"It's the oddest thing. It's not really a journal or a diary. This is more of a list—recordkeeping of air raids or some kind of drills. Must have been from the war. See?" She pointed a manicured fingernail up under the date in the corner. "20 März 1945."

"Thank goodness I can read numbers. The entries are from '43—those are hard to make sense of. I'd say this kid was really young. Then they go to March of '45. That's the last entry."

"Really?" She flipped a few pages ahead, but they were empty. Only paper yellowed and curled at the corners. No more logs or carefully penciled alphabet lines. No outlets of prose for a child dealing with the gruesome realities of war.

Just . . . lost space.

Her heart squeezed, daring to consider the worst might have happened and there was a reason the child didn't finish.

"So what do Arthur Woods, who died in 1940, and this journal, which ends five years later, have in common?"

"That's the question, Foley. There are remnants of WWII all around this town. There's a plaque at the Church of St. Michaels commemorating the servicemen from the village who lost their lives. The old control tower at the airfield has been turned into a museum. And you can't go anywhere without the shadow of castle spires behind you. Even in this pub the people seem to know most of the tourists are here because the 390th Bomb Group was stationed at Framlingham Castle. We can dig into that."

Keira released a breath she hadn't realized she was holding back, for the journal felt like gold in her hands. "So now we have another chapter in this story—one of war."

"This chapter was always out there; we just had to know to turn to it."

The journal wasn't a classic or the musings of a famous author, yet it had been carefully preserved in the highest place of honor at Parham Hill. Tucked away in a library that had been sealed off from the world brick by brick. The only things she could think were that the little book was dear to someone and that someone very likely held it in as high esteem as a portrait of a queen.

But why?

She closed the journal and pressed its cover beneath her palms, almost brought to tears by the beauty of it all. "Emory. This book . . . It's a treasure."

"I agree with you. But why would a record of air-raid drills be saved at all? Why would a kid even care? That's what I'd like to know."

"There's no name in it?"

"No. No names."

"And nothing in the library to indicate a child lived there other than the Curious George storybook?"

He shook his head, his eyes registering something had sparked them back to life. Gathering his things in a flash, he pulled euros from his jeans pocket and dropped them on the table. "You ready to go?"

Keira popped up from the bench, the journal hugged to her side as she followed. "Go where?"

"I hate to be the grim reaper of this operation, but I think we might have an answer that's been staring us in the face. It may not give us everything, but at least it's one idea I can tick off as mine." He smiled and slung the backpack over his shoulder, then held the door so she could walk under his arm. "If we need names, there's an easy place to find them. And one more piece of the puzzle to slip into place while we wait for Victoria to spill her secrets."

Spill her secrets indeed.

If only Victoria could talk, Keira wasn't sure it would be with the most supportive words.

She imagined Her Royal Highness had an Austen-esque wit that matched her letters and enough moxie—even at barely five feet tall—to tell the truth to any parliamentary gentleman who dared oppose her. Certainly she had enough confidence to commission the Winterhalter portrait that during the Victorian era was an outright scandalous undertaking in the end.

No doubt Victoria would have said it was painfully obvious Keira was falling, and falling hard, not for the playboy viscount but, heaven help her, for the soft-spoken Yank who jogged them across Bridge Street, oblivious to the deliberations trailing behind him.

What are you doing?

With each step, Keira demanded an answer of herself.

It was too easy to picture Cormac rolling his eyes. Quinn slapping a palm to his forehead. And Da taking a cricket bat to the unsuspecting art thief. Problem was, the tiny flutter that had sprung up in her midsection when Emory looked at her was growing into a nag—and one with growing strength at that. It was Alton Montgomery all over again, just with a prettier smile and less in the bank account.

It would not end well. And she could find her heart broken. *Again.*

Emory led them down the sidewalk, its cracks growing the last of the season's flowers, a red phone box standing bright on the corner. They whisked through an iron gate with a hinge that creaked its welcome to the Church of St. Michaels.

No, she wasn't a besotted schoolgirl. This was research. This was for Victoria, after all.

Keira shook off her thoughts, instead focusing on the lofty stone-and-stained-glass masterpiece of a cathedral before them. But before they headed up the path to the stone steps and arched front doors, she slowed. Then stopped. And a lightbulb flicked on in her mind.

Names.

They were everywhere.

Engraved in chipped limestone markers. Nearly worn down by time on others in rows of crosses and monuments, taking up the grassy space between the brick wall lining Bridge Street and the scattering of trees that had lost nearly all their autumn color to the ground beneath their shoes.

Keira leaned in to read the stone marker in front of her, for a
wife and mother laid to rest in the late nineteenth century. It was
one of hundreds of names in the cemetery. All stories. All tied to
Framlingham, just like Victoria and her library. A web of names
and generations intertwined, they were always there. Right in front
of them.

"Ever thought you'd spend a morning smiling in a cemetery?"
Emory walked up beside her, that laid-back stroll of his becoming
unnerving.

"Did you?" She straightened and turned to face him. Emory
didn't need to explain what they were doing. Though it was a brilliant idea—enough to win the smile she sent in his direction. "I'll
take this side."

"Right." He nodded and dropped his backpack in the leaves so
he could fly through the aisles without being weighed down.

Keira moved between the stones, clutching the journal with a
protective squeeze over her core, as her riding boots collected dew
and leaves on chocolate-brown leather. She rubbed her fingertips
over moss to reveal names, stooped to read every set of dates on the
headstones low to the ground. For all the history represented by each
stone, none clicked with their story.

She looked far across the cemetery—Emory seemed to be as out
of luck as she by how quickly he moved from stone to stone. Until
she parted ways with the rows and stepped over to a path that led to
a tiny grove of willows, it seemed a fruitless task.

One marker stood out alone, tucked against the brick wall border
with iron-spindled benches standing in a semicircle and knobby
trees growing in a gangly cover over the top of its ledge. She knelt
with her jeans pressed to the ground. Reading. Breath escaping on
a fog when she couldn't hold it in any longer.

"Emory?" Keira called out over her shoulder. "I think I found one."

"Me too," he shouted from behind, his footsteps crunching fallen leaves closer as he came to meet her. He tipped his head toward the far corner of the cemetery. "There's an Arthur Woods over there by the side entrance. Died April 14, 1940. Has to be him. We should ask questions inside. Why—what have you got?"

"More questions, that's for sure." She pointed to the marker. "Look."

What she had was a stone with a faded apple blossom branch and honeybees carved along the border—a memorial to commemorate those who'd perished in a rogue German attack that bombed the Framlingham countryside on March 20, 1945.

They knew the exact time the sirens began their cries—that much was penciled in the child's journal.

All they needed were the names of those who'd died.

TWENTY-THREE

The note arrived at Parham Hill just before breakfast.

It was easy to match the address on the envelope to Thompson's scrawled print from Darly's many soup receipts. As postmaster and official roof climber for the night watch, the old innkeeper would know more wartime headlines than just about any newspaper or radio broadcast on their eastern shore. As unofficial sleuth helping Amelia search for the fate of the Schäfers, he might have provided another piece in the puzzle to find Luca and Liesel's parents.

Amelia dragged her nail under the envelope seal only to wish she hadn't.

It wasn't headlines or names found on a transport list but a few words overheard from loose-lipped Yanks down at the pub.

Planes were down.

Men were dead.

And . . . Wyatt's cot had lain empty for days.

The wind punished Amelia for wearing her one coat that wouldn't present her as a field hand at the gate—an opera coat of delicate powder blue, thin wool lined in ivory satin and a smart bow at each cuff. She must have looked foolhardy, primped as if she went on jaunts to a London play every other night. But it was the last of the lovely things she owned, besides the dress from Darly, and she hoped presenting herself as put together with a poppy-red tam and hair that coiled in a soft chignon against the curve of her neck would be enough polish to convince her way through the gate.

If not, a red-lipped smile and a stack of books just might do the trick.

The guard post was small—buildings no bigger than a butler's pantry staked on either side of the road—with iced-over roof tiles and open windows and a gate that stretched wide in between. The wind penetrated her coat, blistering as she stood before a young serviceman, doing her best to resist tapping her toe as he read over a clipboard in his hand. He shivered but gritted his jaw and kept reading as another layer of icy breeze blew over them.

Amelia pitied him and the rest of the poor devils who were not acquainted with their Framlingham winters, even if he was doing his job thoroughly by delaying her way through.

She pulled her coat tighter around the neck and waited.

"Sorry, miss. You're not on the list."

"*Amelia Woods*. I'm a supplier at the base and owner of Parham Hill—where we're housing officers from the 390th. I've brought books from the library, so I should be on the approved list."

Light eyes said he found humor in her presence rather than a threat, an almost-smile emerging on clean-shaven cheeks that had turned pink in the cold. A smirk and a tipped brow later, he chortled. "You're a librarian? I never seen a one with gams like that . . ."

Amelia raised her chin a notch higher, as matter-of-fact as she could make herself appear. "It is my understanding that you receive regular shipments of books for the troops. Well, I'm here to sort through them. Kindly check again, or I'm happy to wait while you telephone your superior—a Lieutenant Colonel McHenry, I believe? Of course, if he's otherwise occupied in battling Hitler at present, I'm certain Captain Stevens can come and sort this out."

The young soldier halted and looked up, meeting her with a blank stare as his clipboard paper flapped in the breeze. "Captain . . . Wyatt Stevens, you say?"

"That's right."

"From the 571st?"

Amelia stood tall before him, trying not to show trepidation as she nodded.

Was that his unit? Why couldn't she remember anything but the contours of Wyatt's smile or the depth of hazel in his eyes? All of a sudden she could see every detail of his face. The way he walked. And held her when they danced. The way he talked of books or furrowed his brow when he was worried. Why could she summon all the inconsequential whispers her heart murmured, but not what mattered in that instant?

"I believe that's his unit, yes."

He nodded. "You just wait here, miss," was all he said before he disappeared around the corner and into the shack.

Maybe she'd miscalculated and gone too far by dropping names.

They were the highest ranks she knew, and in the US Army, wasn't that how things were done—by issuing orders with brash, knowing they'd be followed as long as they had big names attached at the end?

Amelia watched through the guard post window, keen to settle the heart beating a wild dance in her chest as he picked up a telephone and whispered unintelligible words into the receiver. He paused. Shook his head as he looked down at the clipboard, then tipped his hat back and brought his gaze up to rest on her. There was nothing to do but endure the wind, jut out her chin, and stand confident as ever under his inspection.

This time Amelia could read his lips as he spoke into the phone: "Yes, sir. That's her."

The base had a long, barren stretch of road snaking behind the gate. Beyond that, the cold metal of round-top buildings that seemed like dollhouse miniatures dotted the horizon. Jeeps wheeled on a road between them, coughing exhaust like tiny puffs from the end of a cigar. She couldn't see the airfield or control towers or the rows of great birds that made up the B-17 fleet, but they were out there somewhere. Their roar never seemed to cease overhead, even with the wicked cadence of wind cutting across the moor.

"Very good, sir." The guard snapped back to attention, replacing the phone in its cradle.

He paused to glance through the window, snow and salt residue creating a film on the glass between them. It wasn't enough to mask the softness that had come over him. What was all duty mixed with bravado moments before had switched to concern, and heaven help her . . . he was not very clever at masking sorrow.

She hugged the books tighter to her chest, her fingernails digging into the bindings of the stack she'd brought for Wyatt.

"Excuse me, miss. They're sending someone over. If you'll just wait."

"I don't understand. May I not just go in and make my way to the library?"

"No—they have someone coming from the interior gate. Just a moment and they'll take you where you'll need to go."

A jeep cut down the road toward them, dusting the way though it was drizzly outside. Just for a moment, Amelia thought the uniform-hatted man behind the wheel could have been Wyatt. She held her breath. Hoping. But as he neared, the halo of overcast skies darkened behind shoulders that were not broad like his, and a youthful face took shape over the top of the windshield.

"Lieutenant Hale!" Relief washed over Amelia to see a familiar face among the mass of uniforms and cutouts of army buildings.

"Milady. Come on then." C. B. had jumped down from the jeep and now held out his arm for her to climb into the front seat. Amelia did, so fast the stack of books nearly tumbled from her arms, and he had to help catch them or their bindings would have been soiled in the slush.

"What's happening?" Amelia whispered, righting the books in her lap.

C. B. didn't wait, just hopped back in and shifted the jeep into gear, sweeping them off down the road. "The cap wouldn't let us send for you," he shouted over the roar of the engine. "If you come on your own though, that's a different story."

"So he's . . . ?" Her voice quivered—where were they going? "Please say you're not taking me to speak with a chaplain. I'm not sure I could handle that."

"Don't worry. The cap's alive." C. B. smiled, though concern haunted the corners of his mouth.

Amelia could breathe again, even in the blast of icy air hitting her face. She glanced over her shoulder, watching as the gate grew smaller behind them and the young soldier watched them go. And all she could think was why Wyatt hadn't come himself.

If he'd been able, wouldn't he have come?

"He's been injured then?"

"Yes, milady. I'm sorry to say."

"What happened?"

"I can talk a bit now that it's over. Supposed to have been low priority—a routine mission to bomb out an underground oil storage unit on German soil. But nothing's routine around Berlin these days. We took massive flak over Derben. Didn't expect such a great resistance but had to battle through something fierce. And our bird just took more than she could handle."

He turned them down a road past a gaggle of buildings, one a massive H shape with scores of men lined up out the front doors.

She sat straight and held on to her hat, though her insides felt like the mush beneath the jeep tires. "I'm sorry. What is flak? I'm afraid I don't know the right words."

"Just a fancy word for enemy fire," he tossed back as they passed brick buildings, scores of trucks and trailers carrying munitions, and men hurrying about like working bees in the estate hives. "In the end, we lost nine planes to the Boches. It was a bad outing. We're still reeling from it, milady."

Oh my word . . .

If they were all fortresses, was that ninety men? Or fighter planes with only one pilot apiece? Any one loss was too much. But she understood now why the pub was rife with talk of it. It was too terrible to imagine.

Nine planes, just . . . gone.

Another building came into view—a brick-faced front with square window cutouts and round-roofed buildings stretching far behind. Two army-issue trucks were parked at the curb out front, with heart-sickening white crosses branded over green on their sides. One had doors open at the back and insides exposed, as if it had only just been deserted as the wounded were carried inside.

She tore her eyes away, the sight of white crosses and hospital wards an induction to panic if she let it overwhelm her.

"This is it—Station Sick Quarters," C. B. said, wheeling them to a stop and hopping out before the tires had time to make treads in the snow.

"He's here?"

"Yes, ma'am." He offered an arm to take the books so she could step down without slipping on the ice.

When Amelia felt certain of her footing, even in heels, she took them back. It was the first time she'd looked at C. B.—really seen his face—and noticed cuts, bruising over one cheek, and a wrist that was wrapped with white gauze under the sleeve of his uniform coat. But he stood tall and, for the young chap he was, gave the impression he'd grown inches since she'd met him back in September.

"C. B., whatever's happened to you?"

"Just a scratch or two, milady. But you'll need to know the gist of it before you see the captain . . . We went down on the coast. Lost seven of our crew, including Lieutenant Barton. But not for Wyatt not doing everything he could to save them."

Oh no.

The smiling, jesting member of the crew? Dead. And the rest of the boys—one by one she thought of them, remembered their faces. Seeing them about town. At the Castle House. Asking the girls from town to dance at the USO events. Stopping by Parham Hill though only the officers stayed on nights there.

Which ones would only live in her memory?

Amelia stared through the darkness beyond the window cutouts on the hospital's façade, as if she could see all the way through to Wyatt's bed. She grasped C. B.'s arm, holding tight. "How terrible is it? Please, tell me."

"Burns to his right side—arm and neck. Hit his head hard in the crash, but they say he'll heal. Seems he's more busted up inside his heart than anything. He's taken it on himself hard. Like I've never seen. This time it may well have broken him." C. B.'s voice choked and he righted himself, with as stiff an upper lip as any RAF pilot could have mustered.

He cleared his throat. "We couldn't bail out—happened too fast.

We saw England. Thought we were home. Then flak hit off the water and the wing was gone, and down we went. Cap pulled us out, milady. Went back to the wreckage onshore over and over, battling for each man on his crew, dragging us from flames. Lieutenant Colonel says it's a miracle any of us made it. Miracle or not, I'm standing before you today because of Captain Stevens. I'd never have gone against his wishes by bringing you here, but seeing as you came on your own . . . this is where you should be."

It was the one time Amelia wished she hadn't an imagination.

C. B. recounted what happened with just enough grim detail to make her feel like she'd been socked in the gut of her pretty coat as he led her down the hall. It was busy—too busy for her liking, with uniforms buzzing about. Nurses moving through the halls. Even a medical team wheeling a gurney and soldier so fast that C. B. had to yank her against the wall or both of them would get flattened.

She caught her breath as he slowed them near the end of the hall.

"Here we are, milady." He stopped at a door that opened wide to a room with a host of beds lined against the metal walls.

There was space between beds and officers spread out among them—not with crowding like the general wards they'd passed by. The hum of quiet hung on the air as C. B. pointed her to the far corner and a bed by a window, where the cool light of morning sun shone down on a figure leaning his back against the white metal frame. He looked away from her, staring out the window like something was there, though she could see the glass was frosted over.

"Will they let me in?" She eyed what she assumed were surgeons who flitted a glance up at them and nurses who pretended not to notice them standing in the doorway.

"It's an officers' ward, and I'm letting you in," C. B. whispered, as if that explained it all. "I'll just wait outside."

The sound of Amelia's heels clicked on the floor, echoing off the ceiling like they were all packed up in a tin can. She unbuttoned her coat with her free hand, one button per step, gazing past the lot of officers and beds, swallowing hard as she drew near to his side. "Wyatt?"

He turned at once, slow, like he was lost in a dream, revealing red blotches of burned skin that snaked up from gauze to the underside of his right jaw. Skin around his eye was bruised a wretched purple and black, with an angry cut over his brow stitched but raw. It might have shocked her to see him in such a state had she not been warned. And had his eyes not softened when they rested upon her, Amelia might have been more devastated at the physical damage done to him.

But he was alive.

And breathing.

With blood pumping warm through his veins. And Amelia couldn't be sorry for feeling joy. Thinking of all the young boys who had been lost broke her heart—but she hadn't lost *him*.

"I told them not to telephone you," Wyatt said, his voice rougher, as if it had been raked over gravel.

"They didn't," she whispered, readjusting the stack of books cradled in her arms. "You never came back. I was worried you'd miss out on your reading. The library seems empty now if it's not being used. I know how fond you are of it."

"Fond. Yes. Of books? I suppose I was once."

It wasn't boldness that drew her—Amelia wished she could claim that. Maybe relief more than anything. It had been four years in coming, and she'd not so much as looked at another man since Arthur, let alone danced with one. Until Wyatt. And now she was the one coming to his sickbed in the way a fiancée or wife should have. She hadn't a clue what that meant, but Amelia stepped closer, watching him for any sign he wished her to leave. But he didn't bristle. Didn't move, actually. Not even when she sat on the edge of the bed.

Amelia placed her hand to the blanket, just shy of grazing his. "I've never heard you talk like that before."

"I have no use for books today."

Was that his way of telling her to leave? This little game of books and notes and Christmas Eve dances in liquid-satin gowns was over—just like that?

"Why is that? Have books offended you in some way?" She'd meant it as lighthearted banter. Something to ease the heaviness in the room. But Wyatt had never looked at her like that, as if he was exposed. Broken, even. And she was certain somehow that it was not from the burns or the bump on the head.

Instead of giving a reply, he leaned over to the bedside table, taking a Bible from the top. Without words, he turned to a page from somewhere in the middle and pulled a photograph from the binding. He offered it to her.

Amelia took the snapshot in hand. Looked at the smiling face of a woman with sculpted curls at her crown and an exquisite smile that brightened her face. In her arms, wrapped up in a fur-collared coat, was a mirror image of the woman—a little girl with a dimpled, missing-toothed smile, and the same sugared plait that left no room for error that they were mother and daughter.

"Abigail, uh, my wife. She never wanted to move to New York. She thought we could live on my family's land . . . work the farm . . . be content with Iowa sunsets for the rest of our lives." He raked his good hand through his hair, pausing every couple of words. "And then Susan came along . . . and something changed. Abby agreed to give it a try. We wanted more for our daughter and the city seemed the next big step—even if her husband had to work his way up from a lowly publishing clerk to make it. We both believed it was right.

She knew I wanted to escape and that books were our ticket. So we went."

The beautiful smiles and happiness were so bright, the photo should have felt like sunshine in Amelia's palms. If he'd mentioned anything else but having a wife, it mightn't have been so tough to swallow. She glanced at the ring finger on his left hand, panic telling its own story in her middle.

Empty.

Heavens—what was he trying to tell her?

Wyatt had never gone this far. Never opened the book of his heart to tell her anything about his story. Even when she'd told him about Arthur, and the library, and got *this close* to trusting him enough to share her own brokenness . . . To hear him talk of it felt as holy as if they'd stepped under the vault of a grand cathedral, instead of sitting in a tin can that vibrated as plane engines roared overhead.

"And what happened?"

"I was late for dinner—again. The all-consuming business of the publishing world and a man climbing the ranks of his own selfish ambitions had become a habit. I aspired to be the youngest publisher in Houghton Mifflin history, so much I'd almost become sick with the chase. I didn't show for Susan's birthday night out— five years old and she wanted to go to a hole-in-the-wall shop in Little Italy because I'd made a flippant promise once that someday we'd go there for meatballs and cannoli. She must have figured if she chose that, I might actually come." He let loose with a smile, shaking his head at the memory. But it faded away like a shot, and he grew somber again. "They waited but I never showed. Or showed too late, rather. They tried to hail a taxi and never made it home. I got there in time to find twisted metal and a box of cannoli spilled on the corner of Mulberry Street. One accident. One decision and my life was over."

"Wyatt, is that why you—?"

"Why I run toward flames instead of away?" He nodded, bruises illuminated by a shaft of sunlight. "Wouldn't you?"

"It's not your fault. You couldn't have known what would happen that night."

Amelia clutched the treasured photo in her hand, feeling the prickles of guilt that she'd only ever seen her pain. Felt her wounds. And all the while, Wyatt had remained quiet about how close he was to completely understanding the heart's worst devastation.

"I enlisted, came here thinking I could battle my enemies until the war took me out too. I'd volunteer for every mission that might end the pain with a single bomb blast. Imagine wanting to die and you battle for years, only to be the one man God doesn't choose to take. It's the worst kind of flipped fate. But then I walked into a library one day and found the only person I've ever met who might understand. And books had the audacity to try to befriend me again. So much so that I no longer wanted the bombs. Instead, I wanted them. And *her*. And I wanted to ask if she could ever dare to care about someone again."

He swallowed hard and his eyes glazed. "Books almost killed me. Then they saved me. Now I don't know what to do."

"No?"

"I so wanted to kiss you on Christmas, but I felt . . . It felt wrong. I wasn't ready. And I may not be ever." He stopped. Started again, chin heavy in the sunlight. "I'm dead inside."

"Dead doesn't feel, Wyatt. And you still do," Amelia whispered, battling tears like a schoolgirl. "What happened up there is not your fault either. You did everything you could. You're in this bed right this moment, and C. B. is waiting outside the door—alive—because of you. There's something beautiful in that. Even this horrible loss has something in it that can be redeemed because you had enough feeling left inside to do what you knew was right. You'd have given your life for any man on your crew. There's beauty in that willingness to sacrifice."

"But how do you ask someone to forget their pain, to dare to heal when you know how deep it goes and how unforgiving it can be? I have no right to do that. Not for myself. Not for them. Not even for you, though God knows I want to."

Amelia returned the photo, just brushing her fingertips against his empty ring finger as she turned his hand and placed it in his open palm.

The books she set on the bedside table so she could shed her coat. And pulled the pin to release her tam, then set the red felt hat on the stack so it became a siren that said she was staying put. As long as he wanted her, she wasn't going anywhere. She looked around, spying a metal chair under the window, and dragged it over to his bedside.

There was something about the power of silence to punctuate what the heart couldn't say. Amelia felt it as she cleared her throat, composing herself though tears tripped over the edge of her bottom lashes.

She slid the top book from the stack, opened the cover, and flipped to the first page.

No explanation was needed. No words of affirmation to pretend grief didn't slay like a rabid beast. It was just wrapping his good hand in hers, the photo perched under his fingertips, and holding on for dear life as they clung to the moment—both desperate to heal.

"Chapter One," Amelia began, her voice a soft song against the metal roof. "'It is a truth universally acknowledged, that a single man in possession of a good fortune, must be in want of a wife . . .'"

Wyatt smiled at the opening line.

Amelia held his hand, reading Austen's classic aloud with a soft cadence of words long after exhaustion had swept him into sleep.

And when evening drew near and she finally gathered her things to leave, Amelia brushed his hair back, kissed his bruised forehead, and left a note on the top of the stack where he'd find it when he woke.

One word penciled, meant only for him:

Yes.

TWENTY-FOUR

"Why am I never allowed the same maid for more than a few months before she is replaced?"

Ma-ma barely looked up in her flitting about, adjusting the tiara of diamond-encrusted ivy and fine gauze veil that iced Elizabeth's honeyed locks and filtered sunlight from the chamber window in a halo around her.

"What did you say, dear?" Ma-ma muttered, completely absorbed in smoothing the ivory trail down Elizabeth's back so that the veil stretched out in a liquid train on the chamber's hardwood floor.

"I said, why do none of my maids stay on more than a few months?" Meeting her mother's glance in the gilt floor mirror, Elizabeth challenged her with a fierce stare.

It had been but days since her unexpected visit to the Theatre Royal on Drury Lane, but the odd encounter with the theater owner there had awakened questions Elizabeth hadn't been willing to explore in the years after her father's death. She'd pushed back grief. And loss. Instead allowing herself to be driven by justice alone. Even memories she should have been able to look back on with fondness—taking walks in the gardens, sketching at the mill, seeing real life for what it was, with her father's gentle coaxing and welcoming smile always at her side—they'd been buried under by her pursuit.

But justice came at a price. She'd allowed herself to be managed, hidden by a suffocating maternal force that now had no right to hide the truth from her.

How completely she'd been fooled.

Invitations to balls were received, yet Elizabeth never saw them. Letters came to her on a silver tray, but only after they'd been opened. Ma-ma accompanied her to every call. And Elizabeth was allowed few, if any, acquaintances outside of the revolving rotation of staff who seemed to sweep in and out of their manor with curious frequency.

All of this she'd pored over while pushing food around her plate at the viscount's dinner table or while sipping tea during calls in London, attempting to fit a mask over the absolute fracturing of her world behind the scenes. She was haunted by names like Christopher Churchill . . . Thomas Whittle . . . and above all, the great mystery that was Keaton James.

The viscount would sit at his dining table and endure the onslaught of syrup-dripping her ma-ma chose to employ—whether complimenting the decor of his drawing room, or the masculinity of the library, or the way he'd managed his staff so precisely as to lay a table with such elegance. There was no doubt, said she, that his London home must be as fine as Her Majesty's. Why, their upcoming visit to Buckingham Palace would confirm it.

Yet every once in a while, as Ma-ma droned on and Elizabeth stewed in the mire of her thoughts, Keaton would emerge from behind the veil of propriety and look over at *her*.

Without a word passing between them, those eyes would reveal something was at play. As if he knew Elizabeth had begun to question the very fabric of who she was. And after days of demanding answers in her heart but never summoning the gumption to demand them in real voice, somehow, in those brief moments of feeling she was wrestling alone . . . she wasn't.

Those looks gave her enough courage to confront her suspicions now.

To stand in front of a grand floor-length mirror in his London home, wearing a veil so delicate and pure, and to be unafraid to confront what she never had before.

"You have no answer, Ma-ma?"

"Elizabeth—you needn't trouble yourself with the trifle of service staff when you are to be wed next month and must concentrate on the happiness of your husband. Managing your households can be learned after the wedding." Ma-ma reached for the hand Elizabeth had left dead at her side, squeezed and patted it before she let go. "Do not worry. I will help you."

"*No.*"

That was the attention-getter Elizabeth had sought.

One word cut like a knife, searing the air with her defiance.

"I beg your pardon?"

"I said no. Not until you answer why our maids never take confidence with me. And if they do attempt familiarity, then they are gone soon after. And why am I disallowed from opening my own mail? Or from taking a coach to town? Or knowing any detail of the finances that govern our provision? And why am I prevented acquaintance with any young women my own age?"

"You have tea with Lady Everess's daughters, do you not? Why, we paid call to them just a week ago, now that we are in London."

"You paid call to them. I was made to come along in the carriage."

"Made to come along? Honestly. Elizabeth, it is your duty as a viscountess-to-be to set an example for society. You must take your place. That requires calls."

"You make them then. At your leisure."

Ma-ma smiled. Smiled! She looked at Elizabeth through the reflection and actually found humor enough to judge her questions a worthless folly.

"Oh, you are tired, dear. That's what this is. As all brides tend to be. Why not rest for a bit? Let me see to the remaining preparations."

"I am not tired. And I will not rest." Elizabeth reached up, sweeping the glittering tiara from her crown, pulling the looping ivy design from her hair until wisps dragged loose from the sleek center part of her coif. The attached train she swept up—carefully, in complete control, not the least bit put off by her mother's audible gasp—and began looping the airy white fabric around her forearm with her hair in a state of disarray.

"What do you think you are doing?"

"Putting an end to this sorry charade."

The pastel tailor's box on the bed was soon full again, as Elizabeth tucked the gauze inside its peachy-pink tissue. The viscount's family jewels she deposited back inside the velvet box on the vanity, ignoring the shock on her mother's face as she placed them in the deep plum lining and clamped the lid shut.

"What charade? I haven't time to lose. We have many details yet to decide upon." Ma-ma paused, though the argument in her voice spoke of mounting urgency. It moved to shrill, even, as she watched Elizabeth take dress shop boxes and stack them by the chamber door.

"I shall assist you in simplifying then—cancel the appointments."

She ripped a veil from Elizabeth's grasp and tossed it to the floor in a heap of fluff. "Stop this at once! Do you not remember that the caterer is to arrive this afternoon—the same chef who has outfitted celebrations for the queen? And the dressmaker coming for a final fitting! What am I to do if we fall behind schedule? Pluck yards of satin from a tree?"

"Your schedule, Ma-ma. Not mine," she whispered, then turned back to the mirror to press her hair back into place. "And I do not know if I should marry at all. I'm most aggrieved to have to tell you, but I haven't yet given the viscount my answer. It seems an ill use of his time and yours to choose from veils that will not be worn in the end."

Nails dug into her arm from behind, Ma-ma grasping her so swiftly that a shockwave of pain ripped Elizabeth's attention from her manufactured busyness.

"What do you mean you do not know if you should marry? Of course you will wed the viscount. What nonsensical talk is this?"

"I decide. I shall marry whom and when I choose. It is freedom of a sort that Pa-pa's assets crumbled in the wake of his death. If I came to a marriage offer with a large income, a mill and estates perhaps, then I should have no choice, should I? But the poor artist that I am—she may choose her own fate."

"You have no choice. The viscount is the last—your only choice!"

The day she'd stood up to a wrathful stable groom flooded Elizabeth's mind.

Then she'd summoned strength she didn't know she possessed. It was as if someone else had fled across the meadow at Parham Hill and thrust her arms spread-eagle before the wretched horse. But the animal had been the wounded one then. She'd saved it, or tried to. And now, who would save her?

Now she was the wounded one.

The hurt and abused.

And if she didn't stand up in that moment, her life would bleed by in an endless parade of dress shops and afternoon tea visits, in a marriage of duty with love having been surrendered for a lifetime of privilege. And household management enforced by a manipulative overseer who hadn't any true affection for her at all, only subservience to financial security.

If Elizabeth submitted, justice for her pa-pa would be buried for good. She'd rather die herself than let that happen.

"Who is Christopher Churchill?" She stared at her mother as if each syllable needed its own infusion of strength to make her point. Folding her arms across her chest helped.

Ice befell the room.

No longer was Ma-ma's primary panic that a wedding would be put off or a viscount's offer discarded in favor of the next eligible lady in line.

Stark. Cold. Emotionless . . . Elizabeth saw the worst of her mother's character bubble to the surface and roil upon her face like a reed tossed in a current. She tipped her eyebrows in cool challenge. In truth, the dowager countess seemed almost impressed that her daughter should challenge with such precision, though she gave the distinct impression that she'd been challenged before.

Challenged and won—and would win again.

"Where did you hear that name?"

Elizabeth tilted her head. "Where did you?"

"That name belongs to a spurious criminal who sought to profit from your father's death. Forget it."

"How would anyone profit from Pa-pa's death when we haven't a quid in our pocket and I have but one good gown to my name?"

"This is about more than quids. And gowns. And the stubborn streak your father never suppressed in his only daughter. The criminal professed to have knowledge of an earl's death but would only share what he knew in exchange for money. And the London magistrate had no evidence whatsoever that he was tied to the crime. Just an absurd thespian who thought he should profit from a nobleman's death."

Elizabeth shook her head. "He didn't appear to want money."

"Didn't appear . . . You mean you've met this man?"

Ma-ma's fury boiled over like a babe in a fit for a sugar bowl. She pounded her fist on her palm and turned away, as if the view would offer her the chance to build her wall of composure back up.

"Why would anyone wish to profit from *us*? We are not prizes. We haven't any inheritance left to live on, let alone to rise again from the ashes of a crumbling estate. I haven't a clue why we'd even receive an invitation to Parham Hill in the first place, and yet we did . . ."

Elizabeth stopped, feeling the shades of truth flash through her. Of course.

She hadn't caught the viscount's eye. Hadn't received an invitation to a ball because of her late father's name. However she'd managed it, the entire trip had been carefully crafted by her mother's expert hand.

"You did this. You arranged this marriage to a man you knew was there the night of the murder. You've known who he is all along. And you kept this from me all these years!"

"*Yes. I. Did.*" Ma-ma spat out the words with venom flying. She crossed the chamber as though her feet were aflame and tore open the wardrobe. She rifled through a drawer for a split second and retrieved a shiny metal object that just caught the light—the revolver.

"You think I did not know? You may not have loaded this, but you still carried it. Everywhere." Slamming it down on the vanity table, ironically next to the velvet keepsake box for a wedding tiara, her ma-ma left the weapon like a snake coiled between them. "And what did you think you were going to do? Behave like a man? Challenge your father's murderer to pistols at dawn?"

"I don't know . . ."

"You were set to ruin your future, that's what. I sent a letter to the viscount—he being the brother of a business acquaintance of your late pa-pa's. I posed the arrangement to him and he extended an invitation—why I do not know. But neither do I care. Who would accept a plain and aging daughter with no dowry? She being an artist. So like the drudge of the theater crowd. Unruly and uncouth. Unfit for the gentle world. I would toss every one of your sketchbooks in the fire if it meant you would submit that stubborn will to the duty of your station and forget these fanciful whims and swirls of paint."

"It is those sketchbooks that brought us to London after all. Have you forgotten? I am to paint the queen of England."

"You are to tag along behind a master. You are to meet the queen and then marry well. That is your aim. Paint is merely a stepping-stone to our future."

She'd tripped into finding the name Churchill, and Elizabeth refused to back down without answers. Or some truth that had been denied her for too long. But instead of uncovering truths, it had locked a thousand new doors. And unless she could open them, one by one, she would wither, suppressed and imprisoned, as long as she stayed under her mother's thumb.

"Good-bye, Ma-ma."

Whisking up her hat and reticule, and the revolver from the vanity, Elizabeth breezed past her, heading for the door.

"Where do you think you're going?"

"To the Adelphi Theater in Piccadilly to ask questions after London's wretched thespians. And then to every theater I can find in the city until I unravel the web of secrets you've spun over us. Care to come along?"

"And what will you do at a theater? Find more names that do not matter? Unearth the past that has been buried in peace these ten years? You haven't a carriage. And you haven't a ring on your finger with which to demand anything." She stared, her eyes trying their last and best effort to exert control. "*You need me.* Or else how will you survive?"

It was Elizabeth's turn to smile.

To find the challenge of a bitter dowager countess a folly and her words nothing but the imperious conjecture of a fool tugged the corners of her mouth up to where Elizabeth was powerless to stop it.

"Perhaps I will survive on my own."

"Those are the only intelligent words you have uttered. The viscount will not allow his bride to go traipsing all over the city, associating with the guttersnipes of London's underbelly and thereby sullying his name. You dishonor your father by your defiance. Do you hear me? You would be dead to him."

"Then perhaps I was never meant to be someone's bride or have worth because of someone's name," Elizabeth whispered, the hinges crying out like punctuation when she turned the knob. "Perhaps God whispers my name instead, and gave me an artist's heart all along."

The shouts were drowned out as Elizabeth closed the door.

JUNE 9, 1843
216 STRAND
LONDON, ENGLAND

It took little convincing for the coach to be let. None at all, in fact.

Keaton's promise when they'd arrived in London had been true. Elizabeth was given every right of property—to his home, his staff, even his coach and four he'd left behind. With a mere request the coachman set them out upon the streets of London, asking no questions as to why she'd ventured out without her mother in tow. He'd simply readied the horses and they were off within moments, with only his nod and an assured, "Very good, milady," as he steered them toward the theater district.

The coach turned up Strand Street, the horses' hooves clip-clopping like the ticking of a clock. That was what it amounted to—counting the minutes until Elizabeth might continue her quest in the open. Seeking out unknown men . . . asking after names in theater back halls . . . Perhaps she'd return to the Theatre Royal and beat her fist upon the frosted glass of Mr. Churchill's door until he let her in, then point the revolver at him until he finally surrendered answers.

And then perhaps she'd go back to St. James's Park, to the town-home of the man who was still a mystery, and even without the companion of a loaded weapon, bluff well and demand better until he told her the truth.

The Thames roiled outside the coach, churning as the bright June sun shone down on the way. Her mother had taken them to all points of London, to every dress shop and milliner and perfumery in the new parts of the city—those rebuilt after the Great Fire had torn through and eaten centuries' worth of London's history.

But they'd always avoided the Strand.

Until that moment Elizabeth hadn't realized how well she still knew it.

The haunts and hollows were familiar as the coach rolled by, most buildings unchanged from the dark blot upon her memory. She gripped her sketchbook in her palms, pressing hard to the worn leather as the coach moved on. And remembrance began a slow claw-ing in her midsection as the coach eased to a stop.

She could feel the release of the coachman's weight when he jumped down from his perch. And she remained frozen as he opened the door and waited for instruction.

"216 Strand, milady."

Talons shredded her insides as memories seized upon her.

Elizabeth hadn't a clue as to how long she sat there. Staring out when she should have been brave and stepped down to the sidewalk. But ensconced in the safety of the velvet interior, she couldn't move a fraction.

Twining's still stood, the one-story shop sandwiched between two multistoried brick structures on either side. She remembered the façade, its frame so petite it was not much wider than the front doors. The polished wood gleamed out from behind the waves of falling snow. The gaslight lamp shone on the cobblestones beneath the coach wheels. And the warm glow of shop windows revealed how far back the interior stretched, with row upon row of leaves tucked in jars and bins, and patrons weaving their way through—both men and women, unlike the rule of "men only" posted at London's coffeehouses.

And then the *crack* of a firearm discharging through the night.

Cathedral bells chiming.

The wind howling.

A body falling . . . and her world shattering into pieces.

Elizabeth gripped the windowsill with one hand, fingers grasping for something solid to cling to, with the sketchbook hugged to her chest in the other.

How was it she could still feel the coldness prickle her skin? Could see the passersby not in light linen or cotton fashions of the mild summer afternoon but bundled and rushing about through the harsh December wind? And was that a young man with eyes of gray and a jagged line of gold leaning against the lamppost, tapping a walking stick against his boot, top hat shielding his face from the gaslight's glow?

"Elizabeth?"

She started at an outstretched hand that had reached through the coach's open door.

The coachman had been replaced—unbeknownst to her—and not by an apparition of memory, but by the ten-years-older version of Keaton James. Without top hat or cane. And no candy-striped ascot dancing on the wind. Just him in a deep-ink coat and white shirt, his tie discarded somewhere, as though he'd loosed it and neglected to tie it up again. His dark hair stirred in the gentle summer breeze that filtered through the streets, and he waited, hand outstretched, as he searched her eyes, palm patient as it asked to receive hers.

All she could do was stare at it, unable to move unless to slink back from him.

"Elizabeth . . . may I help you?"

"How did you find me?" She held the sketchbook like a shield across her front.

"Your mother. I returned to the townhome after you'd gone. She was in a state—said that you were bound for the Adelphi Theater and begged me to go after you."

"You followed me."

"No. When you didn't show at the Adelphi, I thought you may come here instead." Keaton gave in, dropping his hand to his side, and climbed into the coach, gingerly taking a seat upon the bench opposite her. She slid a hand over to the reticule on the seat, keeping her metal pet close in case she should need to point it between his eyes.

"So you don't deny it," she breathed out, exhaling long and low, allowing tears the liberty to sting her eyes, even if she was sitting in the presence of the one man she wished to remain in complete control in front of. "You were here that night?"

He nodded. "Yes. I do not deny it."

"How could you?"

Elizabeth trembled, so overcome that her hands dropped to

her lap and the sketchbook thumped down to the floor of the coach.

It was wise that Keaton did not move to retrieve it. Nor to touch her. Anyone knew a caged beast would bite back, and Elizabeth had never felt so hemmed in and threatened at the same time. Whatever she showed him though, it didn't scare him off. Keaton leaned in, pressing the void between them with his body, resting arms on his knees so his hands opened in front of him, fingertips within brushing distance of hers.

"I'd have told you. Anything, Elizabeth. If only you'd asked. It was my one condition in your coming to Parham Hill, and for our journey here—I'd not hide the truth from you if you simply asked me about it. No matter what your mother's wishes were, I'd not keep it from you."

"The truth? How do I know what that is?" She stared out at Twining's. And the innocence of Londoners waltzing by in the street. And the carriages that angled around theirs. A daze of disbelief made her feel as if she were floating outside of herself. All that time. Ten years. Whatever the story was, her mother had known.

Ma-ma had kept Elizabeth in the dark, wasting away in bitterness and grief, until the dark almost consumed her. And those eyes she'd sketched, and the drawing that was yellowed and curled at the edges for how many times she'd looked at it since that wretched day . . . Those eyes that had been the portrait of her pursuit for so long suddenly felt like they might be the only anchor she had left.

Would Keaton answer her?

Would he vindicate himself of any part in her father's death? Or would he tell her the truth—that he'd made an ill-conceived choice in one brash, youthful moment he could not take back, no matter the consequences?

Elizabeth stared into his eyes, daring to trust when everything in her said she mustn't.

"Who is Christopher Churchill? And Thomas Whittle?" She waited, heart thumping a wild drumbeat in her chest. And then, before thinking better of it, she whispered, "And who are you?"

"If you can trust me . . . I'll show you."

TWENTY-FIVE

Worshippers didn't take kindly to being interrupted in the pew on Sunday. But on a weekday morning in a quiet country chapel, it could be downright heathenistic.

"She's the one," Emory whispered when he rejoined Keira at the back of the aisle, pointing out the petite Englishwoman as if she wore a bull's-eye instead of a violet gabardine blazer and a delicate string of pearls. She sat alone, her ivory pixie cut bowed as the sun's golden glow began to dwindle and the sky rumbled with the distant threat of rain.

"You're sure she'll talk to us?"

He nodded. "Why not? She comes in here every day, apparently. And knows more about the history of this town than the castle itself. The volunteers say if we want to ask questions, we're lucky she's here to answer them."

Keira was getting used to Emory's moods by now—his tells and ticks—the way he remained quiet but shifted from one foot to the other when deep in thought. His tone meant he was going to insist upon answers, whether the woman was inclined to produce them or not. And the stubborn streak that said he'd bend over backward where the cottage was concerned fairly guaranteed he wouldn't leave their jaunt to town without some sort of forward progress.

"Right. Let's go talk to her then."

Keira led the way, and they traversed the aisle together, the country cathedral stealing her breath with each step.

It felt like a tucked-away legacy the town would have been most eager to share had more tourists ventured far enough down the lane to discover it. But the stone walls were quiet. Rows of polished walnut pews, each with backs straight as a spade and carved in a cross design at the anchors, lay near empty, except for the woman. Keira looked up to the gold chandelier hanging low over the altar and stepped through refracted light that stained glass cast against the stone floor in myriad rainbows.

What had these walls seen, and heard, and lived through? Armistice Day ceremonies, no doubt, as evidenced by leftover poppy garlands strung about stone columns like bowers of remembrance along the wings. Sonorous melodies from the organ swelling against burnished stone walls. And the legacy of war that had not quieted in the many decades since—a plaque dedicated to the fighting men stationed at an airfield that had been nearby.

Might it all help untwine the tangled history of Parham Hill?

The woman turned at Keira's pause beside her, a smile sneaking out from the corners of her lips with lines that hinted she laughed well, and often.

"Excuse me, Ms. Addams?"

"If you're looking for a tour, dear, the volunteers are at an information desk out at the front. Just there." Prim and proper, she whispered, directing the lost pair with a knobby finger to venture back down the center aisle and leave her to her prayers.

"I'm sorry, but we're not here for a tour, though we may have to take one now after standing here even for a moment. It's so beautiful. I hate to disturb you, but we were told you might be able to speak with us. You're Ms. Evelyn Addams?"

"I am," she confirmed, but seemed like she thought better of it as she looked up—way up—at all of Emory's height standing just behind. "Unless you're the taxman come for a small business owner. If that's the case, we're closed."

Hmm. Cheeky.

Emory stood like a statue, his backpack slung over his shoulder, and waited with a glance that said he was quite as interested as she to disturb the woman's morning worship if it netted a few answers, but he might be a little less inclined toward polite conversation.

Keira slid him a little *hold your horses* side glance and slipped into the pew next to the woman, carefully, so as not to assume they were at liberty to join where they'd not been invited, and sat. "No. We're actually looking for information about the manor past Framlingham Castle—Parham Hill. The volunteers suggested you might be able to help us. Is it true you've lived in Framlingham your entire life?"

She blinked at Emory and folded her hands in her lap as if praying for his poor soul. "Who's he? The new owner? I hope not."

And Keira honestly had to stifle a laugh. It seemed they'd managed to locate the one person from the four corners of England who apparently wasn't wooed by their charismatic employer, even if she hadn't met him outright. Emory bristled under his leather jacket and shifted his weight to the opposite foot.

Please? Keira mouthed and flitted her gaze to the pew, asking him to sit.

Emory rolled his eyes but gave her a smile. He dropped his bag in the corner of the pew and slipped in beside her.

"Uh . . . no. This is Emory Scott and I'm Keira Foley. We're not the estate owners, but we do work for him, as advisers for a restoration project he's undertaken."

"That viscount? *Pssh*." Ms. Addams flicked her wrist and adjusted her collar, as if mention of him would make one woefully untidy.

"Mr. Wilmont has uncovered some interesting history at the manor, and we would like to ask a few questions to try to sort it out. If you don't mind, that is."

Ms. Addams peered over the top rim of her spectacles. She inspected the two of them, her internal deliberations cranking gears that could almost be seen on the surface.

"Miss Foley. I'm sure you mean well, dear, but that whipper-snapper inherited an estate he has no business managing. That's what happens when London boys think they can come out to the countryside and know a thing or two about the locals without actually staying on. All he's been about is whizzing off in that sporty set of wheels and bringing in trucks to chew up our country roads and create a heap of noise."

Keira shot a glance to Emory, asking what in the world she was going on about. Chickens squawking in a barnyard came to mind for how ruffled her sensibilities. And for what? A few trucks and a skeleton crew?

He sat without comment, apparently as confused as she.

". . . That estate owner of yours is causing so much ruckus that it drives good tourist money away. You two best tell your employer there he's not popular in the village. I would not suggest he run for mayor anytime soon or he'll get a right proper thrashing from the people of this town."

Do something, Keira. Turn the tides of this conversation or you'll hit another dead end.

"Um—you said you own a small business." She brightened, sending the woman her best and, hopefully, sweetest smile. "A shop perhaps?"

Ms. Addams righted herself, the question apparently demand-ing a prim posture and she'd give her best effort at it. "Bertie's." She smiled. That must have been the sweet spot to ask after because her demeanor softened to one as amiable as the violet she wore. "It's a lovely little dress shop just out on Bridge Street. Have you seen it, dear?"

Keira looked down at her distressed jeans, time-scuffed boots, and dependable fisherman's sweater—the ensemble worked for the unpredictable East Suffolk weather but didn't do much for the girlish whims of dress buying. Even in London, thumbing through racks of gowns at Harrods and poking through vintage shops in Notting Hill had been more out of M. J.'s pushing than true excite-ment on Keira's part.

She allowed a smile to cover the surface. "No, ma'am. Not much call for dresses these days."

Ms. Addams paused, her shock indicating the mere idea was a tragedy.

"Well, Bertie's Dress Shop has been a fixture in Framlingham since my grandmother first opened its doors in '26. Even during the war she kept the women as fashionable as though they were stepping out to a Mayfair ball—rations or no rations, she made do. I remem-ber the stories. My grandmother was a prestigious lady herself, and she dressed them all. Even up to the most distinguished lady of this entire village. So if you want to learn about the people of Parham Hill, you might start with who dressed them."

Intriguing. Keira brushed her shoulder against Emory's, mak-ing certain he caught what she did. "Which distinguished lady do you speak of?"

"Why, the viscount's bride during the war. But all the way back, they say, to the nineteenth century that manor has stood as a pillar of pride in this fair part of the country. It's grown over the years—added a wing here. A cottage there. That's due to the appreciation for the arts by the most famous viscount—Keaton James. You've not heard of him?"

"No. I'm sorry."

"How could you work there and not know the viscount who started the honey making?"

"We found a list of the title owners but didn't know the significance of their contributions." Emory nodded, taking the lead on questions for the first time. He took out his phone and started scrolling through notes as Ms. Addams eyed him. "Here. The viscount you're talking about brought the honey-making venture to the estate and built the beekeeper's cottage by the road, didn't he?"

"He did, young man. The cottage is special, isn't it? Any eye can see that."

Emory leaned in closer at Keira's side, absorbed when the research overlapped the one spot that had won his affections. He eased over and rested his hand on hers in a silent bid to ask more questions.

Keira sat silent, hoping Ms. Addams and her firebrand wit wouldn't notice the hitch in her breathing or the added color that surely painted her cheeks when his fingertips grazed—and stayed over—hers.

"Ms. Addams, why isn't that viscount in the cemetery? We just looked through all the names. A Keaton James wasn't accounted for on any of the gravestones."

"Wouldn't be. The family keeps a private cemetery. Somewhere on the grounds of the estate."

"Where?" he asked, his thumb brushing over Keira's like an electrical current.

"I wouldn't know. That'd be a mighty fine question to take up with your employer, if he's not too busy to get his trousers involved in duties to properly manage his affairs."

"But why would Arthur Woods be buried here then—wasn't he one of the family too? He was viscount at the estate from 1936 until 1940, according to the list I found."

"Ah. Of course you'd ask that. But everyone who lives here knows the answer."

"I'm sort of living here," Emory added, his voice soft—so much so that Keira wondered what he wasn't saying that could be layered under the comment. "Thought it was for the time being, but this place grows on you after a while, doesn't it? You slip into an appreciation for comfort without having realized it. The pub. The castle spires. Country roads with sunsets that seem to linger a little longer and with more color than in the rest of the world. And the sunrises behind the willows here are unmatched. All of a sudden you look up and you're standing in a place that starts to whisper, 'You're home.' And what's funny is, you believe it without question."

"Very eloquent, young man." She tilted her head up to gaze at a plaque on the wall. "Everyone who died here during the war was given a place of honor, much as you say. Even the Americans have a plaque honoring their 390th Bomb Group—those who were stationed here through '45. As an RAF officer shot down in the line of duty . . . well, that's worth honoring, is it not? The fighting men and women and those townsfolk who died in the war—they're all together in the same section as his lordship, Arthur Woods. He was the first. But they were one family in loss."

Keira felt something tug inside. "And how do you know that?"

"Because my grandmother, Florence Bertram, is with them." Ms. Addams looked back. The lines on her face softened with eyes so blue and words so open Keira felt they could have been friends had she not a suitcase and a home back in Dublin that kept calling her to come back, come back.

What would it have been like to be one of those locals, to buy a dress from Bertie's, and to know the stories and names and history that mattered so much to them all? Boisterous trucks flogging country roads and noise scaring off tourists aside—Ms. Addams seemed genuinely touched by the little bit of care Keira and Emory had shown toward the town. They'd taken time to inquire about the local tales that had long since been buried. Forgotten. Lost even, like the manor down the hill.

A veil of appreciation fell to disarm what defenses the woman seemed to put up against their employer.

"You're a nice couple," she whispered, nodding as if her approval had been won and, if it were, that was quite a feat. "But that employer of yours doesn't know much ado about his own ancestry, does he? So why is it you two are here asking the questions and not he?"

It was the same question Keira had asked herself. A hundred times, maybe.

Why was she able to step into a story with Emory—to care about Victoria and a crumbling cottage—in a way Carter couldn't seem to? And why did it feel so right not to correct the woman that they weren't an actual couple but instead to remain still, loving the warmth of her fingertips cradled in his?

Ms. Addams smiled, patting Keira's knee in a motherly fashion. "My grandmother dressed every bride who walked down the aisle of this church, from 1926 until 1945. Can you believe that?"

"I can." Keira's spine tingled and her cheeks flooded with warmth.

"And would you like to see them?"

"See who? The brides?"

Evelyn Addams, the reluctant interviewee from Framlingham's most important shop—or so she boasted with a note of authority on the matter—whisked Keira and Emory to the back of the church and a tiny hall leading to the bride's room, where those dresses of satin and lace had skimmed the stone floor in the same long walk to the cathedral's center aisle. Where photos were lined, framed stories, one by glorious one . . .

"Here." Ms. Addams pointed to a black-and-white photo framed in silver with a slight tarnish at the corners. "The viscount and his bride. 1938. Before it all began."

And there she was. Amelia Woods, Viscountess of Huxley, standing at an altar with a smiling gentleman at her side. Light hair. Eyes that sparkled even through sepia. Cute little posture. And he—tall. Broad. Thin nose, and softer smile than his vivacious girl.

So the couple had faces. Lovely faces with hope-filled smiles, unaware that war was coming and everything would change.

They had a story.

As Keira leaned in to run a fingertip along the bottom edge of the frame, wondering why in the world she'd not understood before then that story held significance, Emory cut the space between them, laced his fingers with hers, and didn't let go.

Rain had the power to make romance dodgy.

Every square inch of Keira was drenched, down to jeans and waterlogged cable weave, when they hustled in through Parham Hill's front door.

Sconces were lit down the great hall, cutting the grayness from the windows with a soft glow against the black-and-white-checked floor. But no music this time. And no lights in the entry. Just an echo as Emory shut the door on the rain and pinged the security code on the wall, then knelt to sort through the inside of his backpack.

A far-off light trailed out the library door into the hall, but all was still from inside.

"Ben and Eli?" Keira asked.

He checked his watch. "Noon. They never work over a meal. Must've missed them on their way out."

Keira turned away, a bundle of nerves as she stripped out of the sweater and let it fall to the floor in a soggy lump, then wrung out the tips of her hair over her tee, like there wasn't the biggest lump in her throat at the same time. "So it's just us."

He didn't answer.

Why was that? Just slid out of his leather jacket and walked over to hang it on a wall sconce. He ran his hand through his ebony hair, his palm catching at the nape as he shifted his weight to one leg. "Look—I'm not good at this."

"Not good at what? Slogging through a healthy English rain?" She tossed the hair at her shoulders, fluttering air through it in a bid to get something to dry. "Better get used to it, Yank, if you plan to make a go of it by staying on at the cottage. England invented rain boots for a reason."

Keira had meant it in cheek, hoping to calm the fluttering in her midsection. But total ignorance turned out to be something she owned in spades, because Emory looked torn to strips. He stood with his arms braced at his sides, like something was trying, and failing miserably, to stay tamped up inside him.

"What Evelyn said is true. Why are we the ones doing this?"

She swallowed hard. "Doing what?"

"Hunting down a story that's not ours. Finding out about Victoria's past. Putting up walls in an old cottage—that should be Carter's job. Why are we still here?"

There were maybe a thousand answers.

He liked research. So did she. Victoria was stunning, whoever's work she was. They were being paid. It was a gully washer outside, and who wanted to brave the Framlingham roads to trek home through that? There was a manor with free coffee, art that begged to be researched, and enough painted sunsets to last them the rest of their lives, were they keen to stay.

Those answers tried but weren't nearly good enough.

Keira didn't know why, except that Parham Hill, Victoria, the cottage, and Emory . . . they'd awakened something in her that she'd been ready to give up. Dublin was home, but it didn't call her the same way it used to.

Not like a darkened entry with Emory in it did.

"I don't know." Keira put herself in the last position she should have—taking a step closer to him that felt more like a leap across a chasm. "Why are you still here?"

"You want the truth, Foley?"

"Yeah. I could use some truth right now."

Truth turned out to be snogging that stole her breath in the dark . . .

Emory Scott kissed to his own tune, with arms he slipped around her waist like they'd always belonged there, the feel of his heart slamming against her chest, her lips forgetting anything but what it felt like for his to explore them. It was the craziest sense of home she'd ever come back to.

He felt like home.

Then there was a minute of catching their breath and grinning like fools, and he pushing locks of wet hair back from her forehead with the heel of his palm, and she taking the liberty to wipe a smudge of dirt from the side of his nose.

"I couldn't put that off a second longer. I didn't think it was right to pull you into all this. But I haven't done it in a long time—"

"I have a hard time believing you haven't practiced that a bit."

"No, Professor. I meant I haven't been able to trust anyone like this."

"Trust?" She pecked another kiss on him, lingering a moment.

"Look, I'm just about to ask you to spend Christmas in Ireland with my family. I think I should be the one worried right now, especially given that my brothers' overprotective vibe could mean I'm putting your very life in danger if you agree. And I'm kind of used to having you around by now."

When he didn't reply, just took in all she'd said with a blank stare, Keira's nerves kicked in.

"You need a family to spend Christmas with, right? I'd hate to leave you frozen in that pitiful cottage out there. So . . . you know. Just a holiday. But no strings, of course."

He stepped off, keeping his fingers laced with hers, and tugged her toward the hall. "Come here."

"Where are we going?"

The line they'd crossed began to fade as Emory walked her down the hall toward the light spilling out at the end.

The library greeted them, rain still beating the manor walls and lightning creating flashes of white that lit up the room. The scaffolding had been lowered as the wall came down, and aged boards had been nailed up to cover the window that had once been behind it. But other than the reams of books lining all corners and her lovely Victoria holding court on the far wall, it was silent and still.

"What's going on?"

"You mentioned it a while back, that the fade marks on the wallpaper meant there must have been a window behind the wall."

"Right. I did. So what?"

"There were at least eight more paintings we haven't accounted for. And I've been looking for them. Behind locked doors. In the cellar. Shut-up rooms. The attic . . . So now I need to know if you meant it," he whispered, staring through her. "And if you can really trust me."

"Emory—you're scaring me. Of course I trust you. Why?"

He nodded. Just once, then turned away.

It wasn't when he reached for the tarp in the corner and pulled it free to reveal a shipping crate underneath. Or when he muscled a crowbar to peel back nails at each of its four corners. And even though the heart sinking in her chest tried to understand what was happening when he pulled the wood face free and a gold-embossed frame emerged in the center . . . it still didn't seem real.

Keira shook her head, her breath quickening with shock.

An *Empress* lay before her, bathed in Klimt's unmistakable gold—turning Emory into an art thief, with his long-lost Farbton masterpiece that wasn't lost at all.

TWENTY-SIX

After the weariness left over from the long winter of war, spring returned.

Framlingham winters were long and chilling to the bone, but the promise of warmth always brought a thaw that was worth the wait.

Hedgerows woke in muted yellows and soft greens. Hawthorns and willows bloomed, creating bowers of white along the road to town. And the air seemed scented with sweet violets no matter where you trod. Darly had fixed Amelia's bicycle—with new tires from goodness knew where—and she'd regained the freedom of wheeling about town again.

She'd set out for Wickham Market and the weekly shop with ration coupons at the ready, gliding past Bertie's shop with another dress in its window display. She had just enough time to drop in at the Castle House before she rounded back to the cottage at midday. If luck was on their side, Wyatt would be on pass after being on duty for nearly a week, and Amelia would get to see him before he went up again. He'd healed enough that his burns had begun to fade on the outside, but it was the courage from someplace inside that said he wasn't through fighting just yet.

Amelia bit her bottom lip over a smile as she shrugged her bicycle against the stone wall of the Castle House pub. She'd felt an uncommon spring in her step after visiting Wyatt for weeks. After reading together and falling into a gentle rhythm of affections that had turned openly toward one another. She plucked two jars of honey from her basket and thought seriously about skipping her way to the pub door.

A cry split the street in two before Amelia could reach for the front door handle.

Sirens screeched a breath after—so loud her skin crawled—and she fumbled one of the jars. It dropped from her hand and shattered in a pool of glass and sticky gold at her feet.

Amelia shot her gaze to the sky, clutching the other jar in a desperate, white-knuckled hold as she searched the clouds for angry black birds. There was a distant roar of planes, wasn't there? Or was that just her imagination?

They were so used to the hum of engines blighting the sky that it felt normal to doubt the background noise now. The nearest bomb shelter was the largest—the underground in the Church of St. Michaels. There was nothing to do but calmly and assuredly walk toward it, and pray with each step that it was only the madness of another drill.

Patrons bustled from shops, spilling into the street—Bertie among them with tailor's tape draped over her neck, her face calm but her eyes terror stricken as she led women to the church in their various states of incomplete dress. The bookshop emptied of its horde of book lovers. The Castle House, too, saw diners flee, though Thompson was nowhere in sight—the crowd growing too thick to make out his face among them. A few US Army uniforms were in the fray—flyboys on leave, no doubt, though none Amelia recognized as Wyatt's familiar build.

She trekked with the villagers through the church graveyard.

How could this happen? An air raid so early in the day? That only occurred in London. Or Norwich. And a few other fateful ports early in the war. But not as far off the beaten path as the East Suffolk countryside. Even if there was a base nearby, Framlingham was no prize of a target. Not like Westminster or Buckingham Palace might have been. And certainly not a thought to happen now that they'd come so far, with wits that had brought them within distance of beating the Nazis at their own devilish game.

The Reverend Canon May stood with the church doors flung open, ushering the townspeople through the arched wood frames as he watched the sky beyond the trees and the sirens continued the urgency of their warning wails.

Amelia ran in with them, block heels feeling loaded with lead as she climbed the stone steps into the lofty nave, following the backs of those in front of her. Which way was fastest to reach the underground?

If only they'd had time.

The walls cracked as though they were made of ice.

Stones flew as a bomb blasted, splintering the air with shards of stained glass that pummeled the central aisle like rainbow rain.

Amelia tumbled down to the ground, her knees hitting stone with a fierce slap that shot white-hot pain through her limbs. She crawled on all fours, glass inflicting tiny stinging cuts to her palms and knees with each desperate advance. A gentleman in a tweed suit and cracked spectacles ushered women to safety in front of him, moving her through a row of polished wood pews. And what must have been seconds felt an eternity of coughing and moving past debris that had crumbled in piles around them until she reached the nave's wing.

Silence drowned out the sirens' mournful wails as Amelia hurried to curl up in the corner, under the shadow of the great Thamar organ. Townspeople followed. Some she knew. Others she did not. Packed in a tight sea of bodies with hands and arms covering heads.

The organ echoed resonant tones and eerie whistles as the walls shook again. None cried out, even when another blast enveloped them—this one closer, taking down the wall behind the altar. A few strong voices—perhaps the canon or servicemen from the pub—worked to calm the people. And they were calm. They were Englishmen and Englishwomen, after all. And they'd withstood five years of death and destruction. What was one more bomb blast for a people who could stiffen their upper lip at the worst an enemy could chuck their way?

Despite soothing voices and a stone slab floor that felt solid as a rock beneath her, the moments of Amelia's worst remembrance came flooding back. Crippling in a wave of tears she didn't choose. Couldn't anticipate. And was powerless to stop.

It was 1939 again.

The library's Palladian window shattered over her head, dumping glass in her hair . . . her mouth . . . and cutting into her body like razor-sharp shrapnel. All she heard was the whistle—a scant second of terror before the library wall crashed down around her. Then came the eerie silence. The sense that she'd bumped into things and tumbled down but didn't know how or why. And black smoke from the fire choked every breath she dared try to take. She drifted through a sea of blackness until arms plucked her out of it, and she saw Arthur's face hovering like a halo of light in the storm.

And then . . . pain.

She'd doubled over, crying out as the ferocity of it nearly sawed her in two.

That was the end of life as they'd known it before the war reached out to claw them. And all Amelia could do some five years later, as bombs searched the earth to consume her once again, was hug a honey jar to her chest, cry, and pray.

She cried for Arthur. For the unborn future they'd lost that day. For everything that had slipped from her when he'd enlisted as an RAF pilot and took to the sky out of blind, driving rage. But he'd never come home. Even after all the time that had passed, it felt fresh as the day the War Department telegram arrived.

Everything had changed, but somehow she was thrust into the same nightmare once again.

How could she tell Wyatt the truth? When the war was over, her pain wouldn't end when plane engines fell silent and children were packed on trains to go home. If they wanted any future together, she couldn't give him what he'd lost. They could never be a family unless he'd be content with a pile of books and a party of two to read them.

Sobs racked Amelia as she pressed her cheek to the cold stone floor.

God . . . where are You?

Amelia all but tossed her bicycle on the garden path and blasted through the Anderson shelter doors, immediately counting heads. She called out names. Pressed fingertips to little crowns, desperate for the feeling of silky hair beneath her palms, relief bouncing back each time a voice returned in answer.

"Liesel?" No reply. She tried again, calling out, "Liesel—answer me! And Luca?"

The Anderson walls echoed with her shouts, the children sitting in an evading silence as sunlight streamed through the open doors and Mrs. Jenkins stood guard over them.

"We hadn't time, milady." She wrung her hands over the kitchen apron still tied at her waist. "Not to check the manor. Nor the out-buildings."

"But the officers—hadn't they a plan for things like this?"

"The officers about weren't but a few. It's the first light day of spring and they ventured into town. Those who were here helped as best they could to get the wee ones in first. They bid me to stay on while they went back out." Mrs. Jenkins stared back, eyes wide. Lip quivering like she'd spent a night outside in winter. "Luca is missing."

"No . . ." Amelia's insides clawed with the beast of panic, though for the rest of the children's sake she fought it. "What happened?"

"The sirens started in the midst of morning lessons. We rushed the children out—just as Captain Stevens had instructed. But no Luca. And no time. We *saw* them, milady. The planes in the sky." Mrs. Jenkins sobbed into a handkerchief embroidered with pansies on the edge. "And heard their whistles cutting through the fields."

The meadow at Parham Hill was wide open—of course they'd seen them. How could they not? By the time the planes had reached town, it would have been too late. And as Amelia had run across Bridge Street, the terror overhead blocked by the bower of trees with spring blossoms, the children would have had a perfect view of great black death birds winging their way to the gardens.

Amelia shuddered, her heart nearly breaking with empathy for what innocent eyes had seen—the dragon of death chasing them from London to the perceived safety of a countryside manor years ago, yet finding them there once more.

It was too much.

"Liesel refused to stay, even as bombs fell out in the fields. She went about looking for Luca, with Darly—they fled across the meadow together. Several of the officers went out too, milady, but we've not seen hide nor hair of them since this all began."

"And Wyatt?"

"No sign of Captain Stevens, milady."

"Right." Amelia exhaled, instinct kicking in. "Stay here! All of you."

If she was right—and her gut told her she knew exactly where Luca had gone—the path to the cottage was all that separated her from the boy. As was his way, he'd have clutched his journal, with pencil in hand, and through the waves of sirens would have documented the date and time and ferocity of the blasts in his own little ledger.

Or because he cared for Mr. Arthur's memory nearly as much as she, Amelia had to consider he might have run to the cottage for another reason—to keep a watchful eye on the prized painting that had hung on the wall of Arthur's private library since the day of the library bombing.

No matter the reasons, Amelia fled back into the sunshine at a run.

Feet pounded the path of fresh earth beneath her in a cadence that matched the fervent dance of the heart slamming in her chest. Breathing in and out, running over the rise, trying not to turn an ankle in block heels. She slowed at the telltale horror of smoke in a line of wispy black that rose above the trees.

Bodies—two?—emerged from the trees. Walking slowly. Too slow to be running from trouble, they seemed resigned to a sluggish trek back to the manor.

Amelia's breath locked up in her lungs as Wyatt cut a line down the path with a soot-covered bundle in his arms. A tear-streaked Liesel cradled a book, holding Luca's hand and fumbling her footing every few steps at their side. Luca's mop of curls rested against the crook of Wyatt's neck.

"Wyatt!"

Run.

"What's happened?"

Liesel spotted her and sprinted her way, not stopping until she slammed them to their knees in the dirt and buried her face against Amelia's shoulder. Liesel's tears wet the collar of her blouse as she wrapped an arm around her shoulders.

Amelia held her away, cupping Liesel's face in her palms, seeing that whatever happened had covered her, too, with a film of soot, and tracks of tears had run right through it. "Are you hurt, darling?"

Liesel shook her head, but no words left her quivering lips.

"Answer me . . . Please." Amelia brushed the matted brown hair back from the girl's brow, checking her over, making sure she was whole. But Liesel collapsed again with her face buried in the cable weave of Amelia's cardigan, breaking apart against her.

There was nothing to do but look to Wyatt and pray the limp bundle in his arms was not who and what she feared. "Wyatt?"

"It's alright, Amelia." He patted the back of Luca's head, prompting him to raise his head. "We found him."

If war made men out of boys, it made warriors out of women.

Amelia took Luca in her arms as if his flesh and blood were hers, or as if she shared him in some way with the parents he mightn't even remember. Every moment of the last five years came back in a torrent. Watching him grow . . . losing teeth and stretching in height . . . learning English . . . reading his books and hiding away in a beekeeper's cottage like they had their own secret world that the war couldn't touch.

But it could. And did.

And war ravaged her now, demanding her arms cling tighter than they ever had before.

"You're alright, my darlings," she whispered against Luca's ear, holding so tight, his little heartbeat thundering against hers. Amelia wrapped her arm around Liesel's shoulders, squeezing the three of them together. "See? You're just fine. We'll get you cleaned up, spick-and-span. Just like new, *ja*?"

She winked at them—German their little secret—then reached past the children, desperate in gratitude, and held out her hand until Wyatt took it. He squeezed her fingertips but let go, instead bringing his hand up to wipe something from her cheek. It must have been blood because his brow tipped down with the familiar deep crease as he looked her over.

"You're hurt?"

"No," she breathed out, pressing her face into his palm, loving the feel of warmth and life in it. "No. Bombs fell in town too, but . . . I'm well."

Wyatt pressed against the three of them, his arms enveloping, his lips pressing a hard kiss to Amelia's brow over the children. He was affected too—dirt-smudged uniform, hat lost somewhere along the way, and the ghost of his burns shielded over by the same soot that covered the children. But it was more.

There was a shock about him—even a tremble in his embrace.

"How can I ever thank you?" she whispered as she gazed into his eyes, but he seemed to look through her. "Wyatt?"

Was this what it was like to pull crew members from flaming wreckage? She'd never get used to it, as long as she lived, the carnage of bomb blasts and the search for loved ones beneath piles of rubble. It had happened to Arthur at Parham Hill, when he'd had to pull her out. And now, whatever it was that caused the smoke curls in the sky, they'd lived.

Wyatt had saved them.

Amelia squeezed his hand, trying to draw him back to her. He hesitated, like he'd lost his voice and needed a slap in the face to find it.

"You were caught in town?" he asked again. "What happened?"

She nodded. "Yes. German fighters. They came in past the air-fields. Dropped their load on the way, then one pointed his nose at the church and let the engine do the rest. The wreck took out the entire altar at St. Michaels. I don't know how many might have been killed . . . I couldn't stay. But I pray none. Buildings were bombed out—shells of brick and stone remaining right across the street. The bookshop is gone—*gone*, Wyatt. Singed paper floated down from the sky like some ghostly ticker-tape parade. I've never seen anything like it. And all I could do was get back here. To you."

"Are you sure you're not hurt, love?" He examined her again, his thumb lingering over the tip of her shirt collar. "You're shaking. And blood has stained your blouse."

"No harm done. I'm just relieved to see you all in one piece. You weren't caught in it, were you?"

Wyatt stilled her hand and pressed his lips to the curl of her fingertips, terrifying her with the tears that gathered in his eyes. But he didn't shake his head. Didn't deny what she knew deep down. Where there was smoke, fire ate a meal. And if there was fire burning up the willows beyond the path, there was little doubt in her question of it.

"The cottage, Amelia . . ."

Be brave. Buck up. Take it.

"So the cottage is gone, is it?"

"Not gone. The men are putting out the flames. But I'm so sorry." He stopped, emotion thicker than the smoke and ash heating the air around them. "Sweetheart—Darly's dead."

TWENTY-SEVEN

JUNE 9, 1843
DRURY LANE
LONDON, ENGLAND

London had begun to cry a dreary, steady rain.

Elizabeth imagined the front steps of the Theatre Royal swarmed over by patrons on a high summer night—ladies dripping in their velvet and diamonds, bare shoulders hiding under demure wraps, and gentlemen preening in their starched and stuffed white-tie dress. A peculiar thing to arrive now: this time instead of tiptoeing her way through a stage door to a back hall teeming with props, they rode straight to the grand front doors on a rain-soaked street clouded under gray.

Keaton exited the coach under the front portico and reached for Elizabeth's hand. As she took it to step down onto the sidewalk, they might have looked the noble pair—a contented couple heading into the theater for some sort of elegant business or to purchase tickets for a night show, instead of what they actually were—a couple who couldn't claim the delights of the theater were even on their list of present concerns.

His was a swift and purposeful march inside, adding a courteous, "This way," as he led Elizabeth through the front entry. Its marble floor and grand staircase were shrouded in shadows that would linger until the gaslights were lit one by one, burning bright for the shows that evening. The building appeared to have slept through morning—the gentle sway of wind and smattering of rain against the windows and chugging of carriages that breezed by outside making the interior seem like a lost world. And though the corridor of offices might have been hidden from view to the average theatergoer, Keaton knew his way behind the curtained alcove and marched off in that direction like a shot, his bootfalls echoing loud against the groin vaults in the ceiling.

"Churchill!" The office lay dark and still behind the frosted glass door. Keaton knocked but turned the knob anyway, not waiting for an invitation to enter.

Empty.

The open window from days prior had been shuttered and curtains drawn tight with gold cords dangling at the sides. Stacks of loose papers and ledger books had been left in a tower upon the corner of the desk, piled high in some semblance of order as it was when Elizabeth had last been there. A map of the country hung on the wall—she'd not noticed it before—with show advertisements pinned to its edges like a great feathered bird composed of paper and ink, and tattooed letters that called out oddities such as *Nicholas Nickleby—Tremendous Hit!* in bold block print.

All lay quiet, the walls and hallway, and even the entry, as if London and its famous bustle in the theater district had vanished into the deluge outside. Elizabeth could almost hear her own heartbeat in a wild cadence against the stillness.

"He had to have known this was coming, sooner or later." Keaton sighed, shaking his head, hands anchored at his waist as he scanned the office.

"You mean Mr. Churchill."

He nodded. "I suspect he'll make plans to avoid the city while you're here. Now that he's seen you, he won't want to take it any further."

"Take what any further?"

It was absurd that Elizabeth should wonder if she should add, "Who am I?" in response to his statement. Who was she but an earl's daughter from Yorkshire, a lowly sketch artist forgotten these last ten years? And now the past felt closer than ever, the sidewalk in Piccadilly running over in her mind like the snow had just fallen around them yesterday.

"Why would Mr. Churchill leave the city because of me? I'm a complete stranger."

"You may be strangers in practice, Elizabeth, but there is more to it than that. I couldn't care whether Churchill wishes to reveal this or not—it's a decision that's already been made by your coming here. As you've managed to unravel much of this yourself, I won't stop you from knowing. You have every right to be here."

The gasp of a match sparking to life drew Elizabeth's attention, and she smelled the flame he used to light the oil lamp on the desk. Keaton replaced the glass hurricane and tossed the dead match in the dish on the desktop, then moved about the room like he knew exactly what he sought and had an idea about where to find it.

He thumbed through the ledger books for a brief moment. Pulled books from the shelves and fanned the pages of a few, as if expecting something to fly free from the bindings. He turned, spying the advertisements pinned to the map on the wall, and stalked to them.

"What are you looking for?"

"One of these." Keaton pulled on an advertisement until the pin ripped a trail through the top of the paper and gave it up to his hand. "It's dated, but I knew one of them would still be here."

He stepped over to her so the advertisement was cast in the glow of the lamp's light. It flickered against bold typeface promoting an opening night performance of *The Christening*: the advertisement boasted "from Dickens's 'The Bloomsbury Christening.'" It was dated 13 October 1834—almost one year after her father's death.

It wasn't the play itself that had any bearing on the situation but the portrait of one of the lead actors. The man's visage was sketched, much like the image of Keaton she'd captured so many years ago, but this image stared back as if she'd seen it before. A strong jaw. Elegant brow. Similar cut to the hair. And though his eyes didn't boast the rarity of Keaton's, they did pierce the viewer with an uncommon impetuousness so that had it been hung as a poster on the street, the portrait certainly would have beckoned passersby to halt in their tracks.

His presence was regal—almost royal—and far too familiar.

"Who is he?"

"Thomas Whittle—the man whose name you asked after when first you walked through this door." He pointed to the tiny typeface in the cast credit list. "You'll recognize him among the list of billed cast for this play, and any number of others in London—at the Adelphi and here at the Theatre Royal, until 1834."

Elizabeth looked up at him, his eyes open and exposed before her.

"Few knew Thomas Whittle was his stage name. A young gentleman whose interest in theater would have been quite unacceptable for his station. It was to keep his name and title secret. But he was known to me as Fenton James—my elder brother."

"Your brother," she breathed out, running a fingertip over the familiarity of the profile—so evidently akin to Keaton now at a second glance. How could she have missed it? "Yet you inherited your father's title and the estate at Parham Hill. Why? Unless . . ."

Keaton took the advertisement from her slowly and laid it on the desk as if he were done with reliving it.

"You mean why does a man inherit unless the heir apparent is out of the equation? My brother was killed in a riding accident. Not a year after your world was torn apart, mine was upended as well. And the younger James brother who'd never considered himself a grand anything was thrust into a future that never should have been. You sought a dead man, Elizabeth. A man who cannot tell any tales about what occurred that night outside the tea shop, any more than I wish to hurt you by reopening old wounds."

Elizabeth crossed the space of a few steps between them, no longer afraid of what those eyes made him or who he was underneath a gentleman's exterior. That image dissolved as if the sketch from ten years before had been set aflame. All she wanted was answers. Whatever he could offer, it had to be better than wondering a second longer.

Even the truth—whatever it was—she needed it more than breathing.

"Hurt me if you must. Just help me to understand," Elizabeth whispered, looking up at him, watching the flickering lamplight dance against his shirt collar and flutter in lines across his face. "You said you'd tell me if I asked. Well, I'm standing before you now. Asking. I cannot believe it was you who pulled the trigger that night, no matter how my memory tries to sway me . . ."

She swallowed hard, her fingers aching to reach for him instead of twisting into knots in front of her. "I've come to know *you*, Keaton James. I have seen who you are. And I know you cannot now be what I once thought. My innermost will not allow my heart to believe it."

Keaton wouldn't meet her eyes. He stared down at his boots on a deep inhale, his jaw battling with an unconscious flex.

"You thought me a beast that night. Watching from the carriage as I stood by the streetlamp, waiting. Elizabeth, I've lived these last years as a monster in your eyes. There is no reclamation from that."

"There is no monster in you," she whispered, but this time she reached out a hand and ghosted her fingertips along the jaw that battled so with whatever he refused to say. She left them there, holding him with her touch until he finally looked back in her eyes. "If you care for me at all, please—do not leave me in this senseless oblivion any longer."

Her words must have struck in a way that arrested him. Keaton caught her hand, warming the back of her fingertips with his palm. There was no dining table between them now. No silent coach rides, forced marriage contracts, or chance meetings across a meadow. Either one of them could have walked out of the office, leaving the other behind.

But they stood together. A single flame cutting the darkness all around. Hands lowered but fingers still entwined. The truth-battle raging between them as he leaned down, as if debating whether he could—or should—press his forehead to hers, brush his lips against her own.

"I wouldn't have . . ."

"Wouldn't have what?" Elizabeth asked, so close she could have run her arms up to his collar, slipped them around his neck—so close she could almost feel the pulse of his lips against hers.

"I wouldn't have kept anything from you if your father hadn't made me vow it. Please know that. Even now it feels like a betrayal to have brought you here. But my conscience cannot keep you in the dark any longer."

She backed up, steps that felt like a chasm to cross in an eternity of breaths, the bookshelf and her skirt meeting in a fluster of misaligned half steps.

"You knew my father then."

Keaton looked up, eyes sharp though finding her through the darkness. "Not well, but yes. Fenton and he were business associates."

"What kind of business—at the mill?"

"No. That was a business venture all his own. But you said he took you there when you were young, to the textile mill in Manchester?"

"He did. On many occasions."

"And what do you remember?"

What on earth did the mill have to do with a street corner in front of a tea shop? Elizabeth shook her head, untangling memories she hadn't visited in so long.

"I don't know . . . The operations? I was to engage in learning the mill owner's trade. I'd one day have a husband, after all, and what I brought to the marriage must be understood."

"There must be more than that or you'd not have mentioned it before."

"The lack of real attention given to learning the trade was a bit of a secret. Pa-pa took me along and looked the other way as I indulged my fancy for sketching the doldrums of the poor worker's lot in life. How completely imperious that neither one of us saw the reality behind what we were doing—he employing workers in near-scandalous conditions and I moved about, fancying myself clever for sketching the plight of the downtrodden. But I never helped them. Not once.

"I look back now to the memory of children scurrying under the machinery, trying not to get eaten by the grinding of metal tines that chased their feet and ankles. The men and women . . . They worked until they were near ragged with exhaustion and could barely carry themselves home at the end of a day. That is the legacy I now see. I may have been surviving in my own grief these ten years, but they had long before."

Elizabeth shuddered, knowing she'd changed due to her own years of reduced circumstances. How arrogant. How cold and unfeeling and plagued by apathy she'd been. As if an artist's job was to put on a grand performance with the skill of the eye and hand but never care what heart beat beneath the surface of the subject in the picture.

"So you recall children working in the mill up until the earl's death—even in 1833?"

"I believe so. Why?"

"I regret to tell you, but your father was in very dire financial circumstances at the time of his death. In part because of the child labor he attempted to keep secret, but also because of the conditions in which he'd employed them."

"You are certain of this."

The layers had begun to peel back. Causing pain in remembrance. With the words he spoke, with every breath and open glance, it seemed the false memory of Elizabeth's childhood chipped away and her father became more and more distant. The smile on his lips, the care in his voice, even the stately way he held his shoulders when he walked—all were in jeopardy of falling apart.

Summoning bravery from whence she didn't know, Elizabeth whispered, "Go on."

"Parliament passed a series of laws leading up to August of that year, meant to protect workers—primarily children. The Factory Act made it illegal to employ any younger than age nine. And it severely limited the hours that child workers could labor in a day. Your father's interests were hit hard when it was discovered that he'd not only ignored the laws and continued the harsh working conditions put upon children, but that a five-year-old child had died in his mill as a result, in November of that year."

"A child died . . . I never knew." Elizabeth covered her mouth with shaking fingertips as the image she'd built of her father crumbled into memories of dust. "How could he do this?"

"He was wracked with guilt over it. Truly. And never wished you to know. But as a result of this negligence and the impending investigation, he faced losing all that he owned—the mill and all his properties, including your Yorkshire estate. A series of risky business speculations had come to light and in order to cover the reason behind them, he'd gambled . . . and lost. The only option that awaited him was the poorhouse, prison, or both."

"My father faced prison that last Christmas?"

"Yes. It turns out one of his speculations was with a less-than-reputable character who wanted payment before he was able to render it, and bullets fired from an alley were the price he paid instead."

"And why were you not questioned after the events of that night?"

"Because we both know only *you* saw me there. And you never spoke of it, did you? Not with the one detail that would have given me away."

It felt as if a fist had just been thrust into her midsection. Elizabeth sucked in a deep breath as the toxic mix of disbelief, anger, and fury conflated inside her, swirling so fast she had to grip the side of the desk to prevent herself from losing her balance.

She looked back to Keaton, feeling the wind of accusation shift within her.

"And you were there that night. Why?"

"It's complicated."

"Complicated? To say the least, Keaton. All this time . . . you knew. And you didn't tell me?"

"No matter what may have compelled me to tell you the truth before now, your safety demanded I not. I have wrestled with this for years, Elizabeth. And have always come to the same conclusion. I would injure you more with the truth, and I was not able to do that to you."

"Whatever does that mean?"

Breathing raggedly and feeling as though she were going to boil for the temperature of the blood pumping through her, Elizabeth kept space between them. "What kind of business did you say tied my father to your brother . . . and to you?"

He exhaled. Long and low. Weighted, like the truth had been a great burden, and it tired him even in breathing.

"With Fenton James and one Christopher Churchill, Hamilton Meade shared ownership in the Theatre Royal, Drury Lane."

"This theater. This very one we're standing in? You jest! My father never owned a theater. That would have been my mother's type of fancy, had she not an ill view of the theater crowd. But you say he willingly entered into this partnership?"

Keaton nodded, just once. Her father never showed the least interest in the theater, save for the fact that the streets around Drury Lane were clogged and he'd much rather have avoided them altogether than be trapped in among carriages and horses and breathing in soot from the city's smokestacks any longer than he had to.

"And Mr. Churchill . . . how does he play into all this?"

The shift of weight from the hardwood floor and its creak echoing across the room signaled a presence in the doorway. Elizabeth turned, finding the young Mr. Churchill standing there, a curious bent to his brow, as if he questioned not their intrusion in his private office but something altogether different.

Keaton slowly stepped up next to her, his shoulder brushing hers in a silent show of solidarity.

"What are you doing here, Huxley?" Churchill shifted his glance to Elizabeth. "With her."

"This is Elizabeth Meade, but I suspect you know that already.

And you know that she has the right to hear the truth, Christopher. If anyone does, it's she."

What did it mean that the man wouldn't look at her? Churchill fixed his glare upon Keaton's face with all the ice and stone he seemed to possess, but he still refused to acknowledge her thereafter. That, coupled with everything else, rendered Elizabeth unable to resist speaking the one thought blasting through her mind.

"Who are you?"

Keaton crossed his arms over his chest, waiting as Churchill deliberated from across the room. "Elizabeth wishes to know why her father would financially support this theater—*your* theater. Would you like to tell her, or should I?"

It must have been only a series of ticks on a pocket watch—not nearly enough time for it to feel like the eternity it did. But the silence permeating the room was the only preparation Elizabeth had for what was to come. And the sneaking suspicion that invaded her mind and trickled down to her heart . . .

"Hamilton Meade, Earl of Davies, supported the Theatre Royal out of respect for my late mother," Mr. Churchill whispered. "He did so because he was my father too."

TWENTY-EIGHT

"You said you could trust me." Emory's plea sliced the air without hesitation.

The instant Keira had seen the gold shimmer of Klimt's *Empress* staring back from the crate on the library floor, she'd begun to shut down and to back away, step by crooked step, toward the hall. "What have you done?"

"I'm the same person I was five minutes ago out in that entryway. I brought you in here of my own accord, believing that you meant what you said. You *can* trust me."

"Oh no . . . You can't ask this of me. Not now." She held out a palm in the growing distance between them. "Why would you ask this of me?"

"Keira—"

She blasted him with the first cliché that flooded through her. "Don't you dare say 'It's not what it looks like,' when it absolutely is! It is exactly what it looks like. That is *Empress*, every stroke of paint and square inch of gold that's been missing these four years. A hundred million dollars sitting on the floor . . ."

Feeling her head swim a touch, Keira backed up even farther, bracing her shoulders against the wainscoting that met the library door frame.

"I didn't steal it."

"No? Then who did? It just so happens that the prime suspect, who absolutely swore to me that he had nothing to do with it whatsoever, now happens to have said painting hidden at a country manor?"

"*Empress* or not, I don't even know if it's real. That's why I need your help!"

"My help? Emory—I won't help you. Not with this!"

He stood in the dim light, breathing heavily over their shouting, rain-dampened tee still clinging to him as he stared at her.

No overdue snogging needed to snatch her breath now. Keira stood in the library, wet and cold, waterlogged and pain-struck as rain battered the manor, echoing the broken silence between them. Emory stepped forward a pace, like he desperately wanted to reach for her, but Keira shot back and on a whim pulled her phone from her back pocket.

The threat of dialing she braced like a shield between them.

"How long have I been the fool in this story? From that first day here, or does this plot go all the way back to Dublin? Find a pathetic female with a backstory of heartbreak, lure her from home with the promise of a handful of euros and a few artfully placed promises, then she'll do anything, right?"

"Never, Keira. You're no fool. Not to me. You never could be that to me."

"But why, after all this time—after you dared turn into a completely incredible human being—have I been thrust into another nightmare I absolutely cannot see my way out of? Have you any idea what choice you put before me?" She raised the phone level with her shoulder, holding it out. "You make me fall for you and then this? You leave me no option."

Emory stopped. Exhaled, like he'd held the same desperate thought that she'd just spoken.

"It's not like that. Please, Keira. Just listen? I found the painting in the attic. Looking for the ones to fit the fade marks on the wall-paper in this library. It took some time with the sheer size of this place, but Ben and Eli and I have been going over every space with a fine-tooth comb. And this morning I found it. I was going to tell you. Then all that happened at the church and we came back here and . . ."

Don't you say it . . .

He rubbed the heel of his palm against his forehead, swiping wet hair back from his brow. "There are eight more crates up there, but older than this one. I believe they're what we've been search-ing for."

"Don't lie to me."

"I would never lie to you. Keira—I care too much to do that to you."

His voice shook, trembling behind the words in a way she'd never expected. Not from the assured non–art thief he'd sworn he was not. And all the while, she'd dared dream of something beauti-ful—an idiotic farce about breathing life back into a broken-down cottage.

Why had it all seemed so perfect?

"I could go to jail for this, Emory. We all could. Ben. Eli. Carter and M. J. How could you do this to them? Don't you care about that at all?" She cried, the tears refusing to be put off an instant longer, and the shouts feeling so good to pummel him with. "I don't do this. I actually called my family—my sister-in-law, the one I trust, and told her I'd met someone special this time. He was different . . .

Why did you have to make me love you? Why couldn't you just leave me be? You manipulated this whole thing, concocted a story about the cottage, about Victoria and this library, all to draw me in. How dare you—"

The sound of the front doors slamming shut and the echo of footsteps trailing in the entry shocked them both. They were no longer alone.

"Boss?" The Irish lilt called down the hall. "Ye there?"

M. J.

Keira's bottom lip trembled as her footsteps drew closer. She wrinkled her forehead, the searing pain in her chest triggering her decision to click the screen and dial the phone.

"Em?"

And Carter too.

They were back—their famous viscount reappearing, just in time for the grand show.

Keira had dropped the number to the Suffolk Constabulary into her phone some time back. It was in a professional's arsenal of tricks when working with high-priced art to connect with the local authorities at the start of a commission. Who knew what could happen, after all?

"Yes. I need to report a crime." She nearly choked over the words when the Woodbridge dispatch answered the line.

Please don't do this, Emory mouthed as M. J. and Carter swept into the room.

Their viscount stopped in his tracks, feet iced to the hardwood. Had he and M. J. any smiles before that instant, they'd faded to dumbfounded glances by the time they caught up with Keira on her phone and Emory standing guard over the stolen painting, hands braced at his hips, eyes closed as he hung his head.

"Yes. This is Keira Foley and I'm a historian contracted at Parham Hill Estate. I need to report a theft and possible receipt of stolen goods," she said, then, turning to a curiously despondent Carter, added, "Yes. The estate owner is here. Carter Wilmont, Viscount of Huxley. He can corroborate what's happened."

M. J.'s eyes were about to pop from her face. Carter wore a shade of green that said his insides were churning turbulent as ever. And Emory, in what should have been anger or vehemence against her righteous indignation, instead looked at Keira with eyes that were open and unashamed, almost as if he were proud of her somehow for doing the right thing but ever so sorry it had to impact him.

The buzz of the dispatcher's voice stirred in Keira's ear, drawing her back to the moment.

"Yes. The nature of the crime? Uh . . ." She stared back at Emory, her heart breaking at the fact he wasn't even angry. "It seems a painting stolen from a Viennese gallery four years ago has turned up here in East Suffolk. I need someone to come and take receipt of it immediately."

How a morning of coffee and good news at the pub could implode so, Keira couldn't comprehend. Nor could she have imagined the Suffolk Constabulary would be so on point in their response to her call.

The day ended late—with questions of the entire team and paintings being carried off in the backs of police vans. Dear Evelyn Addams must have been having a field day with the tabloid-worthy exploits of the viscount now. But Keira couldn't worry about it. Couldn't do anything, really, but toss clothes in a suitcase in between tears and book the next flight for Dublin.

The last memory she'd have of Parham Hill was not another glorious painted sky from a Framlingham sunrise. Instead, she was forced to watch the man she loved be led away in handcuffs, shock-ingly, with their employer in tow. The back of a police car swallowed Emory Scott into the English countryside, and with his absence, her life fell apart all over again.

TWENTY-NINE

A lost kingfisher darted through the cottage study and landed upon the fireplace mantel, fluffing its bright blue and orange plumage indoors instead of where it should have been, chirping about the seashore.

Breezes flowed through the willows that had survived the fire, and tiny dickey birds boldly flitted through the bombed-out parlor like they hadn't a fear to play where they chose. Amelia sat in a wing-back by the small study fireplace, watching imaginary embers burn against the fireplace tiles embossed with Arthur's *A. W.* initials—a custom add in both the study and the Parham Hill library, a Christmas gift in their first year. She sat quietly in the melding of the outside world with the inside, absently running her fingertips over the black band affixed to her left arm.

All that was left untouched was the study. Arthur's study, in a cottage that had been built more than a century before—the then viscount building a space for the young artist he'd hoped to take as a bride. Arthur had always talked of the legacy at Parham Hill. He was quite proud of the little beekeeper's cottage and the painting that had brought a man and a woman together—the painting that they'd moved after the bombing of the grand library in 1939 to this small, secluded place in the world.

Secluded so the image would be safe. And secure. And untouched by war.

Amelia stared at the painting, hanging so regal above the mantel, the beautiful image of a queen having no idea she'd been spared in the same space that a flesh-and-blood man had not. Victoria sat in repose against a chaise of crimson, hair unbound in a rich chocolate coil over her pale shoulder, with a look of longing so intense it swept over the entire room. Walls of an ink gray and wooden shelves painted a slightly lighter hue made Victoria's colors pop and her eyes the focal point of seemingly every angle.

Footsteps approached. Amelia must have stayed too long again. The children would wonder, no doubt.

"I'm in here," Amelia called out, and stood as if to hide the fact that she'd fallen into a chair and allowed herself to fall deeper into memories at the same time. She began stacking the books she planned to move back to the manor library.

Wyatt followed her voice, meeting her from an anchored lean against the doorjamb. With no hat. Hair combed tight. In the same tie tucked into the placket of the dress uniform shirt he'd worn that morning. He slipped his hands into the pockets of his trousers and waited. "What are you doing?"

"Nothing. Just picking through. Deciding what to take back to the manor." She puttered, stacking and restacking books on the desk with no real purpose other than to keep her hands busy. Then a thought struck. "The children . . . are they alright?"

He nodded. "You don't have to do this today, you know."

Today. Of course she didn't. Who went straight from a funeral to tidying shelves?

Amelia looked down at her dress, a sad navy wool weave with covered buttons down the front and cuffs that spread in a gentle ruffle at the wrists—the hopelessly mournful frock she'd worn to Arthur's funeral, to Florence Bertram's funeral two days prior, and to their beloved uncle's funeral just that morning as well.

"I know. But we have to at some point, don't we?"

In her side vision she saw Wyatt glance around the study, scanning the layout of shelves and books, the fireplace that remained cold, and finally settling on the regal image of the queen staring out at them from above it.

Amelia turned, not wishing to meet Victoria's longing again. She lined book spines in a happy little meaningless row upon the desk instead.

"That's the painting you told me about?"

"Yes. Arthur's favorite," she whispered without turning back to him.

"And you said the nineteenth-century viscount who built this cottage and brought honey making to your estate did it for a woman he'd fallen in love with. That she was a gifted portrait maker and he'd hung this painting in his private study not because it was the image of a queen but because his love had painted it. Did I remember it all?"

It was true but felt foreign to have the story Arthur had always had such pride in be told back to her in Wyatt's voice. "Is love as simple as all that?" she wondered aloud.

"Not simple at all." He moved from his spot leaning against the doorjamb, the floor creaking its protest as he took slow steps into the room. "Tell me about Arthur. How he brought you to the cottage."

Amelia looked up, the books unable to hold her attention, even if it was manufactured. He'd crossed the space between them, birds still chirping in the background as he walked up to her side and stopped, placing a hand over the one she'd left on the books.

"You want to know how I came to be here?"

"I want to know your story. I want to know why you're here in a bombed-out cottage after you just buried your husband's uncle—a man who was as much a father to you as any could have been. I want to know how I can help," he whispered, offering a gentle squeeze of his palm against hers. "Most of all, Amelia Woods, I want to know *you*."

Amelia nodded, and though tears threatened to make an appearance, she was still able to smile.

"How I came to Parham Hill? It was an accident, really. A complete folly that I'm even standing here. It was the books for me too," she said, still smiling, liking the feeling of a fond memory able to sweep away the cobwebs of pain. "Can you believe that? This paper and ink and beautiful words all wrapped in a binding . . . I never would have come here if not for the magic of that library. I worked in a bookshop in Westminster in '37. It was an ordinary day. Rumors of war swirled everywhere, but I like to believe it was an inconsequential autumn morning that I broke my heel just as I was hurrying across Victoria Street. Down I went, and the books I'd been balancing spilled over the pavement. I thought I would get flattened by an oncoming auto, but it seemed the worst kind of death, leaving those stories to a sad fate in the gutter."

"And what happened?"

"Arthur showed up out of nowhere. Sprinted through traffic. Even forced a taxi to go around us. And instead of scolding me or whisking us off and leaving the wretched books behind, he saw in an instant how important they were to me. So he helped. Without a word, he picked up every one, dusted off the covers," she said, and ghosted her hand over the cover of *A Tale of Two Cities*, mimicking the memory.

"And he carried the stack to the curb with me. Then we laughed when we were safe, I think out of the sheer madness of it all. I could have simply left them and purchased the same titles again. Would have been glad to do it. But somehow he understood me and it didn't seem nonsensical at all. I tried to repair the damage of what I must have looked like—mad hair and knees scraped like a hapless schoolgirl. I was a mess. But he didn't seem to notice that."

Amelia pictured Arthur's smart suit and striped mustard tie. So young. And alive. And the way he'd moved quickly to retrieve the books but still peeked at the titles of a few, as if he just couldn't help himself for wanting to know what made her literary heart tick. He raised his eyebrows once or twice, as if intrigued by her eclectic taste. And handed the books back to her, so that his fingertips just grazed hers when the bindings switched owners.

"You know? We left the shoe, burgundy leather, dead in the middle of the street. It didn't matter. I like to think it sat there until a good snow in December and was banished into the sewer thereafter. But the books . . ." Amelia shook her head. Looked down. Patted the spines like they were old friends. "We saved them together, and I walked lopsided all the way to the coffeehouse, where we sat and drank three cups in a row and fell in love over a handful of words. One faulty shoe, one tripped step, and here I am, lady of an estate and keeper of his past long after he's gone."

"And now you're here, talking to me, inviting me into the story too."

"Yes," she whispered. "I suppose I am."

Amelia searched the room, the piles of books, the charming layer of dust. The scent of sweet English violets perfuming the air from the gardens outside. And then, Victoria. The painting had always been what she'd safeguarded. In a way, keeping his books close and his portrait safe was supposed to keep Arthur with her. But keeping a tight grasp on precious things . . . it was no guarantee of a story's survival.

A musty old swiss-cheese sweater hung over a chair in the library. The turtle soup tin and pipe had no owner, and a liquid-satin gown that now felt like a kind of treasure hung in Amelia's wardrobe. Remembering the dress, she felt a stab of pain at the reason she now wore the black band on her arm—another treasured one was gone from this life.

"And my story of New York. And flying thirty thousand feet above our heads only to feel more freedom in a library than I do in the boundless sky. What had to happen to bring me here, right now, to this exact spot in a cottage with you?"

"Life is a tapestry of mischance and fate then, is it? I don't want to believe that."

Wyatt shook his head. "Not mischance, Amelia. And the only fate I know is that God knew my story had to be tied to yours."

It was unexpected—a veiled declaration of love. But Amelia wasn't sure the forbearance she read in him was any less beautiful for the timing. In that moment it was what she needed most: under-standing. It spoke of romance and depth of feeling like few things ever could. A simple "I love you" could get tossed around by eager flyboys at a USO dance. But real, abiding empathy? Never. It was too precious.

"I have a gift for you." Wyatt pulled a small card-stock envelope from his pocket scrawled with *Amelia* in his familiar block print on the front. "Go ahead. Open it."

She ran her index finger under the envelope seal. Inside was the note she'd left at the hospital, the familiar cursive *Yes* penned in her own hand, telling him a thousand futures might be possible if she could imagine caring for someone again. If she could leap and do it with him.

Beneath her word was his invitation to a future that wove them together:

Me too.

Yours,
Wyatt

They'd not spoken of the note since the first day she'd visited him at the base hospital. Maybe Wyatt didn't know it was there until he'd looked at the photo of his beloved Abby and Susan once more. Amelia imagined her note falling from the binding of his Bible, fluttering to the concrete floor like a wish, making him think they could move on together, that they could forget this terrible nightmare that was war and build a family from the ground up.

But in the weeks since, she hadn't the bravery to tell him what it was—that the impulsive whim to pen a note was one she wished she could take back. Amelia stared at the penned words, tears stinging like exposed skin in the bitter cold of winter.

"As you can see, there's a reason why I stick to reading and publish books other people write," he whispered, and how heartbreaking that she could hear the genuine smile and the hope alive in his voice. "But if I ask a question I can't keep in any longer, will you give me an answer?"

"Wyatt . . . I won't do this to you."

"Do what? Imagine some healing can come from this blasted war?" The note fell from Amelia's hands when he reached for her, slipped his palms to the sides of her face in a soft bid for her eyes to meet his. "I don't care what happens up there as long as I know you'll be waiting on the ground when I touch wheels to the runway for the last time. This isn't about a library or a painting, or even a story we're keeping alive in this place . . . It's about daring to believe there's something left in this busted-up world. Isn't it worth it to try?"

"I can never give you what you've lost."

"I'm not asking you to replace anyone." His gaze clouded and his hands softened, drifting to her jaw like one more word might have them drop to his sides. "What do you mean, you can never give me what I've lost?"

Amelia clamped her eyes shut, shame flooding her insides.

Never had she said the words out loud. Never heard them spoken, save for when the doctor had pulled a chair to the side of her bed in the aftermath of a library wall in pieces, and their world crumbled too. Arthur stared on from the metal footer, a supportive smile on his lips though his eyes were tearing and his fists were balled like he wanted to punch them through the nearest wall.

She'd listened, drinking in the horrible words . . .

"Do you understand what I've said, milady? You can have no children. There was too much damage . . ."

"What we've both lost," Amelia whispered, peeling Wyatt's hands from her. Taking a step back, thinking he wouldn't dare touch her now. "Wyatt, I can never have children."

"Amelia . . ."

"There was a bombing here in '39. It hit the library. It hit *me*."

That truth seemed to find a target in Wyatt's core because he shifted, hands looking lost somehow, like they wanted to be buried back in his trouser pockets but she would pick up on the move as too telling. Had it devastated him? Surely he would wish to have more children. A family. A future, only it couldn't be with her.

Truth, Amelia. Spill it, and then let him go.

"Arthur pulled me out of the rubble in the library. It was only after we knew I would live but that we'd never have children that a flame ignited within him. His family line had been snuffed out and he was driven by a rage I'd never seen before. It drove him to the skies. He signed on with the RAF the next day, and within four months, I was not only childless but a widow with a grand estate, and beehives, and a library I hadn't the first clue how to manage without him. And I've been lost from that day until this."

Tears shouldn't have been so free to fall, not five years later. She should have been stronger than that, to crumble again and again for what might have been.

Amelia stood before Wyatt, the truth let, expecting him to . . . She didn't know.

Birdsong continued then, spring alive and awake in the open-air parlor. She stood before him, watching what looked like shades of indecision melt over his features. He didn't cry; not like she. But he did feel. That was clear. Wyatt nodded, so softly she might have missed it had she blinked. And then he stooped, reaching for the note that had fluttered to the floor, and offered it back.

"You are not childless, my dear, beautiful Amelia." He pressed the paper into her palm with both hands, back side up. "I'm so, so sorry."

She obeyed the silent bid, hands trembling as she read the words penciled on the back:

Jürgen and Lea Schäfer: transferred to Hartheim, Linz, Austria. Died 18 June 1942.

"Westminster came through. Thompson gave me the news at the funeral. He asked me to tell you. To help you tell Liesel and Luca what's happened to their family. And I thought if you knew I wasn't leaving—that I'm in this as long as you want me to be . . ."

A course of anger surged through her, and Amelia crumpled the paper in her palm, then pounded her fist to the desk as tears began their tumble. Wyatt reached for her then, enveloping her, letting her cry with her forehead pressed in the crook of his neck. And she felt sure he cried too because he kept his lips pressed up against her temple for the longest time. Whispering soft words. Prayers, maybe. Nothing and everything.

They'd been her children for nearly seven years.

Seven years.

Never had Amelia wanted to earn a family—not like this. Not with the realization that Luca's little journal would have no one to read his entries. Liesel would keep her little brother in line, mannered and disciplined as their mother wished, but she'd never see the impact it would have as her son grew to become a man.

It was the worst kind of precious tomorrows that would never be.

"How do I tell them? How can I possibly tell them something like this?"

"We'll do it together."

"Together . . ." She breathed out the single word, its promise steadfast and anchored like so few things could be. The cottage stood silently, somehow stilled of birdsong, and Victoria looked on as two broken souls clung to each other for rescue.

"Amelia, I already knew. Darly told me you couldn't have children when I asked him if I could . . . ," Wyatt whispered against her temple. Paused. Breathed deep, his heart thundering beneath the palm she'd pressed to his chest. "I asked for his permission to marry you. He told me you couldn't have a family, not in that way. And I told him I didn't care. That you were my family and I was prepared to do whatever it took to show you that."

She saw no question in his eyes as they searched hers.

"I meant what I said. 'Me too.' Us. Them. All four of us. I'll stay here or we can go to New York. Whatever you choose. But I'm not afraid to dream this war will end soon. When it does, I'll be here with you. And I always keep my promises."

THIRTY

"You are quiet on our last day, little bee. Perhaps too many thoughts buzzing about that head of yours?"

Franz examined his canvas at Elizabeth's side, as if the work in progress could stare back and produce the final image he desired without any effort at all.

Sunshine bled through airy gauze curtains, brightening the sapphire walls of the palace's petite salon and the crimson settee where the queen would sit in the center of the room. Elizabeth thumbed through her pochade box, removing paint tubes one by one to set aside, focusing only on shades of rouge and deep azure and bright ivory instead of being drawn into another of Franz's witty banter sessions.

He was prying and knew it full well.

No secret as to why.

They'd arrived at Buckingham Palace for the series of sittings with neither her ma-ma nor her fiancé in tow, and Elizabeth hadn't a word to relay about any of it. The palace was breathtakingly elegant and refined, with chandeliers dripping crystal. Royal red carpets spread as far as the eye could see. Gold-encrusted walls, mirrors, ceilings—it was every palace fairy tale she'd ever read about as a young girl. Even so, Elizabeth endeavored to remain all business on their last morning with the queen.

Though it was still her first ever commission—which just happened to be for royalty—Elizabeth meant to take the experience fully within her grasp. She opted to inspect her canvas, with the extra step of adding a sketch behind what would be the crimson cushion above the curve of the queen's right shoulder.

"You have no answer?" He refused to be put off.

Sketching, dusting charcoal pencil to canvas, and forming the outlines of a honeybee, Elizabeth ignored the bait. "No, I do not. I prefer to work."

"And what are you sketching before our queen even arrives? The wall?" Franz leaned in, enough that his profile invaded her side vision. Elizabeth noted his tip of the brow when he saw what she was putting to canvas.

"You said all artists have a signature. Well, this can be mine."

"The signature of a bee that no one will ever lay eyes upon? Curiously, we have been admitted to the palace on several occasions now, yet I must assume from your lack of conversation that this is all rather intimidating to you."

"You grievously misjudge me, Mr. Winterhalter. I am not intimidated."

"As clever and unplain as you are then, I wonder if you fear wolves might spring out of the woodwork and devour us at our easels?"

"There is no fear of that," Elizabeth whispered back, then set about moving her easel a touch to absorb a better angle of the natural light. "I am already devoured—inside and out. Shouldn't we now leave it alone?"

The mention of wolves took her back to the library and the remembrance of a conversation from the first night Elizabeth had stepped into Keaton's world. Conversation about marriage. And fortune hunting. And the very world in which she'd been reared now upended in the course of a single day—with a brother she never knew living and working but streets away from where their father had died . . . With her own mother having known all along yet never revealing an ounce of the truth. And with Keaton having retreated to Parham Hill, allowing Elizabeth and her mother the courtesy to stay on in London as long as they wished but with the understanding that she could no longer imagine a marriage between them.

She would not become a viscountess, and her dear ma-ma had gone to bed with smelling salts and a broken heart as her lone companions. And after Elizabeth should paint a queen, what in the world was she to do with the rest of her life?

"That is quite unacceptable." Franz clucked a *tsk-tsk* under his tongue, the notion rejected as he reorganized his brushes around jars of water and turpentine. "The queen shall be here momentarily. But until she is, you work and I will think out loud."

"But I really don't wish to—"

"You sketch. I'll talk." He paused, the one soft rebuke enough to halt her protest. He turned to her, eyes as serious as she'd ever seen them. "Do you know where I met Viscount Huxley?"

I can't do this. Don't want to do this . . .

Elizabeth drank in a deep breath and determined to go on, rounded her pencil along the curve of the bee's wing. "No. I do not, sir."

"It was here, at this very palace." He spread his arms wide, rolled shirtsleeves coming unfurled about his forearms as he laughed in Her Majesty's prim and proper royal salon.

"Here? But how can that be? Keaton never said he'd taken

audience with the queen." Her hand drifted from the canvas until her pencil floated on air.

"*Bitte.* Sketch." Franz motioned for her to continue with a finger point to canvas. "Perhaps we should have asked him. Of all the odd places in the world to discover a friend. I expected Huxley to be one of those pompous wolves I am so gratified to disesteem. It is an odd war, this taste for opulence. I have become accustomed to battling the righteous pretentions of nobility. But Huxley stood out as honorable in a way few men can boast when they enter these gilded halls."

"What do you mean?"

"He was here with other noblemen—a Lord Shaftsbury among them—when a dinner conversation degraded into politics on the plight of the working class. But it was not the men from the House of Commons who earned attention from both Her Majesty and the prince on that night. Huxley spoke of the poorest of London, how the children are set upon in hovels of the filthiest sanitation, water, and housing one can imagine. Huxley believed improvements of industry, economy, and education could benefit them, and he spoke with such eloquence and passion that his voice overpowered his peers in the House of Lords as well.

"It is indeed why our viscount makes regular visits to London, to honor a vow he made to an old business acquaintance of his late brother's—an earl, says he—that he would give back to the poor in any way he could in reparations for a grave mistake the man had once made."

The tirade of revelation rendered Elizabeth dumbfounded and quite unable to sketch at all. She'd turned away from the canvas, listening with every heartbeat in her chest.

"You mean my father, the Earl of Davies."

"Your father, *ja.* And the brother you now know you possess, because Keaton James supported Christopher Churchill these ten years . . . and from afar, he watched over you."

"Me? How could he watch over me?"

"Wolves are wolves all the time, but only great men are compassionate to those who can do absolutely nothing for them in return." As if Franz knew exactly what he was about, his eyes twinkled. "I wonder whether you and I both misjudged the viscount at our first meetings with him, hmm? I think if we were to look deeper than the surface of a man's portrait, we would find the truth we seek has been there all along, layered beneath the paint."

The door opened, cutting the moment short.

Elizabeth did her best to compose herself after such a heart-rending declaration.

Beautiful and young—barely older than Elizabeth herself—Victoria entered with her gathering of attendants close behind. Though standing at five feet tall, she didn't need a crown or precious jewels to present a regal entrance. The queen presided over her salon in a gown of simple design, with white gauze ruffles drifting about her shoulders and the usually tidy knot of chocolate hair unbound so it tumbled in waves across the front of her bodice.

"Mr. Winterhalter." Victoria addressed Franz as he tipped in a courtly and much-practiced bow. "We meet again."

"We do, Your Majesty. And this is an honor, as is every such occasion."

"Are we quite prepared? I'm afraid I cannot contain my jubilance at such an undertaking! How my Albert will be surprised by our 'secret picture.' I have been telling my ladies about your latest masterpiece, so much so they wished to accompany me this morning to meet the artists in person."

She turned her attention to Elizabeth, those light eyes and porcelain skin glowing in the sunlight. "And, Lady Elizabeth, I am most gratified to have seen the progress on your portrait as well. You are quite the young apprentice—a woman who is a skilled portrait maker in her own right, I'd say."

"Thank you, Your Majesty. I'm sure."

"Mr. Winterhalter hasn't insisted upon an invitation for a student before, but I must admit that a break with tradition can have its virtues. Now I fear I shall have quite a task to choose which portrait will go to the prince for his birthday." Victoria settled on the chaise, settling the folds of her gown around her in a pose regal yet unbound by the constraints of her position. "Let us begin our competition, Winterhalter, and discover who the winner shall be."

"Of course, Your Majesty." And then, turning to Elizabeth behind her canvas, he said, "Are we ready?"

Elizabeth blasted him with the most vehement whisper she could. "By all accounts, sir, I should throttle you for the absolute dastardly timing of your chosen revelations. How am I to focus at all with such questions flying through my mind? And with the queen of England sitting just there, breathing the same air as we?"

"Questions are powerful when matched with a brush. Use them to your greatest advantage." Franz gave a slight bow to the queen and a nod to Elizabeth, effectively declaring they were off.

They fell into the artist's rhythm—Elizabeth indolent at first, her heart beating wildly and her hands defiant in their wish to tremble. But soon she fell into a world of discoveries in line and light. Shade, shadow, and rich hues. Victoria sat still, talking with her courtly ladies about the room as Elizabeth captured the scene, softening lines around the queen's locks, dusting the slightest pinch of blush to her cheeks and light to a pert nose. Stroke after stroke she perfected the queen to canvas, until daylight shifted in the room, signaling time had escaped before Elizabeth had even the chance to realize it.

A few more moments and she may be finished.

"Fine work." Franz leaned in on a whisper, tilting his head toward the queen in her setting. "But I ask you before you lay down the brush . . . look deeper. What do you see?"

Elizabeth stilled her hand about the canvas and gazed across the salon.

Azure of the flower on Victoria's bodice . . . deep crimson of the settee at her back . . . the graceful white gauze and unbound hair sweeping across bare shoulders . . . While not the typical posture of a queen, it was no doubt a royal pose.

She'd captured it all, hadn't she?

"The morning is wearing thin, so I might suggest moving the settee closer to the window. I want to get this right."

Franz shook his head. With careful fingers, he eased the brush out of her hand and held it captive in his palm. "This is not about light—you have already mastered that. But if you can, forget that she is a queen for a moment and, instead, paint the woman." His fingertips hovered over Elizabeth's canvas, where Victoria's eyes were set. "What is alive *right here*? How does she wear her heart for all to see?"

Elizabeth swallowed hard, watching the queen who sat before them.

She was royalty. Majesty. Beauty and perfection in a deceptively small package. Victoria ruffled her hair again, smoothing the coil just right over her collarbone, and then looked to a chair across the room. She gazed at it, a simmer of a smile tending her lips as if she'd tumbled away, lost in thought. Perhaps she was able to picture Albert himself was there to receive the secret language of a look passed between lovers. And try as she might, sitting with queenly posture and ladies all round, Victoria could not help but show an intimate display of unbound affection for her Albert, though he was not even in the room.

What she bore in that instant was the stunning natural longing a wife had for her husband—one Elizabeth hadn't considered might ever exist for her until that very moment. The memory of a sidewalk in Piccadilly shifted somewhere within her. The snow and gaslight and view of Keaton's eyes changing with it so that the remembrance faded . . . and was replaced with something new.

Elizabeth's heart thundered in her chest as she considered the real reason he might have been on that street corner. And longing struck without warning, in a deeper place than what she'd expected, so that Elizabeth wished the chair had been filled instead with someone she had come to care for.

Franz exhaled, as if he could read the very thoughts flying through her.

"*Das ist gut.* Now paint it." He smiled, placing the brush back in her fingertips before he returned to the delights of his own canvas. "Only someone who's felt that look could ever hope to capture it. I believe you can. And I wonder who would be in that chair across the room from you, were he given the opportunity?"

JULY 17, 1843
PARHAM HILL ESTATE
FRAMLINGHAM, ENGLAND

Stonemasons had set about a curious task of raising an outbuilding on the estate—a cottage tucked into the tree line, nearly hidden from view. Elizabeth peered through the carriage window as the coach emerged from the grove of willows.

"Stop here, please, driver," she called out, searching through the trees.

The carriage slowed along the ruts of the rock wall–lined road, and she pressed a hand to the crated painting on the coach floor, holding Victoria still against the dusty violet linen of her traveling skirt as the coach drew to a stop.

Burnished stone and leaded glass greeted her at the end of a cobblestone path. Elizabeth stepped out of the carriage and walked toward it as birdsong filtered through the trees. On this day the sky shone a brilliant blue instead of the rainy gray it so often appeared. A moss-green door waited for her. She reached for the latch and it gave easily, the new hinge silent instead of crying out like an aged one.

Inside boasted a parlor. Humble but pleasant with flock wallpaper in cheery yellow and floor-to-ceiling windows, their abundance of natural light welcoming views of the meadow behind. In the corner stood the cottage's lone inhabitants: a pochade box and easel, their gangly limbs creating long shadows to streak across the hardwood floor.

In the silence Elizabeth turned, gazing down the length of a deep hall that led to a study with empty shelves—the oak smell still fresh and clean—its ledges aching for book spines, and a fireplace that longed to be used for the first time. She followed the hearth up to the mantel, and with a deep inhale, she rested her gaze upon the only splash of color about the room.

A heart-stopping portrait . . . *of her.*

Elizabeth removed her bonnet as she walked to it, then released the wide ribbon to allow the ivory satin and straw to dangle from her fingertips. She drew closer, staring back at the mirror image of herself captured in oil paint. She stood in a ballroom of robin's egg–blue walls, in her soft yellow morning dress, an easel at her side and a paintbrush gently angled in her hand. And the telltale script of *Winterhalter* sang out from the bottom corner, signed and dated in the bright titian script that was his hallmark.

Did gentlemen run? Keaton was either unable or uncaring to hide the fact that he arrived quite winded, with his tie missing and shirt haphazard about the neck as he stepped into the light cast by the open door. Their gazes locked with the length of the hall between them, his eyes of stone and a jagged line of gold showing he'd indeed hoped to find her there.

"Elizabeth—you're . . ." A deep breath. "You're back."

"I am." She looked through the window to the coach that lingered on the lane, still sheltered by the protective haven of the willows. "But how did you know?"

"Franz. He stopped me at the front gate, relayed that the dowager countess remains in London but that he'd accompanied her daughter back to Framlingham—in a separate coach, as was proper for a woman of her station. But he said in no uncertain terms before he shoved off to a commission in Paris that I'd be 'zhe grandest fool in all of England if I didn't cut across zhe meadow at all possible speed and meet zhat charming portrait artist before she gets away.' Something to that effect. And I didn't even wait to hear his laughter behind me as I headed in this direction."

"Oh. He said all that, did he?" Elizabeth hoped the presence of her portrait, the pochade box, and the easel meant what she'd dared hope. "What is this place?"

"A beekeeper's cottage." His brow furrowed a shade. "Built so you might feel at home here. So you could have a studio. Your own library. And bees, just like at your father's estate."

"You thought I should wish to feel at home . . . and bees were the best way to accomplish this?"

Not taking himself too seriously at her humor, Keaton bounced back with a smile. "Your sketchbook said as much. I hadn't anything else to go on but a series of drawings of bees and blossoms."

Yes. My sketchbook . . . and your image tucked in the back.

Elizabeth allowed the satin ribbon its freedom, and her hat drifted to the floor as she walked to him. She looked up, his profile not bathed in shadows from a gaslight nor snow crying from a winter sky. This time the sun shone down upon him. And he didn't hide his eyes under the brim of a top hat. He chose to meet her where she stopped, but paces away, his posture revealing an openness to answer her questions.

"And what else did it say, my little book of pictures? I suspect it revealed the image I captured of you on a street corner in Piccadilly one wretched night. But for a reason from which you've never sought to defend yourself. And if I'm right, Keaton James"—she dared to say his name in the softest of tones—"I'd like to know why. Was that why you were there that night, to watch over me? To keep me safe somehow?"

"You know it was."

One truth. One nod. And he didn't hold back.

His arms enveloped her. Those eyes that had always been evil's companion in her memory drifted over her face with warmth, affection . . . and love. And she sank into him, meeting the softness of a kiss as if it had always been that way between them, instead of the enmity of the first time. Lost and somehow at home too.

Keaton pulled back, eyes ardently searching her face. "I couldn't allow a man's family to be threatened. Harmed. Or worse. It so happens I was at the Theatre Royal that night, unsuccessfully attempting to draw a thespian brother back to the reality of duties at his estate. But there was an incident at the theater—men came hunting for your father. As reproach for his debts, they intended the worst. We attempted to find him first, Fenton and I. And even Christopher, at great personal risk were your mother to learn of his involvement. Please know we tried to warn your father. I knew I might be recognized, but—"

"Yes. The top hat." Elizabeth felt the warmth in her cheeks even before her lips could spread in a smile. She took the liberty of running her fingertips against his forehead, brushing a swath of dark hair from his brow. "You tried to shield your eyes from me but couldn't."

"I failed terribly."

"You didn't fail," she whispered. "They brought me back to you, did they not? They are why I'm standing here. And now they look on me and I no longer feel afraid. Or alone. Or wracked with thoughts of vengeance. Instead they show me *you*. I see a man who commissioned a secret painting from the greatest portrait maker in Europe. I see a cottage so beautiful and perfect that it could be its own painted castle. And I see a man who honored my father's memory for years after his death. It was you, wasn't it, who sought to ensure we had an income?

"It makes sense now, Ma-ma controlling the post, who I spoke with, and what invitations we'd accept . . . She was afraid I'd find out about my illegitimate half brother. And then what would we have? Every future she was trying to build for me could have come crashing down. And she thought her only recourse was to broker a marriage with you."

"I'd never have spoken of it."

"I know. But you couldn't have kept me in the dark. There's too much honor in you. And though I don't expect this to be an easy path to walk—not with Christopher, nor with my mother—I'm still willing to try. That is, if you should like . . . I'm ready to give you my answer. And if you'll pray forgive me, my dear Keaton, it is long overdue."

"Say yes because you want to. Not for any other reason than because you could love me in return as I do you. As I have from the moment you walked back into my life."

"Then it is a yes." Elizabeth had dared to dream it, that he'd stand before her so open. Honest. With his arms ready to receive her, and she had but to take a step into them. "And I know I obtain the better bargain. In case you've forgotten, I am one of those penniless artists my mother would warn you about."

"Warn nothing," he said, the slightest hint of humor alive in those beautiful eyes.

It was nothing to come home to an estate. Or a cottage he'd built for her. But to slip into his arms and feel an overwhelming familiarity like she'd never known . . . his kiss was home.

He was the turnabout of fate that she wanted, needed, and she fell into his embrace as they threaded arms and melded their future.

"I'd never have believed it," Elizabeth whispered when he pulled back for a breath, staying nose-to-nose close to her. "But Her Royal Highness, Queen Victoria herself, gifted me with my first commissioned portrait."

"Is that so?"

Elizabeth tilted her head to the windows. "It's in the carriage—you'll be delighted to know Franz was struck down with envy that mine was dubbed her favorite of the two. But it should go home with me, she said, because I'd managed to capture longing in eyes that were not hers. So Winterhalter's portrait will be gifted to her great love, and I was allowed to bring mine back . . . to you."

THIRTY-ONE

Cormac motioned for Keira to pull the earbuds from her ears. She obeyed, pausing the music on her phone so Grace VanderWaal's sultry soul cut off and was replaced by the crackling fire in the hearth and rain that cried down the glass of the pub's street-facing windows.

"I said, are ye ready to go?" Cormac stooped by Keira's chair in the dining room. "I vote we close up early an' go make merry wit' the rest o' the family. It is Christmas, ye know."

"I know. But it's my gift to you—I'll close tonight."

There hadn't been but a few customers trickling into Jack Foley's Irish House, but the last thing Keira wanted to do was toss poor tourists out in a steady downpour. It was why she'd chosen to wait in the cushy leather chair by the old stone fireplace—somehow the dance of flames helped her get lost when she'd needed to, and she could forget that it was a sloshy mess outside on O'Connell Street instead of the snowy wonderland it should have been on Christmas Eve. But the room was still. Only a few empty pint glasses lingered on random tables.

She'd come home to this view once before.

It wasn't like when she'd left New York. That had been about losing a job. Being wronged by an affluent family and their wayward son. But now, everything felt different—Emory had made it different. This time Keira wanted to stew. To let herself feel the loss of something she'd really wanted, Christmas or not. Between Victoria and the cottage and all the maybes that had come along with taking a chance—she wanted to pause and just feel sad for once, without her brothers trying to swoop in and fix it.

"Look, it's nearly closing time. Go." Keira gave him a playful shove in the shoulder. "You have a family now, Cormac. I'll lock up and then I'll pop in at Ashford Manor for a bit after. I promise. I'll be fine."

"'Tis freezin' rain out there. Do ye think Laine's goin' to speak to me tomorrow if I let my little sister drive o'er the backroads to Wicklow by herself in all that? Don' make me sleep on the sofa in my own house. I don' see that workin' out too grand for me in the end."

She couldn't help but laugh. "When are Ellie and Quinn supposed to turn up here? I can just ride over with them."

"Change o' plans. Quinn took Ellie straight o'er to the cottage at Ashford Manor so she could see Laine an' the girls. Said he'd come back after—had somethin' to pick up before mornin'."

"Honestly! You two. Must you leave your shopping until Christmas Eve every year? I cannot think of anything Quinn could need but a pocket calendar, and he could have picked that up weeks ago."

The front door bell chimed over her last words, followed by, "Heard that. Some welcome. Thanks a lot."

His accent wasn't nearly as thick as Cormac's, but the rest was so familiar she turned, finding Quinn had just stepped in from the downpour. He pulled a rain jacket hood back from his head, the never-shaven face, Foley green eyes, and chin-length dark hair of his tied tight at the nape, same as ever.

The return of a gleaming smile was new though. Bright futures did that.

"Quinn!" Keira jumped up—uncaring that he was rain-and ice-pelted. It had been months. Too many since she'd last seen him. And she hadn't a chance to hug him for the many years he'd been split from the family and not at all since Ellie's reclaimed health news, so she met him in the center of the room and threw herself up into his arms, squeezing tight so raindrops dusted her cheek and ran down her neck beneath her ponytail.

"I didn't mean it." She leaned back. Smiled at that familiar face. "Okay—I didn't mean *all* of it. You really should get to your shopping a little earlier next time. But I'm a grown woman, remember? If I'm trusted by restoration teams to handle their fine art, I think I can manage to close a pub dining room and wash the lot of pint glasses on my own. You didn't have to come all this way just for that."

"Look, 'tis not my fault. You heard him—had to pick somethin' up so he met me at the airport. Cormac was insistent that we both go. Just squeezed in on the last flight. What do ye think of that?"

She turned, finding Cormac standing by the polished wood snug frame, hands buried deep in his jeans pockets.

"What are you going on about? Last flight to what? What could you honestly need to pick up at six o' clock on Christmas Eve, and that Cormac had to go with you?"

"That'd be my fault."

Keira didn't turn to look at Emory but knew with a flutter in her midsection that he was standing just behind. Instead, she tossed her glance to Cormac, who'd moved over to the snug wall and leaned against it, his mouth iced shut. Not telling her what to do. Not bristling at a Yank coming all the way to Dublin to chase after his little sister.

He just waited. All respectful like.

Very un-Foley of him to duck out when she needed him most.

"You two know he's here?" Keira folded her arms across her chest and faced Emory, waiting in the deserted dining room, the glow of the firelight dancing against his shirt and jeans and black leather jacket with racing stripes down the sleeves.

Cormac answered with a nod and a short and sweet, "Aye."

"And you don't have a problem with this?"

Her brothers ignored her—classic evasion tactic.

It was Emory who walked forward with the casual stroll she knew, as if he didn't just come from an English jail all the way across the Irish Sea. No worse for wear though—same easy smile, except he was a bit rain-splotched. He stopped when there was only a pub chair in between them.

"I'd write that negative review I talked about before if I wasn't scared out of my socks about the two Irish hotheads giving me the evil eye in this dining room. I honestly thought I'd been found by a hit squad when your brothers showed up in Framlingham. Between that and a stint in jail, I'm surprised I'm still breathing right now." He glanced at Cormac. "No offense."

"Wait—what? You said you were taking the day off to spend with family." She turned to Cormac, still holding up the wall. He pushed away with a shrug and crossed the room to the bar.

"He did." Emory answered first, as if the men had reached some sort of understanding that said though he'd wounded her already-skittish heart, they still forgave him enough to let him speak and repair the damage. "Cormac and Quinn—finally met him by the way—they went looking for me, found out I was released from jail. Then just showed up, pounded the front door at Parham Hill and stood over me while I tossed clothes in a duffel. Said we had a family Christmas waiting and to get my passport because we were going to the airport. And then I ended up here. That's all I know. Do you honestly think I was in a position to argue with—" He tossed a glance to the brothers, staring them down. "Well, that?"

"Don' blame us," Cormac cut in. "If'n it was me alone, I'd have left ye in that broken-down English cottage of yers. But my wife stepped in after she got a call from Keira sayin' she loved the Yank, an' she got our da to go along wit' this whole thing. If I were ye, I'd be countin' my lucky stars they didn' see it the other way around, or ye might not be standin' here at all."

"Merry Christmas, Keira." Quinn, ever a man of few words, smiled and stepped back outside to the rainy bustle of O'Connell Street, the brass bell over the door chiming through the dining room as he went.

Cormac lingered a bit longer in the shadows behind the bar, sweeping a towel over the polished wood top, then folded it behind the counter. He turned off lights and flipped the switch of the digital Open sign, bathing the dining room in darkness save a few lights from the kitchen and the fire's glow.

"Make sure the fire's out before ye two leave." He winked at Keira. Then shifted a cool glance to Emory. "Better not take longer than it ought to talk this through an' then drive to Wicklow, yeah? I'll be timin' ye."

"She is an adult, you know." That vibe wasn't going to work. Cormac fired him a look loaded with a subtle layer of gunpowder, enough that Emory added, "Yeah. Right. Got it."

Cormac's features softened, his true heart unable to play the protective act the entire time. He reached for his rain jacket, pulled it from the coatrack's wooden peg, and reached for the doorknob, then stopped. "Take care of her."

It was the classic hand-off line from one guy to another. And Keira thought he'd leave it at that. But with a look at her so layered with care over everything they'd lived through together—he the brother who'd raised her after Mum had died and who'd always been Keira's safe place—he amended the thought with very Cormac-like wisdom.

"No. Take care of each other."

The bell chimed again, and they were alone. Just the pub. Rain. The fire, and a bit of a spark catching between them too.

Emory stared back, waiting with hands buried in jeans pockets. "You had me arrested."

Keira tilted her chin up a notch. "You lied to me."

"I never lied. You didn't give me the chance to explain," he said evenly, causing her to acknowledge the truth in his words. "But I don't blame you. I can imagine how it must have looked. To tell you the truth, I didn't even know what was happening, it all went down so fast. But the detective called you and told you the truth—that Carter has a royal mess waiting for his London lawyers to untangle."

Keira needed something to focus on other than the convincing case he was making. She was scared and she knew it. Moving to wipe down a pub table or two gave her precious seconds to think. "They had a few more questions for me, but yes. The police did call. And told me that apparently there's a problem with *Empress*."

"It's a fake."

"A forgery, yes. But then, you don't seem surprised."

"I had my doubts from the beginning. Carter's father was on the gallery board and arranged for the purchase, with a certain percentage as an acquisition fee. It seemed a little too buttoned up. Too fast. But the board needed the notoriety of it and so I was overruled. And in my distraction over Elise and her death, and in Carter's naivety to remain a loyal friend at my side, it seems his father used the opportunity to slip the painting out before it could be authenticated—and proven a forgery. But it was never found, until now."

"Sounds like some odd remake of *How to Steal a Million*. But how did it end up at Parham Hill?"

"Well, that's Carter's question to answer, and his lawyers to deny any knowledge of it outside of his late father's sins having caught up to him. But Carter did step in the gap of all this and demand my name be cleared. Had to pass muster with the police, of course, and the fact that I told the truth helped quite a bit. They may have more questions, but as of right now I'm a free man. I can go where I please. And it's sure not to step back into my old shoes, even with a restored reputation. I'm pleased instead to be here in Dublin. With you."

"We both know you don't stay planted for long."

"What if I did?" he offered without a breath of hesitation. "For the first time in my life I think I'm actually jealous of something Carter has. M. J. is standing by him. But I have to wonder if you have faith in me. Is that what you're trying to tell me?"

"I did." She slipped her fingers around two glass rims, then swept the tip up into her pocket.

"But you don't now?"

"Emory, it's Christmas. You think you can show up, flash a charming smile—" When he looked like he was going to comment on the last two words, Keira set the glasses on the bar and challenged him. "And don't you dare read into that. I'm not a schoolgirl wilting over a spot of charm here. If you meant what you said to me, that this job was more than Victoria, a library, or a cottage . . . then why didn't you tell me about the Klimt right away? I admit it—I fell apart. All I could see was the past repeating itself."

"I only found the *Empress* that morning. And I should have told you right away. But I was afraid that when you saw it, you'd have to make the decision of whether or not you could trust me. And for the life of me, I couldn't risk it. Not when I loved you too. More than you know. More than I could say then, but I'm sure not letting the moment pass now."

Keira held for a moment on a shaky breath.

Those "I love you" words were terrifying to hear for the weight they carried.

"What Alton did isn't your fault. But I suppose I won't settle. I want truth. And I want something real. If you can give me that, I'll believe what you just said."

"Alright. Evelyn Addams."

The sweet old dressmaker from Framlingham?

"Okay . . . Evelyn Addams. Meaning what exactly?"

"Funny thing is, she wanted to know what my eight hours in the slammer were like. She's got something of a rebel streak in her. But turns out she also shared a few things that changed my perspective about the cottage." Emory turned to fetch a backpack he'd discarded by the door. He knelt, unzipped it, and pulled out a book.

He stopped in front of her and held the binding out to her—a worn red cover that she'd seen in the glass sideboard but not examined.

"Here. A Christmas gift."

She took it, then turned the cover over in her palms.

Peter Pan in Kensington Gardens.

"While Carter's working out his battle in court, I'll be staying on to manage Parham Hill. So I've been spending time in town. At St. Michaels. And accepted Evelyn's invitation to take tea with her. In her shop this was hanging on the wall." He moved closer with boldness, then flipped the cover open and grazed her fingertips when he pulled out a photo. "Here."

A bride smiled back—one they'd seen before.

Amelia Woods stared out from the photo in a drop-dead gorgeous gown—less wedding like and more Hollywood like than what one would expect for a wartime bride. But she glowed, standing next to an American officer in perfect uniform dress. He had an arm slipped around her waist, and she must have been surprised because her wildflower bouquet drifted off her hip like she was about to lose it from the smile, and laugh, and complete joy they shared.

"It's Amelia, from the photos of brides hanging in the church. But we never saw this one." Keira looked up, her heart aching for someone's story to have had a happy ending. "What happened to her?"

"She met the love of her life at Parham Hill and married him—a Captain Wyatt Stevens of the 390th Bomb Group, apparently. But before they went to make a life in New York with two children they adopted after the war, it seems Amelia Woods shut up the manor to keep a story alive in its walls. You see, you were right. The chemical analysis you had done confirmed it—the official letter arrived at Parham Hill after you'd gone. Victoria is exactly how old you thought. But along with her, there's a painting among the eight in the attic . . . I don't want you to think this is in any way a bribe to get you back to England, but it's signed 'Winterhalter, 1843.' And the inscription on the back states that the woman in a yellow gown, with an easel and paintbrush in hand, is a portrait of celebrated artist Elizabeth James, Viscountess Huxley."

"So what you're saying is, Carter may have owned a Winterhalter all along?"

"Authenticating that and, you know, the job of revealing Elizabeth James and her portrait of Victoria to the world will keep me pretty busy. I could use a hand from a professional. Oh, and I have no idea what I'm doing, but the beekeeping on the estate is going to need management. You can't honestly tell me you don't want to laugh at my stubborn hide every time I get stung. I can't believe you, of all people, would want to miss out on that."

In the dining room where they'd first met, with a good Irish rain outside and the firelight dancing within, Emory closed the gap between them. He looked down on her, as if reading that her heart couldn't decide whether she needed to laugh or cry for being so happy. He lifted his fingertips, and the tears that fled off her bottom lashes were softly, sweetly wiped away.

"There's a cottage that needs new memories, Keira. A new story. A new start. And heaven help me, but I can't imagine watching a single one of those Parham Hill sunrises without being able to share it all with you."

THIRTY-TWO

MAY 9, 1945
CHURCH OF ST. MICHAELS
FRAMLINGHAM, ENGLAND

"I can't help thinking there's something decidedly unlucky about this," Wyatt whispered as Amelia reached for his hand and gripped tight. "Seeing the bride before the wedding? I seem to remember my gran warning young grooms about it. Something about wedded bliss. I sincerely hope I won't miss out on that part because of a pair of shoes."

"I'm sorry, Captain, but I can't possibly get these on unless you hold me up. There's no chair in here and I refuse to sit on the floor in this remarkable dress. Darly would agree with me. Are you going to argue with that?"

Amelia struggled with the buckle on her strappy golden heel, draping the liquid-satin train over her ankle and laughing as she pressed against his side because hadn't she sworn she'd never wear them again as long as the sky was blue?

"I wouldn't dream of arguing with someone as pretty—or as stubborn—as you, my love."

"You fancy your wartime bride tripping her way up the aisle, hmm?"

"Why wear them then?"

"You Yanks don't understand English girls. These heels may induce pain, but they're lovely. And the best I own until rationing decides to leave us for good. So I'll bite my lip during the ceremony and, if necessary, through having our photograph taken. I promised that we'd allow the dress shop to hang our photo of Bertie's prized gown behind the counter, and I refuse to be caught grimacing for the rest of eternity. Afterward I'll throw them in the bin on our way out of the church, and you can carry me back to Parham Hill for all I care."

"Careful." He pressed a kiss to her lips as soon as she'd straightened against him. "I might try it."

Amelia reached up, tilting his uniform hat a shade to give him just enough of an off-kilter look to add a little mystery.

"There. Now you're perfect," she said, pecking him back. "Now shoo. Get out to that altar before I race you to it. And see that Luca looks smart in his suit. I've a feeling he's going to try to get out of wearing a tie, and I'm afraid I must insist upon it today."

"I'll keep an eye out, milady. I love you enough to do your bidding any day of the week. Not just today." He winked, adding a more tempered whisper: "Don't keep me waiting too long?"

A slight vulnerability dropped over his face, the kind that said the moments to come meant everything to him, and he wasn't ashamed to say it.

"I wouldn't dare."

He smiled in that dashingly quiet way of his, fluttering her midsection as he slipped out the door, then clicked it closed behind him. And Amelia was alone for the first time that day.

The radio called it V-E Day—a victory over Europe.

What might have been an inconsequential Wednesday in May turned into the biggest exhale the Allies had breathed in more than four years. And as the victory celebration kicked off, and Framlingham remembered the lost alongside the triumph that was the Nazis' unconditional surrender across Europe on May 8, and surrender of the Channel Islands on this their wedding day, Amelia Woods stood in a bride's room. Glowing. Relieved and heart full. Having struggled to buckle tiny gold straps on evil, toe-pinching heels with her American groom anchored at her side.

The bouquet Liesel had gathered for her leaned in the window-sill, one of her golden-yellow hair ribbons wrapped around marigold and camellia stems, sprigged with English violets and ropes of ivy in a homemade nosegay from the estate gardens. Amelia walked to it and gathered the blooms in her palms.

It was then she noticed the spring scene through the leaded-glass window—the green grass, the bowers of fully leaved trees, and the gentle sway of a breeze rustling their color against a blue sky. And there, underneath it all, was a gravestone in the shadow of the afternoon, set off from the rest: *Arthur Woods, Viscount of Huxley. Royal Air Force. Beloved husband. Died 14 April 1940.*

My love . . . Do you mind at all if I smile today?

She whispered who he was: her first love. Not Viscount or His Lordship. Not pilot in the Royal Air Force. Not even Arthur, which was the name he'd so sweetly given as they gathered books and taxis whizzed by them in the middle of Victoria Street during that first meeting. But "my love."

The war was over, or would be soon.

The children would be loaded on trains to London and Norwich. And Lakenheath . . . bound for wherever home was. Flocks of B-17s would fly off across the Atlantic and the flyboys back to their own nests, leaving the airfield silent and Framlingham Castle with only the ghost of humming engines in the sky. Parham Hill would lose its temporary tenants, the 390th officers all discharged back to life in a changed world. And the library would play host to the story of the man she'd lost, to the legacy that Amelia assured wouldn't die with Arthur or Darly, or any of those who'd given their lives in the pursuit of freedom.

Wyatt and she had agreed to close up the library once all the children had gone, keeping Arthur's story safe and untouched, until a new owner would come along and discover a cabinet of books and Victoria's beautiful visage and, maybe one day, would breathe new life into a cherished beekeeper's cottage.

Amelia pressed her fingers to her lips, kissing a good-bye before she walked down a hall with photos of former brides and grooms—knowing a photo of Arthur and her would always hang among them. She'd walk down the aisle in a beloved liquid-satin gown, and terrible shoes, to stand beside a captain with a rare heart, with a full future ahead for them both.

New York City, a family, and a fresh start.

Just like authors H. A. and Margaret Rey, whose lives were saved by a story they carried with them, Wyatt and Amelia Stevens became the protectors of a beautiful story left behind.

One day Victoria would be found and protected again. Until then, the cottage—their own painted castle—would sleep.

EPILOGUE

Titus Vivay may have lost his sight completely, but Keira doubted that hampered her grandfather's eagerness to walk the road to the newly renovated Sleeping Beauty.

From the moment he'd stepped through the scrolled-iron front gates, Quinn holding him at the elbow to brace his steps, their enigmatic patriarch appeared enraptured to imagine the awakening of the long-sleeping castle on such a perfect Loire Valley day.

Sweet blossoms of wild plum trees and French violets perfumed the air. Birdsong twittered overhead. Scores of patrons had purchased tickets, their excited chatter lifting through the forest that shrouded the castle grounds from the outside world. The tourists stopped along the paths, snapped photos in the gardens, and brushed fingertips along the top edge of a rock wall that bordered the family's vineyard rows.

Cormac and Laine trekked along the castle road with their daughters, his arm draped over his wife's shoulders as they paused a stroller at the hushed chapel in the woods—the little steepled sanctuary with stained glass windows that had been where their own story began. Ellie walked along with Quinn and Titus, a brilliant smile upon her lips as she described the fruits of their restoration labors in the last year. A breeze toyed with the tips of her favorite merlot pin-dot scarf, just covering a crown that was defying the memory of chemo and slowly—but beautifully—growing back her ebony hair. And Keira smiled to feel the warmth of the sun on her legs beneath a blush spring dress, and Emory's fingers laced with hers as they lingered on the road behind everyone else.

Before them was the lost castle's moat and bridge and stone spires that kissed the sky.

Open window frames no longer allowed little birds the freedom of flight from outside the castle to in. Instead, they were lined with glass and ivory brocade curtains. Scrub trees that had once sprung up in the cracks between ancient stone walls had been uprooted and cleared away, replaced by bright blooms in window boxes. The ivy they'd left to climb high as it wished, painting the burnished stone in a blanket of deep, abiding green. And the high-arched wooden doors, polished to a rich cognac, had been opened wide and were ready to greet guests to the restored château for the first time in over two hundred years.

Keira paused with a squeeze to Emory's hand. He slowed, turning back to her, and raised her knuckles to peck a kiss to the underside of her wrist. "You okay, Mrs. Scott?"

"I'm brilliant," she answered honestly, for the sight had fairly stolen her breath away.

She twirled the wedding ring around her finger, reliving the memory of when he'd whispered, *"Why don't you marry me?"* when they finished restoring the beekeeper's cottage at Parham Hill. For Emory's laid-back ways, Keira had thought he was just tossing a joke out between them and laughed it off as if he'd asked her if Victoria was hanging straight enough for her liking above the mantel. But then he'd climbed down from the stepladder and went down farther to one knee, asking her right then and there if she'd stay with him always. To marry and live in sleepy little Framlingham. Together, to make the country cottage their little piece of good in the world.

"If you're brilliant, as you Irish-Brits love to say, then why are you tearing up, sweetheart?" Emory brushed a fingertip against the apple of her cheek. "You thinking of your mother?"

"No. Mum would have loved this—all of us together again." She looked up the path. Jack—her da who'd never seen eye to eye with his only daughter—also walked the road with his family. With his former father-in-law at his side, when the last time they'd been together had been before divorce and death, before their story had taken painful turns. It wasn't all ironed out, but he was trying. And that's what mattered to her. "I was actually thinking of home. Of our little cottage along a country road in East Suffolk. It's not grand as all this, but it's . . . well, perfect, isn't it?"

"For me, it is. And you are."

The breeze rustled Emory's hair and she smiled, the perfectly pomaded style from that first meeting in Dublin now long replaced by hair he allowed to fall naturally over his brow. Emory wasn't the trust-fund kid or the high-end art world dealer buttoned up in a suit and tie. He'd slipped happily into farm life on the estate—worn tees, jeans, and all. Even trying his hand at beekeeping, of all things. Spending his days working at restoring Parham Hill while Carter wrangled his family's legal troubles. And nights they spent by the fire in their cottage and woke up mornings in each other's arms, watching every painted sunrise that bled over the top of the meadow.

"I still defy anyone who says that life is without troubles or that all stories will end in walking a road to a fairy-tale castle. Along the way there's bound to be brokenness. Laine lost her first marriage. Ellie and Quinn battled a cancer diagnosis that could have stolen everything. Even my grandfather has had to go on after losing two wives and a daughter to death." She looked up at him, squinting a touch at the bright spring sunlight that shone behind him. "Should I also fear this moment won't last?"

"Don't be afraid. It's never about the end of a road, is it? It's about living and loving in the journey we take to get where we are. Right now. Right to this very moment." Emory stilled her fidgeting with her wedding ring by closing her fingertips in his palm. "Remember what I told you after Elise passed away, that I made a deal with God? I wouldn't hate Him for taking her if He could show me something good in every day that came after that pain."

"I remember."

"You know that was wrong of me, right?"

Keira couldn't help smiling, not when her husband dared to admit he was wrong about something.

"I know if you're clever enough to realize I'm right most of the time, then we have quite a guarantee of a happy marriage."

He tipped his head a fraction, blocking the light just so she could meet his gaze. "No, I meant it was wrong to even ask that of Him. Because if I'd had my wish back then, I'd have missed out on this moment with you. And I wouldn't dare jeopardize that. I have to believe there's no guarantee of anything good in this life outside of the One who offers it to us. It's like the castle stones over there. They've gone on for generations. What lasts isn't what we build on our own, but the stories He builds within and around us."

"So you mean unraveling stories like Victoria's, or the cottage's, or even our own—that's worth everything in this life?"

"Yeah. It is, Mrs. Scott." He smiled and dropped a kiss to her lips. "The question is, are you ready for whatever comes?" Emory glanced out to the end of the castle road and her brothers waving them on to join the family through the castle's open doors.

"Look at this beautiful castle. It's not lost anymore, is it? That tells me every story can be redeemed."

"A castle or cottage . . . I don't care. As long as this story has us together, I'm good."

"Then I'd like to think you can stop looking for those good things every day and rest in the knowledge that we've already got them. Right here. Right in this moment," she whispered, falling in step alongside her husband as wind loosed blossoms to fall from the trees like pink snow. "I'm ready to keep walking this road with you, because I know it will always lead us home."

AUTHOR'S NOTE

The first time I saw Audrey Hepburn and Peter O'Toole light up the silver screen in *How to Steal a Million*, I think I fell as much in love with them as their characters did with each other. Witty dialogue, a storied European cityscape, brilliant chemistry between the main characters, and fashion from famed icon Givenchy combined to create a pitch-perfect setting for a love story about the high-end world of fine art.

Imagine a would-be art thief falling for a girl locked in a high-society world, only to find out they're both keeping a secret, or twenty. What if the suave gentleman really was an art thief? And what if the fine art in question really was a forgery? That spark of tension between main characters became the inspiration behind Emory and Keira's story, and the mystery behind a forgotten library and a lost portrait became the intrigue that brings them together.

Though Franz Xaver Winterhalter was a much-sought-after portrait artist in the throne rooms of nineteenth-century Europe, little is known about his private life. While this story takes artistic liberties to imagine his character with jovial eccentricity, history does confirm Queen Victoria entrusted Winterhalter with the commission of her "secret picture" in 1843 (as she would refer to it in her journal on July 13 of that year). With the queen's hair unbound, wearing a plain pendant containing a lock of Albert's hair instead of stately jewels, and with an unceremonious posture and intense longing in her features, the portrait was considered an intimate look at the behind-the-scenes lives of the royal couple. Though a common practice was for copies to be made of Winterhalter's royal paintings (especially later in his career, when apprentices worked in studio to mass-produce copies of paintings for a larger public audience), the portrait in question had but a select few miniatures made, and no formal copy is known to exist.

The gift was presented to Prince Albert on 18 August 1843, for his twenty-fourth birthday. We've fictionalized parts of the queen's journal entry to add Franz's "little bee" into the storyline, but the queen did refer to the portrait as "my darling Albert's favourite picture" and wrote of the secret picture: "he thought it so like, & so beautifully painted. I felt so happy and proud to have found something that gave him so much pleasure." The prince is said to have indeed dubbed it his favorite portrait of his bride, but found the image too private for public display and instead hung the portrait in his personal study at Windsor Castle. While not shown publicly until 1977, the secret picture was more recently included in a royal exhibition at Buckingham Palace in 2010, in conjunction with preservation by the Royal Collection Trust, United Kingdom.

Like Victoria and Albert, history is still painted over by the stories—in portraits, photographs, and letters—that connect our own yesterdays to the present.

My grandfather served as a B-17 copilot in the 390th Bombardment Group, his 571st Squadron having been stationed in Framlingham during WWII. While I wish he were still here to share his firsthand accounts of those years, one poignant line in this book is directly from him. He once told me what he remembered most about the war—a sobering reality of the WWII generation: "You don't make friends, because the moment you do, the next day they're gone."

While D-day had darkened the skies over Framlingham with planes headed to the Normandy coast in June 1944, the 390th embarked on more than three hundred combat missions of its own between 1943 and 1945. Most were supply drops over a war-weary France and bombing raids on strategic targets in the lifeblood of Nazi industrial resources, such as marshaling yards, train depots, railroad bridges, ports, aircraft factories, and oil refineries across Germany, Belgium, Holland, and Czechoslovakia. While fictional for Wyatt's crew, mission #243 was a real combat mission to bomb oil storage units at Derben, Germany, on 14 January 1945. Flying Fortresses saw an attack from some one hundred single-engine fighters that tore through the skies over Berlin, becoming one of the group's greatest battles of the war.

The mission would cost the 390th nine planes.

Though the bombing of St. Michaels Church was also fictionalized for our story, a Pathfinder wreck did occur in February 1944. A German Ju 88 combat plane managed to evade detection and sneak into the airfield on its tail, resulting in a crash landing into the brick wall surrounding Glenham Church. Despite carrying a heavy bomb load, members of the 390th flocked to the crash site in an attempt to save those on board—rolling live bombs away from the wreckage and pulling both the pilot and copilot to safety.

Of the thirteen crew members, all but three were saved.

The Battle of the Bulge was hitting a fever pitch in December 1944. The Eighth Air Force had sent a dispatch for two thousand bombers to respond, but on the return, thick fog along the coast prevented many from landing safely at their own airfields, leaving hundreds of servicemen stranded with no place to stay on Christmas Eve. It was noted that someone had seen the 1944 film

The Canterville Ghost—about a group of servicemen who were bivouacked at a country manor during a similar situation. Owners of a nearby manor house—aptly named Parham Hall—were contacted in the middle of the night and opened their doors to some two hundred displaced servicemen from the Allied armed forces, hosting them for an impromptu Christmas holiday.

At the writing of this novel, the restoration of the lost castle that inspired the series—Château de la Mothe-Chandeniers—is now becoming reality. Just as our Foley family walks the road to their castle restoration, you and I can now do the same at the castle that sparked this series years ago. The concept of history as a witness to the stories of people living in vastly different times, places, and cultures became the heartbeat of this series. To end it in any setting but the fairy tale–inspired "Sleeping Beauty" castle from *The Lost Castle* wouldn't have felt right. Weaving the Foley family's story through castle stones spread across France, Ireland, and now England added the perfect punctuation to the legacy of stories and how we live them. From Victorian England to Churchill's war-torn world, and from those years until the modern day, the absolute, constant, ever-flowing current to the human experience is that our Creator is the same yesterday, today . . . and for all eternity.

Like weathered castle stones, His story—God's story for each one of us—lives on in the journeys we tread with Him.

ACKNOWLEDGMENTS

For the last many years, I've kept a stack of WWII-era photos and postcards on my desk while I write. I flip through them from time to time, thinking about the fighting men and women of the "greatest generation," feeling those pinpricks of pride in my heart that my grandfather, Edward "Big Ed" W. Wedge, was counted among the brave in what is penciled on the back of one photo of smiling young flyboys from the 390th: "A swell crew."

I have vague memories of attending the annual reunions of the 390th Bombardment Group during the formative years of my youth. I have boxes of WWII-era memorabilia that tracks his time in Framlingham—a book issued by the United States Army that includes airfield maps and Framlingham town photos, and chronicles the firsthand accounts of the 390th missions and general life both on and off base as servicemen invaded this country hamlet. Also helpful were an original newspaper from his Michigan town dated December 7, 1941 (Pearl Harbor Day), medical records, B-17 flight logs, crew yearbooks, dress uniforms, and a postcard of a young lieutenant smiling in a photo sent to his parents (my great-grandparents) before he shipped off to war.

For the heroes of the 390th, and all who fought so brilliantly during WWII, whose history and legacy we are losing to time every day . . . For those who ran toward trouble instead of away from it . . . For the evergreen courage that is a testament to us all . . . And for being willing to put their lives and futures on the line so descendants like this granddaughter can sit in a home office, thumb through photos and postcards, and pen a novel that is as much a part of my heart as any I've written before it . . .

Thank you.

To my ever-patient, protective, and completely wonderful publishing family at HarperCollins, I thank you for your belief in me: Amanda Bostic, Allison Carter, Jodi Hughes, Paul Fisher, and Savannah Summers. To Kristen Ingebretson—many thanks for your absolutely brilliant cover designs. And to my dear friend, editor extraordinaire Becky Monds—you make every day better for allowing me to share the stories of my heart. To Julee, for your beautiful skill and patience in helping this author gal take a story from manuscript to shelf-worthy book. To author sisters who stood in the gap, encouraged, or supported through the writing of this book: Beth Vogt, Sarah Ladd, Katherine Reay, Sara Ella, Rachel Hauck, Susan May Warren, and Colleen Coble. And to Rachelle Gardener: You are the best. You inspire me to be a wildly imaginative thinker and dreamer, and above all, you are a first-class friend. Thanks for all you do.

Oh, how I adore a good character name supplied by reader friends! Thanks to those who helped name characters in this book: To Maggie Walker, my bestie from high school, for embarking on a beekeeping adventure with this author gal, and for loaning her unique brand of awesome to Maggie Jane (M. J.); to the real Cebert Byron (or C. B., as you're known), for mailing my many book packages at the post office; to my nephews, Ben and Eli, for naming two members of the modern-day Parham Hill crew; to beloved friend

Marlene (Amelia) and her prince charming, Steve (Wyatt Stevens), whose Christmastime wedding inspired the love story between our WWII-era characters; to our oldest son, Brady, who suggested the enigmatic Henry Darlington (Darly) his delightfully rumpled yet very British name; to our youngest son, Colt, who inspired the curiosity of young Luca; and to our middle son, Carson, whose sketch of a curious figure in a top hat became the character of Keaton James from the very first lines of this novel.

For noticing a young art student who stumbled into class the first semester of college, and for the more than two decades of investment made in me since, I send my most ardent thanks to Anne E. Guernsey Allen, PhD, professor of fine arts at Indiana University Southeast. You helped shape my love of art and history, and to fill the space for which God was counting on someone to step in and encourage what seemed an incredibly faraway dream, He used *you*. Thank you for changing my life.

Thanks to curators at the 390th Memorial Museum in Tucson, Arizona, for allowing this curious author to peek through your archives and benefit from the absolutely brilliant information and legacy of stories you've gathered on this brave group of fighting men.

Big, bee-buzzing appreciation goes to Tracy Hunter and the rest of the farm family at Hunter's Bee Farm in Martinsville, Indiana. Not just for the research tour of the honey-making world you've been experts at since 1910, but for helping this sometimes-fearful author gal and her bestie to buck up and be *fear-less* for one glorious beekeeping day. Many thanks!

To the amazing community of women at Southeast Christian Church in Louisville, Kentucky; to my momma, for reading the messiest of first drafts I could ever come up with; and to my best friend—my husband, Jeremy—for whispering, "Why don't you marry me?" long before Emory did in this story and changing my whole world because of it. And to our three adventure-seeking sons, Brady, Carson, and Colt . . . Thank you. I love you all.

And to my Savior, who defines all that I am—every story begins and ends with the grace and ardent love I can only receive from *You*.

DISCUSSION QUESTIONS

1. At its core *The Painted Castle* is a story of redemption for three women in very different life circumstances. All are navigating loss, battling to heal, and learning to love again. What are the common threads of Elizabeth Meade, Amelia Woods, and Keira Foley's stories? How do their healing journeys differ?

2. For more than a decade Elizabeth Meade believes seeking justice for her father's murder will bring her peace. What happens when the man she's held responsible for her father's death begins to unravel what she's always thought to be true? How does Keaton contradict the image she'd built of him in her mind?

3. Through the generations we see a shift in the roles of women in society. Elizabeth's expectations in a Victorian era are different from Amelia's during WWII and from Keira's in our modern day. How have the roles of women changed from the nineteenth century to now? How did each character navigate the social construct of her surroundings in order to use her gifts and talents to benefit both herself and those around her?

4. Amelia and Wyatt find themselves thrown together at Parham Hill during the last years of WWII, but it was books that really began their journey to one another. How did their mutual love of books affect their ability to heal from past brokenness? What books have impacted your own story?

5. By accepting the commission to authenticate the painting of Victoria, Keira Foley hoped to find a quick fix to repair her career and hide from a romantic life that had completely fallen apart. Instead, she finds herself thrown into the middle of a situation that tests her in both areas. How does Keira begin to heal from both the pain of her childhood and her broken engagement? Does learning of Emory's past brokenness soften her heart toward him? What wisdom have you gained from being tested romantically? Professionally?

6. *The Painted Castle* turns a spotlight not just on main characters but on many beloved secondary characters— the most famous being real-life master artist Franz Xaver Winterhalter and Queen Victoria herself. How important is weaving in secondary characters to the fabric of a story? Whose stories affected the main characters the most and why?

7. Each book in the Lost Castles series includes a castle or manor house—or beekeeper's cottage—largely forgotten by time. Can a character with no voice still affect the characters' lives? How do the legacy and longevity of castles mirror God's ever-present involvement in our own stories?

8. A constant theme in this novel is the beauty of creation: art is shown as paintings, books, or even a carefully

preserved library. How did each character view the art placed before him or her? Can artistic expression be used to glorify God—whether it's from the past, present, or future?

DON'T MISS THESE OTHER FABULOUS NOVELS BY
KRISTY CAMBRON!

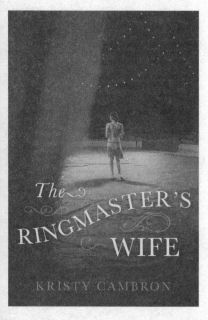

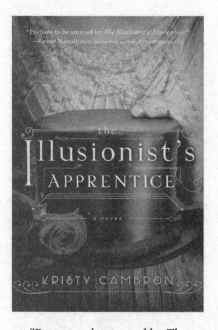

"A vivid and romantic rendering of circus life in the Jazz Age."
—USA TODAY, *Happy Ever After*

"Prepare to be amazed by *The Illusionist's Apprentice*."
—Greer Macallister, bestselling author of *The Magician's Lie* and *Girl in Disguise*

Also Available from Kristy Cambron, the
Hidden Masterpiece Novels!

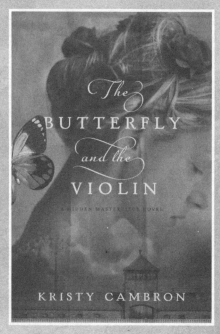

A mysterious painting breathes hope and beauty into the darkest corners of Auschwitz—and the loneliest hearts of Manhattan.

Bound together across time, two women will discover a powerful connection through one survivor's story of hope in the darkest days of a war-torn world.

ABOUT THE AUTHOR

Photo by Whitney Neal Photography

Kristy Cambron fancies life as a vintage-inspired storyteller. Her novels have been named to *Library Journal Reviews*' list of Best Books of 2014 and 2015 and have received nominations for *RT* Reviewers' Choice Awards Best Inspirational Book of 2014 and 2015, as well as INSPY Award nominations in 2015 and 2017. Kristy holds a degree in art history from Indiana University and lives in Indiana with her husband and three basketball-loving sons.

Website: www.kristycambron.com
Instagram: KristyCambron
Facebook: KCambronAuthor
Twitter: @KCambronAuthor
Pinterest: KCambronAuthor